WAR
OF THE
WORLD MAKERS

by

Reilly Michaels

———————————————

Del Sol Press
Washington, D.C.

War of the World Makers
by Reilly Michaels

Published by Del Sol Press
Washington, D.C.

Copyright © Del Sol Press 2017

First printing 2017

Cover art: Scott Richard

Printed in the United States of America

ISBN 978-0692919637

If you can look into the seeds of time, and say which grain will grow and which will not, speak then unto me.

- William Shakespeare

_____

царица

1

A Hail of Giants – Since The Time of Babylon – Zolo's Fate

SPELLCRAFTER ZOLO BOLD WOULD SOON FACE DEATH for the final time at the hands of Temujin Gur, the most ancient and dreaded of all Asian sorcerers. Zolo's strategy to arm the Kazakh Khanate and its tribes with a dragon's horde worth of cannons, muskets and spells, and lead them against the tyrannical Chinese Emperor Qian Long, had forced the Emperor to stir the blackest of magic into life. Though the act of awakening a monster like Gur was fraught with unspeakable danger, the Emperor weighed this fear against an onset of panic. Zolo's followers were pouring in from all over Asia. By the tens of thousands, they prepared for war, the likes of which had not been seen since the age of The Great Khan.

Zolo knew that defeat of the evil Chinese government was paramount. He would triumph over their armies, free the Chinese people and spread terror to the civic agencies of Qian Long. With the help of his own magic he would later conjure a fair and just democratic utopia, one that even the English philosopher, John Locke, might find satisfactory. But before Zolo could finalize his grand strategy, a horrific catastrophe was destined to spread his new army on the winds.

As soon as the midnight clock struck the year 1744 A.D., the black clouds of winter above the tents of Zolo's sleeping soldiers began to moan like dying women—an unholy moan far more frightening than mere storm. Kazakh sentries on patrol that night froze in fear, staring at each other like mystified children until one of them broke the spell by screaming, his head and finger pointing upward. As one, the sentries lifted their eyes to see flaming giants raining down on them from the fathomless black. Scores fell in thunder, their bodies searing the air like lightning, and once they finished their call to gravity, the noise as each one struck ground sounded as if God himself were pounding a weeping Earth.

And no respite was allowed.

From west to east along the Bukhtarma River Valley, the hail of fiery giants mercilessly descended. Thousands of soldiers died at the moment of first fall, others shivering with horrible burns. All those not paralyzed, dead or wounded, ran shrieking into the darkness, their heads filled with a vision of unforgettable Hell.

Zolo was jolted awake after an impact of giant less than twenty yards from his tent. He sprang from his bed of horse blankets, believing an earthquake had cut short his dream of the Chinese Emperor humping a huge rat. As he scrambled for balance, his ears already hurting with the shrieking death sounds of his men, his black-and-ivory striped djinn named Azamat bowed to him. No taller than a cat on hind legs, Azamat calmly parted the tent flaps and Zolo, wearing only his camel-hair trousers, ran cursing into the flaming night—still blinking and woozy, but mad for answers.

Several terrified camp guards and soldiers whined and hopped past him in every direction like twice-bitten dogs, and then he saw it, the source of their terror: a colossal human-like body on fire so close he could almost touch it. What was it? An angel? *Was God once again culling out rebellious divinities and hurling them down to the hell of Earth?* Zolo heard cannon-like booming in the distance and gazed up to see more giants falling from the black sky not only close to him, but many miles down the valley, some vanishing behind a distant ridge of hills in the southwest. The forest there, as well as the trees surrounding his camp, already licked and snapped with heat. A firestorm of enormous size appeared inevitable.

All of his men would die unless he acted quickly.

But towards what end?

He knew not the identity of his enemy and therefore could not strike in retaliation or reverse the terrible spell that dropped the fireball goliaths. Instinctively, he realized the Chinese spell captains of the

Forbidden City must be involved. Who else? But even all their powers combined could not have wrought such profound annihilation.

Sparks flew in his face and he waved them away. Fire-glowing smoke roiled over his head. The *pop-pop* sound of musket fire echoed up to him. He looked down to see a line of his Kazakh musketeer guard firing their weapons at the closest flaming giant. The giant's burning face turned towards them and Zolo saw the lips move.

The thing is trying to talk!

He ran towards them all shouting, "Let it speak!" "Let it speak!"

At least 15 musketeers turned at the last second to see Zolo. Their gun barrels still smoking, their faces contorted with fear and shock, and though elite troops created by Zolo, they appeared to him in the horror of the night like black imps or demons celebrating the fall of a fire god. Before anyone could react, a word filled the air. A single hot word spoken by the flaming mouth of the giant:

"YOU."

The voice like a groan of monster drowning in lava.

"YOU."

Zolo pulled a gleaming scimitar from the scabbard of a musketeer closest and brandished it before him. For the first time, he saw the giant's eyes through the tongues of flame. Golden eyes big as his head. The eyes appeared sad and suffering.

"Are you a fallen angel?" Zolo asked.

"NO. I AM AN IMPERIAL CONCUBINE OF EMPEROR QIAN LONG."

"What?"

"ALL OF US... ALL OF US FALLING ARE CONCUBINES. WE ARE BURNING UNDER THE SPELL OF A SORCERER."

"His name? Who is he?"

"HE WILL SAVE THE EMPEROR."

"Who is the sorcerer?"

"I HAVE HIS ANSWER."

The giant pursed her flaming lips and blew a sulfurous yellow vapor at Zolo that billowed into a rushing cloud of gas. It only stung his spell-ironed flesh, but it oven baked the Kazakh musketeers behind him. They howled and ripped at their armor, holding their faces and falling to the earth. The gas ate deep into their flesh. Skin slid from their hands and face in smoking sheets. Zolo cried out and clutched at them, desperately mumbling spells over their seared bodies, but it was no use. They dissolved down to bone and hollow armor in less than a minute.

Zolo!

Someone yelled. He recognized the voice as he rose to his knees weeping.

Do you know who this is?

A voice within his head speaking slow and deliberate. He decided to answer.

"Niccolo?"

I have caused your powers to lessen. You cannot save your men in any case.

"My God, it's you!... How could you do this?"

I ordered you not to open a new front in China. It cripples our cause.

"Would not a China free of tyrants impede Godfellow's utopia?"

The Chinese cannot fathom the democracy you desire.

"But we can guide them, help them... change them."

Non possibile.

"Then return my full powers, Niccolo, and help me reverse this massacre. You are a World Maker with—"

I cannot.

"Then let me save my men at least... I beg you!"

Sono quasi morto. They are nearly all perished.

"How can you allow this?"

I had no hand in the rain of death. It surprised me also.

"Then who is the sorcerer she speaks of?" he said, pointing back at the giant.

Temujin Gur.

"What?... That's not possible!"

There is no doubt.

But he died at the Czarina's hand."

He lives in 1744. Do you not recall your boyhood?

Though only 46 years of body age, Zolo had lived more than three centuries working for his lord and mentor, Niccolo Paginini, so in reality he was nearing 400; therefore, recalling his boyhood wasn't easy. He needed a spell to tweak the electricity of memory, but it all seemed to drip from his body. He felt helpless as his magic fell to the dirt and grew nothing. But he vaguely imagined the Great Hall of a castle in Prussia. He'd worked there when a teenager, his job to keep a watchful eye on Princess Freddie von Anhalt who would later become Catherine II, Czarina of all The Russias, as well as a supremely powerful World Maker.

Parties took place, balls, and the coming of Empress Elizabeth.

"I cannot remember. Master Paganini... Tell me."

But he would not answer. As a shadow is moved by sun, so too had he soundlessly departed the mind of Zolo Bold.

Then the world caught fire.

The giant suffering concubine burst into a wind of fiery shards that blew about with such force it caused the gas-burned corpses of the Kazakh musketeers to vanish. Bits of the human detritus burned his arms and chest until he cried out, and when the bombardment ceased moments later, Zolo turned to see the forest-birthed firestorm go avalanching down the hill sides with a black-magic velocity before exploding into ferociously roaring tornadoes of flame that began to sweep to and fro across the Bukhtarma River Valley.

He was dumbstruck by the sight of it.

Despite his centuries of witnessing things no normal human could even imagine, he was shocked to see bits of men and horse and wagon swirled like flaming black cinders in the maelstrom. Tears brimmed in his eyes and burned off to steam as he watched.

Nothing could be done.

No one could be saved.

Even the air itself began to depart his lungs as his camel-hair trousers crumbled to smoking black pieces.

Naked and gasping, using his remaining magic to screen the

heat, he ran back to his tent to gather his spell-protected garments, weapons, horse and his adored djinn, the faithful Azamat. But once arrived, he found little Azamat lifeless. A burning shard of iron had cut through the tent and struck him. With a shaking hand, Zolo pulled six inches of metal from his old friend's head.

The open wound bubbled over. It sputtered and coughed before speaking these words to him:

Your only chance is Prussia.

* царица *

ZOLO RODE SOUTHWEST TO EUROPE VIA SAMARKAND. His ultimate goal was to reach the castle of his youth in Prussia—the place Niccolo had helped him recall, and where the future Czarina lived. But a detour to Samarkand he believed a prudent step. Certain ancient spells fused like magic fossils into the stones of that city and he knew the right incantation would make them fluid and easy to absorb—after all, he needed weapons like black lightning to stay alive; and even though his horse, Kublai, was a magical breed capable of preternatural velocity, it would still take weeks to make the perilous journey. Besides, Temujin Gur might be searching for him, and the 12th degree black warlock was at the peak of his powers.

Would he forget Zolo now that the Emperor Qian Long was safe?

Other dimensional creatures known to Zolo as "The Night Brethren," beings who had gathered his dark intelligence on enemies for the past century, could not foresee Gur's intent or even know his position, but they whispered to Zolo of a young World Maker coming into her power in the Holy Roman Empire. She was known as Freddie von Anhalt, and one day soon would possess not only the ability to defy Temujin Gur, but even Time itself.

Yes, he knew. She lived in that Prussian castle.

Perhaps the two of us can destroy Gur.

A small chance, but one he would take. What other choice was possible?

Zolo's magical grand Arabian named Kublai carried him across the southern plains of Kazakhstan in record time, but upon reaching the rocky shore of Lake Balkhash, it broke a leg in a fall. With what little magic Zolo had left, he fixed the leg, but then it broke again. He fixed the leg one last time and set Kublai free. He soon found another horse, but three Russian bandits stole it on the border of Transoxiana. After those unfortunate and nearly fatal setbacks, a wandering Turk traded a horse to him named Blister for a pistol, and he soon goaded the hapless Blister into hauling him to just outside Samarkand.

Now, many days into his flight, Zolo straggled into a caravanserai beside the abandoned watchtower of a long dead race. The one colossal eye of that tower, solitary and morose, stared forever across the lake to the distant mountains beneath the full moon. At the local inn, Zolo fell upon his bed, exhausted, perhaps even too exhausted to be afraid of death. He groped in a pocket within his robe and withdrew a small figurine: Alexander. Zolo had carried him since he was a child, for Alexander still served as inspiration. Unknown to most, the ancient Greek struggled through war after war to create a world ruled by just laws and wisdom. Zolo desired the same goals for his own world of the 18th century.

A short prayer he mumbled to the old, soft-featured god, and once done, stuffed him deep in his robe. Before drifting to sleep his final thoughts were of his long lost mother, Avizeh. The god Alexander, and the nearness to Samarkand, had cajoled him once more to feel her tender caress and a soft kiss on his forehead. Avizeh had vanished quite suddenly when he was only seven. His father had vanished days before. He never understood. Before she disappeared, he recalled her terrible fear of a bee. She saw a bee in the mouth of a street vendor in Samarkand. It stood on his tongue and stared at her with cold anger. Zolo remembered it also: the strange cosmic blackness of the eye, the odd looking head of the vendor and his evil toothless grin.

That was all he considered.

The next morning, as the caravans of the Silk Road arrived laden with treasures from the West, he awoke in a panic, thrashing and yelling. He'd dreamed himself pierced by a hundred bloody nails within the body of a Virgin Mary—an evil iron maiden used by the Pope's agents in Rome to murder heretics.

The sun, already high, clued him that too much time had passed. He cursed himself and leapt from bed, the pain of nails fading. He sprinted downstairs, paid the innkeeper for the night and rushed out to the stables. As he strapped down a bedroll on a sagging Blister, his stomach complained to his brain that many days had slipped by since he'd swallowed a hot meal. Within moments, his stomach began quarreling, promising to ache if his brain refused to surrender. Cursing again, and with a quick look over his shoulder, he returned to the inn where he positioned himself in a corner and ordered food.

It all seemed safe enough, for the time being anyway.

Zolo glanced around the room and verified he was alone, except for a solitary old man at a small wooden table nearby. He dismissed the fellow without a second thought and brooded to himself, planning his strategy for winning over the Princess von Anhalt. Minutes later, the innkeeper brought a side of lamb and a bowl of hot barley. Zolo ate like a famished serf, and once more, pondered his situation. As he imagined a chance at final salvation, the old man spoke:

"Back already?"

Zolo turned to examine him. He noted the long white beard, the old furs and rough woolen clothing of a mountain peasant. Nothing unusual. The old man's beard dipped in his tea cup when he spoke again. "Your stomach brought you back," he said.

Zolo tore a chunk of lamb from the bone with his teeth, wiped the grease from his face with a dusty sleeve and said, "Do I know you?"

"You have, and *you will*."

Lifting a bowl of hot barley, Zolo shoveled it into his mouth. The ache in his stomach slowly faded.

"Well, I don't *know you*."

The old man cleared his throat and said, "I hear you dabble in democracy?"

Zolo stopped eating and stared suspiciously. It wouldn't be beyond any one of dozens of sultans or princes to have sent an assassin to claim his head for preaching European Enlightenment.

"Dabble? What care you if I dabble in monarchy for that matter?"

"I simply find it fascinating that a wanderer of the wastes like yourself cares a wit about people ruling themselves."

"Why? Because—"

"In fact, I am more inclined to believe that wandering the wastes has burned away what little wit you have left," the old man croaked and laughed to himself. "*Ha,ha, hehhhhggg!*"

"I need not defend my political views to you. You would never understand."

"I do understand that you are a fool. The people of Asia would rather feast on your carcass than follow you to a republic of tyrants."

"What?"

"They know their place, and their limitations."

"What do you mean a *republic of tyrants?*"

"Athens, a city run by tyrants who were elected by idiots like yourself. It took Alexander, a great warrior king, to unite the Greeks and bring glory to them."

"You're forgetting about others like Pericles who—"

"Pericles? That oaf with a head like a stew pot? He cultivated the lower orders and it justly brought him to ruin, his country following along. I would have told him, but I wanted him to fail."

Zolo laughed. "Ahhh, so you were a contemporary of Pericles, eh old man? You are truly far older than I thought."

"Yes, I am. Since the time of Babylon. Before that I wandered the waste, much like you."

"I am relieved you are simply insane. At first, I thought you were an assassin."

"But *I am an assassin,*" he said and grinned. "And I want to tell you, that's a fine horse you have. He's strong, sure-footed and handsome... Will he run for office in your new democracy of Asia?"

"He has bad teeth, and he's stubborn. No one would vote for him."

The old man cackled and slapped his knee. "I'm going to enjoy riding him through the mountains."

"He's worn out and perhaps ready to die, much like me. But he's my horse, and he's going to take *me to Samarkand.*"

"Oh, ho ho! You don't need a horse, for you are not going anywhere."

Zolo laughed and shook his fist. "By Allah's thumbs, you're a bandit?"

"You still don't recognize me?"

Zolo saw nothing familiar. "I am not Pericles, so I have never met you."

"Careful, you are wading in blood," the old man said, his face darkening. "Maybe you remember these?" He reached inside the folds of his blanket and withdrew a bundle of smooth black sticks inscribed with Chinese-like symbols. He waved one of the sticks and a blinding white-hot pain exploded at the base of Zolo's brain.

Yarrow sticks! The most powerful magic instruments on Earth.

Zolo wanted to move, to run away, except he was frozen to the spot. His antagonist laughed and tapped his knuckles with the stick and the burning pain crawled down Zolo's spine to his tailbone. "Stop!" he screamed. The pain was so intense he wanted to throw up his lunch. He watched the old man skim his hand over the sticks and they glowed with an ominous, purple light. A hammering sound filled his ears, a thick strident beat that grew in volume.

It was his heart and it wanted to explode!

For the first time in many years, blind fear paralyzed Zolo. His head throbbed as he finally realized the truth: the decrepit ancient must be a twelfth-degree black warlock, for no one else could have mastered the yarrow sticks and accessed their power in such a way as to affect him so profoundly. Only three spell-crafters in the whole world had ever possessed that kind of knowledge. One in Wales, one in India, and...

The old man spoke again, his eyes gleaming like hellish meteors. "And I can see from the pain in your face that you have been reminded of the Virgin Mary box where I put you at age 16. Do you remember? The scores of nails piercing your weeping flesh? DO YOU REMEMBER, ZOLO BOLD?"

"*Temujin Gur*," he gasped.

"Yes, I am he," said the old man. "In a moment, I will be on my way and your soul will be scattered on the winds of time. Even the future Czarina cannot save you. Indeed, she will be the last to fall, and you, Zolo Bold of the Kazakhs, will be in Hell to greet your beloved whore when she arrives!"

Gur raised a gnarled fist that held aloft three yarrow sticks. He tossed them into the air where they floated in space, whirling slowly in a circle, slowed in time. In the center of the space between them, a blue light pulsed, casting a severe shadow across the room. The entire room began to vibrate with earthquake-like force, and shrill howls pierced the air, as if Gur were being cheered on by a chorus of hellish invisible demons. Terrified, the innkeeper ran for his life and out the door.

With no magic left, Zolo drew his dagger to pounce on Gur's old body and bury the blade in his foul heart, but something stopped him in the way an upraised spear point stops a charging horse. Gur had opened his mouth, ever so slightly, and within, Zolo saw a gleaming black eye, like the eye of a bee, an impossibly enormous bee. At that moment, Zolo's knife dropped to the floor. The warlock raised a hand before his mouth, palm up, and the bee strolled into the evil blue light. "Your old friend, this ancient god," Gur said and cackled. "He knows how much you worship him."

Zolo could not speak. He felt an odd tingling in his own hand. He smelled a scent like that of corrosive acid cooking flesh and glanced down to see his fingers blackening to a mummy-like husk, thinning and curling upward towards his wrist.

This moved him.

Whirling like a mad dervish, Zolo sprinted for the door, the vision of that hideous bee swelling in his brain. Gur mocked him as he fled with a voice thundering so loudly that even camel drivers a mile away heard it booming across the steppe:

"THE MAGIC OF THE WORLD MAKERS WILL NOT SAVE YOU,

ZOLO BOLD! TELL YOUR MOTHER AVIZEH I HAVE SENT HER SON
HOME!"

Outside in the bright sunlight, Zolo ran, first one way, then another, shoving aside two camel drivers in his way who cursed him
vigorously. But as he sprang upward to mount his horse, he burst
into a cloud of shiny powder, a glittering smoke that refracted the
light into a rainbow of color as it wafted into the air and rushed
away, higher and higher, lifted by a hand of hot wind into oblivion.

царица

2

The War for Utopia – Hellish Magic Technology - Freddie and Zolo

AS SHE KNELT AT THE ALTAR FOR HER CORONATION in the year 1762 as Catherine II, Czarina of all the Russias, the former Princess Freddie von Anhalt felt like starting a new war. She'd already endured two hours of a five hour ceremony while wearing twenty pounds of silk coronation dress and nine pounds of Great Imperial Crown, and the excessive pomp and boredom drained her of goodness. To distract herself from the seemingly endless drone of the Russian Orthodox Patriarch as he recited Old Testament scripture, as well as the oven of suffocating heat created by a hoop dress big enough to hide twenty dwarves, Freddie lifted the curtain on theater by replaying to herself memorable events in the war of all wars, the ultimate war to define the fate of human nature itself.

Her old violin-playing mentor, Niccolo Paganini, called it "The War For Utopia."

No matter the name, so it was, and would be again. How many utopias had been created as a result? How many fallen? She'd lost count. No doubt her future struggles would ceaselessly birth new utopias from the carnage. And speaking of carnage, people die in wars, of course. Even magical beings die. But it never ceased to strike her as curious and odd that despite her great powers she could not *stop dying.*

Already, she'd grown tired of it, and it was never convenient or easy. Her first death at the hands of Eréndira Marquez, the Wizard Goddess allied with her blood enemy, Edison B. Godfellow, was still the most painful because of the many serf families, even children, whose souls were sacrificed to restore her life. Such an act of sorcerous barbarity forced a guilt she carried all her days and sleepless nights; and what did "the white knights" of war have to show for the battle?

Yet another crater on Mars?

And of course, more needless deaths.

For all she knew, she could be dead even now. The French philosopher Descartes, to prove his own existence in 1644, said to himself, "*I think, therefore I am*," and Freddie could do the same, but could she trust her "I" to be the real one?

As she would later note in her memoirs begun many years before:

Perhaps my own body and mind were grown from a pot by that damnable Godfellow and I existed at the royal coronation as a living copy of my original self. Though entertaining such thoughts might result in the onset of insanity, I must nevertheless admit that I live in a world of games within games. I am never completely sure of what I am, or the reality of where I am. I only know I must proceed as if all is real, and morality is within my grasp.

Musing further on the insanity while the aged Orthodox Patriarch stumbled over a dull reading of Genesis inevitably took the new Czarina back even further, to the very beginning, that distant time at age fifteen in the Prussian castle of Bärenthoren.

Had she really died at the hands of Master Paganini as the vision foretold? She wasn't sure. Not anymore.

Regardless, it all began that afternoon with a sound.

A barely audible titter, like distant footsteps on decayed leaves.

At first, she did not understand and tried to ignore it, believing it to be the scraping sound of a mouse, or some other invading creature, for every now and then a cat bird or a dove flew in the study and fell to the floor, finally tiring itself out with fearful flutters. So truly, it could have been any number of things. She vowed to forget the disturbance and return to her prior tasks: recreating the Greek mathematics of Eratosthenes in an attempt to determine Earth's circumference while imagining herself Sir Francis Drake sailing the Azores in search of Spanish gold.

Putting quill to paper, Freddie sketched the hull of Drake's ship, *The Golden Hind*, before jotting down a few notes on the logic of Eratosthenes, and just as she measured the miles between the two cities in his equation, Syene and Alexandria, the strange tittering repeated. But louder this time. Enough to make her hand slip, the point of quill jaggedly defacing her work. *What in Hell's name?* That irritated her, to say the least, and the disturbance became too curious and odd to allow any further progress on the circumference of Earth.

Though Freddie hated breaking personal vows, she rose from her writing desk, her ears straining to understand. She soon realized the sound stirred from a corner of her study there in the Prussian castle of Bärenthoren, from a dark place in the shadows between a George III globe and a stand of antique books given her by her father, Prince Christian.

The tittering again.

Suddenly afraid to look—for she knew that nothing in her experience could have made such an eerie stir—she nevertheless felt overwhelmed by curiosity, and her own need to find courage in the face of a growing fear she found humiliating. Despite her instincts, she tried to explain it away once more. Could it be a mouse? A trapped bird of some kind? *Or perhaps a trick of yours, mother? It wouldn't be the first time you employed the spirits of Bärenthoren to frighten me.*

She sought courage in the newfound belief that Princess Johanna might well be to blame, and she resolved to face whatever it might be. A chance to defy "the witch of Prussia" should not be missed!

She stepped closer to the sound. Her eyes peered into the shadows. At first, she saw nothing, but her fingers felt as if tiny needles suddenly pressed into them.

By the pricking of my fingers, something wicked nearby lingers.

She knew it to be a sign of supernatural evil lurking nearby, her fingers pricking on other occasions whenever demonic spirits wandered the halls of Bärenthoren Castle seeking redemption or revenge; but the only object demanding her attention near the George III globe was the painting her mother had purchased from Augustus of Poland two years before in 1741—a work by the Dutch painter Vermeer entitled, *Girl Reading a Letter at an Open Window*. But then, about to turn away from the painting and search further, Freddie noticed a frighteningly odd thing:

The image of the girl in the painting had vanished.

The princess blinked. Nothing changed.

Only a dark silhouette remained, and she believed it a trick of light. Or was she going mad? She knew of elixirs that tortured the victim's mind with apparitions before they died.

Are you trying to poison me now mother?

Before she could consider it further, she heard the titter once more, cold and low, poking out from that dark corner just below the painting... and *something moved, I know something moved. Fight or flight, Freddie?* She saw a roundness, a vague shape take form, and she imagined a head nearly a foot above the floor.

But no, it *wasn't* her imagination.

It floated towards her out of the shadows, and what emerged into the light appeared like nothing she had ever seen: a thing so twisted, so out of place in her world, in any world dreamed by women or men or God that it made her doubt her own sanity even more. The upper body of the unholy thing hovered in the air above the floor without legs or support.

The Vermeer girl!

Freddie recognized the muddy blond hair, high forehead, the thin coils of curl, the colors of the old dress, and that face now dour and smirking, as if it knew a dark secret or a wicked event that would soon harm her more than she could imagine. Freddie trembled like a cold little animal and moaned, and as she did so, the unholy thing from the painting spoke to her:

Princess von Anhalt, do you know who I am?

The voice was mousey and girlish, yet evil, an echo of black abyss and death in the tone. More words were then spoken by it, and in a coarse, alien language she did not understand, though with a spell-like cadence she would come to know in future years.

And as the alien voice spoke, an even stranger thing happened.

The huge George III globe snapped free of its wooden frame with a loud crack and rose into the air. Freddie shook so much she could barely stand. She wanted to scream at the horror of it all as the globe floated up, higher and higher until it covered the dark gaping hole in the Vermeer painting where the girl's head had been. Then it began to spin on its axis, faster and faster. It spun to blur and brightened to a red sun, a fiery disk turning dark, blackening to full eclipse, far away and low above a range of snowy mountain peaks even taller and more rugged than the Alps she had visited when only a small child.

The air before her dimmed to fire and shadow, and upon a smoking rock of earth beneath that sun-black alien sky, the future Czarina of all the Russias, more terrified than ever in her life, witnessed an apparition: no bigger than her outstretched thumb in the distance, a hovering ghost that grew legs and became a woman stumbling forward, her body sheathed in a torn white coat of fur, her breath coming heavily.

Freddie recognized her.

Her own dark chestnut hair flowed down to the woman's waist, her own hazel-dark eyes flashed with fury and terror as the body shivered. The woman was her. An older version though, perhaps by ten years or more, and too, Freddie saw a clamoring mob of machines closing fast behind her. Clacking over the rock and whining like dogs, the machines appeared like gigantic Indian locusts, but each one frog-faced and glaring with the eyes of a hideous reptile. The nearest one opened its mouth and screamed like a saw cutting metal—the language that of the haunted Vermeer girl, coarse and alien, echoing to the distant mountains like a great beast in agony.

Freddie gasped and called to her older self:

"It's me! COME TO ME! I WILL SAVE YOU!"

The woman heard the shouts. She raised her head and stared back at Freddie, saw the younger version of herself looking anxious and fearful. She immediately recalled this same circumstance centuries before when at the age of 15 she'd watched herself stumbling forward like a pitiful drunken serf chased by whining hell-machines beneath a sky of black sun.

As the older woman recovered from her initial shock at the sight of her innocence and naivety from so long ago, her eyes hardened to desperation, and she shouted:

"I am Catherine, the woman you will become! A war is coming and the time you know will be no more. The future of your world depends—."

Then nothing. The young girl was gone.

The vision from centuries past had evaporated, as if on cue, just as Catherine had remembered—just enough glimpse to tease her, frighten her.

Only fear mattered then. Now also.

Catherine turned around to see Paganini's Fracas Machines gaining on her, relentless as hounds and driven by beings of dark and terrible magic. She knew it was a race to the cliff with only moments remaining before she would be torn to pieces. Her bleeding feet must do what her own magic could not, for her voice and invincible aria were no more. She could not sing the mountains into cloud, or the terrible machines into the black oil from whence they came.

She could do nothing but seek her own death.

* царица *

THE AIR BEFORE FREDDIE VON ANHALT DIMMED AND SHARP-ENED once more to the familiar walls of her study in Bärenthoren Castle. The horrible screeching machines, the black sun above the snowy mountains, all dissolved. The George III globe back in place.

Was it all over?

Not quite. Once more she heard the tittering, that frightening voice crawling into her skin and reaching for her throat. Still trembling, she closed her eyes, steeling herself to run from the room.

Then she heard a different sound—a clattering of dishes on the other side of her study door, and she could only scream one word in response, the loudest scream she'd ever made, for she realized this new sound signaled the arrival of her salvation:

"FATHER!"

The door to Freddie's study flung open as if by a gust of giant's breath, smashing into the wall with a force that shook the floor boards. Prince Christian burst through with a tray of his daughter's lunch, for he took it upon himself to bring her food during times of study, and never shirked in this task. "What in Saint Dorothea's name!" he yelled, bulling towards Freddie, his eyes the size of ostrich eggs, his white wig askew and gray waistcoat flapping as his body eclipsed the scene of horror. "What is it, my darling?"

"PLEASE TAKE ME FROM THIS PLACE!"

Without hesitation, he threw the clattering silver tray of food onto the night-table, scooped up Freddie in his robust arms as if she were a small child, turned and pounded furiously from the room. Stiff as stone in her father's grip and weeping to herself, Freddie longed to erase the memory of the smirking demoness of Vermeer, to forget that horrid voice, that mousey voice of evil. Little did she know, the memory would never completely fade.

For the moment though, only escape mattered.

Prince Christian clutched his daughter in his arms and rushed down the narrow granite stairs. Yet still, as the distance from the room increased, Freddie swore she heard a sound of rushing air, as if the smirking girl closed on them from behind, still whispering her name. Or was it a thing from that nightmare world of black sun?

Her father reached the base of the stairs, and without slowing, ran across the stone floor and straight through wide open doors into the Great Hall of Bärenthoren Castle. And as his battering-ram momentum carried them forward, Freddie glimpsed the fleeting face of a boy. Perhaps a servant in the castle? ... Yes, it was Willie, her nanny's nephew. *What is he doing here?* But no time to consider. She just saw him staring at her with eyes big and black as those of an owl, his face with the look of a crazed fox retreating into the shadows of the Great Hall.

Her father saw him too, and shouted, "Shut those doors, boy!" Whereupon Willie stopped gawking and ran to the heavy wooden doors like a dutiful servant to begin pushing them closed. But just as the big oaken and iron-strap doors creaked to within a final thread of air, they burst open again.

God and Beelzebub! What now?

Was it the Vermeer girl summoning the strength of a bull to chase her down? A whining hell machine from the land of black sun?

* царица *

FREDDIE'S NANNY OF TEN YEARS OBSERVED PRINCE CHRISTIAN rushing to the stairs, carrying the bundle of Freddie in his arms. She'd been chatting with one of the older maids cleaning the upstairs bedrooms and was on her way to Freddie's study when the girl's shrill, demon-filled screams frightened so much air out of the castle that the nanny almost choked; and the sound chilled her spine too, reminded her of unspeakable things haunting the darkest of European nightmares, for never had the Princess Von Anhalt cried it out in such a manner. Chiseled from the same granite as her father, she had endured things that would have caused even a soldier to faint. It could only mean that something evil, truly evil must be intent on shattering far more than the castle calm.

Babette wasted no more time in conjecture. She launched herself down the hall as fast as her big legs and long dress would allow. In her rush, she almost knocked over Gleb, the dour Russian chief butler who chose to go about his duties rather than involve himself with the mishaps of those far above his station.

"Tend to your own affairs, oh queen of Prussian cows!" he snapped at her as she passed him.

Babette ignored the insult, focused as she was on her mission. Huffing and puffing, she ran down the stairs, chasing the disappearing Prince Christian. She heard him enter the Great Hall and she followed, bursting through the doors just as they almost closed, erupting into the room like Gaia herself, mother of all Titans. She ran up to the Prince and Freddie, almost breathless, and she shouted, "My lord! ... God and my Lord, what has happened? ... Is my precious girl—"

"Yes, Babette, yes ... the princess is of ... good health," Freddie's father said as he tried to catch his own breath, speaking over his daughter's shoulder. "She's just fearful of this castle. Something happened in her room. I know not. There was no time to uncover it."

"Ah, of course, the ghosts of this place. I've seen them many times! Why only yesterday—"

Freddie sighed and whispered, *"Babette"* and her nanny said to Prince Christian, "May I take her, lord? I will care for her. I should have been there in the room to protect her. Please punish me if you must."

"Nonsense! No one will punish you, or anyone else," he said with a hint of irritation in his voice. "There has been way *too much* of that in this castle." He said and gently handed the body of Freddie over to Babette who took her and held her close—no easy task for anyone given Freddie's size. Over the past year she'd grown much closer to full womanhood and astonished everyone in the castle with her maturity.

Babette carried Freddie to a place of warmth while Prince Christian followed. She walked up to stand before an enormous and arching stone-cobbled fireplace now roaring with enough flame to melt iron. Still clutching her princess, she plopped down her ample fanny on a cushioned bench before the fire and soothed her precious charge. She knew just what to say. She knew just what to do. "What happened, my *lapooshka*? You scared the roosters out of me!"

Freddie shivered and struggled for sanity, opening her eyes and glancing about as if searching the dark corners of the Great Hall for monsters.

"Relax, girl, the demons are no more. You're as tight as a drum," Babette said, imagining more phrases of comfort from bygone days, rubbing Freddie's shoulders as her father knelt down, facing his daughter, his hand reaching out to clutch hers. Her nanny knew that the two of them would give Freddie strength and a sense of protection, and she was right. Freddie was moved to reveal at least a shred of the nightmare vision:

"I saw machines ... screaming, chasing me, but *not me*."

"Not you?" Babette stroked the young woman's forehead, her own face darkening with concern.

"I saw myself, older, and I was somewhere in the mountains, the Alps or ... no, bigger, like the Himalayas. My name was Catherine. It was so strange ..."

"And things were *chasing* you?" her father asked." Who sent them to chase you?"

"I don't know. I believe my death was close. It might have been my very last day."

"Nonsense!" her father said, squeezing her hand tighter.

"And she said ... a war was coming."

Babette smiled. "Oh, poof and poop! A war is always coming, and besides, your name isn't Catherine," she said while suddenly noticing her nephew Willie drawing closer out of the shadows, as if he strained to hear their words.

His presence made no sense. What in God's name was he doing there? He should have been in the castle kitchen busy at chores, not lurking around. He was a distraction she didn't need, one that no one needed. Babette wished to chase him away, but felt herself growing more and more alarmed at Freddie's state of being. Had she been poisoned? Babette knew of potions that caused terrible daydreams and nightmares. As the ancient Romans once said, *Whom a god wishes to destroy he first drives mad*. The mere thought of Freddie losing her mind made Babette moan inwardly, but she would be strong for her, no matter what came.

"You are just under a spell, my *lapooshka*, a spell of this castle. You aren't the only one to have visions and nightmares, you know. I myself once had a vision that the Ottoman sultan chased me through the castle halls on the back of a flying goat!"

Freddie managed a weak grin, and Babette stroked the girl's forehead and rocked, watching the great fire as its light softened and calmed the room. Prince Christian stood up and gazed down upon his daughter, and with such love that Babette felt a tear in her eye. Soon enough though, above the fireplace crackle, the two of them heard another noise, as if someone new had entered the Great Hall. Was it a servant? Babette realized she had partaken too deeply of Freddie's fear and now felt terrified herself, so much so she could not move. Bärenthoren Castle echoed with darkness and demons, things not of this world. She'd seen them on occasion, floating in the halls, scampering in the attics, and as the sound of the new thing came closer, only fear for the princess overcame her own.

She began to turn, breathing heavily, catching a fleeting glimpse of Prince Christian's face darkening and Willie's face looking alarmed, his body retreating into the shadows. And as Babette's head turned, she saw the source of alarm on Willie's face. A thing far worse than any imp or hell spawn:

Princess Johanna.

The woman raged with a voice loud enough to frighten away any lurking devils. "Damn you three times, girl!" she shouted at Freddie, ignoring her husband standing off to the side—a man growing angrier by the second. Her arm shot like a bolt from a crossbow across Babette's shoulder to grab a fistful of Freddie's hair and viciously yank her from Babette's lap onto the stone floor. "I told you to dress properly hours ago! Damn you three times!"

Prince Christian said coldly, "No, damn *you*, Johanna."

Freddie just sprawled, her eyes to the ceiling, helpless. Babette whimpered, her own eyes imploring Princess Johanna for mercy as Prince Christian knelt back down to attend to his abused, ghost-shocked daughter, and to protect her from any further harm.

"It's no wonder the little mongrel disrespects me, Christian," Johanna said. "Since your own tongue displays it so well for her benefit!"

"You reap what you sow, Johanna."

"And you've sowed such a precious brat, have you not?" said Johanna. "Perhaps you might use one of your ridiculous mechanical contraptions to muzzle her!"

"PLEASE STOP!" Freddie yelled, her voice cracking.

Ignoring her, as well as her husband's murderous glare, Princess Johanna clapped her hands once and smoothed her face to a stoic mask of stone. Having regained this measure of composure, she looked down and said to Freddie, "Today you will meet Empress Elizabeth. She has come many months on her trip with her nobles to make a grand tour of Europe, and I do NOT want you humiliating me like you have in the past." She bent down, raising a hand as if to coldly slap Freddie. To the side, Prince Christian rose to his feet, one hand reaching around his waist and grasping at air, as though searching for a sword or pistol to draw.

"No, *please* ... I will do what you wish," Freddie said, gazing up at her mother. At this moment, she wasn't the tough as nails veteran of countless assaults. Now, she was only a vulnerable girl frightened by things that refused to follow the rules of the mundane world.

This unexpected response puzzled Princess Johanna. "You will do what *I wish*?" She straightened and her hand fell to her side. "What has befallen you, Freddie?" Her face began to look suspicious.

Babette saw her chance. She jumped from the bench and fell to her knees before the mistress of Bärenthoren Castle. "Please, oh wondrous angel, let me take this young woman to my quarters. I'll bathe her and dress her for the Empress of Russia. She will be beautiful and proper, I promise. I swear it! ... She was just having a horrible dream. It's the castle, the ghosts of the castle. She just—"

"Enough prattle! Take the little mongrel then, and live to your word or you will be whipped and made to shovel the stables for a year."

"No such thing shall ever take place," Prince Christian said.

Babette smiled and whispered *thank you*, but Princess Johanna only sneered her famous sneer at her glaring husband, a sneer known far and wide from Paris to Moscow, and turned and walked from the Great Hall. Babette watched her leave, saw the firelight flicker across her flowing dark dress and imagined her ruling Hell itself, her temper commanding even Lucifer to do her bidding or be forced to shovel Hell's stables.

Prince Christian watched her also, his temper still simmering. He bent down to kiss his daughter on the forehead, whispered something loving to her, stood and turned without another word to follow his wife out of the Great Hall, his steps measured and strong. Babette knew he would confront Princess Johanna in a more secluded part of the castle and resume the conflict. Like the rest of the castle staff, she was surprised the two of them had lived so long without one poisoning or stabbing the other.

Regardless, now that things had calmed in the Great Hall, Babette wished to deal with Willie. She waited several seconds before taking action, for she feared the potential of a sudden and violent return by Princess Johanna—a trick not new to her. Her own princess appeared safe, but she did not wish that woman of powerful rage to burst back onto the scene while she scolded Willie for lurking against orders.

Babette helped Freddie from the floor and settled her gently onto the cushion-covered bench before the fire. Next, she strode into the shadows of the Hall, to a far corner where she last saw Willie. She called out to him in a harsh whisper. He did not respond. She stood in that corner of the Hall, turning around and around, whispering, "*Willie, you scoundrel boy, where are you?*"

But he could not be found.

She saw nothing of him, no trace, as if he'd simply melted away. Could he have slipped out the door after Princess Johanna left, or before? Who knows? Babette would settle things with him later. His ability to read caused all sorts of trouble for her because the writers, or philosophers, or whoever they were, put all sorts of bold ideas in his head. Indeed, they threatened the sanity of the castle!

Their voices must have encouraged Willie to trespass.

The words drove him, like spells ... Yes. That must be it! Like spells of the mind, none of which gave Willie the right to overstep his bounds. Such presumption could not be allowed to exist, not for him, not for anyone in Bärenthoren Castle who did not drink from the golden cup. If only his ability to read such nonsense about "freedom" and "rights" would come to an end. She agreed with the nobles of Europe in their belief that DEMONcracy was "the work of the accursed printing press," and of course, "just a silly idea of ancient Greece."

Babette knew little of Greece, of course, not being able to read herself, though considering what she'd heard she did not care for the place, not a bit.

* царица *

WILLIE SAT DEEP IN THE BOWELS OF THE CASTLE, in a small candle-lit room facing a grand old clock positioned square on a rough oaken table big enough for four people to eat comfortably—the clock trimmed around its face with ornate oak leaf of solid gold, as if created by skilled European craftsmen imitating ancient crowns that once sat on the heads of great kings.

He'd arrived at the room via a hallway within the castle walls, one unknown to the servants and nobles. Of course, Master Paganini knew of it. He knew everything, it seemed. So while the tirade of Princess Johanna continued, he opened a stone panel in the shadows and edged through, closing it behind him with a faint click. He felt ashamed to leave, for he hated the way Freddie was always mistreated by the Princess. He wished to protect her, and even imagined he might be falling in love with her, for he'd been keeping watch on her for many months and his affection grew daily. He prayed that one day he might take revenge on her behalf, perhaps spin Johanna through the air, head over heels around the castle halls before locking her in the Bärenthoren dungeon.

Upon speaking to the clock, telling it a tale of Fracas Machines chasing a helpless Czarina Catherine in the mountains near Saravastra, he reached up and pinched the hour hand, turning it forward one hour to 11. The clock made a musical noise—a few simple notes with a melodic tone that reminded Willie of a woman humming. Once the last note faded, a voice spoke from the clock. It sounded distant and small, neither male or female, and scratchy as fingernails clawing at bark. Despite the distance and interference though, it carried a tone of worry, and when Master Paganini, The Lord of Saravastra and World Maker Supreme worried, it made Willie anxious.

"The princess saw the death of her future self ... are you certain?" the voice said.

"Yes."

"It must be a plan to frighten her, to create suspicion. Part of a bigger plan to turn her away ... And perhaps it was not truly that day, but a version, a conjuring of possibility."

"I believe it was truly that day, Master Paganini."

"Then we must convince her otherwise, Zolo. Very soon now, she will begin to acquire her power of grand aria, and she will work with us to save the 20th century from Edison Godfellow's world wars."

"I know. I will help to mask the truth, I swear it," he said with sadness in his voice.

"Is there something wrong? You sound depressed, young man."

"I know the Princess von Anhalt serves a greater purpose as a future World Maker and Czarina, but at the same time I wish to protect her."

"You will do what you must. I have seen your future, Zolo. You will fight for liberty around the world, in the Americas and beyond. That is your destiny."

"I understand, but—"

"Does Babette still believe you are her nephew? You know how spells across time can dissipate."

"Yes, she does ... I need to say—"

The clock hummed again and went silent. His concern was not heard.

Zolo stood up from the table and looked around at the stone walls of the small room closing in on him. Did he really exist in a prison? And what was "destiny" but another form of prison sentence? To be subject only to The Fates was not what he wished. He desired to change destiny, just enough, for Freddie's sake, even if Master Paganini disapproved. Watching the beating she took from Princess Johanna only confirmed that wish. Besides, Master Paganini did not know everything. How could he? Freddie's vision had shocked him, caught him by surprise. So perhaps *destiny,* the world-to-be, could be changed.

Freddie von Anhalt should live to be a great World Maker and Czarina for the ages, not die horribly at the hands of Fracas Machines.

Standing there, in that small, prison-like room, Zolo Bold vowed to do everything in his power to create a new destiny for her. They could be victorious, even prevent the grand utopian scheme of the demonic Edison Godfellow from taking place, and without the doom Master Paganini believed would inevitably overtake Freddie's older self. Why should living as a slave to one being's vision of destiny be acceptable, and besides, he didn't believe that Zolo Bold of the Kazakhs would ever make it to America to fight for liberty with heroes of revolution. It just seemed impossible. Master Paganini had told him, in a moment of haste, that his adult self would book passage to the New World, and that he would play an important role in the American Revolution, and later, help a man named Napoleon Bonaparte in France.

What an odd name!

Zolo wanted to believe it, more than anything, for having been raised by Master Paganini, he accepted that World Maker's vision of a wise, spiritual democracy for Earth, a veritable utopia to be known as the Pan Buddhist Democratic Union. Besides, why would Paganini lie? He had been like a father and mentor for ten of Zolo's 16 years, raising him in Saravastra together with the Mothers of The Temple ever since that day his real mother Avizeh had vanished from his sight forever. Still, Zolo was supposed to be a great spell-crafter in the future, though why would the heroes of America's new order take up with a common molder of matter and energy?

They made things happen with their beliefs and courage. Causes needed blood to nourish them. It would avail nothing if one day he forced entire British regiments to fire on each other.

That would be too easy, and history would suffer.

The world would suffer.

царица

3

Bleeding Walls and Woggers – The Cooking of Freddie - Anhalt World Storming

"THE ROYAL RHINOCEROS DANCE" SHE CALLED IT. Often she would compare the counts and barons, and other nobles to a herd of bloated rhinoceros—men or women, it made no difference. *All of them so shallow and selfish.* They never stopped croaking like mating frogs about their awfully boring lives and social position relative to the royal courts. They loved their French too, even though the French scoffed at them behind their backs. Fools, all of them! So intolerable. But now, on this day, Freddie welcomed the distraction as she walked through the main hall in Bärenthoren Castle (busy as a Sunday main street in Paris) towards the Great Hall where all present would jostle and puff and climb over themselves for a chance at fawning over Empress Elizabeth of Russia.

She would stoically endure the many flattery rituals because it all served as more distraction, for the apparitions of late had both depressed and disturbed her. Memories of the Vermeer girl, that horrible vision of her older self near death, *those insane machines ...* It must be as her darling Babette said, likely a witchery or curse of the castle seeking a hold on her mind. What other explanation could there be? She was not going mad. No. And if drugged she would still be seeing the visions, unless of course, the drug had ceased its work. If mad by other means, why would she be perfectly fine now?

Fine, yes, except for the memories.

If only a doctor or magician could drill a hole in her head and extract them. Or burn them out? Perhaps Temujin Gur himself, the infamous Mongol spellcrafter of Empress Elizabeth, might do the job.

Though the Mongol devil might replace them with something far worse.

She saw him yesterday, late, only a glimpse after the Empress and he arrived in that massive black Berlin carriage. Like everyone else, she'd heard the rumors spreading like dark plague all over Europe that Gur was the real mastermind behind the Russian throne and Elizabeth only a puppet. Many claimed him more ancient than The Great Wall of China, and said that he presided over the burial of Genghis Khan himself, putting to death all those who witnessed it so they would not reveal the location of the Khan's sacred necropolis.

Prior to the arrival of these powerful beings, Freddie had barely dressed in time. Under the glare of her mother, she stuffed and groaned herself with Babette's help into a full court outfit—the kind she so hated. Whenever she wore it she felt like a cross between a red peacock and a frilly doe. The ridiculously big hoop skirt forced her to go down the castle staircases sideways, one careful step at a time, and with every five steps she took, her mother barked at her from behind, "Damn you three times, Freddie! Be quick!"

Once positioned in the courtyard to greet Empress Elizabeth, what happened next became an event she would never forget.

From the carriage, the Empress emerged into the sunlight, her huge blue eyes flaming with command. Nothing could resist her dominance. Were the very walls of Bärenthoren expected to forget their masonry and bow to her? The walls remained aloof, of course, though all beings of flesh and blood demonstrated obedience. The assembled Prussian nobles from over a hundred miles around in their long coats and powdered wigs, the noblewomen in their frills and jewels and hoop skirts, Princess Johanna and Freddie's beloved father, Prince Christian, as well as the Bärenthoren chief servants, stewards, butlers, valets, and maids in their finest blue-and-gold livery, all ranks displaying themselves in one long line full of bow and curtsy as the mighty Empress of Russia stepped down to the stone.

Freddie watched those royal eyes as they moved, imagining a

grand symphony of music reaching thunderous climax, but then an unexpected thing happened. The eyes of the Empress found a curious object to rest upon, to fixate upon. The entire crowd in the courtyard glanced sideways, straining without turning their heads to see whom the almighty Empress of all the Russias stared at. And those with a view could see the target quite clearly:

The Princess von Anhalt.

The imperious flaming gaze rested on her, only on her.

Freddie gasped in the light of the royal glare. The eyes bored into her like the points of a hot lance. The entire courtyard full of nobles and servants spoke not a word (they did not dare!), and Freddie sensed the crowd growing more nervous as the stare continued.

Why is she staring at me like that? Am I supposed to fall to my knees?

The eyes and face of Empress Elizabeth inhaled Freddie, long and deep, as a person might breathe in a few gallons of fresh air after confinement in a stale cabin. The princess felt embarrassed and looked down. Other eyes glanced from her to the Empress, curious and growing fearful; and at the same time, Freddie's fingers began to hurt. She knew something lay hidden in that carriage, yet to emerge into the sunlight.

An evil thing.

Even so, her patience had come to an end.

Enough is enough! And my fingers are pricking again. At least if an apparition appears, everyone will see it this time.

Freddie swallowed and steeled herself. Glancing up, not wishing to appear afraid, she avoided the eyes of the Empress and focused instead on her curly locks glimmering in the sun like burnished gold. It reminded her uneasily of the Vermeer girl. Was there a connection? The Empress wore a crème silk dress with a low neckline woven in gold thread, a tight bodice, and draped around her shoulders, a gold silk cape, the black wings of the Russian imperial eagle flaring out on either side and caressing her shoulders.

Finally, the Empress walked forward, towards Freddie. The entire courtyard silent, not even a breath. Freddie bowed her head and curtsied as the Empress came near to her and said, "You are Princess Frederiicke von Anhalt, *n'est-ce pas*? I would know you anywhere. Please, rise and lead me inside to the castle. I must speak with you."

Looking up, Freddie noticed fresh blood stains on the neck and bosom of the Empress' dress. She held her tongue though. In fact, the entire affair had rendered her speechless. She could only comply with the wishes of the Empress. Taking Elizabeth's delicate, snow-white hand in hers, she began to escort her inside.

Before crossing the threshold into the castle, both Prince Christian and Princess Johanna took pains to form a new line to greet the Empress—especially since she seemed to be ignoring the usual custom of courtyard etiquette. Freddie politely introduced her parents, and she hoped this would irritate her mother who she realized must already be fuming at the extra attention the Empress was showing her. And as her mother greeted the Empress with a face that could only be described as rivaling the sun itself in warmth and glow, Freddie felt a change in the crowd behind her, as if a sudden eclipse had blackened them all.

It began with a gasp or two from the female servants.

She turned to see a large, red-hooded figure emerge from the carriage and float towards her, following the path of Empress Elizabeth. *What in Beelzebub's name?* Small fluttering things like little moths surrounded it, diving in and out of the scarlet hood as if they nested there, or in the mouth of whatever was obscured. A row of tall black feathers thrust from the hood, running front to back to form a great black fin, all of it flowing into a cloak that hid the rest of the body. And as the floating apparition drew closer, Freddie noted the cloak inked with dozens of mysterious black symbols: curved chisels, sticks, tears and boxes, all collected in groupings like Chinese alphabet cells; and centered on the hood of the cloak, prominent and unmistakable, a Chinese-like pagoda temple encircled by a long black dragon, the mouth of the dragon biting the tail to complete the circle.

The very sight of the thing made her head burn in a disturbing way she had never felt, while her fingers pricked so painfully she pinched them.

Others were affected also.

Just as certain diseases have varying effects on their victims, so too this thing from Russia radiated an evil that touched people in different ways. Two of the castle valets, men of hard and gray age, shook so much their oaken false teeth clacked like wind shutters in a storm. One of the younger maids began to sing, words that sounded to Freddie, at a distance, like lines from an Italian opera. Something by Pollarolo? Another maid nearby shrieked in a savage alien language, flinging words like *"Ho dah, ha dibah!,"* at no one in particular while the maid beside her slapped her own face as if fighting herself. A Prussian noble, the Duke of Mecklenburg, clutched at his chest with a groan and fell to one knee just as a stunned castle guard dropped his musket to the ground, causing it to fire with such a loud report that it slammed the courtyard walls and broke two giant windows. And as the glass crashed to the stones and the smell of gunpowder bit their nostrils, the assembled servants and nobles, mouths hanging open, stepped backwards, for all of them knew this emissary from Hell to be the legendary spellcrafter and Russian royal puppet master:

Temujin Gur.

Before Freddie could recover from the vision and react to her new pain, the Empress pulled her into the castle's gigantic foyer, all full of staircase and statuary, swords and elk heads, and oil paintings of nobility the size of hay carts. The familiar feel and smell of the foyer, as well as the presence of the Empress brought immediate relief. Freddie walked beside the Empress as if her own child. A crowd of stumbling, nervous nobles followed right behind while dozens of castle servants scurried to take positions. Freddie looked over her shoulder to see her mother staring at her with coldly furious eyes. A beating or some other equally brutal punishment would follow, once the Empress left the castle, but Freddie knew, deep down for a reason she could not explain, that she no longer feared her mother.

The awkward and nervous train of the Empress was guided by Prince Christian into the Great Hall of Bärenthoren. He appeared joyful and dignified at once—the perfect host. The Prince wore a long, dark grey coat with broad gold-embroidered cuffs, and beneath the open coat, a gold brocade waistcoat atop a white silken shirt. His white wig was tied at the back by a black ribbon. Freddie knew he desired to lighten the mood after the lunacy in the courtyard. She also felt a pinch of sadness that in all the clatter and craziness no opportunity had presented itself to visit with her father. She respected and loved Prince Christian, and wished to see more of him outside the poisonous atmosphere her insanely jealous mother always created.

Meanwhile, inside the hall, bottles of wine, pitchers of fresh apple cider, and an assortment of pastries, tortes and cakes had been laid upon a long and shiny wooden table. Fires blazed in the eight enormous fireplaces and columns of rose-tinted sunlight, filtered by the tall castle windows, softened the misty air above their heads. Freddie felt as though she walked within an immense Byzantine cathedral, for the presence of the Empress radiated an air of holiness, God-like power and eminence, and this air was breathed by all. The very space itself seemed grand and divine. Only Temujin Gur who trailed the Empress might taint that feeling.

But where was he?

"Your *Excellency*," gushed Princess Johanna. Freddie's attention was drawn to her mother who now faced the Empress. "You must be exhausted after your long journey. Please refresh yourself."

The Empress smiled and took a glass of cider from a tray offered by one of the servants, a trembling butler with the face of a frightened bird. "I'm thrilled to have arrived in one piece. Je *suis béni*."

Freddie could no longer contain her curiosity. "It looks as if you survived a battle," she said, pointing to the blood-stained dress.

To her surprise, the Empress reacted by tearing up, as if on the verge of a strong weeping. "The most tragic thing happened not far from your castle," she said, finding it difficult to speak. Freddie reached out and grasped her hand. The Empress continued. "*Mon*

Dieu au paradis! It tore the heart from my breast. He was a boy of not more than fifteen years, and he ... he rushed into the road without warning from the hedgerow. Something was attacking him and he fled in such a hurry he didn't see us. If not for the timely braking of Ivan Illych, my driver, the draft horses of my carriage would have trampled him." She stopped. Tears streamed down her cheeks. She pulled a handkerchief from within her right coat sleeve and dabbed her face.

Freddie felt a pang of sorrow for this Empress Elizabeth, now transformed in her own mind from a being of godlike power to one far more compassionate and vulnerable. Freddie pressed the hand of the Empress even tighter. The Empress looked up, into the milling crowd, past the faces of Prince Christian and Princess Johanna appearing dutifully concerned, her eyes scanning for someone special. She called out, her voice breaking, "Ivan ... oh, Ivan, come here!"

The driver, Ivan Illych, entered the circle and bowed to the Empress and Freddie's parents. He was a thick-bodied man, classic Russian beard, hands like leather gloves. He'd overheard the conversation from nearby and understood what the Empress wanted. He began to tell the story:

"A large black bear charged from the hedgerow into the road. Before we could do anything, it trapped the boy against the hedge and swatted him across the face. I saw deep and bloody wounds on his face, and as he lay on his back in the road, the bear crushed his neck with a paw. I jumped from the carriage, leveled my pistol at the bear and fired at point-blank range."

Fascinated, Freddie listened to the story, watching the driver and noting his tunic also smeared with the boy's blood. "The giant beast hardly noticed the shot. To him, it was no more than an insect bite. He stood up on his hind legs and roared at us in defiance. My assistant threw a musket down to me and I fired again, hitting the bear, but the thing was a demon, invincible. And then, as if he hadn't a care in the world, he turned from us and lumbered into the hedgerow. We never saw him again."

The Empress, still teary, said, "I rushed to the boy, and held him in my arms. What a cruel and needless way to die. I had to ask my-self ... How did something so evil win the day *so easily?*"

Freddie marveled at the story, and at the realization that the Empress of Russia cared about the peasant boy's death. She *actual-ly cared*. How strange when compared to her own mother and most of the nobility who abused and scorned the serfs, as well as anyone else below their station. The noble class was less than one percent of the entire world, and yet they acted as if they owned a hundred percent of it. Like vampires, they bled it dry to feed themselves. The bullying bastards needed a good forced feeding of European En-lightenment, a few hundred pages of Diderot and Rousseau.

What they needed was a revolution to send them run-ning!

* царица *

MUSING FURTHER ON THE NOTION OF REVOLUTION, Freddie cut a path to the banquet in the Great Hall of Bärenthoren. Servants and nobles alike greeted her with words of *Jours sans, aimables maîtres-se* ("Well days, Mistress kind": one of the French-obsessed customs for servants begun by her mother) and "Good evening to you, Prin-cess von Anhalt," all of them bowing lightly as her red-and-gold hoop skirt, at least five feet wide, swept them away into corners and close to walls.

Within the daze of heads and bodies in the hallway, she no-ticed a single face trying hard to get her attention: the eyebrows nervously bobbing, lower lip quivering, eyes horror struck as if a monster had just screamed holy hell into them. She recognized it as belonging to Benjamin Barth, one of the Bärenthoren servants from a centuries-old serf family in perpetual service to Baron Eichmann of Merseburg.

"*Mistress, please ... I'm sorry for this,*" he said with a frantic whis-per.

"Benjamin, calm, calm. What is—"

"Baron Eichmann," he blurted out and glanced around as though expecting someone to pounce on him. "I would simply write you a note, but I ..." The last words failed him. He appeared like a hollowed-out tree ready to collapse in on itself.

Freddie clutched him by the arm and ushered him away from suspicious eyes into a nearby alcove lit by candles. She faced him, and as the candle light shadowed his face, rendering him darkly sad and fearful, Freddie heard his story, stammered out and caught in his throat between sobs. Baron Eichmann was selling off young serfs to pay tax debts, and had selected Benjamin's twelve year old sister, Daniela, to be one of them. The Baron chose her, and others, from a line up, suddenly rousing them from their beds at night—he and his wife, Baroness Magdalena Eichmann, along with their hired ruffians wielding swords and clubs and harshly shouting *Kommen Sie aus dem Haus!* (Get out of the house!). The Baron wished a proper inventory before the serfs could hide, for the party arriving by horse would have been spotted across the fields a mile away in daylight. And just to make an example, his swaggering ruffians mercilessly beat one of the fathers who dared to question the Baron's need for the cruel affair in the first place.

"Mistress, my soul is yours, my whole being is devoted to thee, I **beg you**. My mother will die—"

"No more, friend Benjamin," Freddie said. She felt sad for him and also a growing anger at the ruthless cruelty of Baron Eichmann whose reputation had inflamed her in days past. "I will look into this. I will even pay that beast-eyed Baron if I must, whatever it takes to save her. You have my word, sir."

Freddie had already paid the taxes for other relatives of Bärenthoren Castle servants, even purchased several herself just to save them from being sold to cruel masters or killed. Prince Christian had reprimanded her once already for turning the Bärenthoren lands into what he called "a free home for Prussia's damned and lost." No matter. Freddie possessed enough gold trinkets to buy many more, and she would, even if her dear father disapproved.

Benjamin slumped to his knees in tears and kissed Freddie's hand. When a noble as high as the Princess von Anhalt helped someone as low as he, it was cause for joyful weeping. Nevertheless, she pulled him back up, steadied him and sent him on his way. She knew the banquet had commenced and her presence would be missed. She could already hear the familiar:

"Damn you three times, Freddie!"

* царица *

THE WALLS OF BÄRENTHOREN CASTLE IN PRUSSIA had witnessed the smoke and shot of titanic violence for centuries. The grand armies of Europe, meteoric in all their steel and pennant, had raged in galloping thunder over its body-strewn fields, burning towns to black skeleton, grinding serfs and peasants alike to marrow and less than memory, thrusting man and horse in charge after charge against the black-granite walls only to splinter them and bring needless death; and too, for so many years, the internecine wars as Lutherans fought Catholic marauders, the Pope in Rome sending his most ruthless swords to cleave the hearts of all heretics until the very flesh-of-war banged fist and wept bitterly upon the walls of Bärenthoren. But the walls never swayed, or showed compassion. They never cried.

Not until the arrival of Temujin Gur.

And then they cried. Not tears, but blood.

Bärenthoren servants saw it first, just before the banquet for Empress Elizabeth, oozing and trickling from the inside walls of several of bedchambers. Their screams brought Prince Christian bounding up the stairs, pistols in hand, to investigate. He touched the blood with one finger. It felt chill as ice and smelled of insect, like a mash of crushed hornets or bees. Princess Johanna took one look and shrieked herself into a faint. The Bärenthoren Castle priest, Father Rolfen Grimm, watched the haunted blood run in rivulets from the seams between the stones and crossed himself seven times seven. But the blood, wiser than they could imagine, possessed purpose, as all were soon to see.

It puddled into images, glyphs and profiles, some of them demonic, others more human in appearance, but all of them unknown and ominous. The kitchen staff swore that the blood on their tiles actually took the form of Empress Elizabeth in silhouette, and that it began to smoke and spit curses at them. A few puddles congealed into full faces that rose into the air, thin as masks, and began to talk rapidly with the voices of growling dogs. It was said later that if one could translate the words, they would know the formula for immortality. Regardless, the phenomena could not be explained. Were they related to Gur? Were the spirits of Bärenthoren bleeding themselves free of the castle in response to the presence of the Mongol sorcerer?

By morning, the entire countryside of Anhalt whispered in fearful tones. Rumors spread from field to tower, each retelling more ghastly or horrific than the one before. The many ghosts, sprites, were-fairies and Prussian demons of Bärenthoren aligned before the Mongol warlock in their ranks and bowed to him—the event witnessed by a butler from Berlin who intruded by accident into Temujin Gur's bedchamber and was blinded for his untimely entrance. Tales also of new windows opening onto other worlds filled with golden towers and snowy mountains, distant and ghostly moanings, and the smells of death mixed with an odd incense, as if from India or Tibet.

Freddie heard all rumors the day after the arrival of the Empress, and from Babette, of course, who signed herself with the cross as she spoke—her voice and manner like that of a child horrified by her first glimpse of war. Even the nobility of Europe spoke of Empress Elizabeth's spellcrafter in hushed tones, believing him to be her source of power and longevity on the throne. No one knew how she secured his services or rewarded him. The peasants rumored that she fed him serf children for dinner. The nobles rumored he walked into her skin and pulled strings on behalf of the Papacy and England's king, or the Ottoman Turks, depending on the politics of the year. Most Russians blamed him for every calamity, from bad winters to dead chickens. Freddie could well blame the apparition of Vermeer Girl and all else supernatural on him.

She shuddered to imagine the magical Mongol beast roving the castle and leaving walls of blood in his wake. What might happen at the banquet for Empress Elizabeth then? Would the roasted meats begin to bleed, or the wine turn to blood, or the ceiling drip with gore? Would he even be present at the banquet or simply bleed things from a distance?

The Princess von Anhalt had no choice but to face whatever came.

At the appointed time, she strolled confidently, head high, into the Bärenthoren Great Hall, holding herself so high because she felt so low, like a moldy leaf in a stream (a sorrowful comparison she would carry all her days). She was out of place, as if she belonged in another world, for the one of European nobility did not suit her. Perhaps her mother, representing this world in her mind, created this general mood of hatred which always led to melancholy. Regardless, the core trouble for Freddie was the European noble mentality, the swaggering sense of infallibility and superiority—all due for a fall in her mind. Way overdue.

So perhaps the infamous Gur will shake things up tonight.

Perhaps even bleed the walls on a few nobles.

What a bizarre comedy that would make!

Freddie passed through the big stone archway of the Great Hall, glancing up to see it chiseled with Roman-like gods and satyrs, all of them leering down at her. Where were they now? Gone to stone memory above a world of apathy. At least this doorway was wide enough to accommodate her stupid hoop skirt. *But never mind the skirt.* The scene in the Bärenthoren hall burst onto her senses, rising up before her like a great stage full of color and pomp, fire and shadow: flaming wax torches, together with the huge Bärenthoren fireplaces, lit the hall along with hundreds of candles set on the white-linen banquet tables, as well as something new: a strange column of trembling white light sweeping over the throng, emanating from a device of science. Raised high on a wooden platform to one side of the entrance, it looked like large circular glass inset within a housing, rather like a giant black monocle, and it squatted upon a thick wooden tripod. The thing was operated by three men who swiveled it back and forth. Prince Christian loved his devices, and no doubt, this one was arranged by him, whereas Freddie's mother loved her rockets.

Yes, rockets, exploding ones, the kind that smashed armies.

One of them she claimed was created by Hyder Ally's father, the famous Indian rocketeer. Princess Johanna couldn't get enough of them, and yes, there they stood, a collection of big iron rockets flanked on either side by two musket-wielding men of the castle guard in dark armor plate. Freddie spotted the rockets to her left, on a metal stand, their black conical tips pointed to the ceiling, looking as if ready to launch and blow Bärenthoren to pieces.

Glancing up, Freddie's eyes scanned the ceiling so high and dark, waving with shadows. One appeared like a giant manta or great hawk. What was it? She didn't know. Her fingers pricked for a moment, and as she stared at the shadows she felt her insides begin to heat, followed by an urge most odd. She heard a voice within herself, no particular words, just a deep and full *ohhhhhahhhh*. It welled up from the oven of her soul to brim above her eyes and rush to her head, and there it throbbed, vibrant, as if from an opera aria, primal and commanding.

Then it was over.

The Princess von Anhalt had received complements on her rich voice from time to time, yes, and her father once told her that her singing would make an army of men lay down their weapons, but now her voice had just come to life on its own, as if willed by someone other than her? Strange. Only her imagination, just that, it must be, so much going on with the terrible magic of Temujin Gur, the sins of the tyrant, this insane banquet, the threatening violence of her mother—all too much for the system.

Fight or flight, Friederike?

Still, oddly enough, the voice within had invigorated her, like a puff of flame heating a balloon to the sky. It felt addicting, so soon. But why had it happened? Perhaps her mind had come to life in a way she never knew possible, working to restore her, to stoke her inner fire back to hope and dreams.

Perhaps.

An explosion of laughter and a dropped glass distracted her back to the scene erupting all about her: Prussian and Russian counts, barons and dukes (the Russians having arrived in dozens of carriages only hours after the Empress) clumping and debating and guffawing about in their long coats and powdered wigs (that smelly white powder she hated). Their shiny black shoes gleamed with their master's chins while their wives roamed and laughed, snipped and quipped from one group to the next, their comically wide hoop skirts of red and blue and white-gold slapping one another as they passed, their puffed hives of hair glittering in the firelight with tiny jewel-lets of ruby and diamond; and as they circulated in the room like bad blood, a small orchestra of flutes, bassoons, oboes and violins played *Water Music* by Handel in the background. Freddie found the piece gay and uplifting. She admired Handel— one of Prince Christian's favorite composers. The music soothed her as scents of almond and cinnamon filled her nostrils, calming her further, easing her mind so recently upset by Benjamin's tale. Calming her, yes, until she spotted her mother joyfully chirping with the Russian nobles.

Oh, how lovely she is. Such a fraud!

Unknown to Freddie, Princess Johanna put on her best face in an attempt to forget the horrific blood seepage throughout the castle. After all, her moment had arrived, and certainly, no one, much less her, wanted blood dripping into the Great Hall and forming grotesque devil heads, at least not until the Empress had left. Nothing could be allowed to upset the presentation of *le grand courvert*, for the French way of dining was considered by the nobles of Europe to be the only civilized way to gobble their evening food; and with Empress Elizabeth present, Princess Johanna's reputation and future depended on the lavishness and pomp of her banquet presentation, and in execution of her service à la française. Even worse, to not display the proper proportions of gold, silver and porcelain on the tables, or to not include enough fancy dishes and desserts, might risk insulting the Empress. Therefore, Princess Johanna, together with the chief steward and other castle staff, had spent months in preparation, pouring over recipes and testing various combinations and layouts of food on the tables, cooking and arranging and fussing like spoiled children as they rehearsed for the big night. And price mattered not. Everyone knew that Prince Christian complained incessantly to his wife of staggering costs, especially as regards her purchases of Chelsea porcelain, fine India China, and the many dishes from Meissen—a business whose specialty was creating such delicate things.

Unfortunately for Prince Christian, his wife strove to mimic the famous service presented recently by the King of Saxony to the British ambassador Sir Charles Hanbury-Williams that included grand and glistening dessert dishes shaped like giant artichokes and sunflowers. Her own unique tastes, noted to Meissen's finest artisans, fashioned leaping wolverines and charging bears, shooting rockets, and huddles of cold but happy serfs scooped out with cupping holes in which to plop various ice creams, butters and jellies.

Next, came Princess Johanna's elaborate and magnificent centerpieces.

All the nobles, even Empress Elizabeth, could not help but *oooooo* and *ahhhhhh* over the grandeur of them. Prince Christian had winced after receiving a bill for the custom-made creations born of his wife's ambition, but there they stood, amazing everyone. Many rose like the gleaming towers of Babylon whose golden balconies and silver terraces bulged with colorful delicacies of all sorts including cheeses, bright fruits, and sweetmeats, while other centerpieces made of thinnest porcelain resembled gleaming white Greek temples and oyster-blue fairytale towers. The chief steward dubbed one of the fantastical creations, "the Hanging Gardens of Cheese Wig"—a pyramidal wonder of blue-white china mounting at least three feet high, each layer an open shelf brimming with plums, strawberries, sliced pears, seven kinds of pickles, and an abundance of cheese wigs (small bread buns coated with cheese sauce, shaped and baked to resemble a man's wig).

To those fortunate few, including Prince Christian, the grand and shining display on the tables appeared in the distance like Biblical rumors of Heaven: a soft whiteness upon which floated a mythical city, one with its town squares and temples and fantastical structures, and all interwoven with silver and golden sauceboats, candle flame, and sails of white napkin.

* царица *

THE PORTENTOUS, COW-SIZED BODY OF THE BARON of Eschenbach obscured Freddie's view in a manner she found extremely irritating, but once she circumnavigated him, imagining herself Sir Francis Drake sailing above an ocean of obese noble, she saw the woman she'd been searching for: Empress Elizabeth of Russia, standing high and regal towards the rear of the Bärenthoren Great Hall. A huge stone fireplace blazed behind her. The flames appeared to lick her waist and rise along the rim of her skirt, and yet, despite the hellish implications, her exalted form presented itself as gift to the ages. Her hair mounted high and white as the English cliffs of Dover, feathers of soft blue and gold inset, and all sprinkled with diamond jewel-lets (accomplished by her French coiffeur). Her forehead high, cheeks plump and rouge rosy, her skin glowing white as her hair, her neck adorned with emeralds and diamonds big as walnuts on a necklace looking as if it could purchase all the ocean's islands with enough left over to buy India. Her dress, the most magnificent eye-warmer of them all: a grand, eight feet of hoop, deep red and gold-trimmed. In the distance, she appeared like a big red rose turned upside down. A low, oval neckline bared her shoulders, bodice heavily-boned, and her elbow-length sleeves were covered with tiers of white lace flounces. All so perfect!

"Princess Von Anhalt?"

A male voice to her left. She turned from the vision of the Empress to see Willie, the nephew of Babette, one hand balancing a silver tray full of red wine glasses above his chin. Costumed in Bärenthoren Castle livery—blue short coat with gold trim and buttons—he appeared all very smart and shimmering. Freddie noticed his hair damp, a bit unruly as if combed in a hurry. His face was kind and fairly handsome, yet stern, his eyes deep brown and reflecting the trembling bits of candlelight.

"I only have a moment, Princess. I must get on with things, since chief butler Gleb is ... uh, watching all of us," he said. The words came uneasily, as if he were a bit nervous, though resolve shone in his countenance. Freddie sensed too that Willie liked her, a lot, perhaps even more than a lot, and her presence had a marked effect on him; but she felt not offended, rather pleased. The common practice of a European noblewoman was to take immediate and often raging offense at any show of attraction, no matter how subtle or imagined, if it came from a servant, or worse, from a serf. Beatings and even execution might follow.

Freddie spoke. "You were in the room when Babette saved me. Last night—"

"Beware of Temujin Gur," Willie said, cutting her off. "He is the author of apparitions."

"What?"

"He lies with illusion."

"Any particular one?"

Willie paused, breathed deeply, and said, "The machines that hunted you, barking your name, driving you towards death in the mountains."

Freddie was shocked. "You must have overheard me say that to Babette. Now this is none of your—"

"What you saw wasn't true. Your future is limitless," he said, his face full of such conviction that Freddie felt awed for a moment.

"You are telling me that Gur *created* those visions?"

"Yes. And ... never mind, I must take my leave, for now, but I want you to share a secret with me. My own real name is *Zolo Bold*, not Willie, and I know you will keep that a secret."

"You *know* I will?" Freddie's temper flashed. She was about to dismiss Willie, or Zolo, or whoever he claimed to be, but an unmistakable look of concern crossed his face, and she realized that he cared for her. But why? She did not know, though the fact served to calm her. "Alright, you have my word. Our secret, *Mr. Bold.*"

He flashed Freddie a brief smile, turned and walked towards a nearby group of white-wigged noblemen who stood chatting. One of the noblemen, a Prussian baron with a thick gold chain about his neck and a face like an otter, saw Zolo coming and shouted at him with a gruff voice, "Hurry up you wretched little wogger!" Upon hearing this, the other noblemen turned their heads and jeered at Zolo.

Wogger? Those hateful bastards.

A word used to humiliate the servant class. An English term given to an ill-fated group of serfs who rebelled against their masters ten years ago in Russia, joining with Cossacks from the north, and raiding farms owned by nobility. They spread revolt until brutally put down by the Russian royal army. Thousands of serfs died before the cannon's mouth. More thousands executed, their families sold or imprisoned, or starved to death. It all reminded her of Rome's servile wars, the greatest of all led by a rogue gladiator named Spartacus. Many whispered that the woggers had formed a secret society, festering and growing in the roots of European shadow like mushrooms, collecting muskets and wogger swords and conspiring at more bloody uprisings.

As Queen of The Woggers, I would gladly lead the revolt.

Before she could sign up for the wogger war though, a loud *kahwoooshhhhh* sound interrupted her thoughts.

A big burst of steam, or?

Kahwoooshhhhh again. But from where? She heard Prince Christian's voice rise above the throng, booming over the hall, silencing all:

"Empress Elizabeth, nobles of Prussia and Russia!"

She turned to see him standing upon the stage, that big roving eye of light behind him, swiveling back and forth, burning him to a black shadow every few moments. He held a long cone of dark wood before his mouth and spoke into it, the cone magnifying his voice across the Great Hall:

"May I present to you ... THE WORLD STORMER OF ANHALT!"

Huh? The what? *Kahwooooshhhhh* once more, followed by the sounds of metal clanking, gears connecting, force applied and lurching forward into destiny. A thing huge, wonderful and horrifying at once went *crannnk clank-toc, zzzzzzt.* Freddie heard the milling crowd of nobles gasp in awe.

Never have these stocking jackals acted so impressed!

Pushing through a cluster of noblewomen, she excused herself while angling her hoop skirt to edge in. They parted for her without notice, their attention directed on a lurching monstrosity, their mouths hanging dumbly open, eyes big as coffee cups. *Crannnnk clank-toc, zzzzzzzt, kahwooooshhhh ... crannnk clank-toc, zzzzzzt, kahwooooshhhh.* Freddie imagined a mechanical death device turned loose by the woggers, now arrived to exact revenge.

At last, she made it to the front.

Her breath stopped.

An enormous machine, bigger than a Berlin carriage, and twice as high, passed like a frightening dream before her eyes. The chassis and housing were painted black and gold, its four gigantic spoke-wheels grinding against the tile floor, cracking it in places—and that's where the comparison to the carriage ended. The rest like nothing Freddie had ever seen. She knew of machines, of course, relatively simple devices that fire or water propelled or turned, but this was as far beyond these as a bird beyond a moth. Upon the platform, above the chassis, she glimpsed the inner workings: brass gears toothing into bigger brass gears, at least a dozen of them connected by rods to a revolving shaft running through the center like an oily black spine. In the rear of this beastly *World Stormer of Anhalt* a tall iron stack spouted sparks and smoke, and in front, tubes of copper and plates of glass intertwined in a great metal dish. Two huge brass globes protruded beyond the dish, hanging in space at the end of curved iron supports, producing a pincer effect while brilliant arcs of violent blue-white electricity shot between them and created a *zzzzzzzt*, followed by *kahwoooooshhhhh* as big jets of steam gushed from the sides. The Stormer's steam and violence shoved the nobles back further, their faces in complete shock, their whole world suddenly become fragile and uncertain.

Beelzebub's beard! Where was father hiding this thing?

A half-moon of crowd retreated, step by step as the thing lumbered forward, the floor tiles cracking, gears turning wheels *clank-toc clank toc*, steam whooshing and the electricity spitting *zzzzzzt*, and all of it going a bit faster with each passing moment. To what end though? Would they all be killed? And as though the present spectacle weren't threatening enough, a hidden hatch in the rear of this World Stormer sprang open and a big pair of menacing guns, dark-steel army killers, swiveled up 45 degrees to click into place—each gun with not one but eight musket-sized barrels forming a circle.

As Freddie watched, astonished as everyone else, the guns cranked up a few degrees then commenced to revolve and fire. The storming sound of the reports crashed against the walls and echoed back and forth until her ears hurt. She also heard a noblewoman or two scream in the background, their husbands cursing. Mercifully though, after sixteen flaming eruptions in five seconds, the guns went silent. Their barrels spun to stillness with a *click-click-click* and began to smoke.

Out of nowhere, a jovial Prince Christian bounded up to the side of his World Stormer and faced the stunned onlookers. But no time for calm. Even though the guns had ceased their blistering fire, the World Stormer itself *zzzzzt*-clanked faster. Air-cracking electric bolts, one after the other, blazed hotter and louder, and the contraption seemed well on its way to destroy all life in Bärenthoren Castle, if not on earth.

And if that electricity touches those rockets?

"Not to be concerned, good noble folk!" Prince Christian said.

He clutched a brass handle on the side of the chassis and shoved it down. *Zzzt-clonk.*

Freddie watched as the entire thing began to slow and stop. The steam whooshed one more time. The smoke and sparks died. The entire quivering mob of nobility in the Great Hall sighed with relief. "Thank God and Mary!" more than one exclaimed.

Prince Christian raised his left arm into the air and snapped his index finger on high. Receiving this cue, Bärenthoren butlers swarmed in from all sides—at least a dozen of them, each carrying a silver tray filled with fine crystal glasses of wines and vodka. The nobles received the alcohol with much gratitude, needing to calm their nerves and reconsider themselves masters of their domain. Even Freddie might have asked for a glass, though she constrained herself and invited only a few deep breaths. She listened to her father explain with much enthusiasm how science-minded men from around Europe had assisted in the creation of World Stormer. Freddie knew he'd been working on some project for years, and his long nights often drained him, made him appear gaunt and worried.

"Are your fingers pricking now?"

Another voice surprised her, but this one dangerous and deep as lava yet to feel the air. She turned to see a smiling face, a Chinese-looking face beaming with care, soft brown eyes twinkling like a Christmas St. Nicholas. *That voice from this face?* The skin clean shaven, just one thin lock of braided black hair dangling from the chin, and a small ornament, like a big silver beetle, piercing the flesh of his right cheek—its surface inscribed with the same symbols she noted yesterday on Temujin Gur's cloak.

Could this be him? Surely, such a happy man cannot cause Bärenthoren to bleed.

He stood a few inches taller than Freddie, wearing a dark red tunic tucked into a wide, black leather waist band inset with rows of rubies and gold circlets. He repeated his question to her, though in a slightly different way:

"By the pricking of your fingers, does something wicked *nearby linger?*"

"No, but how could you—"

"I am not evil. My soul is beyond good and evil, Princess," the Chinese-looking man said.

"You are ... *Temujin Gur?*"

"Yes, and I am Mongolian, not Chinese. There is a big difference. The moon does not believe it, but I am older than the moon," he said and smiled.

"How do you know about my fingers?"

"Through the darkness of future past, the magician longs to see, and I've seen far more than your fingers. But I wish to talk about something else now," he said, his face still glowing. Truly, he appeared like the Asian Monkey King—all chipper and frisky and full of life.

In the background, Freddie heard the excited voice of her father explaining the workings of his new war device. His voice nearby helped to calm her, for despite the friendly appearance of this magical Mongol, the blood still flowed into demon shapes and the legends of death persisted. Yet, at the moment, her fingers felt normal.

He continued. "I wish to discuss a matter with you. I know of your brilliance, princess, your gift for languages—a suitable command of Greek, Latin and French, as well as your love of philosophy, history and opera. I hear that you can even sing an Italian aria with your rich voice."

"I am honored by your kindness ... I hope one day that I can live up to your overestimation of my talents. And what do you wish to discuss with me, sir?"

"A bear."

"*A bear?*"

"The bear attack, witnessed by the Empress Elizabeth, just yesterday. Do you consider it an act of evil?"

"By evil, you mean ...?"

"Your Christian bible tells you what *evil is*, does it not, Princess?" He looked wise as the Buddha himself, seeking to instruct with questions, riddles, and stories to follow. "Your Christian bible, first assembled by Emperor Constantine, later discarded and rewritten with many edits. The final version now serves your Pope in Rome."

"Ahh, yes, *that* bible. But he is not *my* Pope, sir."

"So tell me, Princess von Anhalt, did the forces of evil win the day?"

"I think not," she said, "because the bear's attack is an amoral act."

The sorcerer looked intrigued by her reply. His eyebrows, thick and long as Indian caterpillars, raised high enough to call attention and cause Freddie to stare into his eyes. She saw her face in those eyes, reflected back so plainly and candle-lit white that the Mongol appeared to possess no eye color at all. His eyes had become her face.

She felt her fingers prick at the vision of it.

"Do you deny the presence of evil in the world?" Gur asked.

"That is a question for theologians and priests. I am certain the question of good and evil does not apply to bear attacks."

"And if I were the bear?"

Freddie glimpsed her face again, staring back at her from the sorcerer's eyes, and a small burning began in her head, as if a candle had been lit only a few inches below her nerves. Gur smiled and she noticed gold markings on his upper teeth: Chinese-like symbols, much like the magical symbols on his scarlet cloak. "Yarrow stick symbols," he said, his eyes full of Freddie. "They protect me from poison."

"And who would dare wish to poison you?"

The Mongol laughed and executed a half turn, extending his hand towards the tables where Freddie's family awaited. Having calmed, the crowd had begun to take seats at the white-linen tables arranged for them. The tables formed two long rows facing one another across the Great Hall, at least thirty feet of space between the two—enough to leave room for the entertainment to come. Russian nobles and Empress Elizabeth formed one row, Prince Christian and Princess Johanna, and the Prussian nobility, the other. Servants of all kinds busily carted in the carefully decorated food and placed it on the tables; and to prevent ruining any appetites, The World

Stormer had been pushed into a far corner by castle guards and covered with a tarp of gold-trimmed purple cloth.

"Please, Princess, do not let me keep you," Temujin Gur said, "but just one more thing. I must conclude our marvelous talk."

"Yes, please do."

She stared into his eyes again and noted her face even larger in them, so large that her own eyes now composed half of Gur's eyes. The pain in her head, the burning, felt hotter. What would happen when her eyes finally became his? Would her head burst into flame?

Gur continued. "If a final confrontation took place between the two greatest armies of all time, let's call them the forces of light and the forces of darkness, who would triumph?"

Is the Mongol sorcerer testing me? She believed him to be weighing her psyche. *Flight or fight, Freddie?* She knew she must show resolve, ignore the magical burning and the consuming eyes while also resisting the temptation to criticize the Mongol's obsession with good and evil.

She took a deep breath and answered. "The final battle will be decided by the one who arrives first and has the superior will, but I believe pure force to be a weak form of power."

He smiled once more. "Might you provide an example?"

"Before you cook my brain like a roast?"

"Whatever do you mean, Princess von Anhalt?" Gur looked genuinely baffled.

"Alright then ... in conventional military terms, when two armies meet on the battlefield, the cost in human life is high and the damage to the treasury long-lasting. A weak ruler attacks first with his whole army, but a strong and cunning ruler overthrows his opponent with a cup of poisoned wine."

"Ahh, I see. So you are telling me that—"

The Mongol was suddenly cut off by Prince Christian who appeared in their midst holding a goblet of dark red wine in each hand. He walked up to his daughter and kissed her on the forehead. "Good evening, my darling girl." Freddie kissed him back on the cheek. He then glanced from one to the other and said: "The Empress should be happy to hear that I personally oversee the bottling of all the wine from my vineyard." Offering a glass to Temujin Gur, he said, "Drink up, my friend, and let's have done with all this talk about death. Besides, you'll *never* convince this princess to change her mind. She's a stubborn one. Why, I cannot even persuade her to surrender her homeless serf collection. She's hiding them everywhere!"

Before either Gur or Freddie could reply, Empress Elizabeth, accompanied by Princess Johanna, walked up from behind and joined their circle. The Empress stated, "I think this Princess von Anhalt is brilliant." She paused, reaching out a hand to stroke Freddie's glossy, dark chestnut hair and smile lovingly at her. "She has a real talent for persuasion. But I have the idea she can be *flexible* when she needs to be, hmmm?"

The merry Mongol chuckled, still refusing to notice Prince Christian's hand full of wine glass. He said to Freddie, "I am impressed after our first meeting, Princess von Anhalt. You are only fifteen years of age, and yet, I believe even now you could probably cross the river Styx and convince Hades to let you return to Earth."

Her burning pain vanished. Perhaps the coming of the Empress changed things? The color rose to her cheeks. "Are you asking for a demonstration, Temujin Gur?"

Before he could answer, Princess Johanna said sarcastically, "Well, as you all of you can see, my daughter is also *so humble.*"

Freddie lifted her head high and glared at her mother. Everyone's attention fixed on her. "Well, mother, if you treat me nicely for a change, I'll convince Satan to let me *bring you* back from Hell also."

Nearly all laughed at this comment, Empress Elizabeth more than anyone. "Oh, you darling sassy girl!" she said, and bent to kiss Freddie on the forehead. But Princess Johanna did not share in the laughter, and as the Empress turned to go to her table, Freddie read the clear message her mother's eyes.

Freddie, however, was not prepared to die, at least not at age 15.

* царица *

FOR THE BANQUET, CASTLE BARENTHOREN HAD IMPORTED scores of extra servants from surrounding noble estates, offering their masters special access to the Empress in exchange. They now swarmed the room, nervously tending the many pressing and eccentric needs of the nobles while setting the long tables with final splashes of spice shaker, salt box and cutlery, and small golden cups of red peonies. The chief butler in charge, Gleb Brerezhnoy—a short and very angry Russian with a mustache lip-twitch and teeth the color of fish smoke—presented himself in finest livery and held his head high, and like a general on the battlefield, barked commands to his troops in the Bärenthoren servant army. He knew his head might well depart his shoulders if Princess Johanna became displeased or embarrassed. Once, in years past, a stuttering older butler named Kermit Baumgartner had disappeared, never to be seen again. Rumors claimed the Princess roughed him from his bedchamber at midnight and threw him to the hounds because he had spilled two drops of red wine on the Prince Bishop of Brandenburg (known to be a prickly bastard) during his visit to Bärenthoren Castle.

To avoid becoming dog meat, Gleb Brerezhnoy therefore struggled to instill as much fear in the servant staff as the Princess instilled in him. After all, it was only fair, and besides, did he not fear equal respect and obedience?

Like the night, fear was always rising at Castle Bärenthoren.

No one knew this better than one of Gleb's favorite whipping boys, Zolo Bold (alias Willie Pavel Bukavitsky), who now walked among the guests with his silver tray of spirits, jeered at by the nobles as "a wogger" and avoiding the glare of the chief butler. As though anxious or worried, he glanced at the Princess von Anhalt in the distance who faced the Mongolian spellcrafter of Empress Elizabeth: Temujin Gur—his real identity revealed to him by Paganini.

The bodies of drifting nobles hid her from his vision at times, forcing him to reposition himself to enable even more anxious glances in her direction. He had revealed to her his real name, seizing on the opportunity provided by the banquet to introduce himself, for Babette never allowed him near the princess out of fear they both might be horse-whipped. But all the fear in Bärenthoren could not match the guilt he now carried within himself. Beginning this evening, at the banquet, he knew that Gur would coax forth Freddie's incredible powers on behalf of the World Maker, Master Edison Godfellow. And the World Maker, Master Niccolo Paginini, to further his own aims, would later do the same, both sides raising her as if she were their precious starry child, and both in a race to use the future Czarina to wield a terrible force that would one day threaten the future of Earth itself.

And of course, she was not supposed to know.

Zolo must hide it from her, and even worse, lie to her when necessary. Only minutes ago, he lied when he said the nightmarish vision of her future was only illusion, that her future stretched limitless. But was it really a lie? What about his vow to change fate upon seeing her beaten like a dog by Princess Johanna? *Damn Paganini and all of them*, and whatever ultimate dark force drove Master Godfellow—the identity of this ominous being hidden from Zolo. Just one of the many secrets Master Paganini kept close. Regardless, Zolo Bold vowed once more that the future Czarina would live for a thousand years, as she was meant to.

May her eyes ever shine in the sun, until I am undone, until I am no one.

Suddenly jostled by an obese nobleman, he lost sight of her. This irritated him to no end. He stepped around the man to stare in her direction again and saw an odd, almost pained look on Freddie's face. *What is the demon Gur doing to her?* He understood he must restrain himself, fate must take its course, for the moment. Nevertheless, a surge of rage welled up in him, his legs beginning to quake with the emotional violence of it.

Just before confronting Gur, come what may, a hand fell hard on his shoulder. Zolo turned to see the face of Gleb, the Russian chief butler, scowling at him.

"I hear you've been called a wogger, Mr. Bukavitsky. Are you a wogger?"

"A wogger? No, I am not a wogger, or a grogger—"

"Eh? Never mind. Enough blather! To the kitchen now or I'll have you shot as a wogger spy. The first course of soups is ready and seven more courses to go. And no more gawking at the Princess von Anhalt. Her mother would **have you** made into soup if I told her."

Zolo swallowed his anger and returned to the kitchen. He took his place in line with the other servants, the perspiring and nervous kitchen staff handing off bowl after bowl of soups and stews, each servant grasping one in each hand and returning to the hall for placement beneath the waiting mouth of the nobles. And this process continued in one giant loop until all the individual settings had gleaming china bowls of steaming hot soup set square between sterling silver cutlery.

After Zolo had walked out of the kitchen with full soup bowls for the third time, he glanced around for any sign of Freddie. He did not see her and this bothered him. Within moments though, he passed the entourage of Empress Elizabeth, all full of hoop skirt and white wig, moving slow and chatty ha-ha towards the grand table. He averted his eyes and looked down at his feet, not wishing to be beaten for "noble staring" and thus bring attention to himself. Besides, he might kill Gleb rather than take a stick or whip beating from him, and all hell would break loose. Paganini would be furious too. No, he just had to go along with the custom, play the role, his powers hidden.

As the last of the flatterers passed him—Countess Magdalena of Nassau grinning like a jaguar—a figure detached itself from the entourage and the shadow crossed his path.

Zolo watched it change.

What had resembled the head and body of a man softened to formlessness before assuming the shape of an insect. Perhaps, a bee? Zolo shuddered with the memory of that long ago day in Samarkand, and glanced up to see the Mongol warlock Temujin Gur smiling at him.

"Do not be alarmed, Zolo," Gur said, his voice low and quiet as death, his eyes filling with the rising moon of Zolo's face. "I know you doubt whether or not you will one day travel to America and fight your revolution. The answer is, you will not. You will die before that happens and I will be the instrument of your death. As a matter of fact, I killed you only last week just outside Samarkand. You died at age 46, powerless and abandoned by your beloved violin-loving master ... And now, with this knowledge, you can rest easy. No more need for plans."

Zolo stood paralyzed, watching Gur's eyes moving over him, those black warlock eyes like a hundred spiders walking over his skin. He shuddered once more. Without another word, the Mongol smiled big as a china plate, his spider-legs of eye leaving Zolo's body as he turned to rejoin the train of the Empress.

Zolo remained unmoved as the banquet swirled around him. He heard a "Wake up wogger!" harshly spoken by one of the Prussian nobles nearby, and he struggled to recover enough anger to push down his new fear. He told himself that Gur must be lying. How could he have died last week at age 46? Master Paganini always said that Gur twisted reality whenever it suited him, as well as took pleasure in the pain he inflicted on others. Put these two virtues together, and what do you have?

Nothing but lies.

царица

4

Smell of Serf - The Coming of Aria - A Stick Becomes a Man

A LOUD *TAN-TAHHH-RAHHH* BOOMED AND ECHOED in the Great Hall of Bärenthoren, almost as loud as the guns of the Anhalt World Stormer. Those present who survived what happened next by holding on to their fragile sanity were nonetheless later subjected to the blackest of oblivion-cursed nightmares.

It all began with a troop of masked actors parading into the space between the two rows of long dining tables, waving to the audience and lifting their legs high as they stepped. The nobles, accustomed to such trumpets, behaved as if they barely noticed, so consumed were they with chatter and food and bad memories of the World Stormer. The actors, however, were determined to correct this mood. A half dozen of them blew into big black serpents—musical wind instruments covered in black leather and looking like slithering snakes. They blew and tooted and the remaining actors, at least twenty, skipped and marched.

Freddie watched them while finishing her soup and straining to remain polite to the young noblewomen to her left and right: Princess Hermine Reuss of Greiz and Princess Théodolinde de Beauharnais. Both were seated by Princess Johanna to "provide fitting company," but in reality to torture Freddie. Hermine wouldn't stop whining about her "scratchy bodice" and "the smell of serf" on the soles of her feet, while "Théodo the Terrible," as Freddie nicknamed her, blathered on and on about Prince Whoever of Whatever and how rumors said he often donned a golden codpiece etched with a Zeus hurling lightning bolts.

"Perhaps, dear Théodo, this cod-piece Zeus of might hurl a bolt at Hermine's feet and burn the *smell of serf* from them?" Freddie said. Both princesses stared at her as if she were impossibly difficult, for they wished only heaping doses of astonishment and sympathy for their petty ills and ambitions. Nothing else would do.

Another blast of trumpet. ***TAN-TAHHH-RAHHH.***

Freddie welcomed the opportunity to ignore the princess duo and relieve herself of the desire to slap them. Before her eyes, the actors, in black masks and wearing clothing that symbolized both royalty and peasant class, staged a silent performance while the six serpent blowers stood outside the circle and played a mournful dirge. This performance, Princess Johanna's favorite, symbolized the ascension of royalty over chaos, and therefore, the establishment of rightful order in the universe. The peasants, fleeing chaos, found the stable and regal royalty waiting for them and fell to their knees in gratitude. Freddie had seen this stupid performance way too many times and it bored her to death. It dragged on like smallpox and gratefully ended as the third course of the meal was being delivered, a course that included boar, turkey, and peacock pie.

Before the performance ended though, as the servants scurried like mad and the general noise level in the Great Hall increased because Empress Elizabeth was braying loud as a drunken donkey, one of the actors in sack-and-rope peasant garb removed her mask and stared at Freddie from across the room. She was old, surprisingly old, especially since actor troupes were usually composed of young and penniless peasants. As Freddie watched, two of the other masked actors, both men, broke away from the group and escorted the older woman towards her.

The woman stared at Freddie as she walked forward, her eyes never straying until she stood a few feet before the table. Her two escorts, still masked, released her without a word and returned to join the performance. The old woman's eyes dropped to the floor and Freddie looked her over. There was nothing special about her. Her garb plain, hair white and roughly brushed, her face resembling a water-starved desert of lines and cracks, as one would expect.

Before Freddie could speak, a voice nearby said:

Sing the body young.

A voice from the old woman? No. The voice belonged to a man, and it sounded strange and deep in tone.

Sing the body young.

Again. She looked around. Nothing. Only Hermine and Théodo acting witless as usual, and not even paying attention to the old woman. *Why are they not seeing her? Do they not realize how odd this is?*

The voice once more:

O poder é a vida ea morte, Princess von Anhalt.

Freddie knew that language. Galician, yes. A rare language of Spain, heavily influenced by Roman Empire. It translated to "The power is life and death."

Sing the body young.

Her fingers pricked for a moment and she realized the source of the voice: Temujin Gur. *It must be him!* And as she made that realization, she abruptly felt the heat well up within her. She reached for a goblet of water and gulped it down in an attempt to quench the heat and stop the voice. But she could not. It formed words and they rose up from the depths of her being into her throat, each word like a ball of warmth blowing onto her tongue:

"Meu segredo está oculto."

My secret is hidden ... He made me say it. That spell crafting demon! She strained her eyes for him. Zolo, Willie, or whoever was right. *Tricks, illusions.* And what did the words mean? What secret was hidden?

Sing the body young.

The words forced her to look at the old woman again. Now the woman's eyes lifted and bored into her. Freddie's face began to burn. Her skin felt as if dozens of small fingers walked lightly over it, almost spider-like. *What in Beelzebub's name?* The woman's eyes implored Freddie to act, as if a terrible thing would happen if she did not.

Sing the body young, Princess of Anhalt!

Upon hearing this, she felt more words heating in the oven of her being, desiring to erupt from deep inside, and this time with an aria-like force. As before, the Galician song words brimmed above her eyes and rushed beyond her lips even as they moved:

Como os ollos de Ahriman luz dadaaaa
Deixe a maldición do temmmpo
Ser levantada a partir de ti.

(Like the eyes of Ahriman given light / Let the curse of time / Be lifted from thee.)

With an operatic voice, Freddie sang, and the words sounded alien-rich and blended, as if another voice sang them, a nonhuman voice perhaps, though waving rhythmic and repeating with clear vibrato, stressing and held:

En nome de Deus e Saravastraaaaaa,
Eu restaura-lo á belezaaaa!

(In the name of God and Saravastra / I restore you to beauty!)

Freddie and the old woman locked eyes. The old woman's face flushed red and twitched, her eyes watered, and as Freddie watched, the face began to change. Like a ripple that begins from a stone striking water, the water of the old face shook. A transformation began. It flowed out from the center and spread to the edges. The desert of her skin softened, the cracks dampening and evaporating, on and on, until her youth was restored.

But only for a few moments.

My God!

The woman's body began to shake terribly. Tears ran more heavily from her eyes. Her face quaked and sagged again, as though the magical force that stretched her skin had evaporated, and she grew old once more. Freddie gasped. Still, not as old as before. Then all was quiet—the woman having gained at least 20 years of youth. She now appeared 50 or so, and Freddie appeared stunned.

Was it all a trick?

You are a World Maker. Your powers will not be denied.

The voice again. *My powers?* Powers now or more trickery? And who or what is Ahriman? Freddie turned around to futilely search for the source of that irritating voice, believing Temujin Gur hid behind her, but a shrill scream brought her around. Princess Hermine bellowed like a wounded warthog, lurching up from her chair to point downward. Freddie looked to see the woman collapsed dead on the floor.

My God and father! Have I done this?

From out of nowhere, the two masked actors appeared again and whisked her body away. Freddie felt dazed, stammering inside herself. Hermine simply sat back down, her face baffled for a moment, then stuffed a cheese wig into her mouth before resuming her prattle. In the background, the black serpent horns continued to blow. The nobles never stopped their chatter and posture, and the castle servants never stopped scurrying back and forth with drinks and plates full of food.

The woman's death was of no more importance than that of an insect.

Before Freddie could react, the trumpets blasted again. *TAN-TAHHH-RAHHH, TAN-TAHHH-RAHHH.* The actors turned and high-stepped out of the Great Hall, waving to the nobles and bowing before Empress Elizabeth as they passed. Empress Elizabeth shouted out, "Long life to all of you!" Her left hand raised a wine glass as if toasting the troupe while her other hand banged on the table—her expression portraying the amount of fun and wine she'd been gulping nonstop. The two hundred or so European nobles in attendance likewise raised their glasses and banged their hands, harrumphing and "Long Life" muttering like a bunch of stupid sheep.

Freddie realized the callousness of it all. *Long life, yes, except for those who drop dead before your eyes!* But seriously, did she need to grow up? Was it realistic to expect the momentum of the royal banquet to slow and stop for the death of a peasant? Or to expect the selfish sheep to care? Of course not. Still, that did not justify the absolute invisibility of the death, represented most profoundly by that damnable cheese-wig munching Hermine. As for the other princess, she had acted absent, as though the woman were invisible to her the entire time.

TAN-TAHHH-RAHHH, TAN-TAHHH-RAHHH.

Empress Elizabeth rose up from the table, her left hand lifting a wine goblet into the air as if to toast. Most of the nobles hadn't noticed yet. Prince Christian, a few places down from Freddie, stood and thrust his wine glass into the air, calling across the room, "Empress Elizabeth!" The nobles turned and stared at her. She held the glass in the air, saying nothing.

TAN-TAHHH-RAHHH.

Finally, the Empress spoke: "A toast to the marvelous company here and the hospitality of Prince Christian and Princess Johanna of Anhalt!" The crowd of nobles raised their glasses and echoed her toast, almost in unison. Prince Christian opened his mouth to say something, but Empress Elizabeth cut him off. "As a treat for all of you, my personal aide and friend, Prince Gur, heir to the throne of Mongolia, will provide more entertainment! I know you will enjoy it!"

The room went silent. Freddie froze. Her eyes scanned for the spellcrafter. He was not beside the Empress. Where was he? She looked over at her father, Prince Christian, and he appeared surprised. A glance further to her mother confirmed the surprise. None of this was planned.

The Empress sat back down.

TAN-TAAAAHHH-RAAAAHHHHHHHH.

The blast, even louder and longer than the others, shook Freddie. Prince Christian turned in the direction of the trumpets, his face curious and annoyed, as if he were saying to himself, 'Who keeps blowing those damn trumpets?'

Then everything changed.

A gigantic black stick, at least twenty feet long and three feet thick, entered the Great Hall. It twirled end over end in the air from one side of the hall to the other. Back and forth between the rows of tables it went, way above the heads of the nobles—all of them too dumbfounded and fearful to say a word. It was round as a peg and inscribed with Chinese-like symbols etched in light red gold. It made no sound. Only the air whooshing as it revolved on an invisible axis.

On the fifth pass, it halted and behaved like a windmill above the space where the actor troupe had performed only minutes before. It turned faster, and faster, and a whirlwind began in the Great Hall. The dresses of the ladies fluttered and men's wig tails flapped, and the candles winked out, hundreds of them. The Great Hall sunk into a hellish, firelight darkness. Long and monstrous shadows were cast by the castle fireplaces now roaring even hotter due to the wind while all present watched in awe. Still, no one spoke, though a few of the women began to moan as if possessed, Princess Hermine among them.

Freddie watched the thing *whoosh-whooshing*, hovering and spinning in the darkness, and within moments it began to glow, end to end with the pale light of old parchment, a jaundiced light of yellow-eye sickness. Freddie looked down to see the face of Empress Elizabeth in that pale light, and she was grinning. Apparently, the phenomenon not only failed to surprise the Empress, it actually amused her. This fact dampened Freddie's alarm a bit, though not entirely. Too many questions to ask, and that giant stick whipping about in the air, glowing like a mad magician's disease. And the wind, and the threat.

A man's voice shouted, "By Joseph's beard, *look!*"

The stick began to slow and stop. For a few seconds of silence it rested in the air, parallel to the stone floor, and it growled. Yes. That was what Freddie heard. A loud and earsplitting **GRROWWRRRRR** sound exploded from it, louder and more savage than the growl of any earthly animal. And once the dragon-like echo of it died, a single dropped glass broke the silence that followed. Dozens of servants fled to the kitchen, the sound of smashing china reverberating in the air as they fumbled stacks of plates in their rush to escape certain doom. A noblewoman shrieked too. Then another, and Princess Hermine began shrieking, and Princess Théodo, and the air in the Great Hall went shrill with one big shriek as the noblewomen found their courage for terror—all except for Freddie. Though shaken like everyone else, she felt an echo of her previous power and wished for words to sing the thing to black ashes.

TAN-TAHHH-RAHHHHHHHH, TAN-TAHHH-RAHHHHHHH-HH.

The return of the trumpets drowned them out to whimpers and sniffles, the voice of Empress Elizabeth arriving next like the voice of a Titan:

"BE SILENT AS A DEAD MOUSE, ALL OF YOU!"

Behind her, Freddie heard a clanking commotion of steel. She turned to see her father, followed by a contingent of the castle guard armed with muskets, racing behind the tables and curving around to the back of the Great Hall. Did they plan to restart the World Stormer of Anhalt and pit it in battle against the giant stick? But no time to consider. The thing began to glow brighter, the once-pale light pushing out to jaundice the eyes and flesh, to make all faces in the Great Hall appear wan and mummy-like; and too, fetid odor accompanied the light, arriving as if from a place of death.

Freddie felt the urge to gag. Princess Hermine doubled over and vomited out her cheese wigs. Freddie reached for a goblet of water, and as Hermine continued to heave, Freddie watched the floor before her evaporate. The stone tiles of the Great Hall, directly below the floating black stick, sizzled and steamed to nothing, leaving a giant black hole big enough to drive five World Stormers into at once. And neither Freddie or anyone else could have prepared for what came next—indeed, no mortal could, not even Empress Elizabeth who now jerked her head around as though desperate to find someone important who was inexcusably missing.

Freddie gasped. A swarm of black things blew suddenly up from the hole.

They flew into the air above the stick and swooped back down. Seven of them. Each a black shadow shaped into a human-like body. Thin threads of soft light interwove within the limbs, head and torso, like glowing webs of nerve shimmering a delicate blue. No mouth or eyes, though small, soft balls of bluish-green luminosity floated in their heads. A home for a soul? They made no sound, only rushed past each other in the air, circling and diving, up and down, forming a big ball of frantic yet deliberate movement in the way of black crows when attacking a predatory hawk.

Everyone in hall just stared, utterly stupefied, until the Duchess of Saxe-Altenburg shouted, "Satan's servants are among us!"

Then the music began.

It emanated from the hovering black stick, eerily similar to the music played by the actor troupe on their serpent horns, but a mind-twisting version that grew louder and louder, and as it did, a few of the nobles began to violently lose their minds. The pale jaundiced light, the fetid odors, the macabre apparitions darting about, and now this sickening music proved all too much for them. Despite the order of the Empress, new screams broke out. Freddie heard a banging sound and saw the Prince of Halberstadt on her right, several places down, ramming his head into the table. Two other noblemen, stirring up much clatter as they did so, sprang up and ran in a panic from the Great Hall—one of them, the immensely fat Duke of Oldenburg, tripping and falling, losing his wig in the process, though scrambling to his feet like a frightened pig to resume his bolt to the door.

Princess Théodo shrieked out, "Our escorts to Hell!" and began to weep hysterically. And the Empress heard and saw all this. Freddie watched her eyes go flaming mad, and she rose up, high and regal as the goddess Hera, and shouted:

"I SAID BE SILENT, YOU WHIMPERING CROCODILES!"

As though in response to the Empress, the music stopped.

The seven swooping black figures halted also. They lowered their arms to their sides, and as they did, a thunder shook Bärenthoren Castle. Freddie heard it and felt it in her feet and up to her eyes; and in the midst of the thunder rattling Princess Johanna's priceless china, as well as the nerves of all present, downward the figures drifted towards the open black hole. As they drew near, the floor reformed itself in a moment, became whole again. The black figures landed soundlessly, standing erect in a circle, their faceless heads turning about as if taking measure of the considerable fear and awe in the room. A moment later, they swiveled to face each other and began cavorting about, high stepping and leaping in a grotesque manner that made no sense to Freddie until she realized:

They're mimicking the entertainment troupe.

Was the intention to mock the nobles? They poked fun at Princess Johanna's beloved chaos-to-order theme, and the Empress began to laugh. Those nobles closest to her on the Russian side stared at her and tried to laugh in imitation, and in a few moments, the entire hall was engulfed in throes of weak and strained laughter. Even if forced, it provided some form of relief, and yet, it all struck Freddie as so very dark and bizarre.

Are we all dead then and in no need of escorts to Hell?

Next, a voice, from everywhere and nowhere, booming far louder than Empress Elizabeth and melding with the thunder:

"THE WORLD MAKERS BRING FORM TO CHAOS!"

Temujin Gur's voice. All human sound in the hall stopped in mid laugh, like a talking man shot dead by a musket ball.

"ROYALTY SERVES THE WORLD MAKERS!"

These words stunned the nobles into further acts of fear and confusion, and then, more gasps and shrieks from the crowd as the giant black stick suddenly swiveled upright and lowered to the floor. The black shadow figures stopped, turned and leapt towards it. Drawing near, their human form was lost, for the stick, acting like a magnet, snapped them forward and absorbed them until all had vanished. Once done, only it remained, ominous and still. The thunder dimmed, as did the sickly yellow light, and all the candles in the Great Hall flickered magically back to life. The fetid odor vanished also, and Freddie could once more smell the roasted meats of the banquet.

At that point, the stick became a man.

How insane, how terribly insane!

Both women and men fainted at the sight of the ungodly transformation. A few slumped in their chairs while others smacked tables head first, their bodies toppling to the floor as the stick shortened but grew thicker in seconds, contouring and shaping itself like hot tar into a single human body. Before the last noble hit the ground, the thing popped with a loud finger snap into Temujin Gur.

And he smiled, so happy was he!

His arms lifted up and out, his hands open, and he revolved in a circle, looking at all the nobles as if seeking applause for the performance.

"BRAVO!" Empress Elizabeth shouted.

She rose to her feet and clapped. The shocked and reeling nobles began to imitate her, a few at a time, until all of them stood clapping and shouting "Bravo, Bravo!" All except for Freddie. She glared at them with disgust and cared not a jot if she made the Empress mad by remaining seated. She then noticed, far to her right between the tables, her father's castle guard in two firing lines, one kneeling, the other standing to the rear, their gleaming muskets raised and prepared to cut the Mirza down at father's command. But as the Great Hall rumbled with sounds of approval, the guards lowered their muskets at father's command.

"Thank you! Thank you!" Temujin Gur said and lowered his arms. Empress Elizabeth sat down and quieted herself. The nobles took note and did likewise. He continued, "You witnessed the power of my magical yarrow. It is the power to dry oceans and wither forests ... But we are almost done here." He paused, still smiling, and shouted to nowhere in particular, "Now, I call on Prince Manuchar of Abkhazia!"

Gur turned to stare at the Prince who sat on the Russian side of the hall. The Prince stared back at him, looking confused; but as Gur's stare intensified, quieting the Great Hall to perfect silence, the Prince steeled himself with as much defiance as he could muster. Freddie admired him for that, and realized this Prince Manuchar to be very different when compared to the other Russian nobles. From a principality in Georgia, heavily influenced by the Ottoman Empire, he was rumored to be an enemy of Empress Elizabeth. Apparently, here at castle Bärenthoren, the Empress practiced the ancient maxim: *keep your friends close, and your enemies closer*. Freddie knew she hated anything with a hint of Ottoman influence, and Prince Manuchar fit the type: flaring black mustache on a stern face beneath a cap rimmed with bear fur, a silken brown shirt, white sash, and baggy dark pants. Only the gold head-rings on his fingers, and his regal bearing, suggested he was of noble blood.

"Prince of Abkhazia! Come to me!" Temujin Gur shouted, and

laughed in a jovial fashion. Many of the nobles chuckled also, apparently becoming amused at the baiting of a noble from Georgia who most of them intensely disliked anyway.

"Prince of Abkhazia! Come TO ME!"

Prince Manuchar obeyed in his own fashion. With one arm he roughly pushed aside a massive porcelain centerpiece that looked like the Athenian Acropolis, stood from his chair and leapt atop the dinner table with a loud bang. Smiling and whistling a Georgian folk tune, he jumped to the floor and strolled towards Temujin Gur, his head held high. He opened his mouth as if to speak, but the happy Mongol cut him off:

"So you are a proud man, Prince Manuchar. Let us test your pride after you lose your head!"

Upon saying that, a black yarrow stick darted from Temujin Gur's sleeve and rose to hover at attention before his chest. It glowed a dull green, and the Mongol warlock, still smiling, waved his open hand in a chopping motion, whereupon the astonished Prince lurched upwards, his legs kicking as he flew into the air. His body jerked back and forth above the crowd like a struggling catch on a fishing line, and he shouted, "In Allah's name, no more!" before Gur's spinning finger caused him to twirl round and round. The Mongol obviously took great delight in humiliating him for Empress Elizabeth's benefit.

Unknown to Freddie, fixed on the image of Prince Manuchar who had begun hurtling towards her, Empress Elizabeth's eyes flamed imperious with power. She relished the terror of the Prince. All who dared to steal glances at her saw this, for the power of the Mirza translated to more power for the Empress, and a being of such awesome power must be feared at all times.

Truly, Empress Elizabeth now appeared power drunk.

The Princess von Anhalt, however, remained speechless. The body of the Prince halted and dangled before her at least ten feet above the floor. His face was white with horror, his pants darkening as he pissed them. Such a man could face enemy armies and die with honor, but this insane yarrow magic of Temujin Gur terrorized him.

How could it not?

Without warning, and despite her own shock, Freddie felt the now familiar warmth of words heating in her. Another burst of magical aria perhaps? It must be, else why would the Prince be hovering before her? But she was not afraid. She knew a great power now resided in her, one as natural as laughter and tears. How long would it last? She did not know. Temujin Gur darkly coaxed it forth, yes, and she should be as terrorized as the helpless Prince, though she was not. She felt at peace, oddly enough, and confident.

As she considered this, Prince Manuchar began to turn, face first, end over end. Two black yarrow sticks had appeared to either side his body, floating motionless. He screamed out, "Mercy, Empress of the Russias!" But his spinning grew faster, and as his body lifted upright in the course of one full revolution, a bluish-white light, thin as a clothesline, bridged the two yarrow sticks, and in consequence, Prince Manuchar's severed head shot from his body. The head twirled upward to the ceiling. The crowd in the Great Hall gasped. Freddie watched in disbelief as the shock-faced scream of head drifted back down to hover above the body that continued to spin. Strangely enough, no blood gushed from the open neck.

Gur's magic must be clamping it.

Freddie then felt the inner core of her being heating even more. Just as with the old woman, and within the birthing oven of magical Galician language, deep inside, she heard the somber voice of Temujin Gur: *Sing the body whole, Princess von Anhalt.*

So be it! She resolved herself.

Yes, I will do it then. My hand forced or no, I will save this man.

She stood to her feet, her eyes never leaving the sight of Prince Manuchar, and her voice rose up with a tone of brilliant silver and steel like that of a dramatic soprano, heightening with volume and vibrato, wave upon wave:

Vida a ti, Príncipe Manucharrr.
Eu respiro o aire, terra da sombra da Ahrimannn
Para cantar a todo o corpo,

Cantar o novo corpo.
Sexa o que era, o Príncipe Manucharrrr,
Sexa un home de vida, non a morte!

(Life to you, Prince Manuchar. / I breathe the shadow land air of Ahriman / To sing the body whole / Sing the body new. / Be what you were, Prince Manuchar, / Be a man of life, not death!)

The body of the Prince stopped spinning. The black yarrow sticks snapped back though the air and across the room into the heavy-ringed hands of Temujin Gur. The severed head of the Prince lowered onto his neck and joined his body, and the man dropped like a softening balloon to the floor, landing feet first to stand facing Freddie. His dizzy eyes blinked, his jaw moved, though his mouth could not speak.

"BRAVO!" The Empress shouted from across the room.

Freddie looked beyond the dazed Prince Manuchar to see Empress Elizabeth in a jovial mood while the rest of the Great Hall sat as though paralyzed in time. Apparently, the display of aria power met with her approval; and as the Empress began to nod at Freddie, it became obvious a test had been passed, one arranged with Temujin Gur at the behest of the Empress herself.

Freddie glanced over at Gur, but saw nothing of him, only a black heat wavering in the air, distorting the faces of the people beyond it. No one seemed to notice this effect. Was it real? Indeed, in Freddie's mind, the bounds between the real and unreal had dissolved, and as the distortion evaporated she recognized a woman's face, the face of a noblewoman of Russia, seated at the table across the way: muddy blond hair pulled back from her forehead, thin coils of curl, and the face dour and smirking.

The Vermeer demoness!

Freddie cried out in rage, rebelling at the fear. Enough was enough! She grabbed a cutting knife the size of her forearm, and as if possessing the strength of several men, she heaved the entire table over with unbelievable force and rushed towards the apparition in a state of fury. But as she brandished the knife within a few feet of the startled Russian, Freddie stopped. The noblewoman was not the evil girl from the painting, not even a remote resemblance.

Regaining her composure, Freddie tossed the knife to the floor and said coldly, "Pardon me, madam, for the mistaken identity. I thought you were a demon I needed to kill."

Having said this, she turned and marched out of the Great Hall. In the background she heard the Empress of Russia laughing, another "Bravo!" from her, and the last thing she saw was Princess Johanna's shocked and fearful face.

For the first time in her life, her mother was afraid of her.

Freddie smiled to herself.

царица

5

The Grand Evolution · Love Beside The Methane Lake – War Tracker

EMPRESS ELIZABETH OF RUSSIA TREMBLED AS SHE SAT on the edge of her bed in the chamber reserved for her at castle Bärenthoren. The banquet had lasted hours and she felt exhausted, her maidservants anxiously awaiting her word to enter and help her change out of her dress. But word was not forthcoming, not yet.

Not until certain dark business was concluded.

The Empress removed a priceless ruby ring from her finger, and reaching into a small leather bag sitting on the bed beside her, withdrew a large brass-and-steel monocle—a complex three-layer contraption sprouting small coils and nail-like protrusions, though no glass. She fitted the ring into the setting of the monocle housing, the enormous ruby in the center facing inward, and snapped it in with a click.

She lifted the monocle to her right eye, and with difficulty, due to her nerves which caused her hands to shake, she pulled the monocle's thin black-leather straps around her head and snapped them also. She knew she looked ridiculous, sitting there on the bed still wearing her banquet tower wig, and now with this monstrous gleaming thing on her face, but no other choice was possible.

Communication was mandatory, and actually, now overdue.

The Empress felt anxious, and a bit fearful, as she always did during such occasions of communion with the God One, and the act of it made her feel like a child awaiting disciplinary action from a stern parent. But in this case, a parent with incomprehensible power.

Mon Dieu, sauve-moi, she thought to herself.

She reached up with one hand and flicked a small switch on the side of the monocle. The glowing ruby haze filling her right eye brightened to a screen of red-tinted white, and words in black letters formed before her:

HOW DID THE PRINCESS VON ANHALT PERFORM AT THE BANQUET?

"My God One, I watched her closely," she said. "She was not the same person as the one who became terrified at my manifestation as the girl in the Vermeer painting."

The Empress recalled how hesitant she'd been to join with that faceless black shadow sitting calmly on the seat beside her in the Berlin carriage on the way to Bärenthoren. Temujin Gur assured the Empress of no danger, that his yarrow sticks dominated the "possession demon" as he called it, and that the experience would be fantastical and exhilarating. And he was right. She edged over in the seat and allowed herself to be consumed by the shadow being. Almost immediately, she stared out from the Vermeer painting at Freddie working at her writing desk. Then she felt herself emerge from the surface of it and become dimensional, freely floating and determined to terrify the Princess von Anhalt.

How exciting that was!

YOU REPORT TRULY. I HAD EYES AT THE BANQUET WATCHING ON MY BEHALF. ARE YOU COMFORTABLE WITH HER TRANSFORMATION?

"If you had eyes at the banquet, then you already..." The Empress checked herself. She knew she must not question. "Yes, I am comfortable. She seems to have the courage and iron in her to conquer the world. But how, my God One, can such a being of power be contained?"

SHE WILL BE CONTAINED, I HAVE ASSURED YOU OF THIS. YOU WILL HAVE IMMORTALITY AND ENOUGH POWER TO SECURE YOUR THRONE. THE PRINCESS VON ANHALT WILL MARRY YOUR NEPHEW PETER IN MONTHS TO COME AND BE UNDER YOUR INFLUENCE IN MOSCOW.

"Yes, thank you, God One, but are my powers sufficient?" She swallowed hard. "I do desire power like Temujin Gur and the princess. I cannot hide that desire. I wish dominion—"

OF COURSE YOU CRAVE MORE POWER. IT IS IN YOUR NATURE, EMPRESS ELIZABETH, BUT SUCH POWER IS ONLY FOR THOSE LIKE TEMUJIN GUR AND THE PRINCESS VON ANHALT, AND TO A LESSER EXTENT, THEIR APPOINTED GODS AND CAPTAINS OF SPELLCRAFT. THERE WILL BE NO FURTHER DISCUSSION OF THIS MATTER.

"Yes, yes I understand ..." She trembled more than ever and regretted mentioning it. But she could not help a terrible stab of jealousy that a mere princess should be entitled to such power.

JEALOUSY WILL AVAIL YOU NOUGHT, EMPRESS ELIZABETH. IT ONLY MAKES FOR SCHEMES YOU WILL NEVER REALIZE, AND WHICH MIGHT WELL JEOPARDIZE YOUR LIFE.

"Yes, I know, I am sorry, but please, just one last thing."

YOUR FEAR OF TEMUJIN GUR?

"I trust him as far as I can, God One, but I know he schemes and he is monstrous."

YOU HAVE NOTHING TO FEAR BECAUSE I HAVE A WATCH ON HIM. ONCE HE COAXES THE PRINCESS VON ANHALT'S POWERS TO FRUITION, HE WILL PERISH FROM THIS EARTH.

"But once he is gone ... I mean, what will the princess do with her powers besides most likely turn my wretched nephew into a snake? She will be so powerful and power yearns for expression."

YOU DOUBT ME?

"No, no, I—"

HER POWERS WILL SERVE MY AIMS IN THE FUTURE. THAT IS ALL YOU NEED TO KNOW. DO NOT SEEK TO LEARN MORE OR TO USE TEMUJIN GUR IN AN ATTEMPT TO SATISFY YOUR UNNATURAL CURIOSITIES AND STUBBORNNESS.

"Yes, please forgive me, I ..."

The screen before her eye darkened. This meant the communication was finished. With her trembling hands she reached back and unsnapped the monocle and let it fall to her lap. She reached out to her bedside table and picked up a goblet of red French wine and drank it all down without a breath.

She realized she must learn the habit of desiring self-preservation over unbridled ambition.

* Оверман *

THE GOD ONE ENDED HIS DIALOGUE WITH EMPRESS ELIZABETH and stood up from his patio chair on the balcony of the Dubai Towers, early one evening in the fall of 2038. And as his personal chronocom—engineered with magi-tech and looking like a small disk of yellow-hued glass—hovered in air only an inch from his eye, he stared out over the city of Dubai.

Now *his city*.

He chuckled to himself. The "God One" indeed!

Edison B. Godfellow found the moniker amusing, though even more amusing was his ability to terrify that egomaniacal diva, Empress Elizabeth, whenever he wished. Such games were good sport, and his boyish desire to behave like a Zeus or an Old Testament Jehovah every now and then (a desire undiminished after thousands of years), served him well.

"Put the fear of God in the bastards!" his friend Winston Churchill always said.

The Dubai air was chilly, so he slipped on a leather bomber draped over the chair and resumed his overview of the city. At least a decade it had taken to realize this utopian vision: the City of The Overman. His crowning creation, The Dubai Sun Towers, each one like a galaxy of stars, rose for miles into the atmosphere. Three times higher than even the tallest building in New York or Hong Kong—vast mega-plexes above the clouds. His gravity-dampening invention allowed this, as well as The Dubai Sky Isles: floating platforms of suburb strung with lights, their underbellies glowing a soft burnt orange, drifting above and beyond the city over the Persian Gulf. Lines of aero cars connected the Sky Isles and the uppermost levels of the Dubai Sun Towers, and in the distance below, the Palace Crescents, dozens of them like luminescent embryos of spiny crustacean afloat in the dark Gulf, all covered with hundreds of shimmering palaces competing with the vast and silent constellations above.

Dubai: capital of The Overman, birthing oven of the next phase in the human condition, mother of "The Grand Evolution" nourishing the children of the father and raising them as her own. And as father to The Grand Evolution, as well as ardent admirer of the philosopher Nietzsche, Edison Godfellow could do no less than be an enlightened patriarch. Though he found Nietzsche himself to be a rather puny and irascible fellow given to bouts of migraines and sudden vomiting, he embraced the philosopher's concept of The Overman.

Like the philosopher, he was beyond good and evil, and like Nature herself, he realized he must guide humanity to a new utopia, no matter the cost in lives or torment. Earth's two World Wars, and the rise of Communism, had ignited a time stream that created his Dubai. No different than an extinction event that ended the dinosaurs, the 20th century world wars had made possible events leading to the "Grand Extinction" of Homo Sapiens and the coming of The Overman, not to mention his greatest inventions to date: a fleet of magi-tech starships like giant black mantas the size of towns—all under construction beneath city-sized domes several miles outside Dubai. Dubbed by him, "The Sorcery Stars," the ships would rule galactic space, as well as assist in the building of the Dyson Sphere—a utopian creation conceived by the famous physicist Freeman Dyson—that would entirely envelop Earth's sun so that future generations of The Overman, in their trillions, might live with a near endless supply of energy.

The Grand Extinction Event, c'est moi.

No one could threaten his own utopia plans, or him, not in his time of 2038, especially not with his domination of the American military who in turn politically dominated Earth with their greatly expanded robotic drone divisions and teams of black ops assassins. As for other World Makers still alive on Earth, they were little or no threat. Few if any possessed the time powers to challenge him, and most were now alcoholics or drug addicts living their days in Persian brothels or in New York art studios, bitterly wasting their lives.

But one remained in his employ, a half-blood World Maker: the Wizard Goddess, Eréndira Marquez. Formerly the Oracle at Delphi, Empress Theodora of Byzantium, and Catherine de Medici, the manifestation of Eréndira demonstrated her loyalty to the God One by murdering as many thousands of humans and Saravastra spell-crafters as necessary, no matter the year or place. Eréndira was the kind of terror who made fingers prick. In her opinion, the current human species was weak, stupid, and smelly. "Enough of them!" she shouted one day. He knew she could hardly wait to plow the new killing fields. She bragged to him that she could kill a quarter million humans in minutes simply by flying through Calcutta or Hong Kong at supersonic velocity. "Taking a shower" she called it. She even begged him to allow her to personally kill the idealistic Princess von Anhalt when the time came.

Such loyalty born of jealousy.

Contrary to Eréndira's will, Edison desired the powers of the future Czarina to mature to their full capacity, aided in this maturation by that bastard Mongolian Temujin Gur. By means of inducing violent conflict, Gur would succeed, and when the time came, Edison would use her magical aria to challenge Ahriman himself for full Earth mastery, and if she did not cooperate he would trick her, and if that proved impossible, he would siphon her, and if that proved impossible, he would unleash Eréndira to torture her into compliance. The future Czarina would not grow to become the woman she is now. She would grow to become his pawn.

Speaking of the Czarina, where was the current version at the moment?

He knew she flitted nearby at age 32, untouched by him and only a few years away in 2033, probably up to one of her schemes with Paganini no doubt. The two of them were so laughable! It amused him. Their "war for all time" went nowhere, for he checkmated them at every turn by means of his ultimate, magi-tech invention: WAR TRACKER.

Sensitive and desirous of pleasing her father, Master Godfellow (even to the point of growing legs to search for him), the energy-soul and magic body of War Tracker remained locked in capsule, protected from harm, and from itself within a solid diamond block coated with two feet of vanadium alloy and enough magi-tech black armor plate to withstand a direct hit by fifty gigatons of nuclear force. War Tracker's interior was further reinforced by layers of sizzling force screens that would fold aside only for her father.

Years of his inventive genius and his most powerful sorcery had created War Tracker, and he valued her above all other inventions. In her 52 inch wide "monitor eyes" he could check the status of what he termed "the world history death games"—a little like watching the frantic jumble of numbers the European or American stock market produced on any given day: the facts and figures of kills and rebirths, hundreds of symbols representing names of spellcrafter captains and gods, columns and boxes divided according to year, time and place of interventions, etc., all in 24/7 flux. It would change even as he watched, representing the status of the conflicts being continuously waged between his *Dio Soldati* and the forces of Paganini. Only yesterday, while examining various battles and results, he grinned to see the ancestors of Karl Marx, the author of Communism, being assassinated one more time, then alive and resuming their copulations seconds later as his own forces restored the stream. When would Paganini and Catherine learn?

Human evolution must be allowed to take its course.

He laughed to himself. Endless entertainment those two World Makers—though he grudgingly gave them points for courage and tenacity.

Amosar Catherine. Amosar Princesa Anhalt, Edison Godfellow whispered to the air.

He shivered in the cold of the desert night, now magnified by the 9,000 foot height of his balcony. He wished for a warm drink, like a hot chai tea, and as it formed in his cupped left hand, the image of Catherine, the former Princess von Anhalt, appeared in the chronocom floating before his eye. But where was she exactly? On a plane perhaps. Yes. The flight from Washington to Paris, June 28th, 2033, 10:02 AM EST.

She looked striking as usual. Her long dark chestnut hair flowing down one side of her head and onto her chest, her eyes like small dark-blue moons that men might worship as twin goddesses for their gleaming display of wisdom and iron, and too, her strong yet handsomely curved body dressed in blue jeans and a black cotton shirt, brown leather boots with flaring tops—so much more comfortable when compared to those absurd 18th century hoop skirts. What comical torture those things were! Edison Godfellow smiled to himself, but as he stared at her simmering beauty and realized her Earth-shattering force, the power to even sing rivers onto the moon, he felt an abrupt surge of passion. After all, his DNA was still that of a human being in most respects.

Such passions were undesirable though, not helpful in the least. He must not allow simple animal mating desire for the Anhalt princess to temper his will. He must not only be beyond good and evil, but beyond love also. Given his romantic nature though, denying the call of real love was always a struggle.

He examined the scene further. To her right on the window side of the plane sat a middle-aged woman in a baggy flower-print dress. She sniffled with a bad cold. Her information appeared in his chronocom as subtitles below the image:

Mrs. Emma Rabinowitz

Age 62

POB: Hoboken, New Jersey

Class: Human

Edison felt mischievous. Time enough for another trick? And why not? Besides, hope springs eternal. He chuckled to himself again, and while staring at the sniffling middle-aged woman Mrs. Rabinowitz through the chronocom, he spoke the words:

Asumir esta forma (assume this form).

Within a few milliseconds he had a sore throat and felt like a clogged sink. In one word, miserable. He rummaged in his host's bag for tissues. All in all, he believed suffering now and then to be a good thing, a reminder to stay humble. He smiled to himself, sneezed and said:

"Oh gracious!"

Beside him, Catherine II, Czarina of All the Russias, glanced over and smiled warmly. "Do you have enough tissues, my dear Mrs. Rabinowitz?" she asked. Then her face became confused. She lifted her hands and stared at them, and as she did, her mood shifted to dark anger.

Edison spoke first. Using the woman's old voice thick with virus, he said, "By the pricking of your fingers, does something wicked nearby linger?"

"Which Overman cult freak are you? Speak or I'll burn your soul."

"*Acaba de falar coa Emperatriz Elizabeth.*

"What? You just spoke with Empress Elizabeth?"

"My dear, does she know you are crossing the skies in a great ship of metal centuries after her death? Would she approve of such behavior?" The nose of Mrs. Rabinowitz made him want to sneeze. "You ... ahhh, you should be at home in Moscow, making even more plans to build hospitals for the miserable serfs," he said and laughed, coughing with the effort of it. "By Ahriman's soul, this cold is a bad one!"

"Do I have the distinct displeasure of now sharing this flight with Sargon of Babylon alias Trajan of Rome alias Leonardo da Vinci alias Edison Bombastus Godfellow—"

"Many more than that. A World Maker my age has lived at least several dozen significant lives." He said this and sneezed. *Ahhhheeeghhhhhh!*

"You are a legend in your own mind."

"No, I am authentic legend. Where is your wisdom and sense of destiny?" he asked and lifting the tissue, once more blew her nose. The amount of fluid issuing from her nostrils was amazing to him. Would it ever stop? He decided then and there to develop some type of "flu curse" he might use against enemies in the future.

"Why does a World Maker of your stature bother with sarcasm? And why should you concern yourself with me?"

"You know the answer, my powerful Czarina ... Because you are still a threat as long as you take orders from Paganini. Methinks you pity the sheep way too much." He sneezed again and dug in Ms. Rabinowitz's purse for more tissue. "My throat is killing me."

"I wish it *would* kill you. Get out of that innocent woman's body!" Catherine almost yelled, but then calmed herself with renewed re-alization of her circumstance on the plane surrounded by ignorant humans with first class tempers.

"As Ms. Rabinowitz here would say, *Gute gezunt* ... What's done is done."

"Your *what's done* has caused two world wars, tens of millions of deaths, not to mention the suffering of countless others living in brutal servitude."

"Did I pull a trigger or force a hand? No. And does anyone on this conveyance care about the dead of World War I or II, or the suffering of Russian serfs? No. Does anyone in America care? ... No. The wars are a source of pride. Militarism makes for jobs and drone contracts. The misery and pain of long ago is forgotten, and the fu-ture is The Overman."

"Wherein you rule, surrounded by your own cult of personality."

"It is my destiny. Thus spake Zarathustra."

"Zarathustra? Are you joking? That is just a stupid fantasy of Nietzsche."

He laughed and sneezed. *Ahhhheeeghhhhhh!* "Oh, please. By the way, my dear, why did you not use your magical aria to sing your way to America, or is your debt to Ahriman becoming too much to bear?"

"You know the answer."

"By the way, even if you did somehow survive me, that ancient and glorious evil deity from Andromeda would one day collect his due. That is your curse."

"Perhaps, perhaps not. But I am growing impatient. What do you *want*, Godfellow?"

He noticed she was getting angrier by the moment. "Why are you flying to Paris?"

"Go to Hell. Again, *what do you want?*"

"What do I always want? For you to stop aiding that *shmuk*, Pa-ganini."

"And if I continue to resist your desire?"

"You will perish at the hands of his Fracas machines, just as you foresaw when age 15 in Bärenthoren Castle."

"And you can change that destiny?"

"I can, dear ... dear ... *Ahhhheeeghhhhhh!*."

"I will not perish at the hands of Fracas machines. I will simply throw myself from the cliffs, first. A quick death."

"No. One of the machines will catch you as you leap, and it will murder you in a *most nightmarish* manner. It will dismember you, and gut you, like a lion with captured prey. " He said this and coughed for a few moments, watching her shudder then regain her resolve.

"*So be it*, monster" she said, her face fierce and determined.

"Mazel tov, Catherine of Russia. Revel in your time!"

Edison waved a ta-ta at her with a tissue and sneezed once more. *Ahhhheeeghhhhhh!* But this wasn't the end of it—just part of a scheme to change her, lay a foundation for making a deal that would later turn her against that accursed Paganini. The crazy Italian violinist was too strong for him to kill easily, though the two of them could manage it. As long as he lived, the future of The Overman, the Dyson Sphere, dominion over the stars, his new utopia and all else remained in jeopardy.

He had much to ponder. *All in good time though, all in good time.*

Later that evening in Dubai, he relaxed and ate a midnight dinner at *Le Petit Sanglier* (The Small Boar), his favorite restaurant on one of the Sky Isles drifting lazily above the Persian Gulf. The waitresses there, all morph-droid models (his invention), who duplicated the appearance of famous American actresses such as Angelina Jolie, Natalie Portman, Ava Gardner and Lauren Becall, even down to the mannerisms and voice, strolled throughout the dining room, smiling and pampering the customers. Other features included zero-grav fountains (his invention) that lifted shimmering water in huge arcs over the heads of the patrons; and a special tele-glass (his invention) set in the walls that allowed patrons to see beyond the rim of the Earth to a golden-red sunrise over the Himalayas.

How pleasant and relaxing to eat and drink in this place, watching as Angelina Jolie served him a fine Italian Pinot Noir while the soft Himalaya sunlight turned the water above his head to a rainbow; and as a bonus, the sore throat and clogged nose of Mrs. Rabinowitz were already a fading memory. No labor or hardship would ever be an obstacle to his relentless nature. And considering this fact, the favorite words of his favorite song, "The Future," by the 20th century singer poet Leonard Cohen came to mind, as they so often did:

Give me back the Berlin wall,
Give me Stalin and St Paul,
I've seen the future, brother:
It is murder.

As he sipped his wine and mused on how Leonard Cohen in his old age looked disturbingly like that old buffoon American president, Ronald Reagan, he was joined at his table by a striking and powerfully built wizard goddess—a former Mongolian queen by the name of Mandukhai. She had arrived fresh off a primary conflict point in the World Maker War: the Battle of The Somme in 1916. Like a cross between a Chinese warlord and a circus acrobat, she was lithe and hung with weapons, also smeared with blood on her neck and bosom, arms and legs. As a bonus, she was missing her right eye.

"Must you wizard goddesses *always* be dripping blood?" Edison said.

Mandukhai refused to respond to his dumb question. Instead, she grew her eye back while reporting with stoic demeanor on the Somme conflict—yet another "futile attempt by Pan-Buddhist Democratic reactionaries to change history." As she spoke of the disposition of forces during the battle, her hand reached under the table and smoothed up to his groin, whereupon he instructed Angelia Jolie to bring him a bottle of 1938 Chardonnay from Burgundy. And while he and Mandukhai conversed, and the massage continued, Angelina Jolie returned and glared murderously at Mandukhai. Edison realized it was Eréndira attempting to disguise herself and spy on him. Before she could launch herself at the throat of her rival Mandukhai (who also wished to possess The God One and bear him dozens of demi-god children) and thereby destroy the entire restaurant, and the sky island as well, he engaged both of them with these words:

"In a few minutes, the three of us will be on ancient Mars."

The two wizard goddesses stopped glaring at each other and stared at him. He loved excursions to distant planets and star systems now and then. Once he loved Mandukhai for hours on Titan, on a dark shore of that moon beside a quiet methane lake as the ringed planet Saturn and its bands of thunder rose on the horizon. Another time he loved Eréndira within the bosom of a stellar nursery, a nebula off the shore of the Milky Way—the two of them several miles tall at the time, though invisible beside the birthing suns.

Was Master Godfellow planning a threesome? No. They would help him foil an assassination attempt on his life by the Princess von Anhalt, and her older self, Catherine the Great.

"Who told you of the whore twins' plan?" Eréndira asked.

"Your Lord of Saravastra, the fellow with the violin," Edison said. "Apparently, he falsely believes he will somehow gain by my continued existence."

Eréndira laughed so hard she forgot her desire to decapitate Mandukhai.

Politics as usual in the war for all time.

царица

6

Mother Yarrow and Saravastra - Eréndira vs. Freddie – Water and Wind

NEARLY AN HOUR AFTER THE BANQUET FOR EMPRESS ELIZ-
ABETH had come to an end, Zolo Bold and the other servants attached to Bärenthoren still cleaned and carefully packaged the
priceless centerpieces of Princess Johanna. Zolo felt exhausted, not
only because it was two o'clock in the morning and his legs ached
with fatigue, but also because of the stress placed on him by the
warlock Gur, as well as the haunting aura of that hideous bee recalled from the day his beloved mother Avizeh vanished from his
life. He still felt the pain in his nose, still saw the look of terror on
his mother's face. But the aura of bee in the shadow raised another
question:

How was Temujin Gur connected to the events of that day?

He must be, or else the bee-like shadow was a way of shaking
Zolo up, trickery by Gur to confuse him. Or was Gur himself an insect thing in the guise of human? Paganini often spoke of Ahriman,
the distant father of the World Makers (who he claimed would, like
Saturn, one day eat his own children), as a nonhuman magical being
fallen to Asia from the stars.

Might Gur be Ahriman himself in disguise?

No chance to explore the notion. Zolo's musings were suddenly
interrupted by Tobias Bergmann, one of his fellow house servants
and a pray-for-no-beating person like himself. "Willie, my God, what
a horror! Did you see all of it?" Tobias' face appeared strained and
excited at the same time, as if something about Gur's terror theater
actually thrilled him.

"How could I have not, Tobias? I was here the whole time."

"My God, Willie, I hid in the kitchen after those things appeared. Even some of the nobles joined us and we were all like whimpering dogs. Duchess Maria Anna couldn't stop sobbing, and another noblewoman lost her mind and tried to stab herself with one of the chef's big knives. I stopped her."

Zolo listened, half bored, then caught a glimpse over Tobias's shoulder of Princess Johanna facing Gleb Brerezhnoy. They stood in the distance, near the covered bulk of the World Stormer of Anhalt, and well out of earshot. Princess Johanna looked murderous and Gleb fearful, as though his life were being threatened.

Zolo could not suppress his curiosity, especially because the dialogue might involve Freddie. He felt compelled to eavesdrop, though such a feat required a bit of magic, but first he must leave a baffled Tobias behind. He excused himself with a "Back in a moment," and walked to the opposite corner of the Great Hall. Since Princess Johanna terrorized Gleb, no chance the butler bully would notice Zolo's disobedience.

Alone in the corner, he fixed his eyes on the two of them, and though much discipline and time was needed before he would be a seasoned spellcrafter, Paganini had gifted him with a Mother Yarrow. She listened to his head, and saw what he saw, knew what he knew. Her incredible power watched over him and emerged in dire need, though in the meantime, only trickles of her true force fueled his meager requests and spells. Anything greater might arouse suspicion from the likes of Temujin Gur and attract unwanted attention. So he watched Johanna and Gleb, and whispered to himself, *Nai Yarrow, deixe-me escoitar* (Mother Yarrow, let me hear), and the first voice he heard was Gleb:

"... but if I am suddenly rich?"

"It will take him days to die, and you can hide the gold in the wall of your room, just as you have before."

"Then I ..."

"This cannot be delayed. The fool just informed me he will resist *to his dying day* any effort by Empress Elizabeth to marry his daughter to her nephew Peter, and I cannot have this. We must act quickly. His day to begin dying *is now.*"

"Yes, I understand."

"His brat of a daughter will be crushed by his death and that will not be a source of unhappiness to me. And once the deed is done, you will see to the destruction of this World Stormer thing. Do you hear? Pound it to pieces. It humiliated me."

"Yes, mistress. It will be done. I will personally see to its wreckage."

"Fail in these tasks and I will see to your wreckage, Gleb Brerezhnoy."

Zolo heard Gleb moan. It was almost enough to make Zolo feel sorry for the bully, but no time for pity, not for Gleb. And how many other murders had he committed for her? Zolo pondered it all, heard the words repeated in his head:

It will take him days to die.

* Оверман *

PONDERING THE DEATH OF THE OLD WOMAN from the troupe, and feeling guilty in a way she could not dismiss, Freddie resolved to consider the matter further in her castle bedchamber. Despite the adrenaline rush she experienced, the excitement and horror of the banquet had frazzled her nerves and exhausted her.

Upon entering the bedchamber she lit a few candles, changed out of her heavy banquet garment, and warmed herself before a fireplace blaze prepared by the maidservants. Once warmed, she began to tremble. She wasn't sure why. Perhaps the insanity of the banquet had finally caught up to her? She stood and walked towards her four-post bed, desiring to lie down, but her intentions were interrupted by a small teakwood music box on her bedside table. Where had it come from? A gift perhaps? She sat on the bed and felt compelled to open it without hesitation, as though a gentle force inclined her, and once done, she heard strange yet incredibly beautiful violin music. The violin sounded so perfect she knew it must be a Stradivarius. It touched her soul with hope and sadness at once, and tears began to fall from her eyes as she sat on the bed to listen. She imagined great white seabirds riding the breeze of a pink dusk, the crashing of brutal ocean against the windy cliffs of forever. It uplifted her soul while reminding her of her own mortality. It filled the dark smoke of her head and turned it to light.

Nothing but light.

Years later, as she tried to move her body, she felt stiff and tingling, as though she'd been sitting in the same position forever. Then her eyes began to focus. The source of light became a window, an arched window without shutters at least fifteen feet away and over ten feet tall from sill to top. Through this window her eyes beheld enormous, snow-peaked mountains in a misty distance, big as the Himalayas beneath a sky blue as European winter, and in that sky, streaks of cloud and specks of white bird, like gulls, circling and soaring.

Could this be a dream? Gulls meant ocean nearby, but ...?

The violin music resumed.

That same music. This can only be a dream.

She rose from her seat, wobbly and stiff, and walked forward towards the window. From only a foot away she stopped and beheld a sight that stunned her. Before her rose a city, the most godlike city imaginable. Scores and more scores of four-sided towers gleamed in the sun, thrusting up for many hundreds, even thousands of feet, rivaling the snowy mountains beyond in sheer grandeur. Composed of brilliant white and golden stone, they possessed countless numbers of arched windows from base to crest, many of the towers with dark bronze balconies brimming with brilliant flowers, plants and small fountains; and all of them topped with massive roofs of carnelian-red tile flaring out from the tops—like Tibetan structures in paintings she'd seen, but on a scale far larger than she would have ever believed possible. And too, the sound of mysterious wind voices touched her ears, gusts and mellower breeze carrying soft words and melodic whispers incomprehensible to her. Pillows of cloud and white gulls drifted among the towers, and the teary-beautiful violin music became one with the dream city. As she stared, unmoving, one of the gulls soared nearby.

She turned her head to glance at it.

She blinked twice, and realized, it was not a bird at all.

The body of it belonged to a human being.

Man or woman she did not know. The white wings of a gauzy light material tightened over a thin-wood frame, and it reminded her of ... yes, a sketch of a flying device imagined by Leonardo Da Vinci. *That's it. But these fly, actually fly.* The wings lifted these Da Vinci-like magic contraptions to whatever heights they wished.

This is a dream, one of those wherein I can hear my thoughts saying, 'this is a dream'.

She imagined her arms fitted in the flying wings and she raised them before her, as if asking the gods of this city for her own wings, and then she noticed: *My arms and hands are larger, my arms stronger, as though I am older.* And next, she heard words in her head, as when Temujin Gur had spoken to her without lips. The voice male, though richer and calmer:

"Turn around and see, Princess von Anhalt."

She turned around as the dream voice commanded and saw herself in a tall mirror. She appeared older by several years. But how many? She saw a powerful and excitingly beautiful woman, her hair longer than ever and cascading over her full chest, her pure white skin draped in a sleeveless carnelian chemise that fell to her ankles. She felt cool inside of it, breezy and vital, and as her mind cleared, her being surged with a feeling of unbelievable power. She felt as though she could tear down castle walls with her bare hands or squeeze sword iron to putty. *All part of the dream, a wonderful dream, or perhaps this is Heaven. Mother has poisoned me and I have arrived. Let it be so then. At least I lived to see her afraid of me.*

"You are nineteen in years, and Princess Johanna has not tried to poison you, at least not yet."

That voice again. But where? Where stands the god who speaks?

"On the contrary, I am godless ... Over here, princess, to your left."

Freddie turned to her left, and way across the room saw a man sitting behind a four-legged wooden table not more than five feet long. She noted various contraptions and papers on the table top. The man's head was down and he busily wrote with a large golden pen. His clothing simple: a black waistcoat over a white long-sleeve shirt with broad cuffs. She walked towards him and the image became clearer as he stopped writing and glanced up at her: his narrow head framed by wavy dark hair that fell to his shoulders, his skin pale, nose long and craggy, lips thin, and his eyes, small and sleepy eyes staring at her with a look she interpreted as apathy, as if he had spent most of his life eternally bored because he could never be surprised, and her appearance before him now was no exception.

At this point she wished the dream would take another turn. She walked to within a few feet of this odd sleepy man and halted. He placed his golden pen down on the table beside the paper, the head of the pen easily the size of her thumb. She looked more closely and saw an actual head, that of Buddha, for she recognized the placid face and the three-fin helmet.

"This is no dream, my future Czarina, and you are not drugged. You are in a city known as Saravastra, named after the Hindu Goddess Sarasvati. The year is 1898, the country Tibet. Those are the Himalayas outside and my name is Niccolo Paganini. I am a World Maker and known in this place as the *Time King Bodhisattva*, though such title is admittedly my own and not bestowed by Tibet's Buddhist monks, or any other tradition," he said with a weak smile and cleared his throat.

Freddie noticed his long and delicate white fingers placed atop the table, looking like precious sea anemone. His left foot below the table slid back and forth. Such an odd tic!

"You are the ... Bodhisattva King ... on Time?" she asked in a daze.

No answer to her question, though he said, "I do follow the tenets of Buddhism, however, and find them gratifying. You might consider it at some point, but that is a discussion for another time, perhaps in the year 3145, or earlier, in 1683."

Freddie reached over with one hand and pinched her other arm.

Paganini continued. "The woman whose body you inhabit is you, of course, but at the age of 33. The consciousness of your older self is within you now, listening and watching, and freely allowing you to inhabit her. When your own consciousness returns to your castle, your hand will still be on the music box, and all of this will have happened in less than one tenth of a moment, and reside forever as a memory lodged safely in your left wrist."

"My wrist?"

"Yes, in a place where Temujin Gur, as you call him, will not notice. We don't wish him to know your soul has traveled to Saravastra. The images and knowledge you gain here become like a beacon of light in your head because they are so unique and tantalizing. The Mongolian warlock would spot it in a moment. We need to conceal it but allow it to trickle into you as needed."

"I think I—"

"No, you don't understand, not yet."

Before she could answer, another voice, sounding like hers, cut in and said:

But you will.

A whisper in her head, *But you will.* Another voice intruded into her mind. When would it end? It made her realize she might be going insane.

No, not insane. You are me, and you are awakening, the whispering voice inside her said.

It was definitely her voice, no question.

Yes, I am you, but you as you will be many years from now. You must listen to your new acariya, Paganini. Pay no attention to his manner. He is one with sadness and great troubles.

Paganini lifted a single piece of paper from the desk, and handed it up to Freddie. She took it from him and read the words on it:

I love those who can smile in trouble, who can gather strength from distress, and grow brave by reflection. Tis the business of little minds to shrink, but they whose heart is firm, and whose conscience approves their conduct, will pursue their principles unto death.

"Those words were written by the man who is our enemy, Master Edison Godfellow. You know him best as Leonardo Da Vinci," Paganini said, his face flat and demeanor likewise. Would anything ever stir the man to passion? His nose twitched, his foot still sliding back and forth beneath the table. His beautiful white fingers intertwined with each other as though about to copulate and give birth to more fingers. Freddie began to feel irritated, but then she noticed a strikingly beautiful violin sitting on a stand behind Paganini. She'd heard stories of the Messiah Stradivarius, the most wondrous and perfect violin in the world.

Might this be it?

Back to more important matters though.

"Da Vinci? You mean Da Vinci of—"

"Yes, that Da Vinci. The famous Da Vinci. He now has his own cult of personality, so to speak that he calls, the *Quadro del Overman*, or Cadre of The Overman, and his army of spellcraft captains and *Dio Soldati*, or God Soldiers, are spread throughout the centuries like a growing pox. We are waging war against them, a war for utopia you might say."

Freddie gaped at Paganini, looking dumber than ever in her life.

"For now, consider it a deadly chess match in four dimensions, and *you*, Princess von Anhalt, are the only Queen on the board. You do play chess, quite well, yes?"

"I do ... but why am I—"

"Your rare aria power. Only one other World Maker ever possessed it. The demonstration you gave at the banquet for Empress Elizabeth was only the beginning."

"What happened, sir, to the other possessor of aria?"

"You will learn, *in time*." Paganini sat back in his chair, staring at her with his sleepy eyes, his anemone fingers uncurling and resting on his belly. "We were once friends, Edison and I. We were both born in bronze age Italy, blessed or cursed by Ahriman, I am not certain which."

"Ahriman?"

"A magical being who fell to Asia from the stars ten thousand years ago. It is said he instills his power in the World Makers at birth, and we grow to realize it, just as you are realizing yours."

"I am ... yes."

"By age sixteen I ruled the Etruscans, and Edison moved to the Middle East to become Sargon of Akkad, a rather ruthless dictator. I never approved of his militarism, but he mellowed going into the 14th century, content with art and invention until he adopted the dangerous philosophy of a man who hasn't yet been born in your own century, a philosopher by the name of Friedrich Nietzsche. Edison considers him to be a prophet for the next stage of human evolution that he terms, "Age of The Overman.""

"Evolution?"

"You don't know Charles Darwin yet, but never mind. Edison believes he must usher in this new stage of humankind and do so on the backs of millions of corpses and enough tears to create another Atlantic Ocean should it ever dry up."

"Millions of corpses? ... Forgive me for being so ignorant. This is all—"

"Forgiveness isn't necessary. You must know the facts, and that is part of the reason you are here. Two major wars will happen in the 20th century. Both are catastrophic beyond imagining, accomplished with a violence you would never believe possible. Edison supports them as part of his utopian plan to create a new order of human in the 21st century. Whereas, we of Saravastra wish to prevent these ruinous wars and usher in a world both peaceful and wise, and one populated by real humans. We believe improvement of the flesh far less important than improvement of mind and soul. This is our vision of utopia, and Edison and I have debated the opposed visions endlessly."

"This is all ... so much to—"

"By the way, do you know that water falls from the stars? Our tears belong to suns that have perished."

One overwhelming impression on top of another! She found it hard to cope. What happened to the voice of her other self? If not mad yet, she might well go mad soon enough.

You will not. Be strong.

Before she could relax, she heard a familiar noise, a *zzzzzt-click* sound, then another. Might the World Stormer of Anhalt be arriving? If so, no one, not even her other self could convince her of the current reality.

But it wasn't the World Stormer.

She turned to see something far more horrible. *My God!* She let out a gasp and stepped back. One of those evil things she witnessed in her vision back at Bärenthoren, one of those hideous insect things with a frog face that chased her and barked. Now a smaller version, walking on thin legs of gleaming bronze, *zzzzzt-clicking* as it went, and upon its back, a table-like surface upon which sat bowls and glasses of food and drink.

The Fracas mini-machine clattered up to the table and stopped. Paganini sighed and reached over to pick up an empty plate. He chose a large serving spoon and began to place food upon it—what looked like herring, banana slices, and strawberries. "Pardon, we are famished. World making is enough to make you ravenous," he said with sarcasm in his voice.

"This thing ... things like this, tried to kill me. I saw the vision—"

"A lie!" Paganini almost shouted, sounding annoyed. "A lie arranged by Temujin Gur to sow distrust. He is in truth, an ancient Wizard God, almost as powerful as a World Maker, and in the employ of Edison Godfellow ... or so Edison believes. His task is to mature your powers because Edison has plans for you. However, I suspect Gur nurtures his own schemes for world making. He is insane and nearly powerful enough, but the details are vague ... and one of your two major tasks in the days to come will be to help us discover these details."

"My tasks?"

"I feel certain that Temujin Gur will not honor the southern-most war line defined by the Treaty of Nicholas, signed by Edison and myself."

"War line?"

"The treaty draws the line at 1529, the year of the siege of Vienna by the Ottoman Empire. We call it The Nicholas Line, named after the defender of Vienna, and we both agree it is crucial the Ottoman Turks lose that conflict and that events leading up to it remain in place. The Mongol Gur, however, knows no such boundaries. I believe he will cross the Nicholas Line in defiance, if he can muster enough power … I would have him dead, but he is a difficult kill. I annihilated him once and he sprang up elsewhere, like a cancer."

Freddie believed that by all rights she should be in the throes of madness or shock brought about by this glorious and terrible dream that was not a dream. "How will Temujin Gur mature my powers?" she asked.

"Through conflict. Your powers and your ability to control them develop as a result of use. The more you are forced to use your powers, the more easily they become a part of you, and no better way than conflict, hot emotions and actual fear for your life. Whatever does not kill you, makes you stronger."

And a portion of my strength will follow you back to Europe.

"But there is more," Paganini continued. "We must trick Gur into helping us defeat Edison's plans. We must hurt the old Da Vinci where he lives, in his precious Dubai. The future belongs to the bold, my future Czarina."

She knew of the siege of Vienna, of course, but Dubai puzzled her. Before Freddie could respond, she heard yet another noise—a roaring sound, like a volcano erupting in the distance, and growing louder, as if a mountain of hot ash cloud bore down on Saravastra. She swiveled around to see, through another open window way across the room, a ball of roiling light streaking down like a blazing asteroid through the artic blue sky.

Eréndira Marquez comes. She is a monster wrongly trusted by Paganini.

No time to try to understand, for the ferocious light ball, crackling and flashing, drew closer, the roaring even louder. Freddie saw various indistinct black objects churning like debris within a whirlpool of white and golden light, and as the ball grew larger, she noticed a human-like form at the core, half the size of the loud and blasting thing itself.

Prepare yourself. The demon is almost upon us.

Increasing in velocity at the last moment before entering the window, it crashed through with a thunderous racket, and in two blinks of moment, dissolved to a woman standing in a haze of swirling fire smoke.

Though not quite a woman.

Freddie's first impression was that of a uniquely beautiful human crossed with an insect, though upon closer inspection, other contrasting features became obvious: wicked mandibles thrust at least a full foot from her jaw like twin black sabers, and giant thorns the color of fire ant rose from her upper shoulders, while her eyes, big as fists, gleamed a somber, lifeless black like the eyes of a giant shark. But as the smoke cleared and the godlike hybrid strolled forward, the mandibles and thorns withdrew, retreating with soft pops into sockets of flesh. Her eyes shrunk to human eyes, becoming the color of umber, a burnt orange, an autumnal sizzle of things dying and seeking rebirth. And too, this Wizard Goddess stood tall, at least six foot four, curved and powerful as any woman Freddie had ever seen. She wore only a dark armor breastplate that bared her broad shoulders and contoured down to rest high on her hips, the surface patterned with three rows of magical Chinese-like symbols of varying sizes, all glowing soft purples and reds. Her flesh, of a Latin hue, dark as the Moorish ancestors of Spanish kings, and her hair black, flowing behind her and falling below her waist—the most lustrous black night of hair framing a face strong as a cliff, yet as lovely as the setting sunlight upon that cliff, accentuated with golden hoop earrings and a thin golden necklace with a gleaming emerald the size of a thumbnail. She wore no shoes, simply ankle bracelets of gold. To look upon this woman, if she could be called that, was to have one's breath taken away, no matter the observer be male or female.

Eréndira is smeared with blood. She has been on a killing spree.

Freddie saw what her other self made reference to: dabs and streaks of fresh blood on Eréndira's arms and above her bosom, a small trickle from the right side of her lip—as though the blood of her victims was still tasted by her mouth and body. The Wizard Goddess fixated on Paganini, who in turn watched her approach—his face calm, though not quite so apathetic as before. Her head turned ever so slightly as she strolled forward, and her autumnal burn of eye flashed at Freddie, and she knew at once that this Eréndira deeply loathed her. She saw her face in those umber Goddess eyes, and it reminded her of Temujin Gur, the way his eyes appeared to consume her at the banquet.

Yes, she hates you. She is a jealous half-blood who wants you dead.

"You have been fighting, my darling Empress of Byzantium," Paganini said with an emotionless tone.

Eréndira came to a halt before the table, and said, "I saved the stuffy Archduke Ferdinand twice, but Godfellow's forces moved in rapidly and the Serbs succeeded. It's his damn machine, his War Tracker daughter giving him that edge, as we both know. World War I therefore proceeds as usual, and even worse news, the battle for Mein Kampf has finally suffered an Extinction Event. I am sorry to report that Hitler has once again been rejected from art school," she said flatly, her voice possessing an exotic accent Freddie could not trace. Portugese? And the tone deep, nearly the voice of male command, unlike any other woman Freddie knew. But who was Hitler?

With resignation in his voice, Paganini said, "I am not surprised. The Mein Kampf point has seen conflict between our forces at least a dozen times. What are the losses?"

"Surya Command reports a squadron consisting of seven of our best spellcraft captains assigned to that era, along with two gods, Wotanna and Farzoon, and at least a dozen black armor pieces of various sizes including five new War Reapers, several platoons of Alakar, and reports of three to five Magogs, including a female with child."

Freddie still mulled over "Empress of Byzantium," much less the other terms. This Eréndira, an Empress of Byzantium? History recorded no such person. Freddie would have heard of her, history being one of her specialties.

Paganini's calm broke, and he said with irritation in his voice, "Magogs with child are *not supposed* to engage and—"

"It was not my choice," Eréndira said, her voice clam, and turning to face Freddie, her umber eyes burning brighter, she shouted with a thunderclap voice that shook the very molecules of the room wherein they stood:

"AND AS FOR YOU, CZARINA CATHERINE, YOU SHOULD TEACH YOUR BRATTY YOUNGER SELF TO HIDE HER THOUGHTS SO THEY DO NOT FOUL US ALL LIKE CURDLED MILK!" The sheer force of the bellow rocked Freddie back on her heels. "I WAS AN EMPRESS OF BZYANTIUM, AND MY NAME WAS THEODORA!"

Courage. The vile creature is baiting you.

"Do not try my patience now, Eréndira, this is a time for mourning, not petty rancor," said Paganini. "These beings were heroes."

Eréndira turned her face back to him and resumed her flat delivery as though nothing had happened: "You always feel sad for your heroes, especially following an Extinction Event, but why? You know it will occur if a pivotal point in history is contested too often. You know that anyone hurled back in time due to the Event will cross the Nicholas Line going south and our chrono-defense satellites will sterilize them, and whatever burning and bloody scraps are left once they hit the Cenozoic ocean at over a thousand miles an hour will be breakfast for megalodons. You and Godfellow set up your game that way. Your rules, your World Maker craft. You should learn to accept the inevitability and not mope about it like a sissy girl."

"I will not argue my emotions with you, Eréndira. And this is *far more* than just a game. Edison, as deluded as he is, isn't insane. He knows that without rules like the Nicholas Line that all of us would cease to exist."

Freddie decided to speak. It felt ridiculous for her to stand there, mute and afraid of this Eréndira apparition. "But you said to me, Master Paganini, that I am a chess queen in this game, did you not?" Freddie asked him.

Before he could answer, Eréndira turned a glare on Freddie and said, "Look, it's trying to think!" The glare intensified, the umber eyes burning with streaks of fire, like scraps of heroes falling into the Cenozoic ocean. Freddie's fingers began to painfully prick for the first time since Eréndira appeared. "Who said you could speak in my presence, *babooshka*? Isn't that what your castle nanny calls you?"

"My nanny is none of your business, Empress of Byzantium."

The claws are out. Careful!

"So, your fingers are pricking?" Eréndira asked. "Well, one day you will do enough evil to make your own fingers prick, and you will say to yourself ..." And Eréndira cleared her voice and spoke a perfect imitation of Freddie:

"By the pricking of my fingers, my own black soul nearby lingers."

"I will not do evil, so that will never happen," Freddie said with a tone of defiance.

"Gods of Time! The perfect Czarina!" Eréndira Marquez said and laughed in a bitter tone, like someone who had seen too much misery and death. "You will do evil in war, *babooshska*, more than you can dream! So much that your castle nanny Babette would not recognize you. So much that you will make Princess Johanna look like an innocent wood nymph in comparison."

"Enough of you!" Freddie shouted at Eréndira. The comparison to Princess Johanna had proved too much. She felt anger beginning to overtake her, and she welcomed it, for it was far easier to endure than fear.

In consequence of Freddie's defiance, Eréndira's entire body began to fume. The air above her head and upper shoulders turned mirage-like hot, her umber eyes brightening and streaking with meteor. Her face darkened to a sinister death smile while dark blades of shadow whipped like a turning fan across her upper chest, arms and thighs, as though horrid inner demons raced within her, their black forms reflected on her flesh.

"We love, and we fight, like *no human can*," Eréndira said with a savage tone in her voice.

Freddie saw Eréndira staring murderously at her and watched as her own face bloated larger and larger in Eréndira's eyes, and with that growth came the feeling of painful nails scratching inside her head. She winced and groaned. It felt to her as if Eréndira would claw her brain to shreds.

"Enough, Eréndira!" Paganini shouted, "There is work to be done!"

Eréndira ignored Paganini because Freddie was now her chosen victim. "Conflict that does not kill you, makes you stronger, Czarina whore, so let us make you a little stronger now. Do you want me to tell you about THE EVIL THINGS YOU WILL DO BEGINNING WITH ALLOWING YOUR OWN FATHER'S DEATH?"

Damn her lying bitch soul!

The Princess of Anhalt and Czarina Catherine were now in agreement. Freddie glared at Eréndira, her body trembling with rage, and her enemy glared back, and as they did so, magical yarrow symbols appeared in mid-air, flanking both of them. Large as each woman by half, they glowed a blood red and swirled angrily as they underwent ongoing mutation to new symbols.

YARROW WAR SYMBOLS.

Glyphs of sorcery such as these had the power to devastate entire cities, but Freddie was ignorant of their meaning. She did not care, though her older self understood, and welcomed the chance to inflict as much pain as possible on Eréndira.

Paganini shouted at them, "Suppress the yarrow! You will take out half of Saravastra!"

Eréndira's yarrow symbols, hot and snapping, faded from view as their master never let her eyes stray from Freddie. And as they faded, so did Freddie's defensive yarrow symbols.

"I have *no need* of yarrow," Freddie said with an edge of knife in her voice. "I will strangle you dead for speaking of my father with your foul lips."

"You wish to lay a hand on me, hypocrite Czarina? I will snap your head off and throw it over the Himalayas!"

So be it, half-blood monster!

Freddie's open right hand blurred forth and struck Eréndira's face with a lightning bolt slap that whipped the creature's body around for three spins and slammed her to the floor. Without a moment of hesitation, Freddie cried out like a wild lioness and launched herself onto Eréndira with inhuman speed. She grappled the muscular and taller body of the Wizard Goddess, head-locked her and drove a knee into her chest with the force of a wall-shattering ram. Eréndira grunted in pain and Freddie drove in the knee again. The furious Wizard Goddess reacted with a fist driven upward into Freddie's abdomen, and then, with legs strong enough to pummel a tyrannosaurus to pulp, she sprang forward and up, causing the two of them to fly like cannon shot across the room and smack the wall beyond Paganini's desk. The force of the impact quaked the entire building, and they crashed to the floor, Eréndira's legs locked like pythons around Freddie's straining body.

The women screamed in rage, hurling insults in Galician like *Czarina esterco!* and *Can bruxa!* (Czarina dung! and Witch dog!) as they punched each other in the face, each blow with enough force to crater a city street.

Realizing that shouting was pointless, Paganini reached for Skanda, his magical violin, for he understood that only its power might stop the fight before the tower collapsed. He hoped too that the quaking and shrieking would bring the Saravastra spellcraft captains racing up to the room.

Meanwhile, the death grapple between the World Maker and Wizard Goddess continued without surrender or respite. Freddie and Eréndira careened over the floor, wrestling and punching, stopping once or twice to bang each other's head by the hair into the stone tiles before rolling on towards the opposite wall. Eréndira's legs continued to squeeze gasps from Freddie, crushing her with enough force to reduce a boulder to rubble. Once they hit the wall though, Freddie raised herself and yanked Eréndira up by the hair to face her, whereupon Eréndira's mandibles burst suddenly out from her jaw and drove their dark points with a *kerchunk* deep into Freddie's cheeks.

"Saravastra's gods!" Paganini yelled.

He began to play Skanda, his bow striking with anger, his fingers curving over the strings and beating like mad white spiders, but it would take time and ingenuity to break apart this fight between these two powerful and furious magical beings.

Freddie screamed and her face blood streamed down her chest. She let go of Eréndira's hair with her left hand and snapped off a mandible from the jaw of the Wizard Goddess, yanking it from her own cheek at the same time. Eréndira screamed in agony. With a cry of rage, Freddie drove the black saber into the wizard woman's mouth with such force that the point of it pierced through the back of her neck. Freddie then spat the blood from her own mouth into her enemy's shocked face, and as Eréndira desperately yanked the mandible free, followed by a spewing gush of dark blood that soaked Freddie's chemise, a World Maker aria voice echoed in the room, pure and bright as sun from the voice of the older Freddie:

Fóraaa monstro, a cabeza cara a pedraaaa! (Away monster, your head to the stone!)

The shrieking Wizard Goddess unwrapped from Freddie and flew backwards in an instant. The aria spell levitated her to the ceiling before driving her to the floor face first, there to begin ramming her head into the stone tiles. Freddie then leapt high towards her foe, her right arm outstretched as a symbol of moon-blue steel formed in mid-air and congealed to four feet of shimmering yarrow sword, clutched at the hilt by her right hand.

The attempt to impale the Wizard Goddess, however, was hampered by Paganini's Skanda beginning to take effect. The arc of Freddie's flying body, sword in hand, began to slow, and slow even more. Only one chance remained. The older Freddie within her invoked her Mother Yarrow:

Nai Yarrow Maria, concesión forzaaaa me! (Mother Yarrow Maria, grant me strength!)

In defiance of Skanda's magic gaining in power by the second, Freddie completed her arc just in time, dropping down to drive the yarrow sword through the back of her enemy with a force of no less than twenty tons per square inch. The flesh of the Wizard Goddess sizzled hot at the point of entry wound and the blade stabbed deep into the tower floor, trapping her there like a thrashing dragonfly pinned by a dart.

Eréndira howled in such unrelenting agony that the sound of it was like several large cannons firing salvos one after the other, and it was said later, by those who lived in Saravastra, that the howls beat against the Himalayas like storm waves and caused dozens of avalanches, some of which buried whole villages of mountain tribesmen and wrecked more than a dozen Buddhist shrines.

* Оверман *

COVERED IN BLOOD AND SMILING, SHE SAT BEFORE PAGANINI, her chemise in tatters and torn from her legs. Recovering from the fight with the Wizard Goddess, she breathed deeply, unable yet to believe herself wrong for relishing the extra pain she caused the half-blood by twisting the yarrow sword in her body as she thrashed. Nothing but hatred, pure and glorious, had filled Freddie's soul. Both her souls. How satisfactory to have watched Paganini's Bodhisattvas of spellcraft pouring into the room in their tall crescent caps and flowing orange robes to remove a screeching Eréndira Marquez still impaled by the yarrow sword. Their spells, spoken in unison, formed an imprisoning sphere of force around the Wizard Goddess and she looked like a squirming rodent trapped in a glass egg.

"We have known you for years now, and you are hot of head, full of passions," Paganini said, his face dour and exhausted, "That is a strength, and a weakness at the same time. It is amazing you were able to slow my music spell reaching full zenith. Skanda has rarely been defied."

"Skanda?"

"The Hindu god of war. But my Skanda, my violin, is an instrument for creation also, almost as varied and strong as your aria power. But that is a matter for another time. I have more I must tell you. My apologies for the interruption of—"

"What is the source of Ahriman's power?" Freddie asked.

"You cut right to it, yes?" Paganini said, grinning sadly.

"To know the source is to know a being's deepest secret," she said.

Following a long sigh, a weary Paganini said he had no answer for Ahriman's power. And how did he influence the aria, create the aria? Why was it bestowed on Freddie and not another? No answer for that either. The future Czarina's power derived from the same source as the yarrow magic refined by he and Edison Godfellow many centuries before in Spain after the fall of the Roman Empire— the source being the "Tao," the flow and substance of existence into which Ahriman was embedded, like a tree growing from a great stone.

The concepts of magical aria, Tao, and yarrow mesmerized Freddie.

"However, there is a theory we World Makers have ...," Paganini said, looking distant and somber.

"Yes?"

"That the Tao, at least in part, is a balance of visible matter like stars with dark matter we cannot see. The dark matter state will be discovered by Earth scientists about a hundred years from now. The Tao is a *fanciful term*, one belonging to the ancient Chinese. The notion of Ahriman growing into it, also fanciful."

While Freddie still tasted Eréndira's blood in her mouth, Paganini reached over to one of the contraptions on his desk. It appeared like a small, transparent sphere of glass with an elongated neck, a very thin loop of wire inside. It stood upright upon a wooden base, screwed into the top of it. Paganini's index finger touched something on the base and she heard a *click* sound. The sphere filled with white light. Paganini withdrew his hand and said, "Electricity ... the power to change life on an enormous scale, with the help of science and a manifestation of Tao, but the non-magical side of Tao. Few human beings comprehend electricity, just know that it works and has many uses. The same circumstance applies to the magical side of Tao. We call upon it and control it, use it for a number of purposes, though we do not fully understand its nature."

"The two sides of Tao, I understand. But what do you mean by *bestowed* on me by Ahriman? Why me? You honestly have no idea?"

"As Socrates said, the wise man is he who at last understands he knows nothing. If that is true, I am very wise indeed. I only know that one evening my eyes watered and my limbs tingled, and I realized a new World Maker had been born somewhere in the past, in a quietly altered time stream, and one who possessed the rare aria magic. I used my powers and saw it was you."

It both thrilled and frightened Freddie a bit to consider her birth rippling up through the years to tingle the limbs of Paganini. How odd! She did not wish to imagine it. And what did "altered time stream" really mean?

Paganini sighed again, and continued. "The World Makers, and there have been a dozen of us, have a saying, *Ahriman's will is water and wind*. As I told you, he fell from the stars and now exists in a form none of us understand."

"Fallen? Like Lucifer?"

Paganini's face grew dark and pensive. He hesitated for a few moments, then said, "In our dreams, we often see him as an insect-like thing. Whatever his true form, none of us understand his ultimate aim, or why he exists on this obscure planet on the rim of nowhere, or who he prefers in the war between Edison and I for Earth's future. Maybe it matters not to him. Maybe it is all a big test ... The ancient Persians knew him as an evil god, but we know him also as a creator god—like my Skanda, capable of form and chaos ... And he is much like you, future Czarina of all the Russias."

"But I am *not evil*, and I will never be so, not like that horrid thing your spellcraft men dragged from here."

Paganini stared at Freddie, his face appearing saddened. "Eréndira will come after you to settle things, and one of you will perish in the death struggle. War has its victims. I say this for both of you and your older self to hear. We are often forced to do things that may seem immoral at the time."

"If I meet the monster again, I will kill her, and that will be *the moral thing* to do," Freddie said.

"That may be so," Paganini said, "but before you do that, you must undertake an incredibly dangerous and difficult task. It is one that might well shift the bigger conflict in our favor."

"Whatever must be done, I—"

"You must help me destroy Edison Godfellow's War Tracker that lives in the year 2038."

"And this will *save* the world?" Freddie asked, feeling a bit cynical with the taste of blood in her mouth and the dull roar of pain mounting in her muscles and nerves.

Paganini's face hardened, his gaze deadly serious. "Do not be cynical, Princess von Anhalt. This is not a creation of theater or melodrama. Your precious aria power can help us change the course of history for the sake of human civilization. But you must freely choose to help me in this endeavor, and the total choices available to you are two, not three. You can never go back to life as it once was in your Prussian castle. You either choose to aid Edison Godfellow, and his vision, or you choose to aid me and mine."

Freddie stared into Paganini's eyes for a few seconds, and said, "I choose ... to change history for the better, and if this means taking your side, I will do so."

"Well spoken," Paganini said, and smiled.

"I know I have the power to make it happen. I sense it."

Paganini saddened at the comment, as if he felt sorry for her. "Power will be a burden to you, as you will see in time, far more than a blessing."

This statement made her pause. She heard her older self say:

Do not ask what you are going to ask.

Freddie ignored herself and asked anyway, "And evil? Will I—"

"A few more things ..." Paganini said, cutting her off. "You have met Zolo. He is a friend, and will help guide you because he is a righteous soul."

"But I thought he was only a castle servant?"

"He is in my employ, and one day he will be a spellcraft captain of renown." Paganini went on to rumble her mind even further. "Regardless, the end of War Tracker and the defeat of Temujin Gur, as I noted before, are tied together, as you will soon see. But first, we must learn Gur's strategy if he indeed plans to cross the Nicholas, for in theory, your presence now allows that possibility," Paganini said. "Only your power combined with his could possibly penetrate beyond the Nicholas without risking annihilation ... And if we realize this fact, he most certainly does. We must accept that the temptation to betray Master Godfellow and establish his own world order might well prove irresistible, but your powers must first leave their cocoon stage with his help ... It will be painful, very painful."

"What? Painful ... How?"

"I regret having to tell you that truth, though it had to be done."

He actually does regret it, and Paganini is a man without love, Catherine said. *But now the time winds blow, and I must leave you. Mother Yarrow Maria is our bridge, though not without her faults. You will know her soon enough. I love her, and you will also because you are me.*

"*Goodbye,*" Freddie said.

How odd that was, yet how natural it felt, to hear herself and to know for certain she was not going insane. As for Paganini, a man without love? In her universe, she knew of no such man. The nobles of Europe, both men and women, took "love" whenever they wished, and spurned it with equal passion.

"Are you listening?" Paganini asked. "This is very important."

Freddie apologized for daydreaming, and he continued. "If our new fusion of the magical Tao with the non-magical Tao proves successful, a breakthrough is imminent. Edison is not the only inventive genius in this world," Paganini said with a glimmer of pride in his eyes. "We have been working on a particular project for years, assisted by minds like Einstein and Hawking."

Upon dropping even more names Freddie did not recognize, he attempted to explain it:

"Nano-magic Neural Infiltrators."

"Master Paganini, such words do not—"

"Imagine atoms that when combined appear to make a solid thing. The NMNI are not nearly as small, but small and magical enough to enter the mind undetected, and once there, listen and record thoughts. All you must do is tightly hug Temujin Gur's body for at least two seconds, and that will enable the transfer of the NMNI."

What? Oh my God! She could not imagine anything more revolting than holding Gur close.

"Zolo will provide you with the details upon your return," Paganini said and began to examine some papers on his desk with his beautiful anemone hands, as though hunting for a last second detail he needed to tell Freddie. His foot slid back and forth as he sat there. "One last thing ..."

"Forgive me, Master Paganini, but I have one last thing I must ask *you*."

Paganini stopped and glanced up at Freddie's worried face. His foot continued to slide beneath the table, back and forth. He did not appear puzzled, rather resigned to whatever Freddie would ask.

"Master Paganini, the Eréndira monster said I would allow the death of my father. That cannot be so."

"We do what we must," Paganini said, his face unmoved. "You have a destiny."

"I will not allow the death of my father. I *will not*," she said with iron in her voice.

Paganini retreated to his customary look of apathy and exhaustion. He removed a golden watch from his pocket, dangled it by the chain before his eyes and said, "Now you must return to your castle in Anhalt."

"Did you hear me? Will you not answer?"

"Your older self, Catherine, has a flight to catch out of Paris in

2033, bound for Washington."

"I will make my own fate then, Master Paganini."

"Catherine has a flight to catch out of Paris in 2033, bound for Washington."

"A *flight?* ... Washington?"

царица

7

The Agony of Destiny - Nobles Might Torture John Locke - A Dream of Bee

SHE MUST ALLOW HER FATHER'S DEATH, AND ACCEPT IT," the voice said to Zolo, sounding distant and dulled by a low drone of static. "It is destiny, and without this, the Princess von Anhalt will never be Czarina."

If Zolo were ignorant, he would not believe this voice belonged to Master Paganini. He sat in his small, candle-lit room deep in Bärenthoren Castle, facing a grand old clock on the table. He'd been talking to the future for a few minutes, hearing of what happened in Saravastra, and now it pained him to consider how devastated Freddie would be by the death of her beloved father, Prince Christian. He only hoped he, Zolo Bold, could bring comfort to her, in some manner.

To the clock, he spoke these words:

"She cannot be willing to accept it yet, sir. We need time. Please let me to signal the possibility of this acceptance with you before we allow the death of the Prince, or it will crush her. *Please, sir*. I am closer to her, and truly, there is no rush."

"This is against my better judgment, young man. Time will heal."

"There is no rush, Master Paganini. I plead."

"As you will, Zolo. You must therefore delay the plans of Johanna. Work with Mother Yarrow carefully. She is sensitive to the presence of Temujin Gur, but you must be wise also."

"He already knows I am your agent."

"Yes, but he does not suspect you have a Mother Yarrow in you.

We do not wish to make him suspicious enough to dissect you in order to find her."

"Gur told me he will be the instrument of my death, and that, as an older man, I am already dead."

A pause, then Paganini said, "When did he tell you this?"

"At the banquet for Empress Elizabeth ... He said I would never go to America."

"Young man, you know he sows seeds of mistrust and fear whenever he can. It gives him *pleasure* ... Gur was referring to an attempt he makes to kill you when you are an older man, but fails to do so. My magic simply makes it appear to him that he succeeded."

"Why did you not speak of this, sir?"

"I did not wish to distract or alarm you."

"He would be the true instrument of my death, if he could. That would also give him pleasure. He is a sadist, Master Paganini, *pure evil*, more evil I believe than Master Godfellow."

"He believes in a cause, and that makes him dangerous, but Gur would burn the Earth to a cinder just to serve his personal ambition. We must uncover his scheme, and right now we can only guess. You will obtain the nano-magic data, once the Princess von Anhalt exposes him, and use Mother Yarrow to translate."

"I understand."

"You must also understand there is a chance that you will have to kill Prince Christian."

For a long moment, Zolo could not speak, and then he said, "Master Paganini! No, it cannot be me! I *cannot murder* this man."

"By foiling the plans of Princess Johanna, you might delay the death for too long, or in such a manner as to cause Johanna to forsake having him murdered, or worse yet, approach Empress Elizabeth asking for Gur's assistance. If that becomes the case ..."

"If Freddie ever—"

"Whatever happens, she must not be able to prove her mother is behind it, even if she suspects, which she will. In any case, you *must* work with Mother Yarrow to disguise the true cause of the murder. We do not want the princess burning a hole through the castle to kill Johanna, and we certainly do not want her to suspect you, if it comes to that."

"Why is her mother's evil life so important?"

"She will work with Empress Elizabeth to transition the Princess von Anhalt to Russia, as well as help arrange the marriage to Peter. It must play out this way, in all its parts."

"So the good must die, and the evil live."

"I wish it could be otherwise, young man, and I understand your sadness. But Princess Johanna must play her role and Prince Christian must die."

No different than when told of his own death by Temujin Gur, the fact that he might actually have to murder Prince Christian shook Zolo to his very core. Bad enough to be forced to allow the death of someone Freddie loved, but now, to think he might drive the dagger in himself? Besides, he liked Prince Christian, the one noble in castle Bärenthoren, or Anhalt for that matter, who did not treat the servants with cruelty or contempt—unlike his evil wife who beat them every week.

"Can we not use Mother Yarrow Margaret to change his mind?"

"Princess von Anhalt's path to becoming Czarina does not include the presence of her father in Moscow. It is history. I am only the messenger."

"You sometimes ask too much of me, Master Paganini."

"Destiny asks too much of us all, Zolo Bold."

* Оверман *

MOTHER YARROW TOLD ZOLO THAT FREDDIE'S SOUL was hers once more. The princess had returned from Saravastra in 1898, and less than one tenth of a moment had passed in castle Bärenthoren since her departure. Whenever Zolo heard his Mother Yarrow's voice, it sounded soft yet firm, like the voice of wise mother. It always soothed him and made him feel secure. She connected to his time and place via her yarrow bridge—a "frequency on the Chrono

Wave Continuum" as Master Paganini would say—created by the World Makers long ago. Since bonding with his Mother Yarrow, Margaret of Anjou, years before in Saravastra, she had never failed him, and her power shielded both he and Freddie from the poisonous influence of Temujin Gur—as long as reasonable precautions remained in force, such as no blatant displays of power.

Gur must be kept ignorant of all soul trips to Saravastra.

He must believe that HE is in control.

Before going in search of Freddie, Zolo Bold left a snoring double of himself in his small servant chamber in Bärenthoren (a room half the size of the average closet and containing only a narrow bed and a bronze chamber pot), for he believed it prudent not to give the appearance of being absent, and entered the inner walls of the castle via a hidden door. Over the past many months before the coming of Empress Elizabeth, he wisely used Mother Yarrow in the creation of secret rooms and doors, and in the boring out of more inner passageways, so that now, all vital points could be reached easily. Without these new passageways in the castle, magic would be required to pass through the walls, and such magic was an alarm bell to a warlock like Gur.

Zolo made his way to Freddie's bedchamber. He halted outside the entrance and waited while Mother Yarrow Maria quietly looked inside, using no more energy than a fall of light snow. In a moment, the image of the sleeping Princess von Anhalt filled his eyes. She had changed out of her banquet clothes and fallen back on the bed. Her mind must have been so exhausted with the trip, as well as the terrible fight with Marquez, and she needed to process the explosion of information and new sensations thrown at her.

Who could possibly deal with it all?

His own trip to Saravastra as a small child, upon losing his mother, was shocking and strange enough. The mother Bodhisattvas descended on white wings from the godlike city of Saravastra and escorted him through the air to a place they called "The Tower of Mothers." Once there, he received warm food, a hot bath, and loving embraces. They were his mother's aunts, they said, and would care for him always. So far though, Freddie's bath in the waters of the future was not only very different, but also hot with violence. To imagine the evil Eréndira Marquez seeking Freddie's death drove a spike of fury into him. He only hoped good fortune would one day allow him to kill Eréndira, or at least, help the future Czarina accomplish the task.

Zolo pushed open the hidden door to Freddie's bedchamber and walked in, softly and without a sound. The room, dark and huge, scattered with furniture and life-sized wooden statues of famous heroes. Six of them were created by a talented craftsman in Anhalt known to the castle. Among them, one of Zolo's favorites: Alexander the Great. There he stood, the world's greatest general and leader, crouching for battle, his round shield before him, his spear thrusting at an invisible enemy. Perhaps the mighty Darius himself?

But no time for musing on Alexander's wars.

At the foot of the four post bed, Zolo stopped and stared at Freddie. The Czarina-to-be wore a simple robe of black cotton, tied at the waist. Her bosom rose and fell, her glossy dark chestnut hair spread across her chest and over the pillow. To a love-hungry young man like Zolo at age 16, she appeared divine, a cross between Greek goddesses Hera and Diana, symbols of true power and pure love. He recalled Paganini saying to him, "*The Czarina will one day sing rivers on the moon*," and he imagined the two of them there, on the shore of a dark moon river, staring up at the blue ball of Earth while breathing the air of stars.

Zolo closed his eyes, and as he made love to his passionate Czarina beneath the shine of Earth, he heard a soft sound, like the opening of lips. He lifted his eyelids, and in the light of the small candle burning beside Freddie's bed, he saw her staring back at him. He gasped in surprise, and said in a whisper, "*Princess ... my apologies for waking you, it's just that we must talk. I was sent—*"

"I know who sent you *here*, Mister Bold," she said with a calm, firm voice.

In silence he watched as she rose from the bed and stood to face him. Her expression showed calm and courage, though he knew she must be fearful for her father. He said to her, "We must leave this room and descend deeper in the castle if we are to be perfectly safe. Mother Yarrow has created a sphere of solitude that will protect us from any spies or senses of Temujin Gur."

"Lead the way, sir," she said and smiled at him. The smile took him by surprise and stopped all motion. "Please, let us not tarry," she said, reaching out with the palm of her hand to gently touch his arm and nudge him onward.

Recovering from his daze, Zolo turned and walked towards the hidden exit, and Freddie whispered at his back, "*Where in Beelzebub's name are you going, Mister Bold?*" He turned and quietly told her of the secret passageways, one leading to her room. "I had no idea ..." she said. "My mother could have—"

"Your mother knows nothing of this," he said.

The invisible door in the wall swung outward at Zolo's touch and they entered the passageway, the door closing behind them.

"There is no light in here, and yet I can see," Freddie said.

"Your power is like a child awakening in your body. It becomes smarter and stronger every day, and now your eyes pierce the dark, like mine," Zolo said, and turned to lead.

The two of them walked for a full minute before entering an arched doorway on their left and descending a narrow stairwell into the lowest bowels of Bärenthoren Castle. They passed the level of the castle armory on the first floor and continued even deeper, into the purple darkness wherein the walls grew slimy and the air decayed and chill. As they descended, Zolo felt Freddie's hand touch his shoulder and slide down to the back of his arm, and it stayed here, clutching him. Zolo could not have asked for more. The thought of her looking to him for comfort or support was the most thrilling thing imaginable.

Soon enough, they both began to cough a little, and after a tedious descent, reached the lowest depth, stepping from the stairwell and moving into a low-ceilinged stone chamber with a dusty concrete floor. Nothing else visible but a large gaping doorway to their right—the wood of the door half rotted, hanging loose on rusted hinges.

Simply curious, Zolo walked over and peered in the room. What he saw stunned him. He swallowed hard, and returning to stand before Freddie, said to her, "We can talk here. This is fine."

"Mister Bold, what did you see in *that room?*" Freddie asked, her eyes suspicious.

Zolo realized he had poorly concealed his emotion. The room spooked him. "Nothing, nothing," he said. "We must—"

"I will see what disturbed you," she stated with an air of command and walked around him to stare into the room. She paused for a moment, silent, before stepping inside. He followed her, and in a few moments they both stood on the fringe of the old Bärenthoren Castle dungeon.

Though the ceiling was low, the room itself was huge—the floor plan in the shape of a wheel, dozens of iron-barred cells lining the rim. But in the center, the many machines of body-shredding torture rose in the darkness like hideous goblins. To Zolo, the entire placed smelled like a giant black wound, one hidden and festering in the body of the castle. The odor of old blood touched his nostrils and the sound of shrieking filled his ears as both he and Freddie moved closer to stare in amazed horror.

Zolo saw crucifiers, large upright slabs of wood upon which victim's hands were nailed in imitation of Christ's crucifixion. Many of the victims must have been Protestants or Jews, or simply innocent serfs accused of heresy by their neighbors. And three large wheels of oaken wood and iron, at least 15 feet high, their spokes thick as his leg and fitted into a cast iron tower with a large turning lever; and below the wheels, fire pits in the stone floor, their mouths still black with the charred wood whose flame once cooked the bodies of the wheel's crying victims as they turned and roasted like pigs. He noted long, thick tables upon which torture implements such as thumbscrews, skin flayers and breast rippers were laid, water buckets for blood washing, as well as an assortment of "turning wrenches." Two rack tables also, necessary for pulling quivering limbs out of their sockets or ripping them off altogether.

But the crowning glory of the Bärenthoren Castle torture dungeon consisted of two Virgin Mary cocoons, each six feet high and facing one another from across the room, their eyes sad and needful, their hands folded in prayer as if asking God for each other's forgiveness. At first, they appeared to Zolo like life-sized painted statues of the Mother of God, though he understood their true and sinister nature.

"The Madonna in this place?" Freddie asked.

He explained the statues were hollow, filled inside with a spread of at least 40 iron nails, so that once the Virgin Mary door slammed on the intended victim, who had been stripped naked, the nails drove deep into their exposed flesh in dozens of places from head to foot, including their eyes—not deep enough to cause immediate death, just enough for a slow death, many hours of agonizing pain, shock and blood loss. The Virgin Mary would shake and rumble with pitiful sounds as their trembling victims died a minute at a time, their blood trickling out of holes in the Mother of God's toes into waiting pails while a presiding Papal priest mumbled prayers for the victim's salvation.

Freddie gasped and coughed, drawing close to him, clutching his arm once more, and he felt her full bosom pressing against him as she said, "My God, what *monsters* of the Church reveled in this hellish place?"

Zolo reached around to pull her body even closer, his arm encircling her protectively, his face in her dark hair and his senses reeling with the closeness of her. And he realized that even this place of darkness and unspeakable anguish could not mask or prevent his growing love for the Princess von Anhalt.

If it takes devices of torture to make this moment, so be it.

"You know that only the poorest and bravest were brought here to be broken," Freddie said with bitterness in her voice. "I once heard of an entire town, the Silesian town of Neisse I believe, that confessed heresy to a team of Papal torturers. It began with a few and spread like a plague as each new group was hauled in and broken on the wheel and rack until they gave the names of others, and so on until *the entire town of hundreds of people*, even women and the smallest children, were shattered and thrown into heaps, out in the night to finally die of the terrible cold. They died Catholics though, having renounced their heresy or witchcraft or whatever false accusation befell them, and this was all the bloodthirsty dogs of the Pope wanted. They could report success back to their master in Rome."

"And why do you think the Pope or his bishops wanted this?" Zolo asked.

"Power and money, Mister Bold. What else? Each conversion to Protestantism meant loss of treasury, and a threat to Church influence, and rather than risk these losses Rome gladly burned whole cities to the ground in the name of God."

As Master Paganini once said to Zolo, *power will do anything to protect itself.* "Europe's nobles and priests would certainly use the Virgin Mary on political philosophers if they could," Zolo mused, "especially on men like Diderot or Rousseau, or old John Locke of England."

"The nobility of Europe believe Locke to have been insane," Freddie said, sighing to herself. "I heard a story of Russian court officials surrounding a school teacher on the streets of Moscow and beating him to death with canes for teaching Locke."

"Imps of the Czar. No doubt they were rewarded."

"And do not forget Voltaire," Freddie said, her voice gaining in strength. "The Church would flay him alive before the world if they could. He is one of their greatest enemies in France and they use every chance to hound him and drive him away ... My God, can you imagine if the Pope possessed magical powers? He would send his soldiers back in time to destroy the printing press and kill Martin Luther in his crib."

Zolo cleared his throat and coughed. The horrible air of the dungeon gripped his lungs. "As Diderot said, man will never be free until the last king is strangled with the entrails of the last priest."

"My father says French and English philosophers are dangerous and should be imprisoned. God bless his heart, he believes in the absolute right of kings." Having said this, Freddie coughed more strongly, her body suffering more from the dungeon air. "Damn this place."

Zolo felt a twinge of pain at her mention of Prince Christian. "I also agree with Diderot that no one has a natural right to command his or her fellow human beings."

"But one day I will be a Czarina, Mister Bold, and who will I command, sheep or squirrels?"

Zolo laughed and said, "You will be the Czarina of Voltaire's dreams, a just and wise ruler who cares for her people and forbids the Church from interfering."

Freddie paused for a few moments then turned in Zolo's arms and looked up to him, her hands raising to clasp his cheeks. "Promise me that when we are able, the two of us will return to the past, to this place, kill these torturers and free the innocent, and put such a fear of demons in this castle that my despicable ancestors, or whoever they may be, will never again attempt to torture anyone ... *Promise me*, Zolo Bold."

"Time roving requires much power, preparation and precision of spells—"

"*Promise me*," she said, her face stern and determined. "My power of aria will make this possible, I know it, so you must *promise me*."

"Yes, yes, I promise you ... I swear it," he said, and he knew at that moment he would have promised her anything and given her whatever she desired, overcome as he was by her womanhood and power of will. "Only great passions elevate the soul to great things."

"Diderot again?"

"Yes. I am afraid I cannot get enough of him."

He watched her smile at him for a moment, then she became deadly serious once more, her two hands clasping his face more strongly than ever. "Look in my eyes and promise me too, that you will help me save my father from death," she said and coughed again, her breath coming more heavily as she strained to inhale enough air in the stale dungeon.

"Princess ... there are matters—"

"I know Master Paganini would not speak to me of this. I know he believes my father's death a thing that must be done, but I do not. I can live my destiny without the needless death of my father, most likely at the hands of my scheming mother. She has hated him for years and every night of cold bed feeds her hatred," she said, her manner becoming intense, her eyes draining the soul from his body with their powerful stare.

To Zolo, no more potent magic could exist. He found it hard to speak, but he forced himself, choosing his words very carefully. "Master Paganini sees your future as a Czarina. He knows what must be, and we all know from death comes life, and roads that—"

She cut him off. "I will make my own roads, Mister Bold. I possess the aria power. I am the only one commanding this incredible force. In the scheme of things, if my power is so great, I must have enough to fulfill destiny and save my father at the same time. Does that not make sense?"

"It does, yes, in a way—"

"But first you *must* tell me. Who wishes to kill him?"

"I do not know the answer," he said. A lie, of course, a practiced and perfect lie for the sake of history. "Only Master Paganini knows ... and his death could be an accident, or a sickness even. No one said his death was plotted."

He hated lying like this to her.

A curse on me for this. But what choice do I have?

"That is true. I just assumed my *mother*," she said, her eyes narrowing to a quiet fury.

"Your mother plays an important role in your ascendance to Czarina. If you end her life, as you are probably thinking ... yes?" Freddie did not answer. "This ascendance will be disrupted, and you *must be* Czarina. So much depends on it. So many depend on it," he said forcefully, hoping this would give her pause to consider, to see a bigger picture.

"But you *will help me* keep watch on my father and save him when the time comes. Promise me this also. I trust you."

"Princess, I ..."

Zolo realized he could not speak, only do what nature and the Princess von Anhalt demanded, and he said *"Yes."*

And now, perhaps, he lied to himself. He wasn't sure, though it mattered not. He kissed her, full on the lips, and she closed her eyes and returned the kiss, long and deep, and said, *"Yes,"* and they stood there, saying *"Yes"* and kissing and floating in their passions amidst a memory of tyranny and death, the two of them invisible to everyone in the world but themselves.

* Оverman *

SHE LISTENED INTENTLY AS ZOLO TOLD HER to be watchful of her physical nature, especially since it evolved by the day, and already she possessed the strength of 15 and a half men. Her reaction time, land speed, stamina and senses had also improved, and her flesh was now immune to pointed weapons and capable of rapid healing, even from concentrated musket fire. He told her not to attempt magic in the castle with Temujin Gur around, not unless Gur was present and coaxed it forth—otherwise too risky. The Lord of Saravastra would soon place her soul in the body of her older self once more and pit her against nothing less than Master Godfellow's Cadre of The Overman—all in preparation for the ultimate destruction of War Tracker.

"You are the only queen on the chess board of this war," she heard Zolo say to her, hearing him speak as though from a place faraway. She felt distracted, though she wasn't sure by what. It all continued to seem so unreal, no matter what had gone before. "You will be powerful beyond your comprehension, but you *must remain humble*, Princess von Anhalt, and I will help with that."

"No one can keep me humble if I choose not to be," she said, smiling up at him. Was she joking? Even she wasn't sure. The new power, fleshing itself out to her fingertips, awakened a sense of dominance, and a vision of crushing Princess Johanna passed before her; and what of other petty tyrants like that serf-killing Baron Eichmann?

Let them now beware.

Such a thought warmed her, until Zolo spoke of the confusing new "nano-magic," the NMNI invention thing of Paganini. Once within Gur, it would not only provide them with his thoughts (that Zolo himself will gather), but also filter her thoughts within him as well. The nano-magic will tell the Mongol wizard what he wants to hear. If Gur believes Freddie's mind is an open book, he will trust her. But once she does what he wants, he will certainly try to kill her, and despite her power and destiny, she can be killed and the time line changed. Gur remains one of the few beings on Earth who can make that happen.

"Who else can kill me?" she asked him.

"It does not matter, you—"

"Who else, tell me," she said, determined to hear the truth.

"Only a World Maker, or a very powerful Wizard God."

"Can that beastly thing Eréndira Marquez kill me?"

"Under the right circumstances, yes ... and she will try. You will have to slay her."

The thought of slaying her, for some reason, made Freddie feel even more amorous. How odd was that? Finally, she allowed Zolo to inform her, between kisses that left him gasping for air, of another factor that would also work to keep her humble—while at the same time enabling the injection of the nano-magic: her own Mother Yarrow, Maria of Pozzuoli.

Freddie gasped, her mouth remaining open for a long pause, until she asked, "How? When?"

"You have been inhabited by Mother Yarrow Maria since age eleven. You could never have known. She speaks with Master Paganini."

"This Mother Yarrow has been spying on me for years?"

"Keeping watch, helping to stoke the fires of your birthing aria. She contains the nano-magic within her, and it too has resided within you since age eleven, waiting for the moment to come when you will clasp Temujin Gur."

"Who is she?"

"Maria lives south of the Nicholas line, like all Mother Yarrows. She was a female warrior in the 14th century. I know little about her, but she believes in our cause and is sad to learn that a fellow Italian is our enemy in the future. Nonetheless, she wishes to fight him to the death. Master Paganini has told me all of this."

"She wants to *fight him?*"

"Yes, through you, to live the coming battles through your eyes and limbs. She will always be a part of you. Even if powerful magic separates her connection, her personality resides in the Mother Yarrow stick implanted within the spine of your body. Her soul possesses it."

"This is too much. I cannot ..." All of her amorous nature for Zolo fled her for the time being. A cold shower of new truth bathed her mind. Might she fully believe this new revelation if she repeated it to herself?

I am inhabited by a Mother Yarrow, a warrior named Maria of Pozzuoli.

Zolo smiled and said, "I feel at peace with my Mother Yarrow. If not for her, I would be blind."

Was this Maria stirring my fury as she helped to drive my sword into the wizard goddess Marquez? I felt as if possessed by a warrior soul, though I believed it to be me, the 'me' of those years to come ... Maria? Are you there?

No answer. Perhaps her worthiness to speak to Maria was yet to be proved, or her power not yet strong enough. Nevertheless, Freddie understood she must struggle to recover her senses yet once again.

Will there be any more mind numbing revelations?

She became aware of Zolo's strong hands gently massaging her shoulders. She let out a big sigh and held him close. She needed a warm body and a loving smile to comfort her. Her father could do that, but he knew nothing of the truth. He would believe her insane, perhaps even send her to recover her senses in a convent.

As if the whippings and biting of nuns could change anything.

How well she knew! The Princess of East Frisia was once sent by her husband to a convent in Luxemborg that had a reputation for being cruel. Upon arrival, the nuns wasted no time in stripping her naked, and like a coven of crazed witches, held her down and bit into her body. She suffered over a hundred bites and died of the untreated wounds, not to mention starvation. "As God willed it," the Mother Superior said.

"Who is your Mother Yarrow?" she asked Zolo.

"Her name is Margaret of Anjou."

"That name is familiar. I have read of her, somewhere ... Yes, yes, she was a leader of Lancastrian forces during the War of the Roses. Her armies defeated the Duke of York and the Earl of Warwick."

"Is there any history you don't know, my Princess?"

* Оверман *

SHE SAID GOODBYE TO ZOLO WITH HER LIPS, having been escorted by him to her bedchamber, and once done, he turned from her without a word and vanished into the wall. Soon, in the fire lit darkness, she stared at Paganini's music box. She wondered when he would summon her soul to future war. The thought of it frightened her a bit, and thrilled her too, and now that the Mother Yarrow news had settled she began to feel bolder, less afraid than ever. Her companion, Maria of Pozzuoli, had driven her yarrow sword home. And how had she summoned that yarrow sword?

Could she do it now?

The world belongs to the bold.

She outstretched her hand, cupped for the hilt.

Maria, Mother Yarrow Maria, please give me my yarrow sword.

In Galician then.

Nai Yarrow, crear a espada, a súa princesa suplica. (Mother Yarrow, create the sword, your princess implores).

Were these the right words? They seemed right, coming to her naturally.

Did Maria put these words in my mouth, or are they a result of my foolishness?

As if in response to her question, the yarrow sword appeared in her hand as before: gleaming steel of moon, a straight and powerful broadsword much too heavy for even ten men to wield, though easy enough for her. Its essence lit the walls of her bedroom with a ghostly glow and she believed she heard it whisper to her. Perhaps illusion? Was Mother Yarrow in the sword as well? She could not be sure. She opened her hand and the sword vanished to a thin line of vapor.

Freddie laid back on her bed to contemplate. Surprisingly, she felt not a bit of fatigue, her body fully recovered from the stale air of the dungeon. She was not invulnerable, she could see that. The ghosts of so many dead must have weakened her, caused her to cough, and even World Makers needed fresh air. And she considered another who was not invulnerable, recalled his jackal face once more:

Baron Eichmann.

The world belongs to the bold, yes, and justice cannot wait a moment longer.

Upon completing this thought, she changed into her riding clothes: close-fitting white pants tucked into tall, black-leather boots with silver buckles; a dark gray waistcoat with gold buttons and black velvet collar worn over a white cotton shirt with frilled cuffs, and a flowing red scarf added for color. In the way of heroes, and acting on impulse, she placed a black mask on her face, one from an old costume ball at the castle. Next, she grabbed a small bag of gold coins hidden in a secret bedpost niche. She left her bedchamber and entered the secret maze of passageways in the castle, and after two wrong turns, found her way down to ground level and out of the main building to the castle stables.

She chose two young black stallions and rode them bareback at full gallop beneath the stars to Baron Eichmann's estate, switching from one to the other to maintain the speed. For an hour of ride, she felt exhilarated and wild, lifting her face to the night and whooping her joy.

In the woods beside his fields, she slowed the panting horses and tied them to an oak. Once done, she ran as fast as her stallions and soon reached the base of his castle wall. She jumped to the uppermost parapet in one bound, over and down to the courtyard, still at a run, never slowing.

Musket-wielding guards stationed before the Baron's palatial residence only had a few stunned moments to react before she cut them down with her fists, their armor helmets crushed. The Baron's heavy oaken door then caved inward as Freddie struck it with her open hands, bursting it off the hinges and flattening it with a loud, echoing crash. After bounding up a staircase and down a hall, she erupted into his grand bedchamber like a masked avenging angel, shouting at him:

"TIME TO RISE, OH MONSTER!"

In full sight of the shrieking Baroness, Freddie yanked the fat, sleep-dazed Baron out of bed and hoisted him high into the air, dangling him like a child as he protested and yelled. She slapped him across the face twice and tossed him through the air like a sack of dead rats. He hit the far wall with a loud grunt, so hard it almost knocked him cold. She calmly walked over to him, and reaching down, yanked him gasping to his feet by the hair. With her free hand she withdrew the small sack of gold coins from her coat pocket and shook them to the floor. Still clutching his head by the hair, she forced it down to stare at the coins.

"There is your payment for all your serfs. You will release them tomorrow and allow them to make their way to Bärenthoren Castle, unharmed. Do you understand? And not a word of this to anyone!"

"Yes, yes, in God's name, no more!" he whimpered. Two of Eichmann's butlers ran in to grab Freddie but her right hand shot out and caught the first one in the chest, sending him flying back against the other. They smashed into the wall behind them, helpless with broken ribs and dazed heads. "Anything, masked *demoness*, anything!" he gurgled and yelled.

Freddie released him and he slid down to a heap. She pivoted on her heel and walked over to Baroness Eichmann who was catching her breath, eyes wide with fear. Freddie backhanded her with a slap so hard it knocked her senseless. Would she ever recover? It mattered not. Vile and hateful creatures such as Baroness Eichmann deserved not a shred of mercy. She and her horrid husband were fortunate to be left alive. Only raw power could ever hope to tame nobles like them into rightness of action, thus preventing them from victimizing even more helpless people.

That was a fact in Prussia, in Europe, and indeed, all over the world.

Much later, upon her return to Bärenthoren, Freddie entered the secret passageways and walked to her room, changed her clothes and got into bed. She was finally tired and fell asleep feeling good and righteous, though in her dreams later that night she saw a hideous black thing. At first, it appeared like a giant shadow in her room, staring at her statue of Alexander the Great.

Then it turned to stare at her.

The features were indistinct, though the bee-furry head of it could not be disguised, much less ever forgotten. Large as the skulls of ten men, it quivered like a bell struck by a hammer, though without sound, and the eyes, six of them big as banquet dishes, looked like enormous black opals twinkling in their depths with tiny glimmers of red light, as if reflecting a distant torch.

As she watched, an image of her face replaced the red light in those eyes.

A dim white speck of her terrified face.

царица

8

Babette Feeds Them Apples - Temujin Raises Welts - The Sun Angel of Anhalt

BABETTE BEGAN THE NEXT MORNING WITH HER CUSTOMARY tune she whistled night and noon. Nothing complex like a Paganini violin Caprice, just simple and lovely. Freddie never knew the source, or even cared for it, until now. Babette had just knocked and entered the bed chamber, dancing and whistling and swaying happily, carrying her silver tray of porcelain plates and cups that contained eggs, toast and tomato juice. Freddie sat up in bed, smiling at Babette, happy to see her. The freshness and care radiating from the woman stood in contrast to the horror and selfishness of the world, and it reminded Freddie that good people still existed, and that she should be grateful. Nevertheless, she must speak to Babette of dark matters, and her nanny would not care for it.

"Any more demons lurking about, my *lapooshka*?" Babette asked with love on her face, smiling at Freddie as she laid her breakfast on her lap. "Today is beautiful, so sunny, and you know the sun is a soap that washes away demon dirt!"

Freddie laughed and accepted the truth of this. As Babette opened the curtains to let the sun fall in one big column over the room, and turned again, smiling just as warmly, the lingering demonic image of the bee thing in Freddie's dream became almost bearable.

"Babette, please, come sit by my side," Freddie said, holding her hand out.

"Yes, princess. Your eyes are troubled."

Babette sat down and stared into Freddie's eyes, her hand

reaching out to hold Freddie's hand. Being a perceptive woman, she saw that Freddie wished to ask her something, and said, "I know you are bothered, my *lapooshka*, so tell me. You have never hidden anything from your Babette."

"It's hard ..."

"Is it about the banquet for Empress Elizabeth? I wasn't there, but Gods in heaven, I'm glad I missed it! The servants won't stop talking about it in hushed whispers, as if they expect a sword from the sky to swing down and cut off their heads ... and that horrible Mongolian magician, the blood on the floors, the smells. They thought they would be killed, and you, I heard you—"

"Babette, this is not about the banquet. It is about my father," Freddie said, her face now darkening. "Do you know of anyone who might wish him harm, other than my mother?"

"Princess Johanna? Wish him harm? ... Does she? I don't—"

"Never mind my mother. This is very important, Babette."

"I know of no one, princess, no one, I swear," Babette said and signed herself with the cross, her face alarmed. "Why do you think he might come to harm? He is a good man, loved by all I know. He makes the nobles angry with his contraptions, I think, but I can't imagine any would wish him harm because of that. What in Beelzebub's name is the matter?"

"I cannot tell you, I am sorry. I just believe ... I mean, I am worried for him."

'And now, I'm worried also. I will keep watch, ask around—"

"No, please say nothing."

"As you wish, my *lapooshka*, as you wish." Babette stroked Freddie's hand, her eyes looking teary. She hated it when Freddie became upset, and was pleased she could now deliver a bit of distracting news. "By the way, princess, I heard a strange tale. A courier riding from town said he saw dozens of serfs on the road to Bärenthoren Anhalt. They are at least two hours away. I asked Gleb to keep it quiet, and that I would tell you. None of your family knows. Gleb thinks they could be woggers."

"Ummm, the serfs? I will look into it. They must have heard we are a sanctuary. I am sure they are not woggers."

"Prince Christian will be very displeased if he learns of them. What will you do?"

"There are empty huts, on the fringe of the castle estate, to the west. Send Eiffel and Freud, under my orders, to ride out to meet them and escort them with respect to those quarters for now. I will see to the rest later."

"Might a few of them be woggers?"

"No, Babette, *none of them* are woggers, only refugees from Eichmann."

"I will make certain they are fed apples and cheese, and bread tonight," Babette said.

Freddie felt overcome by Babette's thoughtfulness. *So shines a good woman in a weary world.* "You know, Babette, if the end of days arrived tomorrow, the Lord would take you to Heaven first."

Babette smiled and kissed Freddie on the forehead, and left the bedchamber. Upon her leaving, Freddie picked at her breakfast, brooding on her father once more. She could not help it. Awake a full two hours before Babette entered the room, she had bounced between two walls: one belonging to her father's possible death, the other to the black dream of that monstrous thing. *What in Hell was it?* A sum of her fears? Eréndira's father? Master Paganini's master, Ahriman, from the dark between the stars? She could not say. But even with Zolo's doubts and possibilities, she believed her mother would be responsible for her father's end.

I know the witch is planning it.

She considered becoming the cause of her mother's death first, to save her father. How could she not, despite her Czarina destiny? Her mind strayed to *Hamlet*, the play by William Shakespeare. She'd read several Shakespeare's plays by age eleven, and Hamlet's words came to her clear as a musket shot at dawn:

Whether 'tis nobler in the mind to suffer the slings and arrows of outrageous fortune, or to take arms against a sea of troubles, and by opposing, end them.

To take arms, yes, and end the troubles!

Just as she'd taken arms against that Baron Eichmann, as she will take arms against the monster Godfellow and his Overman cadre. Why then was it wrong to end the life of a thing so despicable and plotting as Princess Johanna, the tyrant of the castle? Because she plays a role in her ascendance to Czarina of all the Russias—as Zolo said, and so many depended on her coming rule, and that must mean, so many innocents. Being a Czarina she could issue orders to her armies and save many tens of thousands of serfs from brutality and death, as well as do her part to fulfill the dreams of Voltaire and Diderot, squash the influence of the Church, and rid Europe of as many tyrants as possible.

My God! To think that a world of future good depends on the life of such petty evil.

Well she knew that the nagging nature of the argument within herself would not be settled any time soon. She would still balance the thought of ending Johanna's life with Zolo's warning, and her coming destiny as a Czarina.

Pushing aside her tray of cold breakfast, she stood up from the bed, still wearing her robe of last night. She entered her "potty closet," as she called it, on the far side of her bedchamber, and washed her face with water standing in a small pail beside her gold-trimmed porcelain basin. As she wiped her face with an Anhalt cotton cloth, bearing the family coat of arms, she felt an odd tingle in her eyes. She removed the cloth from her face and saw a dark shadow move across the wall like a giant black bat.

What now?

She then felt as if she were rising into the air, and turning downward, around and up again. Still, her feet remained solid. She saw them on the floor of her bedchamber, unmoving, just a glimpse before all went blurry with motion.

She began to spin.

The floor and walls of her room vanished. She screamed in terror. All balance and sense of place lost to her, and she kept screaming, the sound of her voice filling her head like a deafening gush of roaring hot water. End over end, end over end she tumbled, until finally she slowed and stopped, her head dizzy, her lungs breathing heavily.

My God, no more! Mother Yarrow Maria!

Freddie sensed she floated in space. The air about her, dark and flickering with firelight. Where was she? In what other world? Moments after that question, the darkness evaporated and the light changed, as though a thousand candles of sickly yellow were all lit at once. Her body felt squeezed in a vise, her hands tight at her sides, her heart knocking against the invisible walls that closed in on her. She was a prisoner in a box, her powers withered to dead leaves. Even Mother Yarrow seemed deaf to her. And her hearth of aria, where was it now?

Frustration mounted in Freddie until she screamed again. This scream, not one of fear, rather one of primal rage, exploding from her mouth with a *GRROWWRRRRRR*-like sound. She heard it echo, thrumming back and forth as if between the walls of an enormous room—the sound of it like a dragon's bellow, more cruel and frightening that any creature born of Earth.

The echo died.

She heard the shrieks begin.

Two or three, then more, many more. The shrieks of women. A hundred of them at least, their terror pouring out and trembling the very air—the kind of shrieks that only a nightmarish threat of death may produce, but suddenly cut short by a blast of a giant trumpet:

TAN-TAHHH-RAHHHHHHHH. TAN-TAHHH-RAHHHHHHHH.

The trumpet blast followed by a voice:

"BE SILENT AS A DEAD MOUSE, ALL OF YOU!"

The origin of it unmistakable: Empress Elizabeth.

For a second time, Freddie attended the same banquet, but as a prisoner within a magical box of some kind, floating above the tables. A long box perhaps? ... Yes. The only answer.

I am here, within the giant yarrow of Temujin Gur.

In response to her thought, words intruded, just as they had at the banquet, words spoken with a voice of deep lava yet to burn hapless cities to ash. The voice of a Mongolian black warlock:

You are honored to be the entertainment, Princess von Anhalt.

Freddie then felt herself drop. She fell downward until her entire body smacked full and hard against a cold, stone-like surface. The wind was knocked out of her, her breasts mashed and aching, the right side of her face flaring with pain. She groaned and opened her eyes, trying to focus, and soon realized she was laying on the stone-tile floor of her bedchamber, her right eye level with the floor that stretched before her like a dark, flat plain.

As she lay there recovering, her breath returning to normal and the shock fading from her limbs, she heard a trickling sound on the other side of the room, near her door.

Was it water? A leak from the room above her?

Freddie stood up, a bit wobbly, her head still loopy with being a yarrow stick. She examined her arms and felt her hands. All was well, any remaining pain quickly dissolving due to her magical strength, and the fact of this restored a bit of confidence to her, though only a small bit. How could she not feel shaken at the idea that Temujin Gur was capable of such a feat? Of wrenching her from time and space and making her a prisoner, good for nothing but scaring the souls out of foolish noblewomen?

Or was it all a trick?

No answer possible, not yet. The noise grew louder.

One mystery at a time then.

Freddie walked over towards the source of the watery fall, near the door, and glanced around, seeing nothing until her eyes fixed on the door itself. Three rivulets of steaming hot blood oozed from seams in the polished oak, beginning at the top of the door and continuing down to the base; and the blood, having allowed gravity to introduce it to the floor, pooled to a yarrow-like symbol: a dragon biting its tail to form a circle, and within the circle, a pagoda-like temple. Once complete, the blood symbol began to glow a bright umber, and like a bladder filling with air, the glow expanded to become one large ball of umber light drifting upwards, its center softly streaking as if with tiny meteor trails. It reminded Freddie in an eerie way of Eréndira's bizarre eyes, and that in turn reminded her of those brave beings of Master Paganini who suffered death by Extinction Event.

The fall of heroes into the Cenozic Ocean.

Before she could consider anything else, the light burst in a soundless explosion and sprayed the room with a burnt orange hue. It faded in a moment, but left something behind, standing between Freddie and the door: the kindly Chinese-looking face, beaming with care, soft brown eyes twinkling like a Christmas St. Nicholas.

The playful Buddha himself, and wearing the same red tunic and clothing.

Temujin Gur.

Freddie watched the big silver beetle on his right cheek crawl in circles like a tiny dog preparing to nap. Human-sized lips, four of them, fluttered about his ears, all whispering at once. Freddie could not make out the words. They sounded raspy, alien, vaguely like the Vermeer girl, or the speech of the Fracas machines. Gur waved a hand and they swallowed each other until one was left. It stopped to grin at Freddie before darting into Gur's left ear and vanishing.

"Thank you for entertaining the banquet, Princess von Anhalt," Gur said, his mood light and breezy, his voice a rumble of distant ash cloud. "A lesson in humility, and not the first one you will receive today. As your powers grow, so *must* your humility, and thus will your wisdom grow also until you are truly a fitting bride for that useless whelp Peter, as well as a saintly guardian of the dismal and doomed Russian empire." He said this and laughed. Freddie saw his symbol-etched teeth, as before.

Loathing and distrust of the Mongolian was now stronger in her than ever. She decided to never give him the responses he desired. She understood, however, that she must keep her knowledge of his true identity a secret. "My humility and wisdom are sufficient, Temujin Gur, and I will thank you not to make me your yarrow stick circus in the future," Freddie said, staring him straight in the eye. "I have no desire to entertain such cows and foolish bulls."

Gur smiled, genuinely amused, and an image of Freddie's face popped into his black and bottomless left eye. Still amused, he waved his hand before it and the face floated free, looking like a white marble of Freddie's head. It hung in the air with an expression of surprise. Gur blew and the head burst into white dust. He returned his gaze to the real Freddie and smiled more broadly than ever. "Rebellious princess, yes, and I expect *nothing less*. In my own way, I love you."

She pretended his ridiculous comment and showy magic affected her not at all. "Is it true Peter is an idiot? Does he really play with toy soldiers?"

"He is an imbecile and a pretentious brat."

"Why did Elizabeth first consider me to be wife to this future imbecile Emperor?"

"King Frederick of Prussia recommended you. He believes you to be an intelligent and cultured young woman. For a human of your age, he is correct. As a World Maker though, you are pathetically ignorant."

Once said, her fingers began to prick, for the first time in the presence of Gur. "Your fingers prick because I allow it, and they will continue to prick until I disallow it. You are my puppet princess, and I do as I like with you."

"To Hell with you! I am—"

Temujin Gur let out a screech like a great bird of prey, a mythical Roc, a shrill screech so loud and piercing it exploded every bit of glass in her room. His peaceful expression never changed. The force of it socked Freddie's insides like a blow from a boxer. She bent over and wretched, vomiting her small amount of breakfast onto the floor.

Next, Gur said, "Do you know this?" Freddie coughed, unable to speak, and looked up to see a pale object in Gur's hand. "I carved this trumpet from the tibia of a young Cossack girl, and I use it to call the thirteen thunder gods." He lifted it to his mouth and blew into it, and a deafening roar resounded in her ears, deeper and more lasting than the shriek, and her vision blurred. Once done, she leaned forward and vomited once more.

"Damn your black soul, stop it!" Freddie yelled and coughed.

"As you wish, princess," Gur said calmly, pulling a short leather riding whip from within his tunic. "In my day, a young woman like you rode with the best of the men, drew a bow and fought like a tiger. She was made of iron or she died. But I will forge your iron and you will thank me every day until your death in Saravastra at the hands of that accursed Paganini."

Freddie knew Gur watched her closely, but she gave no sign his remark affected her. She said to him, "I know that is a lie, and I will perish when I choose, and a Mongol dog like you will have no say in it."

Gur laughed. "Now, extend your arms, princess. Please, for this dog of a Mongol? My task is to further mature your powers, and I look forward to enjoying it."

Freddie hesitated a moment because she saw it coming. Rolling up her sleeves and holding out her arms, she looked up at the benign face of Gur and said:

"Do your best, son of a *horse.*"

Gur's whip whooshed down on her arms with incredible force and speed. The first blow knocked her to her knees and she cried out. The next blows fell in blurs, heavy and fast as fifty pound hailstones. Gur whipped her ferociously, more than a dozen times across her forearms and upper arms, and even more across her shoulders, shredding her robe and soaking it with her blood. She screamed in rage and spit at him. In response, Gur cracked her across the face with a blow so hard it gashed her lips and knocked her flat to the floor. Blinded with the intense pain, she ground her teeth and water poured from her eyes. Purple welts bloomed on her arms and shoulders, her blood dripping to the floor while her face throbbed as if beaten with an iron pipe.

"Defy me! Are you too weak? DEFY ME, PRINCESS VON AN-HALT!"

As she struggled to stand, he moved around her in circles, savagely slashing, driving her back down. She wept with the searing pain. Against all odds, she rose to a kneeling position to face the Mongol, and he swung one last blow, his hardest one that struck her full on her breasts with a force strong enough to kill a lion. Thrown backwards, she laid there on the floor, gazing up at the ceiling, gasping and moaning. Even the struggle with the Wizard Goddess had not produced such torment.

Never felt pain like this ... not like this.

Gur slid the whip back into his tunic. "Whatever does not kill you, makes you stronger. Now, you are verging on iron, on the bear within!"

After his words died in her ears, Freddie heard a muffled shout outside the door. A woman's voice. *Babette!* She must have heard all the noise. Suddenly, she screamed also, as if terrified, and all went silent. "Darling Babette ..." Freddie blubbered out.

Gur smacked his lips and smiled, then said, "Your castle nanny will return to wipe your royal hole soon enough. But now, you must heal yourself more quickly than your physical ability will permit, and I do not have an hour to wait. I struck you with enough force to kill a village of peasants. NOW STAND! TEMUJIN GUR COMMANDS!"

Her body lurched up from the floor, snapping to attention before Gur. Truly, she had become a puppet, and one shaking in pain, suffering like a heretic broken on the wheel by Papal torturers.

I must end this monster's life. I must. God, the pain!

"SING YOUR AGONY TO MEMORY, CZARINA OF ALL THE RUSSIAS!"

Immediately, the word hearth within Freddie began to heat to aria. But how? How could the Mongolian grip her soul in such a way as to force the magic into air? More importantly though, how could she sing with a mouth full of blood? No choice. She spit it out, big gobs of it, just as she had in her savage fight with Eréndira, in preparation for the aria. She began to sing with a trembling voice, bravely though and strong enough:

En nome de Ahrimannnn,
restaurar o meu corpo.
todos curar feridas,
toda a dor de memoriaaaa
esquecidos pola madrugadaaaaa.

(In the name of Ahriman, / restore my body. / All injury heal, / all pain to memory forgotten by dawn.)

Upon completion of the very last syllable of the aria, she felt a healing wave cascade from her head to her feet, as if someone had drenched her from above with a pail of soothing warm water. Her pain tremors eased and the welts faded to normal flesh. The blood dried and fell as red dust to the floor, and her body returned to normal within seconds. Even so, she stared at Gur with a molten hatred in her eyes. She knew she should disguise her emotions, not give the Mongolian the satisfaction of knowing he affected her so profoundly. But alas, she could not. The hatred that remained behind following that beating was real, and impossible to escape.

Something else too. A truth surged into her head.

Do I owe this to Gur? To the violence and pain of the beating?

Whatever the cause, she realized she suddenly possessed more will over the aria magic. As she understood the math of Eratosthenes, or other tongues like French, so now also the magic language of aria. It awaited, in her memory—not enough yet, not complete, though hundreds of the words presented themselves as Galician, all awaiting her needs and imagination, as well as the hearth of aria. She had used the language already, yes, sung well in Saravastra, against her blood enemy Eréndira, though that had been her older self, not the woman she was now.

Temujin Gur observed her, smiling warmly. "Of course, you want me dead, but do you feel different? I know you do, even if you lie. So please be less predictable."

Before Freddie could answer Gur, an inner voice interrupted her thoughts. A woman's voice. One never heard before.

Princesa von Anhalt!

Freddie did not speak or move, just coldly stared at Gur.

Son eu, María de Pozzuoli. Os oídos do seu poder están abertos (It is I, Maria of Pozzuoli. The ears of your power are open).

The voice sounded strong and kind. Freddie became a statue, staring at Gur, betraying nothing. Could anything surprise her at this point? She did not think so. With the maturing of her power,

Maria's voice had arrived. It felt natural, though so unnatural.

Gur continued. "Your next test is in a few moments, so take your power to heart, future Czarina," he said, his voice lower in tone than usual—a tone of earth shrugging with a prediction of eruption. Freddie imagined his grinning head bursting open, rockets of lava arcing forth and burning Bärenthoren to a char.

Maria of Pozzuoli spoke again. *Non teña medo. O asistente non me pode escoitar* (Do not fear. The wizard cannot hear me).

"I do not," Freddie answered with her thoughts. *"Will you help me end this cur's life?"*

Non é o seu tempo (It is not his time).

Gur continued. "I can rip out your heart or, if you prefer, set you on fire. Your choice," he said with a voice calm as a dead fly.

"What?"

"Heartless or burned to a crisp?"

Freddie sneered at him. "Perhaps Hell would suit *you* better. Does not the Great Khan await your coming?"

"Fire, then!" the Mongol yelled triumphantly.

Coraxe. A morte está preto! (Courage. Death is close!).

Gur thrust his arms before him and two black yarrow sticks darted from his red sleeves. They stopped in the air only a few feet away and began to spin, like the giant yarrow at the banquet, only these glowed red, crackling the air like lightning. "Forgive me, Princess, but I love this drama. I call the fiery serpent—"

He never finished his sentence. Freddie sprung upon him with incredible speed, just as she had with Eréndira, her arms gripping the startled black warlock in a bear hug. "If I burn, then you also, Mongolian!"

Gur shrieked at Freddie in Chinese, "怪物!" (Monster!), as loud as his bird of prey shriek, his face enraged for the first time, but Freddie held on though her hearing was lost and her head shrill with torment. She pushed out with her legs and smashed Gur with great force into the stone wall behind him, causing him to grunt in pain. The Mongol writhed like a hundred boa constrictors rolled into one and Freddie's arm muscles burned with the strain of bear-hugging him.

Mother Yarrow give me strength!

More tears flowed from her, blinding her while Gur's head grew to three times its normal size. With a mouth of inscribed teeth, now red with rage and smoking like embers, he opened wide and snapped down onto Freddie's head, biting down savagely with a loud crunch.

She never saw it coming.

The most terrible scream she has ever known burst from her. Gur shook her by the head, back and forth like a mad tiger shakes its prey, her body helplessly slapped about in the air. He then tossed her with a vicious swing. She flew across her bedchamber to knock over the Alexander statue, and as she tumbled to the ground, Alexander's spear pierced her right shoulder, lancing through the bone to air. She screamed again and thrashed in agony, impaled like a harpooned fish, but the monster-headed Gur did not stop to admire his work. He continued with the fire spell, shouting at her:

"BRAT OF AGES! CZARINA OF FOOLS! LET THIS BLACK FIRE NOW ROAST YOU HARD TO A MISERABLE RULE!"

From his spinning red yarrows exploded two tornadoes of black flame, deadly supernatural flame without external light or soothing warmth, only black hot pain—the true flame of Hell itself. It struck her with a hurricane-force wind and blew her like paper across the room, still impaled by the statue. An indescribably horrible burning sensation spread from her head to her feet. Her skin smoked and blackened. Her heart cooked and her eyes boiled to dark blue water.

This is the end Mother Yarrow. I must go.

* Оверман *

MARGARET OF ANJOU SIPPED HER TEA AND VIEWED worlds beyond imagining, far beyond those of any ordinary queen. While a
house prisoner in the Duchess of Suffolk's castle in 1474, just outside London, the former queen of England delighted in helping Zolo
and Master Paganini as a Mother Yarrow. It not only allowed her
to atone for past crimes (many of which were terrible), but it also
provided a glorious freedom and power far beyond the limitations
of real flesh. She'd traversed the sands of other planets, fought new
battles with tremendous powers as her "will to magic" and connection with the Tao became realizable through the implanted yarrows
of Master Paganini. No struggles for personal gain as in the old days,
only struggles for something bigger, enough that she felt redeemed
in the eyes of God. Best of all, she lived many years as a Mother Yarrow without ageing more than a few minutes, or less, in Suffolk's
castle.

*If the English knew my secret they would kill me out of spite and
envy.*

In truth though, if she told them, all would believe her mad.

With Zolo's eyes, she watched him go about his business in that
Prussian castle three centuries in the future. *So dark and haunted,
those Prussian castles.* She was often tempted to turn his eyes as she
wished, though in truth, she could not. A good thing too. Friends
had always accused her of wanting too much control. Master Paganini, the creator of her Mother Yarrow identity and her physical
embodiment within Zolo, limited her to responding at certain crit-
ical times, to influencing events or Zolo's wishes only when serving a greater purpose. Such was the will and wisdom of the ancient
World Maker Paganini, and she respected him, even feared him. Of
course, Margaret might argue a point from time to time, but she
never pushed too far. She would never risk not being a Mother Yarrow, despite the darkness that lurked at the rim of her consciousness like a stalking demon.

Everything good comes with a price.

Despite her powers, she could not fathom its source. She never actually saw it. Only a vague bulk of shadow, moving, watching.

She knew when it lurked, for she felt it, like one senses a danger or a wicked thing drawing close in the night. The magic words, *A morte está preto*, came to her. She preferred death at the hands of her English enemies, the Yorkists, than to a death at the will of this lingering dark thing, for she knew instinctively that such a death would be worse than death. What unknown and hellish dimension it might use to torture her soul, she would not even try to imagine.

During times of such thoughts she turned to Zolo's life for distraction.

With her help, Zolo placed a watcher spell on Princess Johanna's wretched servant, Gleb, the one tasked with the death of Prince Christian. The watcher spell took the form of an invisible and soundless creature of magic, an *observador paciente* (patient observer), formed like a cell of a human body (one of the secrets of life known to Margaret of Anjou since becoming a Mother Yarrow), composed of magical parts working together. If one could see an *observador paciente* it would resemble a small transparent ball with moving and squiggly parts.

Zolo's *observador paciente* hovered in the air above Gleb every moment. It watched and would alarm Zolo, and Margaret, if Gleb took steps to end the life of Prince Christian. And that's exactly what it did, early that morning following his time with Freddie in the dungeon of Bärenthoren.

While at work on his aching hands and knees polishing the Great Hall in preparation for a dinner buffet on behalf of Empress Elizabeth, Zolo heard a soft bell-like chime in his head, as did Maria. With two inner eyes, they saw the murderous Gleb in a dark corner of the castle kitchen. The butler stooge dropped a white poison from a vial onto the melting butter of Prince Christian's toast and spread it with a silver knife.

Margaret heard Zolo say, *Nai Yarrow, facer este doce veleno como a vida* (Mother Yarrow, make this poison sweet as life). And in less time than it takes to say "Prussia," she did. The poison turned to the sugar of apples in Prince Christian's butter, so not only was he not poisoned, he enjoyed his toast more than usual. Zolo and Margaret watched over the shoulder of a bowing Gleb, via the *observador paciente,* as Prince Christian said to Gleb, "My God, mister Gleb, this is wonderful toast! How did you do it?"

Gleb rose up from bowing, and said to Prince Christian, "My Prince, I did nothing, simply buttered it, as usual. But I am overjoyed you like it."

They both saw the look on Gleb's face as he turned to leave the magnificent bedchamber of Prince Christian: a look of evil, a vengeful sneering evil. Margaret of Anjou wondered at that sneer. *Do the evil sneer because they are evil? Or does an act of evil, once done, force the sneer?* Though such a sneer had been witnessed many times by her (especially when observing that cretin farmer Princess Johanna), it still bothered her, in the way a stocking burr might irritate her to pluck it out.

Before considering the matter further, Zolo said to Margaret, *Deixalo atopar a dor* (Let him find pain), and before their eyes, Gleb tripped on his own feet in the hallway. He stumbled forward and smashed his head into an expensive china vase standing in a wall alcove.

Margaret and Zolo smiled to see Gleb's agony, and fear at breaking the vase. The cost of it would come out of his pay for years unless he could figure a way to hide it. Zolo's eyes then closed to Gleb. The *observador paciente* would continue the watch, and Margaret would take a nap in the Duchess of Suffolk's castle with the smile still on her face.

* Оверман *

DESPITE THE SMALL VICTORY OVER GLEB, Zolo felt a rush of shame, for he was willingly playing a game with people he cared for. If up to him, he would foil every attempt on Prince Christian's life for Freddie's sake. But would she ever allow or tolerate his death without a threat of derailing the future? Damn the Empress of Byzantium for her poisonous mouth! Regardless, it all seemed like a waste of time, and his role, one of the fool—a role he created for himself. He could only hope the Princess von Anhalt would finally accept her destiny without overmuch misery or rebellion, and of course, without ever learning of the lie forced on him by Master Paganini.

At least, for now, he respected Freddie's wish that he protect her father.

On to other matters.

Once the floor of the Great Hall was polished, the huge task ending about four in the afternoon, Zolo and three more servants were summoned by a furious Gleb to the castle kitchen where he demanded to know who had broken the expensive china vase outside Prince Christian's bed chamber a few hours earlier. One of them must have done it since, according to Gleb, "You woggers are the worst of the bunch around here!"

After Gleb finished yelling with such force that spit from his mouth showered them all, Zolo asked him how it was possible given they were all polishing "the ass kissing floor?" Before the evil bastard butler could answer, Margaret of Anjou, alerted by the sound of Gleb's blather via Zolo's ears, speared the toady of Princess Johanna with such a horrible ache between the eyes that he gripped his head and moaned like a child. Gleb could only dismiss the "woggers" by waving them away, unable to talk with his pain.

Zolo then heard his Mother Yarrow softly say to him:

O espía espera por ti, nunha árbore, ao lado da Princesa von Anhalt (The spy awaits you, in a tree beside the Princess von Anhalt).

'The spy awaits'—Saravastra code talk for the NMNI of Master Paganini. So Freddie must have been successful at transferring them to Gur, but at what cost? Zolo felt anxious to see her. Though where exactly, and why in a tree? Had the Mongolian perched like a bird when the NMNI oozed from his skin as a tiny bead of sweat? Or had he actually turned into a bird and crapped the NMNI on a nearby leaf? And why was Freddie there? Had he whisked her outside the castle for ...? Too many questions. He hungered to know the answers, and he must learn the truth immediately!

But I cannot use magic for it would be too strong and alert Gur. Damn it all! Nai Yarrow?

She did not answer.

Nai Yarrow Margaret?

Still no answer.

Margaret was strong on rules. Master Paganini chose her for this reason, among many others. Zolo knew Mother Yarrows underwent careful screenings. All must be disciplined, loyal, needful and grateful. Warrior women in their waning years served well, all of them living south of the Nicholas Line. They were the best. Ordinary women of the noble or peasant classes usually failed in the long run—too selfish or fearful, or overcome with superstition.

Zolo muttered a curse to himself, and just as he prepared to leave the kitchen, a big commotion began outside in the Great Hall. The sounds of many voices and cries of alarm! Before he could think, the kitchen door burst open and a crowd of servants poured through, three or four valets and butlers in the lead. They vigorously waved their arms and shouted, their faces red and strained, their white wigs knocked askew on their heads; and followed by more servants, a mix of lower rank butlers and "wogger boys" carrying the body of a woman in maidservant clothing, her face to the floor.

Clearing a big cutting table with sweeping arms, the men laid her atop it, face down. That is when Zolo noticed the woman's uniform ripped open in the back, torn way to bare her upper shoulders. On her flesh, several inches below her neck, Zolo saw symbols, Chinese symbols big as hands and etched blackly, as though burned into her with a brand:

母 狗 學 習

Zolo noticed the symbols move ... no wait, it was the woman, and she breathed! "Turn her over," Zolo said. "She's alive!" Though the butlers glared at Zolo for daring to bark a command, they clutched the woman's body and flipped her. That's when Zolo saw her face for the first time:

"Babette!" he shouted with a shocked voice.

One of the maidservants, a much younger woman born of serf parents, screamed: "She is cursed by that Mongolian wizard of Empress Elizabeth! We will be cursed in turn!"

"Shut up!" one of the oldest valets named Faust said to her.

But too late. The younger maids and scullery took up the howl of the first, and one of the older valets began looking hysterical, crossing himself repeatedly. In a few moments, the entire kitchen resounded with cursing and cries of doom. The chef, an old bull named Kaufman, began shouting for silence and whacking his meat hammer against an iron pan, but they would not stop. "Throw her from the castle!" one of the butlers yelled. "Yes, out with the cursed sow!" another maid exclaimed.

An enraged and disgusted Zolo picked a woozy Babette up from the table. He slung her big body over his left shoulder, and without hesitation, strutted out of the room, shouting behind him as he went, "I will take care of this matter and this curse!" and before anyone could react he was out of the kitchen and across the Great Hall in a few bounds, vanishing within moments like a ghost.

* Оверман *

BABETTE'S EYES WERE THOSE OF A LIFELESS ANIMAL. Zolo had carried her to a secret room of rest and solitude created months earlier with the help of Mother Yarrow. The room, like a suite in a Paris city hotel, contained running water, a sink, a bed, and more. He laid Babette down and lit a few candles on the end table, his hands still trembling with anger. He could not believe the disloyalty! The vicious dog attack on Babette by servants she had worked with for years. He hated them. Perfect swine, except for very few. If he'd not acted quickly, they might have thrown her off the castle wall like a side of rotten beef.

Zolo could not stop to ponder further though. With Mother Yarrow's help, he placed a rejuvenation spell on Babette. She would be unconscious until the next morning as she healed from Gur's branding—more than enough time for him to rendezvous with Freddie. His concern mounted by the moment. If such a horrible thing had been done to an innocent Babette by the wicked Gur, what ungodly assault had the Princess von Anhalt suffered? *Nai Yarrow Margaret?*

I am here, Zolo, and with you.

Zolo felt relieved she was present once more. He pulled a dark woolen cloak from a big cedar armoire in the room and fastened it with a clasp around his shoulders. He kissed a sleeping Babette on the forehead and exited the castle. Unseen to all, and with magical yarrow as his shield against human eyes, he ran across the fields of toiling serfs and up into the dark forested hills of Anhalt faster than a horse could gallop. Knowing where Freddie could be found, because Margaret of Anjou pointed the way in such gentle whispers as *Sobre o monte* (Over the hill), he pursued his course, gaining speed, leaping small lakes and even gliding from slope to meadow like a soaring hawk. On the way, Zolo asked Mother Yarrow to define the Chinese symbols on Babette's back, and she replied *A cadela aprende* (the bitch learns). The knowledge of this caused even further rage, but he put it to sleep, for only the fate of the Princess von Anhalt mattered to him now.

Many miles later, near sundown, he closed in on her location. A great streak of red and purple cloud filled the sky above him, the dying light soaking sadly into the last autumn leaves; and from the north, the first of a light snowfall blew in from a heavy black cloud drifting south. The snow fell in gleaming, dusk-light flecks, and as Zolo ran up one final hill, a long sloping one of straw-colored grasses, he spotted something very odd at the crest: a white pillar, perhaps a column of pure marble, and upon the top of the pillar, a small dark ball.

So what the devil is this? A monument of some kind?

He drew closer, panting and puffing out his frosty breath, and soon realized the white pillar to be a solid block of ice, one at least eight feet tall and three feet wide, and the dark ball atop it, the Princess von Anhalt's head.

"By the gods of Saravastra!" Zolo yelled. "What has—"

"You were thinking of Dante a while ago. I heard you," the head said quite calmly with Freddie's voice. Its eyes were glassy, darkly simmering with pale autumn light, staring straight ahead. The long, dark chestnut hair fell behind and down the back of the ice. But Freddie's skin had not turned blue and she seemed quite at ease. "Am I not like Lucifer in *The Inferno* by Dante, entrapped in a block of ice?"

"You are ... I—" Zolo stumbled with his words, unable to understand. "Why are you not chewing Judas then?" he asked, attempting to bolster his own courage with humor.

"I have been thinking of things, Mister Bold. You know, there is a birthing oven of stars, in the uncountable miles of night above me, known as the Orion Nebula, and it is so large that not even the best human minds in Europe can ever hope to understand it ... and in this Orion Nebula, a place exists called the *Well of Souls*, and the smoke of this well, the nebula vapor, is hot enough to burn Earth to a black ash in moments. It forms great towers and faces of all colors, the likes of which no one can possibly imagine. I have seen all of this today, sir," she said and closed her eyes as Zolo stared at her in disbelief, still regaining his breath.

In a moment she opened her eyes again and the big pillar of ice, now glowing pink in the sunset, dissolved at once into tiny flecks of snow. The flecks formed a whirlpool that rose above her naked body and vanished in an early evening breeze, carried away to fall on the pines and firs further down the southern slope of the hill. Her body, steaming with foggy vapor and gleaming like fiery white porcelain in the dying sun, drifted to the ground, landing softly before him.

Zolo was speechless. The fact that the Princess von Anhalt stood naked before him, her body exquisite, stronger and more shapely and stunning of limb than he could have guessed, did nothing to prod his words. After a long pause of inhaling her like a strange and wondrous scent, like a white starflower of Samarkand, he unwrapped his woolen cloak and covered her body with it, feeling a bit ashamed he'd not done so sooner. To his surprise, she responded by encircling his neck with her bare arms, pulling him close, and kissing him on the mouth with great passion.

Zolo returned her love and felt overwhelmed with the urge to fully take her, beneath the darkening sky, but she gently bit his lips and withdrew with a big smile to stare at his love-silly face, and said, "In that tree over there, on a leaf about half way up, are the thoughts of Gur. Your *NMNI data*, as Master Paganini says." She pointed to an old oak on her left, about twenty yards away. "The demon Gur brought my body here, nothing but a blackened mummy. He encased me in a pillar of ice then flew into that tree, sat on a branch and began *mocking me* and laughing like a jolly Buddha before falling as black dust to the grass."

"What has he done to you, and Babette—"

"Babette, yes, my darling Babette. I know she is cared for now, by you. She bravely tried to help me and Gur branded her. The beast's cruelty *knows no limit*. I understood that he was filled with hatred and contempt, but never realized he wishes the entire world as we know it to meet a violent end."

"Master Paganini believes this also," Zolo said, still recovering from Freddie's passion.

"And my father? I know you are watching over him."

"He is perfectly well."

Wait now," she said, and opened her hand before Zolo. Atop her palm was an oak leaf. "Here it is."

Zolo took the oak leaf from Freddie and pressed it between both his hands. The invisible NMNI speck of Gur's thoughts, smaller than the eye of an ant, entered his flesh and fed Mother Yarrow. She in turn forwarded it with her open chronocom link to Saravastra, there to be analyzed by Paganini's Bodhisattvas trained in "black magic operations." Unknown to Zolo, she smelled a whiff of Gur's thoughts in passing, as one might smell rotting garbage on a passing cart, and it frightened her. She knew evil existed, once a party to it herself, though this evil of Gur surpassed what she believed possible. Only the dark thing lurking on the fringe of her thoughts could compare, yet it was more mysterious. Gur's evil, in contrast, was a poison arrow to the eye.

No disguise. No retreat.

Zolo knew nothing of Margaret's fear, or her experience with the odor of Gur. He simply hoped the NMNI information would provide a way to end the sorcerer's hellish existence forever. Whether he worked for Master Godfellow, or himself alone, it did not matter. The evil thing needed to perish.

Freddie interrupted his thoughts of Gur with a toneless voice:

"And now, Mister Bold, your Mother Yarrow cannot hear me. I must tell a secret and you must vow there will be no betrayal to anyone in the universe, past or present."

Even if Zolo wished to, he could not deny her request. He nodded his head and his eyes gave consent.

"All three of us have decided to take action," she stated matter-of-factly.

"*All three?*"

Freddie did not answer, only stared at Zolo with that glazed eye he first saw upon arrival before the ice pillar. What was she thinking? *Is she once again entering the Well of Souls?* He did not know.

She gripped him by the arm and gently pulled him to the ground to sit close beside her, the two of them settling to face the final rays of sunset. Only half the sun remained on the dark horizon and Venus shimmered in the china-blue mist of sky. Zolo wished to kiss Freddie during these final moments of light, until she said to him with a voice calm and natural as a stream of water over stones:

"We are going to kill Edison Godfellow tonight."

"*What?*"

"My other self, Czarina Catherine, and the Mother Yarrow we share, Maria of Pozzuoli, came to the decision as I cooled and healed in that block of ice."

Zolo struggled to make sense of it. *Could this be a manipulation of Temujin Gur?* Naturally, he might benefit from Master Godfellow's death, especially if he plans to cross the Nicholas. She continued.

"Their voices came to me as I suffered, gave me courage, and we talked of war ..."

"You talked—"

"What Master Paganini wishes, the end of War Tracker, is important, yes, though War Tracker is useless to anyone but Godfellow. Without him, the militarists lose, and the vision of Saravastra and peace is realized for Earth."

"But Master Paganini has his plans, and we do not know—"

"The World Maker wants what *we all want*," Freddie said, her voice gaining an edge as she stared at him, her dark blue eyes glimmering with a twilight sun.

"Mother Yarrow Maria knows better than this," Zolo replied, "She has sworn her loyalty to Saravastra and our cause."

"She wants nothing more than to help our cause. She is risking *much* also."

"But you cannot kill Master Godfellow, even with your aria powers. He is protected in all his past lives down to the Nicholas by complex and immensely powerful spells. Even if you somehow killed him in the past, his spell sends an alarm that summons both he and a contingent of *Dio Soldati* from a time before the point of death. We know, it's been tried by another World Maker, a long time ago. Master Paganini believes that even if you blocked that spell, Master Godfellow has others that would awaken and undo all you have done."

"Another World Maker? Who was this *other* World Maker?"

"She is dead. And I was not supposed to tell you that."

"Because *she* was the one with aria powers? The one Master Paganini spoke of?"

"Yes, yes ... He did not wish to speak of it, not until—"

"Even my older self and Maria said nothing. What was her name?"

"No one wishes to speak of it unless forced."

"I am *forcing you*, Mister Bold," she said with a flat tone.

"Her name was Dao Changkratok, and she was born in Thailand over two hundred years ago, to a poor family of rice farmers."

"How did *she* die?" she asked him, now with a determined voice. "Since facing death at the hands of Temujin Gur and burning to a crisp of bacon, I am less afraid of death, and more afraid of Gur."

"Gur wants you afraid of him despite your growing powers. That is his game."

"Never mind him. How *did she die?*"

Zolo wished to hide the truth, though the reveal of it might stop or slow her recklessness. Perhaps, or no? ... *No. She will of course go forward regardless. It is a matter of honor now between she and her new companions.* Still, he did not wish to tell her, though little choice remained.

Perhaps he might soften it?

"She was on a mission to end Master Godfellow's life at the point of Nicholas in 1529. He ended hers instead."

"How? I must know. I must *be prepared*," Freddie said, her breath coming faster.

"I can tell you nothing that will prepare you for Godfellow except to say you cannot prepare for him. He is a supreme World Maker, a genius, a commander of deadly black-armor forces, and he covers all possibilities to the finest detail and—"

"I will not accept this as true," she said, her eyes flaring at him.

"Then you will DIE!" he shouted like a madman, jumping to his feet and looking down at her. "Listen to me! Dao appeared one second after the Nicholas Line was drawn, one second, and *Dio Soldati* swarmed her, seven of them, all powerful enough to smash a mountain to dust. Master Godfellow had anticipated such a move. Guardian spells filled his space, globes of them everywhere, invisible, watching everything, every hair on every arm, especially during those first moments following establishment of the line. They picked her out despite a disguise. One of them smelled a difference in the heat of her brain ... I do not completely understand it."

"We do not have to worry about brain smells, and—"

"You must listen! They beat her to death with their yarrow and black armor and war swords while Godfellow rained giant meteors on her like Odin. It took hours, and she destroyed many of them, but they did it, and burned her down to salt. Do you hear? *A few spoon-fuls of salt.* They seasoned fish with her, just for a laugh, and joined with Godfellow to create a spell that obliterated her for all time, from birth onward. We only knew of her because Saravastra's magic saved knowledge of her existence outside the new time stream."

Gazing up at him, in a calm but firm voice, Freddie said, "I do appreciate your concern, but my older self and Maria know of the *Dio Soldati*, and they have conceived a bold new plan."

"To what? Destroy them?"

"No, to avoid them entirely. We will pull Godfellow from the future and send him to another world, as it was over two billion years ago, and kill him there."

"What world?"

"Mars."

"*Mars?* Kill him on Mars?"

"What more fitting grave for Godfellow than the God of War planet?"

"Why not just materialize him in the core of the sun?"

"Because we *must* be sure. We must see him dead."

"Does your Mother Yarrow now have a screen around this place?"

"Yes, and I do also. I sang a shield atop her own. Nothing can see us or hear us. Mother Yarrow Maria has also created decoys a few miles away, and right now they are making love beneath the light of Venus." Zolo paused to consider and blushed. Freddie saw and reached up to hold his hand. She held it tight and stood up to face him. "And I desire that we do the same, if I come out of this alive. I want you too, Zolo Bold."

Zolo blushed again, and could hardly think. All he could say was this:

"I must come with you to Mars."

But the reply was not what he wished:

"You cannot come. I need someone to guard my father and my back," she said and cupped his face with her hands once more. "Only Zolo Bold do I trust."

* Оверман *

THE LEGEND OF THE ANHALT SUN ANGEL CAME INTO BEING before young Zolo Bold's eyes, that late spring day in 1531, as the hot
torture dungeon of Bärenthoren Castle echoed with the screams
of agonized serfs, men and women both—the final outcome of the
famous German Peasant Rebellion begun in 1524 that had spread
from Alsace and Salzberg to shake the castle walls of a frightened
Prussian nobility. Zolo learned of the Anhalt Sun Angel shortly after being sent by Saravastra to take employment at Bärenthoren
as a way to watch over the Princess von Anhalt. A fresco of the Sun
Angel painted on a far wall in the castle kitchen served as his intro-
duction to the legend: a white-robed woman three feet high who
looked very much like the Mother of God, floating in the air, rays of
sun forming a giant halo around her body. Below her, soldiers stood
in a bath of flame, lifting their arms on high to the Mother as if to
ask forgiveness, or relief from the fire, or both.

What the maid did not know was that the Sun Angel had inspired a new heretical religious movement of serfs and peasants
who called themselves Angel Light Protestants. The movement was
put to the sword, and its leaders oven-burned in 1549, because the
nobles feared it might eventually grow to unleash yet another peasant war.

Zolo asked chef Kaufman about it one morning, and he said with
a gruff voice, "It's the Sun Angel," but later, one of the older maids,
Gisela, told him the Sun Angel had appeared suddenly outside the
castle one day, centuries ago, and took revenge on the "evil nobles
of Anhalt" for their crimes of killing and torturing serfs they sus-
pected of wishing rebellion. The nobles of the land, Anhalt included, were in process of raising taxes yet again and they wished to
torture a number of serfs in advance, not only to make an example,
but to gain valuable information, just in case a rebellion was being
cooked up—even though no such thing was actually taking place.

Once Zolo later learned the truth, he could not tell Freddie that her display of magical power, that day in 1531, which freed the tortured souls of the Bärenthoren dungeon, had later resulted in the deaths of thousands in 1549. He would never burden her, and remarkably, due to Princess Johanna's terrorizing of the castle servants, so few spoke to Freddie of anything, much less the Sun Angel, though she'd seen the fresco in the kitchen when much younger.

Upon return to Bärenthoren, Freddie followed Zolo to see Babette. She uttered a spell that would speed Babette's recovery from Gur, turned to Zolo and said, "Now, some unfinished business, sir. Without further ado, we must defeat those torturers of Bärenthoren, as I made you promise."

Zolo tried to argue her out of it, though that proved impossible, of course. It was a loose end, one that need resolution before she joined with Maria of Pozzuoli and her other self to try and kill Master Godfellow. And so, a reluctant Zolo returned with Freddie to the stale air of the Bärenthoren dungeon, and without hesitation an aria that transported them, with the help of Mother Yarrow Maria, to the earliest time possible before the drawing of the Nicholas Line: May 3, 1531.

Freddie crashed in the heavy oaken door to the dungeon with one kick, splinters and fragments of the wood ripping out to fly across the room. Once done, they both entered to witness a vision of horror nothing could have prepared them for. Vomiting at the sight only moments after entry they glanced up to see the castle torture captain, Herr Borman, as well as his seven blood-spattered brutes, staring without even twitching a finger. The sudden explosion of door had paralyzed them. Freddie and Zolo's eyes next witnessed the naked and gory bodies of human beings whose flesh quivered in various stages of torture. Several men lay twisted by the rack, mouths open in frozen scream, others tied to tables, faces and chests bleeding and bruised by torture implements. Three women spun on the wheels, shrieking as they cooked, flame from the black pits licking up below while both Virgin Marys shook and hummed with muffled shrieks, the poor wretches locked within dying slowly.

But the sight that shook Freddie with deepest rage, as Zolo

could see, was that of a naked and crying young boy, not more than nine years old, hung upside down and beaten with a thin rod of iron. His assailant, a rotten banana of cretin wearing nothing but sackcloth like some kind of Catholic monk, still held the rod. Like the rest of the trolls, he simply stared with his gap-toothed mouth hanging open.

Before Zolo could act on his own anger, Freddie unleashed another potent aria, deep and wall-shaking, one born of utter contempt and lived hatred:

Sentir a picadaaaa

do seu propio mal

monstros de Anhalt,

e lembre-se

esta dor leve no Infernnno!

(Feel the sting / of your own evil / monsters of Anhalt / and remember / this soft pain in Hell!)

Whereupon, the torture implements snapped into the air and turned upon the captain and his seven brutes. The torturers shouted and hopped as the objects chased them around the room, burning and biting them. Zolo grabbed the shrieking boy-torturer as he scampered towards the door and with one hand hurled him twenty feet through the air to break his back against one of the Crucifiers.

Meanwhile, Freddie sung more spurts of more aria to suit her enraged imagination, lifting and waving her hands as though conducting a symphony before the royal Prussian court. First, she released the victims of the torture from their bonds. The women separated and flew away from the wheels, and the Virgin Mary doors sprung open, their occupants floating forth. The racks reversed, and so on. All of the serf bodies drifted to one side, quieted and healing, and then, the castle torture fiends got hit by the second wave. Growling imps of flame sprang from the pits and jumped onto the backs of the screaming monsters, and by the shrillness of their cries, one could assume they were not comfortable with such searing pain. Two at a time they caught fire, in rapid succession, and then flew through the air as if hurled by a giant's hand. They smacked face first into the waiting arms of the Virgin Marys, the doors slamming shut and impaling them inside. But just as quickly, the doors swung open again and they hurtled out, only to be replaced by two more until all eight of them had been severely burned and then pin-cushioned by the Virgins.

Soon enough, the torture trolls lay in a heap, moaning in agony while their previous victims began to stand on their feet, amazed at their pains and wounds fading. Freddie waved her right hand at the left wall, and sang, *Un túnel cara á luz* (A tunnel to the light). At once, a black mouth of tunnel gaped open, and beyond it, a long throat that led out of the dungeon into sunlight.

"All of you, go from this horrible place!" Freddie yelled to the dazed and naked serfs. "Go!" They stood up, a few at a time, and scampered from the dungeon.

Zolo Bold would never forget what came next.

Without a glance at him, Freddie followed the serfs out of the dungeon, and Zolo right behind, stopping for a moment to look at the heap of smoldering torturers. He spit at them and started for the tunnel. The climb took only a few seconds, though Freddie had already vanished, and in those few seconds he heard a commotion outside the castle. An intense bright light stung his eyes as soon as he emerged. Where was it coming from? He looked up to see Freddie directly above, floating at least forty feet high in the air and facing the castle. The light emanating from her body was blinding and already withering the grass with its heat.

By the gods of Saravastra! Is she trying to imitate the sun itself?

Zolo heard someone on the wall fire a musket and its report echoed over the field. Shouts rang out as dazed castle guards ran to take their stations. But it was no use, not for them. The glowing light quickly heated their armor and each man ran away screaming, cooking like raw meat in a pot.

And as these men recovered from their burns in the weeks following the incident, they would tell anyone who would listen that God had sent an angel of sunlight to punish the dark evils of Anhalt. Most of them would later join the Angel Light Protestants and die with honor, fighting for what they believed to be a just cause. If Freddie only knew, she would say *God bless those men.*

Zolo felt that to be true.

* Оверман *

STRENGTH RETURNED TO A WEEPING BABETTE. She lay in bed, her hands Christ-crossing her chest as she spoke of her brush with death. Outside the door, she had called out to her princess, fearing for her life, and quite suddenly, a horrible black mouth opened in her eyes and swallowed her into a burning dark place. She shuddered to think of it, and Freddie soothed her by stroking her face, saying "It's all over my precious Babette, all over, and it will never happen again. You are in my keeping now," whereupon Babette reached up to hold her close and they both cried together.

Zolo watched and sat on the bed, his hand on Babette's leg beneath the covers. She still thought of him as Willie, and always would, believing he was a relative; and of course, he would never tell her differently. A lie of necessity and convenience, arranged by Paganini, implanted in Babette's mind. "Willie" had played the part, and even come to enjoy it and feel real affection for Babette. In fact, he rather loved her, being a motherless young man in need of an older woman to care for him and scold him now and then. Nothing wrong with that.

So in truth, a lie has created a good thing for all.

Still, Zolo hesitated at being comfortable with lying, especially when it came to lying to Freddie. He would never be as easy with lying as Paganini seemed to be. Then again, Master Paganini had responsibilities Zolo could only begin to imagine. The strain on the man must be unbelievable. After all, he was attempting to orchestrate an entire new future for Earth, one without needless wars and fanatics. Not exactly a rose garden in spring! So what difference a few lies?

Will the end justify the means?

A question Zolo asked himself all the time, and quite often, the answer was not always clear. If only his clearness of purpose might be as iron hard as that of the Lord of Saravastra.

"Rest easy now, my Babette," Freddie said, still stroking her face, "I have some business to attend to, so sleep now and we will both be on our feet in the morning." And as Freddie stroked Babette's face, she said, *Durmir agora, meu amor* (Sleep now, my love).

Babette dozed off and Freddie stood up from the bed, as did Zolo. His concern for her returned like a pointed crossbow at his head. He faced, reached out to her arm, and pulled her close to him. She unexpectedly kissed him full on the mouth. Zolo could only respond, his head moaning into a daze with the power of it. She pulled back after a moment and said to him, "You do not fault me for killing those torture dungeon monsters, do you?"

"No. How can I? I felt the same sense of rage ... I think I would have been crueler to them, but you had it all under control, my Sun Angel of Anhalt."

Zolo told her of the Sun Angel fresco in the kitchen and the legend. She was amazed. She knew of the fresco, of course, though not making the connection since returning. As for the legend, no servant ever told her. They were all so terrified of showing familiarity with nobility. What other legends and secrets did they hold close?

All for another day.

"Now, take me with you, I beg you," Zolo said. "I will arrange a spell to watch and guard your father."

"But Gur is here, and Master Paganini avoided me when I told him I would save my father, so he also believes he must die. Too many powerful beings, Mister Bold. Too much to worry about. I must *have you here* ... And I must *have you safe*."

"You fear I might die if I join you?"

"This will be a horribly violent struggle with that monster God-fellow. You said yourself how powerful and protected he is."

Zolo felt a sting to his pride. Of course, she was right, though it hurt nonetheless. He wished to be her protector, not the other way around. "You will do battle on Mars without me," he said, fear filling his eyes, "But where are you planning to meet your Mother Yarrow and your older self? On the Martian surface?"

She hesitated, as if uncertain, and said, "No, not on Mars. We will be involved at a primary conflict point in Earth history, all part of my Saravastra training, but during the battle we will use War Tracker's connection to Godfellow in order to pull him to the conflict point from his headquarters in a place called Dubai, and from there, transport all four of us to Mars. It will take less than a moment. I do not completely understand, but the three of us working together can do it, and there will be no trail to follow. Like the cogs of a watch, sir, all *behind the veil.*"

Zolo could not contain his growing irritation. "It's all that simple, eh? You will pull Godfellow into a Nexus Zone while combat is raging with the *Dio Soldati,* and Ahriman knows what else, and then catapult him to Mars while all of you tag along for the ride?"

"I do not know what a Nexus Zone is, Mister Bold, but I *know* this plan will work."

Zolo became angry at her calm certainty. "The World Maker can turn a second into a day, a year into a moment. He can give the centuries one beautiful pair of wings and send them gliding above the ocean at sunrise before setting them on fire. Do you really know who you are dealing with?"

"I am tired of having that dog Godfellow praised to me."

"What? I am not—"

"The die is cast. I will hear no more of it."

"But you still have not told me—"

"I cannot say *which* primary conflict point."

"You do not trust me?"

"I am afraid you might become so fearful for my life that you might give away this conflict point to Master Paganini in hopes of an intervention ... I am sorry, sir."

"Your words cut deep, though what you say is not without merit."

"You must vow to say nothing of my words to Master Paganini, even what little I have told you."

"You have my word, Princess von Anhalt," Zolo said with a solemn tone.

He considered what he was doing. If Master Paganini ever knew of his betrayal, what would come of that? It seemed as though he was fated to betray everyone. Who comes next? Should he just resign himself to being chewed in the jaws of Satan along with Brutus and Judas?

He saw Freddie staring into his eyes. She noted his pain and worry, and softened. She kissed him one more time, told him that when he left this room his memory of her plan will not be seen by Margaret of Anjou, but if he speaks of the plan to anyone, Margaret will know. Zolo watched as she turned and sat down on a chair in the room, a short wooden one with a leather back and cushion, and she smiled and said with a strong voice of cheer:

"For Diderot and Saravastra!"

"For Diderot, Locke and Saravastra," Zolo replied half-heartedly.

Freddie laughed. "Locke too then!" One last brave smile and she vanished as she whispered to the air: "*Nai Yarrow ...*"

Following her departure, Zolo walked over and sat down beside a small table in the corner of the room, watching the chair where she sat only seconds before. He half expected her to return in a moment, flushed with victory, or perhaps minus her head. Anything was possible.

She did not return though, with head or without.

Zolo sat there for an hour and pondered the possible death of the woman he loved, or perhaps the death of Master Godfellow, Earth's first and greatest World Maker, or both of them, taking place two billion years ago on a dead planet so faraway that even the light from it was of less importance than a speck of dust falling on his skin.

царица

9

Battle of The Somme - White Mongol Gods - Stars, Souls, and Fire

THE "CREEPING BARRAGE" OF THE BRITISH ARTILLERY AT THE SOMME awoke Catherine early one morning on July 1, 1916. The Czarina had lived with the German infantry troops during the many days of nonstop shelling begun much earlier on June 24. She did not have to endure it. She chose to do so. She chose to know the unspeakable horrors and catastrophe that Niccolo Paganini spoke of, and thereby finally understand his fanatical aversion to the world wars of the 20th century, to fully identify with his need to change the history of that century for all time.

Were the conflicts as terrible and pointless as he depicted?

Catherine knew the answer, and it was *yes, a thousand times*, and a thousand times more, far more terrible and pointless than could ever be dreamed. Tens of millions dead, and even after just one hour of head-bursting explosion quivering the earth, she realized, as she squatted in a dark concrete bunker with a small group of terrified men, that all her magic and wisdom acquired to this point in her life had not prepared her—her struggles with dark forces, face to face, like the bites of fleas compared to the roaring black plague of World War I in Europe.

Though why this particular time and place?

In the War Room at Saravastra, while planning strategy at "primary conflict points" that could forever alter the 20th century, Paganini told Freddie that history recorded the eight days of shelling by the British on the German lines at the Somme, beginning on June 24, 1916, as creating one of the most "horrific hells" ever known.

As required of all Paganini's forces in the field, Catherine thoroughly studied the history involved, learned it in Saravastra, so she knew upon using a precise aria spell to land in that German army bunker beside the French village of Guillemont near the Somme River on June 24, all the details of the conflict in the way of a good general. She realized it would be different than wars of her century, or previous times, certainly louder and more violent, but "louder and more violent" could not begin to explain it.

Within only hours of arrival, she squirmed and wept, her head aching and nerves wracked beyond belief until, like the rest of the quivering humanity in that hot and filthy candle-lit box of shadows, and like the mud-soaked wretches in the nearby trenches (all tricked into believing war would be a rightful and glorious adventure), she began to physically shake and feel sanity draining from her. Out of all the atrocities she'd ever experienced, this was the worst.

For those seven days, Catherine endured the living hell, without the slightest bit of aria to cure her as the British fired on the German lines with well over a million shells, using everything from small field cannon to eight inch howitzers to their huge siege howitzers that sent crackling metal chunks of fire into the earth with a concussive burst that turned any human head within a hundred yards into ringing bell. Unlucky wretches closer to a blast were battered to jelly. Two of the men now in her bunker, musketeer Martin Heidrich and private Harry Bierkamp, were shell-shocked victims of these same cannons. Catherine had carried them into the bunker one night upon discovering the bodies in a trench, slugged unconscious after an especially heavy barrage.

Slinging them over her shoulders, she ran over the open ground of No Man's Land, muttering a spell to ease their shock. In the darkness all about her as she ran, flashes of shell bursts, scores and scores of them, and the sounds of the explosions, *WHUMP WHUMP BOOOOOOM*, too many to count, *WHUMP WHUMP BOOOOOOM*, echoing and shattering the air into one solid drone of maddening noise. Shells burst above her also and glimmered red in the thick smoke hanging above the ground. In the distance, her ears picked up the sounds of wounded men, screaming and shrieking like scorched animals. She sensed metal shrapnel from a nearby air burst spraying out with enough velocity to sever limbs, hurtling at them, and she spell-covered the men with an umbrella of magical force just before the shrapnel hit. It saved them, but a ground burst less than a hundred yards away blew several hot shards into the Czarina's calves, causing her to wince in pain. She pulled them out as she ran, and in doing so, recalled a diary entry she'd read in Saravastra, penned by a French Second Lieutenant Alfred Joubaire just before he died in WW I:

"Humanity is mad. It must be mad to do what it is doing. What a massacre. What scenes of horror and carnage! I cannot find words to translate my impressions."

She had fooled herself before arrival into believing she understood what Joubaire meant. *Yes, all madness, and for what? Paganini was right. If inhumanly possible, history must be changed.* But it was not until the doomed British assault of July 1 that she fully understood the diary entry. The "creeping barrage" announced the start of her lesson, and her younger self from Bärenthoren Castle in the 18th century arrived in the thick of it. It occurred then to Catherine, that whatever happened on this day of July 1, 1916, she would experience it twice.

As she recorded later, in her Saravastra journal:

I sat in the bunker, against a wall. The floor was full of splinters, since the wood had stretched and broken in places due to quakes caused by the shelling. My skin was not pierced by the splinters, but still, all very uncomfortable. It was early morning and a gray sunlight came through small slits in the bunker walls to make the insides look like a room in Hades. My companions, all German soldiers of the XIV corps, Fourth Army, held rosary beads and drank their black miserable coffee, two of them smoking pipes, one a cigarette. As if we did not have enough smoke! Like me, all were shaking, sleepless and nervous, beaten down after so many days of unending concussion. One of the men had begun to scream in the night. I sent him a dream of pleasing seaside and his sweetheart beside him. Besides wishing to heal him, I knew if he continued, all would begin screaming and sanity would fly from us. I could have used aria to heal or protect myself, but I wished to endure this Hades, this hell of sound and fury like the rest of my bunker mates. Would I not be a coward if I chose otherwise? And too, a suitable cure for my arrogance of late. I knew I wished to punish myself, for much blood was on my hands and thoughts of evil and good had lately become one.

The 'creeping barrage' of the British, as they call it, their prelude to a massive infantry charge all along the line, filled our bunker room; and like other barrages, filled it with a ghastly and skull cracking thunder. Like those thunders of other days and nights, it seemed to last forever. The hours of these barrages I count as the longest and most painful of my life.

As I felt sorry for my pathetic state of being, the Princess Von Anhalt appeared in the bunker, and quite suddenly, as arranged with Maria of Pozzuoli. She stood there in the center of the room looking dazed. The men present, all six of them, saw her as a German infantryman due to my spell, in the same way they saw me, and in this case, one who had just stumbled into the bunker. If anything, they believed her shell shocked—a common sight in this war. She staggered back against the wall, stunned at the persistence of the unending explosive thunder. Nothing could have prepared her. In truth, she was shell-shocked already.

I watched silently as she examined her surroundings, her experience becoming part of my memory even as she did so. She looked around at the men, none of them paying any further attention to her, all just sitting there, smoking and praying and shaking. Her face appeared confused, and then her eyes turned to me. She blinked and saw who I was, and came close. She sat down beside me and continued to stare as I reached out and held her hand. My own hand was shaking, but she held it tight, her eyes suddenly fearful to see herself, her more powerful and older self, trembling like a frightened puppy. She asked me, 'What manner of hell is this?' and I explained as best I could. She was surprised to hear she resided in France with the German army in

1916, and that England was responsible for the shelling; and as we both sat there, clutching each other, rattled to our bones and made pitiful by the bombardment, it seemed ridiculous, even laughable to believe we were beings who could survive the battle much less ever hope to change the world.

* Оверман *

ZOLO FACED THE CLOCK OF PAGANINI'S VOICE ONCE MORE. His Mother Yarrow had informed him—while he sat on that chair watching Babette, worrying about Freddie, and contemplating Fate—that Paganini wished to speak. He left Babette after a kiss on her forehead, and a promise of return, and went to the small communications rooms shielded from all human and magical eyes. Before the clock he sat, turned the hands in the proper way, and listened. The voice of the Lord of Saravastra came through the clock, thin and hard:

"As we feared, the NMNI results prove that Temujin Gur intends to cross the Nicholas Line, and with the Princess von Anhalt. His goal is the Necropolis of The Khan, the final burial place of Genghis, somewhere in the Khentii Mountains of northern Mongolia. There he will resurrect him to mount a new and decisive invasion of Europe in the 13th century."

Zolo hesitated to reply, rattled by Gur's plan. He had realized of course that something strange and nightmarish would result from poking around in Gur's mind, but this? Nothing less than the extinction of all Europe? Given Gur's exposure to Master Godfellow though, it was not surprising that he would think in such grand and world-devouring terms.

"But why does he believe Princess von Anhalt will cooperate?" Zolo asked.

"He will first trick her by not revealing his true goals, then he will hold her father and nanny hostage, as well as her favorite servants. Gur also believes she will fear him enough to not defy him, despite her power, at least not until it is too late."

Zolo shuddered to think of Freddie's fate in Mongol hands. But another question remained. "Why not simply keep Genghis alive beyond his time of death?" he asked. "Why the resurrection, Master Paganini?"

"To create a spectacle and convince the Mongol people of his divinity."

Zolo laughed bitterly to himself, and said, "The greatest monster of all time, now a god."

"As his followers squabble over the empire, he will glide down from the air and land in their midst, claiming to be God of The Eternal Blue Sky, a deity of the Mongol religion. After a grand ceremony he will order invasion plans to commence. The God and his Lords of The Bow will then rampage over Europe with even bigger and more bloodthirsty armies than before, this time inspired by religious fanaticism and aided by sorcery, and as Genghis did in Persia and China, he will follow on Gur's desires to be especially brutal with Paris, Vienna, London and Rome, as well as any future center of western art or learning. Nothing will remain. And once Europe lies dead, he and his sons will begin five years of rape. They will methodically and savagely rape thousands of captured European noblewomen, and thus father a new Mongol Europe of the west, renamed Temujina, and in time to come, they will be known as The White Mongol Gods."

"Gur wants every bit of European culture destroyed ... no democracy, no— "

"All culture, all people, all memory gone. And he will live it, as it happens."

"How do you mean?"

"A portion of his soul will reside in the new God, thus allowing him to live out his fantasy. In effect, he and Genghis will be one in the same. In that black stew of horror that is Gur's mind, he already refers to himself as Temujin Khan, and Lord of The World. He is actually jealous of the mortal Genghis and his accomplishments. Forcing his will and soul on the new divine Genghis solves all problems."

"And what of ..." He was afraid to ask.

"He will brutally kill her after her energy is sapped as a result of delaying and destroying our defense satellites south of the Nicholas. Her access to the magical essence of the Tao is not limitless. And once done, he ..." Paganini's voice trailed off.

Zolo grew curious and afraid. "He will?"

"We do not wish to speak of this."

"You must tell me, sir."

"He wishes to feast on her body. He will toast with her blood and bake her heart in his hand. He will offer it to Genghis for dessert after a grand meal atop the bones of European princes."

Zolo paused before speaking again, regaining his composure after learning the news that Gur wished to make a meal of Freddie. "But how ... how can the Mongol get away it? You and Master Godfellow will still be alive. Saravastra is outside the time stream, so how—"

"Our friend, the Empress of Byzantium, will join him once the Mongol invasion of Europe begins. He has been conspiring with her to kill Edison for some time. But in this new scheme of Temujin Khan, he believes he'll find one more World Maker to help him, one of our comrades fallen on hard times in New York or Bagdad, and together they will assassinate Edison, take over his forces, and make war on Saravastra ... And yes, I have known for quite some time that she is a traitor to our cause, but we keep our enemies close, young man."

"How can we kill this mad beast?"

"We have a plan. We must be patient."

"Even Master Godfellow would not condone this. Even he—"

"Edison will not know. Gur's demise will come in our time, by our hand alone."

"As you say. I cannot help but—"

"Are we keeping Prince Christian safe, for now?"

"Yes, but I do not know if his daughter will ever be comfortable with his death."

"She will be resigned to it. We understand that now ... Good day to you, young man."

"But how will she, sir? How do you know?"

No answer. Paganini was gone. The clock stopped.

* Оверман *

TOBIAS BERGMAN WAS THE FIRST TO SEE THE CORPSE. It dropped from the ceiling of the Great Hall, right at lunchtime. He'd been walking from the kitchen, groaning to himself because his arms ached, holding on high a heavy silver platter of freshly cooked and sliced meats. He intended to rest it on a long table set up for Empress Elizabeth who was dining with Princess Johanna and Prince Christian that day, as well as other select nobles—just a small affair, a simple lunch of several courses.

When only a few feet into the Great Hall, a movement above caught his eye. He looked up to see it drop. It fell from the uppermost reaches, from the shadows of the ceiling, like a big black sack. It hit the edge of the long table just to the right of Empress Elizabeth who faced Princess Johanna in the midst of conversation. It struck with such impact that it flipped the whole table over, spilling food and drink onto the floor with a loud crash.

Tobias froze in place, as did the other servants. The nobles and Empress Elizabeth, also speechless. The first to react was Gleb. He ran over to the thing and knelt down to examine.

"*Mon dieu!* What is it?" Empress Elizabeth asked.

Gleb looked up at her and said, "It is a naked corpse, bloody and eyeless, and all its bones are broken. It is the body of a woman ... I know not who."

Tobias walked closer, needing to see the thing for himself. The corpse appeared more like a lump of bloody meat cut from the carcass of an animal. It had stubs of limbs, a head of sorts, and long dark chestnut hair. No other parts marked it as a woman. Before he could step closer, Empress Elizabeth commanded the corpse be quickly covered and a physician summoned to inspect it. Gleb snapped his fingers and two of the dumbstruck butlers standing nearby pulled the stained white tablecloth away from the overturned table and draped it over the body.

The Empress coldly observed the butlers, and said to no one in particular, "After all the strange happenings in this Prussian castle, I am not really surprised that a corpse has dropped from the ceiling to ruin our lunch."

Then things got stranger.

Just moments after Empress Elizabeth spoke, one of the butlers tugged at Gleb's sleeve and pointed at the cloth covering the body. The cloth lay flat on the floor. Gleb bent down and lifted the cloth.

No body could be found.

"What devil's magic is at work?" Prince Christian asked with an angry voice.

Tobias knew, as did everyone else in the room, that Prince Christian wished to point the finger at Empress Elizabeth's Mongol wizard, Temujin Gur, though he dared not risk offending the Empress by doing so. Ever since Gur's arrival, the castle had suffered bleedings and all manner of madness. Already, the villages nearby believed Bärenthoren to be demon haunted and cursed, even more so than in the bygone days of the Sun Angel. Empress Elizabeth made no comment. She just stared at the bloody spot where the body had rested, her eyes fixed for many moments, as if she realized something important though would not say it.

Before anyone could utter another word, distant shrieks of terror erupted from above. To Tobias it sounded like the maidservants in the upper quarters of the castle, the shrieks echoing down the grand staircase outside the Great Hall. The shrieks grew louder and continued, as if those shrieking had run from the source of terror and were drawing close.

As the day wore on, Empress Elizabeth and Prince Christian, Gleb and Tobias, and everyone else learned, upon weeding fear-based rumor from fact, that within one hour following the drop from the ceiling, the same unrecognizable female corpse had appeared in at least five different locations in or around castle Bärenthoren. One of the maidservants, overcome with hysterics, told Prince Christian the corpse appeared in mid-air as she was making a bed, and chased her out of the room. "It just *floated* after me," she said, "just floated and dripped blood, dripped and dripped!" Indeed, a trail of blood found later in that hallway by castle valets confirmed her story. Two of Prince Christian's musketeers reported the corpse sitting atop a parapet on the castle wall, staring with no eyes to the horizon. It vanished when they attempted to snag it with a halberd. Finally, it came to rest just outside the castle gate.

The guards alerted Prince Christian and they all watched it from the walls for half an hour as it lay there unmoving in the sun. After a cloud rolled in and a light snow fell, the corpse vanished once more, finally coming to rest in the bed of Empress Elizabeth. It appeared beside her as she reclined with a big brass monocle in her eye and a glass of red wine in her hand. That was the story of one of her Prussian maidservants, Frieda Hoffman, later whipped by Princess Johanna for spreading the story of the corpse's appearance, and for the crime of spying on the Empress in the first place.

Later that evening, rumors whispered among the nervous castle staff said the Empress had summoned Temujin Gur to deal with the case of the vanishing corpse. Nevertheless, it seemed to all in the castle that an ugly god or power could not make up its mind. Where did it wish to place the corpse? It reminded them of Princess Johanna using the backs of servants to repeatedly move pieces of heavy furniture from one room to another, not able to reach a decision, and of course, remaining callous to the suffering she caused.

To many it seemed like a prankish joke of some kind.

A very sick one.

* Оверман*

THE *OBSERVADOR PACIENTE* OF ZOLO REPORTED THE PUNISHMENT of Gleb at the hands of Prince Johanna for the fact that Prince Christian was still alive. Zolo sat in the secret castle bedroom suite, having returned there after speaking with Paganini, and while Babette slept peacefully, his inner eyes watched a raging woman confront Gleb in another secluded room of the castle. With both hands she reached out and grabbed a cringing Gleb by his jacket and threw him across the room. The man stumbled and fell to the floor.

"Imbecile, why is Prince Christian still alive?" she shouted, looming above him, vengeful and fuming.

From the floor, a rattled Gleb looked up and said, "He should be sick by now. I don't understand. I gave him the right poison—"

"Not only is he not sick, he says he feels better *than ever in his life*. He even tried to take me to bed last night. He was amorous and lively, and if I had not slapped and scratched him he would have violated me!"

Just as Zolo chuckled to himself at Princess Johanna's fear of sex with her husband, he saw a dark shadow move across the wall, like a giant black manta. It startled him. Zolo then felt as if he were rising into the air and turning downward, around and up again, even though he remained seated.

Suddenly, all went blurry with motion. He began to spin faster within himself, and as he did, the floor and walls of the room vanished. Babette vanished. All balance and sense of place lost, and the sound of his frightened voice filled his head like the roar of a bear deep in cave.

End over end, end over end. And then ... he stopped.

His head spun. He breathed heavily.

He stood nowhere, sat nowhere, simply floated. The air about him was dark and flickering with firelight. Where was he? In what other world? He saw stars, livid stars in the blackest of nights. He watched them, imagining their light piercing him and lifting him, making him one with them. Before he could take comfort, he fell, down and down, and his body hit the earth. The wind was knocked out of him and he gasped.

"*Nai Yarrow Margaret!*" he called out within himself.

No answer.

He glanced to his left and saw a fire, a big fire, and beyond the fire, white human faces, more than a dozen of them, and even more behind them. They hovered above the flames, as though the severed heads of damned souls cooking for Satan's pleasure.

Stars, souls, and fire.

Then he heard a voice, a deep voice of simmering evil:

"Your beloved Margaret of Anjou cannot help you now. I have my hand on her throat."

He turned his head to find the voice. It belonged to the smiling Buddha face of Temujin Gur.

"Your future Czarina is dead," Gur said and grinned at him.

"What? ... Who is dead?" Zolo asked, still trying to recover his senses.

"Your fool girlfriend. Have you not seen or heard lately of the vanishing corpse?"

"What? I ... I have been—"

"Hiding and scheming as usual. So many *schemes*, you little Zolo of white flowers and democracy." Temujin Gur winked at him. The small silver beetle on Gur's face glimmered for a moment and terrible pain stabbed into Zolo's head like a hot needle. Three ghostly lips flew from Gur's mouth, soared down and bit savagely into Zolo's arms and legs with invisible sharp teeth. Zolo cried out and thrashed on the ground.

"You and your Czarina schemed, and you failed," Gur said. "God of the Blue Sky, I hate fools!"

The biting lips released and vanished. Zolo gasped and groaned. "No. She cannot be dead. She—"

"Turn and behold, apostle of Diderot!"

Gur pointed and Zolo turned his head to right. He saw a side of raw bloody beef. The head was lost in shadow. The body soft, almost boneless

"No, this is not—"

"Yes, it is, and you will watch so that you can tell her all about it, from the first scream to the last."

"What do you mean?" he asked, looking up to face Gur once more.

"First, stand and see the woggers. Ask them if they wish to vote on this."

Against his will, Zolo's body jerked him upright to a standing position. He felt dizzy and sick. He lifted his head to stare beyond the large fire and saw that the white heads belonged to a whole clan of naked serfs—men, women and children, several families at least. They stood there in rows, in the cold air beneath the stars, staring at the fire and shivering, gaunt with poverty and beaten down like sad dogs. Their faces fearful, though a few looked resigned, others just glassy eyed. None spoke or moved from the spot where they stood.

No doubt a spell of Gur's kept them silent, and rooted.

Zolo glanced around to the horizon and saw only the dark silhouettes of tall fir trees against the night sky. Apparently, Gur had brought them to some secluded place deep in the forest of Anhalt. He looked down again at the corpse. It sickened him, but the thing, the side of bloody meat, seemed so unreal. He walked a few steps to get a better look, and he noticed the dark hair on the head of the thing: long and dark chestnut hair.

царица

10

A Necessary Evil – Woggers Must Perish - The Godfellow Nuance

THE FRENCH AND BRITISH INFANTRY ASSAULT BEGAN AT 7:30 A.M. Along the curved path of an ancient Roman road, from Albert in the west to Bapaume twelve miles to the northeast, 13 divisions of the British Army and 11 divisions of the French Sixth rose up from their trenches, north and south of the River Somme, and moved forward towards the German positions. The Czarina knew that over 20,000 men would die as they marched, upright in their waves, towards the unrelenting fury of the German machine guns. In only one day, those men perished, tens of thousands more wounded. From her studies, she recalled a few words of the speech delivered to the British Yorkshire Light Infantry just before the attack: "When you go over the top, you can slope arms, light up your pipes and cigarettes, and march all the way to Pozières before meeting any live Germans!" The British believed their massive and days-long artillery bombardment would severely weaken the enemy and cut the barbed wire defenses as well, thus allowing a park-like stroll to victory.

Nothing could have been more of a fantasy.

After the final bursts of the British creeping barrage ended and their guns went ominously silent, I pulled my confused and shaken younger self out of the bunker and into daylight. Such a bizarre experience I shall never forget. As My Youth saw and heard the war, so did memories of these dark visions light in my brain at once, so that in effect, all became déjà vu even as it took place. I witnessed the same horror seen so many years before, when her age, and this made things even worse. To have lived the nightmare once was bad enough. In fact, I even remembered staring at myself that day, looking for strength. How could I fail the one who needed me most? But such bouts of living with her were so uncomfortable that I resolved never to do it again unless forced by inevitable circumstance. All too odd and disturbing. No one can possibly understand it who has not done it.

The shouts of officers, a few at first, then more numerous, shook me to attention. All up and down the German line, for miles in either direction, my eyes witnessed tens of thousands of dark helmets pouring from dugouts and bunkers, all swarming to take positions. Many of them set up hundreds of black 08 Maxims, arranging these big water-cooled machine guns in such a manner as to create a zone of forward and enfilade fire that would sweep the enemy ranks in the front and on the sides.

A morning breeze blew huge billows of white smoke into our faces. We stood upon a wooden walkway implanted in the dirt wall of the trench before our bunker. In a few minutes, far across the chewed and charred remains of a cornfield, I saw them coming, dim and dark in the hazy distance. Rank after rank after rank, so many I could not count. I know that over a hundred thousand French and British rose up and over their trenches that day, and I saw by their colors that the waves of men intent on killing me belonged to an Irish brigade, perhaps two Irish brigades, trudging and stumbling through the shell craters of the past day's bombardment. The ground, now a part of No Man's Land. Nothing remained, not a single stalk; all trees blasted too, uprooted and crushed by fire north and south of the Somme River. For miles in both directions, the earth had been churned to a muddy, tree-shredded stew by the rain of shells and water.

I saw through the lifting smoke that hundreds of yards of iron barbed wire awaited the Irish. The insane shelling had not cut it, not as Field Marshall Haig had planned. He should have calmed the bombardment at night, sent parties out to check the wires, at least once towards the end of it, but he would not consider even the potential of failure. The arrogant fool!

The German 08 Maxims barked in chorus well before the Irish reached the iron, at least 20 of them to the nearby left and right of where we stood. They created a superior sheet of metal fire, the likes of which surprised me. Sprays of bullets whined and spit at the Irish from the front and sides. The men out there, being chipped to pieces, hopped and danced and dropped each moment by the score. I heard them, more than a hundred yards away, over the firing. God help me, I did not wish to hear their sad and terrible cries. "Erin go Bragh!" one yelled before a bullet tore out his throat. An Irish officer shouted "Fritz will be runnin' lads!" just before three Maxim bullets knocked him sideways and threw him face first to the ground as if pushed by a rough bully. A young private stopped to pray "Mary Mother hear my—" over his fallen brother from Dublin, and in less than a second, seven bullets spun hot through his body, one passing through to wound a soldier behind him in the leg.

The Irish brigades, what remained of them, soon hit the black barbed wire. Many frantically attempted to use their wire cutters, but were themselves cut in half as they tried. Others threw themselves screaming on the big loops, their minds in a state between horror and hysteria, pain and panic. The bullets raked them as they squirmed and struggled, and finally, death posed them for all to see. One of the men, stuck in mid-air, appeared to be praying, his head lifted to the sky, hands pressed before him; and as the days went by, the dead men acquired nicknames that defined their pose: the trapeze artist, the swimmer, the hopscotch man, the jockey, the evening stroll, the ballet dancer, and so forth. The German soldiers found a way to define the ghastly and macabre vision of these posed corpses, to make sense of it and toast "the courage of the ballet dancer" or else they would go mad.

The mass killing of the Irish was ruthless and efficient. No choice in the matter, for the mere thought of having a steel bayonet buried in you was enough by itself to keep your finger on a trigger. The unreal tragedy of it became clear to my younger self, and again, to me. Once the waves of Irish, and others, had begun their decay to earth, we stared into each other's eyes, and I remembered that moment and became myself in the memory, staring into my own soul; and she *asked me, "Is there more of this?" and I said, yes, much more, and then another war to follow, and more still, the finest men and women, the most courageous and kind will die, and among their number, millions of the Jewish people, Russians, and so many others, meeting death in ways that cannot be spoken of.*

* Оверман *

IN THE NO MAN'S LAND OF CRATERS AND DEATH, on the field south of Guillemont at dusk, the Princess and Czarina strolled, the day's charge against the German lines having been reduced to smoke and corpses. They spoke of many things while the piteous cries of the wounded created one long moan in the background. Freddie asked if power had become a burden, and Catherine answered yes. "In truth, it will never cease to be a burden," she said. Power meant responsibility, choices between life and death, good and evil, and all in between. And now, a "necessary evil" would be staged early tomorrow morning at The Battle of The Somme in an attempt to prevent a greater evil later, and Freddie remarked, "I will not take part in evil of any kind."

"In truth, you will, or you will not be me," Catherine said, her face cold as No Man's Land.

"I will not be you then."

"Then you will not be here, and this war will go on *without you.*"

"And how will *our necessary evils* make it any better?" her younger self asked. To the south, a new bombardment by the French had begun, the distant quaking of it rolling through the darkening blue air.

"Is it evil for the Germans to defend themselves? Or for the French or British to attack? This is French soil we stand on," Catherine said.

Her younger self hesitated before answering. "I cannot say. They do what they must."

"And we do *what we must,* no?"

"But they are driven by orders, and a belief in rightness of their cause."

"And we are driven by *choice* and rightness of cause. Are we evil then because we are not actually taking orders as would soldiers?" Catherine turned and clutched Freddie by the shoulders and stared into her eyes as the voice of the French guns grew louder. "After this World War I you find yourself in now, a much greater evil will arise in Europe in the 1930's. It will be led by a German political radical, and through fear and lies he will conquer the German people and begin a second world war to conquer everyone else. He will eventually be defeated, but only after tens of millions of deaths, and in dying he will fuel an American war machine that will grow to become Godfellow's army of the 21st century."

"From America? I thought they—"

"The war machine corporations will control America's government in Washington and bleed the country to the bone, and with undercover doses of Godfellow's magic, this symphony of evil will rise to conquer Earth itself. Humankind as we know it will perish."

"But we will kill Master Godfellow before that happens ... or will we?"

"Saravastra's move to alter the Battle of The Somme will lure his forces to restore the time stream. Then we will kidnap him from the future, as I told you while you cooled in that block of Temujin's ice."

"But how can we be sure the Saravastra plan will work well enough to lure his forces?"

"The plan is sound, and simple. Once the German army begins a surprise counteroffensive here at Guillemont at 3 A.M. tomorrow morning, it will break through and turn north, rolling up the British right flank. The French will be cut off and unable to support. This victory will end effective British presence in France and allow the Germans to—"

WHUMP! BOOOOOOM!

A shell suddenly landed nearby and both of them were showered with dark bits of mud and gore. She continued. "... allow the Germans to dominate the war here on the western front."

WHUMP WHUMP BOOOOOOOM!

The French shelling was now joined by British batteries closer to their position, faraway across No Man's Land. Freddie looked confused and jittery in the presence of the shelling. Who wouldn't? She said, "But if the Germans win, then—"

Catherine interrupted, "The plan calls for the Russians to drive the eastern front into Germany and force the German high command ... to retire from France." WHUMP! "In the long run, a peace between the allies and Germany will be made ..." WHUMP! "Germany will remain prosperous and without Allied treaty restrictions." A shell landing only twenty yards away kicked body debris into the air around them. Catherine felt her stomach lurch. "In short, the Saravastra time-war strategy cancels conditions that lead to the rise of ..." A fierce whine of shell cut her off.

WHUMP! BOOOOOOM! *SHREEEEEEEE!*

A violent whistling of shrapnel. Catherine continued quickly for more explanation was needed and she sensed a new shower of shells on the way. "Assuming the Saravastra plan works at the Somme, War Tracker will alert beast Godfellow and his Black Army Corps. Units of *Dio Soldati* will arrive to remove the threat to his version of history. At this point, a Nexus Zone will be formed."

"And then we kidnap the World Maker?"

WHUMP! BOOOOOM! WHUMP! More debris and mud rained down. Thick clouds of smoke began to obscure them, dark purple in the light of dusk, hiding their faces for a few moments. Despite a headache blooming into her skull with pounding force, Catherine said, "We will kidnap him from his headquarters in Dubai, via the chrono-defense satellites, to the Nexus Zone. Before the monster can blink, our aria will reroute him to Mars, and then—"

WHUMP! BOOOOOM! ... WHUMMMMMMP!

"So you know for certain these *satellite things* are talking to War Tracker?"

"They watch events between moments, hours between seconds, as here in the Nexus Zone. If I am right though, we can—"

"What in Beelzebub's name is a Nexus Zone anyway? Zolo talked about it, and said—"

WHUMP! BOOOOOOOOOOM! *SHREEEEEEE!*

Enough! A frustrated Catherine sang a brief burst of aria to temporarily slow time, for she knew she must explain to the nervous Freddie—whose right arm had just been clipped and bloodied by a whizzing fragment of shell casing—a few crucial things about the Nexus Zone:

"*Tempo de ser lento!*" (Time be slow!).

A new rain of smoking debris slowed to a halt ten feet above their heads. She took a deep breath and began, noticing that half of Freddie's face was hidden by a frozen puff of purple smoke.

"The Zone ... it's an invention of the World Makers, a time-space battlefield that prevents our war from devastating the landscape and changing history in an unwanted manner."

Her blinking youth listened as she explained that battles took place within seconds, usually between the first millisecond of the first second and the last millisecond of the next. Within this tiny space of time, hours could go by, even days; and if Master Godfellow lost, he and War Tracker could develop a new strategy within moments and launch it. For example, if they failed to stop the German counteroffensive, they might create a British counteroffensive in the north that would turn the German right flank just as the Germans were turning the British right. Whatever it took, for as long as it took. No end of seconds within which to fight, no end of possible Nexus Zones. But there was always the threat of magical Tao energy becoming exhausted, or too many combat units destroyed or spell captains dead, and the horror of an Extinction Event always loomed.

Freddie said, "I heard Eréndira speak of it. I don't understand. I feel like such a child."

"It's hard to grasp," Catherine said. "Time suddenly resents being started and stopped again, rather like a horse ridden with too much whip. It throws its rider to the ground and returns to the stable. Does that make sense? ... Master Paganini believes the Tao responsible. Edison Godfellow believes it to be Ahriman."

"And so many die?"

"Whole divisions of black armor and scores of magical beings can be scattered to the past, far beyond the Nicholas Line, but that isn't what kills them. Whenever an Extinction Event occurs, the Time defense machines of the World Makers high above the Earth burn all victims of the Event, whoever and whatever they may be, and hurl them to the Cenozoic era, deep in Earth's past to prevent any possible contamination to history ... It isn't kind. We've lost tens of thousands. Godfellow's Cadre of The Overman has lost nearly a hundred thousand."

"What about us? Could we be killed in that way?" Freddie asked.

Catherine decided to answer honestly. "Yes, I believe we can."

She watched her younger self pause to gather courage, shell flashes and a thick haze frozen behind her. She watched her lips and heard her say, "I saw our death, at the hands of mechanical monsters in the Himalayas."

Catherine instantly recalled herself asking that question. "Yes, I remember it also," she said. She really did not wish to speak of it. The issue understandably made her uncomfortable. The thought of being helpless and ripped to shreds by a Fracas Machine was nerve wracking. "I do not know it if is true, or an illusion. I know from history that we live as a famous Czarina, and we will be known as Catherine The Great, but it is possible that Czarina is not really us."

"Not *really us?*"

"Perhaps a double substituted to appear and act like us. Anything is possible in this war. The acts of manipulation and intrigue ... I try not to dwell on it."

Freddie paused to consider, shaking her head, then her face saddened and she said, "Must our father die for us to become Czarina of the Russias?"

The question surprised Catherine, though she recalled it even as it happened. She did not answer her younger self, but the memory awoke, and she remembered standing there in the frozen smoke and flash, anxiously looking into Catherine's eyes for an answer, one that became obvious as each moment ticked by. Into those younger eyes before her, she stared back, creating the memory even as she did so, and at once, both pairs of dark blue eyes became teary. The two women reached out and hugged each other tightly and began to weep in earnest, and as the temporary time spell wore off and the shell thunder grew loud once more, the sound of their crying faded away.

* Оверман *

STARS, SOULS, AND FIRE: ALL PRIMAL THINGS of importance on that fateful night in the black forest of Anhalt. Zolo's anguish and despair at the realization that Freddie had died drove him to recklessly attack Temujin Gur. He launched himself through the air, fierce and flaming as a flying dragon, intent on breaking Gur's neck and frying his eyes, but Gur's magical shields hurled Zolo back through the air to collide with tremendous velocity against a thick pine tree. With a resounding crack, it snapped off at the base. Undaunted though, Zolo leapt to his feet. Channeling Mother Yarrow, he shot spinning blades and beams of destructive magical force from his eyes and hands at the Mongolian, force strong enough to rout the Prussian army, but to no avail. Gur smiled as the bolts of force splashed against him and fizzled to sparks; and as the sparks fell, Zolo snapped himself to Gur's side and in half a second struck the Mongol in the face and body with more than a dozen blows, each strong enough to kill a bull.

But Gur would not go down.

While a frustrated and raging Zolo continued to strike, the silver beetle on Gur's face sprang from the flesh. It grew to the size of a man in a moment, hurling itself at Zolo as it did so. It knocked him to the ground and crushed him, pinning his straining limbs with silver insect legs while his face turned to watch the horror show.

"What will you do with them?" Zolo shouted, barely able to get enough breath due to the weight of the beetle now heavy enough to flatten a suit of armor.

Gur did not answer. He turned his calm and kindly face to the frightened, cold-shaken serfs standing before the fire, and said to them, "You thanked your former master, Baron Eichmann, with disloyalty and betrayal. You thought yourself free at Anhalt, and you were, for a few hours. Keep that memory now as your souls make your savior, the Princess von Anhalt, live once more."

Zolo heard what Gur said. In his state of rage and anguish he only now realized that Gur meant to use the souls of the serfs to restore Freddie to life. Suddenly, his thoughts were mixed. Freddie had rescued them, and he did not wish their deaths, though at the same time he felt a thrill and a relief to know she would live again. But if he could struggle free, would he move to stop Gur? Would Freddie hate him if she ever discovered he let the serfs die? He could not answer his questions, though he became grateful for the weight that subdued him.

Temujin Gur began the ceremony.

Gur lifted his arms and black yarrow sticks darted from his sleeves. Twelve of them shot through the air, spinning out to form a perfect circle of twelve points that surrounded the serfs. Once done, the sticks stopped spinning and grew to three feet in height, their base pointing to the Earth, their top pointing to the night sky. They glowed a pale yellow, that same sickly pallor as at the banquet for Empress Elizabeth. Above them, the stars became brighter until actual rays of starlight, hundreds of them, pierced down through the darkness of eternity to shine upon the yarrow sticks. It appeared to Zolo as though the sticks fed upon the starlight. Gur began to chant while the serfs began to moan and cry out in anticipation of the horrors to come.

"Stop it now, we beg you!" one of the women yelled.

But Gur ignored them all, his eyes closed, his face serene, hands still uplifted. He began to chant. The chanting language of the Mongol was alien and strange to Zolo, like hard wheels on gravel, yet vaguely Chinese. *Hu li zhai xuuu zhahnng, ro lum khahlees, lum khalees.* Perhaps an ancient form of Mandarin, or something else? And then Zolo remembered. In his studies at Saravastra, he'd learned of a legendary magical language known as The Tongue of Ahriman, tens of thousands of years old, spoken by only the darkest demons of the night and the most learned of wizards. Said to be even more powerful and dangerous than Galician because it spoke directly to Ahriman, the mispronunciation of any word could doom the speaker to an agonizing death, for a failure to use his tongue correctly was said to be a great offense to Ahriman. Only legend, of course, and yet it made sense. The control of the starlight, the stealing of souls, the rise from death, all required the most powerful of magic languages, and The Tongue of Ahriman, if really true, would be that language.

Hu li zhai xuuu zhahnng, ro lum khahlees, lum khalees, Temujin Gur chanted again, and the once-pale yarrow sticks, now throbbing with brightening starlight, grew larger and wider, fleshing out in several moments to human-like bodies.

Black bodies full of stars.

Each of the bodies, filled with starry night sky, began to dance, moving around the circle. Mouths formed in the heads of these demonic things and they opened to repeat what Temujin Gur said:

Hu li zhai xuuu zhahnng, ro lum khahlees, lum khalees.

Zolo realized these magical, human-like demons to be the same that had danced at the banquet. Could Gur's yarrow sticks each be a different being, or a soul struck by Gur's magic and forced to be his slave? He did not have time to wonder at it, for what happened next stole all of his attention.

Another yarrow stick darted from Gur's sleeve and spun through the air to come to a halt above the corpse of the Princess von Anhalt. It floated parallel to her body. Zolo watched as it enlarged to over six feet in length and lowered onto her chest, becoming almost entirely transparent as it did so, as if transforming to pure glass. In a moment, the ghastly corpse of the princess rested within the clear yarrow block, rather like a body in a coffin. The block then raised upright and floated up, drifting to position itself above the fire, and upon doing so, the red fire turned black with a demonic groan and licked the base of the block, just beneath the skinned and bloody corpse.

The chanting of the Ahriman tongue grew louder. A few serfs screamed, then more as one of their number, an old woman, snapped from the ground and into the air like a stone thrown by a catapult. Her body flew end over end towards the floating yarrow block above the black fire and collided against it with a fleshy smack.

What happened next was worse than any nightmare conceivable.

* Оверман *

THE GERMAN COUNTEROFFENSIVE PLANNED BY SARAVASTRA went as planned. At 3 A.M. on July 2, the German army stormed the trenches just north of the Somme, and without prior bombardment, catching the British totally by surprise. The necessary evil of Saravastra's plan resulted in over seven thousand British soldiers being bayoneted and shot as they scrambled to a confused state of consciousness. Most of them could not even get their helmets on. Many awoke to a German grenade lobbed into their bunkers. The lucky ones never awakened. Many never knew the difference between dreams of death and actual death.

It all became one.

The German divisions pivoted to their right by 4 A.M. and moved north, sending a herd of British soldiers fleeing before them. The British lines dissolved into complete chaos. Meanwhile, the German artillery had begun a creeping barrage at 3:30 A.M., a hellish meteor storm moving south to north and a full mile ahead of the German counterattack. This kept the Brits pinned down and expecting a frontal assault while the tremendous noise of the bombardment also hid the sounds of the war howling in the south. British command only knew something was horribly wrong when thousands of panicked soldiers, half of them in pajamas or freezing in grimy underwear, came storming into their trenches and tents, all of them screaming that Fritz was right behind them and out for blood.

Freddie and Catherine remained still, beside their bunker. They waited. The stars came out and the Czarina gazed up to see Mars, red and glimmering in the night. She imagined the God of War staring down at them and nodding with approval; and if all went well, she would soon be there, shaking the God's hand over the grave of Edison Godfellow. Deep on Mars she would bury him, and once they returned, the final version of the "God One" would have been dead for two billion years. No Earth spells would alert the *Dio Soldati* to storm the future and save him. He would simply wink out, quietly, and she would replace him with a magically sculpted doppelgänger of her own creation—in short, an identical double of the narcissistic sociopath who walked and talked, fumed and postured just like the real one, but a version not detectable as a fraud, not by anyone, or by any of Godfellow's machines or spells. She would perfect the creature on Mars, train it, scar it to realness, and awaken it. The doppelgänger would be a snapshot taken a moment before the real Godfellow's departure from 2038 Dubai—the whole process like swapping an identical fake art work for an authentic one, and so fast that no one spots the swap.

Oddly enough though, the creation of a perfectly formed yet fraudulent World Maker, transparent to vigilant watcher-and-sniffer spells as well as his analysis technology, would result in a being so realistic, so absolutely Edison "Da Vinci" Godfellow, that in effect, she and Saravastra would be facing the real monster once more. A nuance of difference would have to be included in the new version, but that meant risk.

But the world belongs to the bold, and World Makers should never think small.

She'd been mulling over the "Master Godfellow Nuance" for many months. What would it be? Any shift in his direction, any change in goals, might well irritate the watcher spells and tech, and they would begin to probe. Perhaps then, a change of heart over the course of years? A gradual shift in viewpoint, so slow that no alarm bells sound?

A most reasonable nuance, it seemed.

Though how much havoc in the meantime?

In the distance, the German counter-offensive roared like a lion and hyena war in midnight Africa. The final waves of the German corps clunked across their path, heading for a right turn north across British lines. Freddie looked over at Catherine with a troubled and curious look, and said, "We are not *doing anything*. Why must we be here now?"

Catherine answered. "Mother Yarrow Maria and I are on alert to keep things on track. Small bumps can happen. A Godfellow agent could strike a significant German general with a heart attack and throw all into doubt. We cannot allow that."

"I see ... and what shall I do? I cannot remain useless," Freddie said with irritation in her voice.

"When the time comes, and I am gambling that it will, given the success of our German counterattack, the *Dio Soldati* will challenge us at this conflict point. You and I will then combine our powers with Mother Yarrow Maria and draw Godfellow in once the fighting has started. We must be precise with our aria, in unison, to connect to him via War Tracker's link with the Time satellite machines. Assuming the link is created in that way. I am not a hundred percent sure.

"What? If you're not sure, then why—"

"It will not be easy. Fighting will be happening all around us, the likes of which you cannot imagine. You *must* follow my lead."

"Maybe I can imagine it, but that isn't the point. Maybe you should be sure before—"

"I know how uncooperative you can be at times, of course, I know, but now is not the time."

"I thought we had plenty of time, that we could *make time*."

"I wish to get it right and spare our lives, and maybe even save this world. Now, please stop arguing with me pointlessly!"

Catherine and Freddie glared at each other, almost ready to begin slapping, or worse. The silent confrontation lasted several seconds, each of them breathing heavily, but only Catherine benefited from remembering her anger as a much younger woman, and this softened her, and Freddie could see the change in Catherine's eyes.

"So our forces have a chance of winning this conflict point?" Freddie asked, apparently desiring to defuse the tension.

"Yes," Catherine answered, her own blood pressure dropping again. "It all depends on luck and the amount of force brought to the zone. Other battles are taking place throughout history, so War Tracker might not have enough forces to dispatch ... It's hard to say because it's different every time."

"Does Master Paganini know we are here?"

"He knows I am, but not you. He would be furious if he—" She stopped talking because Mother Yarrow Maria interrupted:

The Dio Soldati come, my Czarina.

Freddie felt "the coming" also, the arrival of the Nexus Zone, the lure and danger threatening at the edge of her mind in the way a passing flame heats the skin. "Do you feel it too?" she asked her companion, and Catherine replied she did. "It is time. Hold my hand. This will all surprise and frighten you."

"I am not frightened," Freddie said, and held her head high.

"You will be, or you will not be me," Catherine said.

* Оверман *

AMONG THE SERFS SACRIFICED THAT NIGHT TO RESTORE LIFE to the Princess von Anhalt included Johann and Magdalena Gottschalk, a couple in their late twenties, along with their seven year old son Edward. "Ugly faces and souls," according to Temujin Gur in his incantation which sent them to their deaths. The elderly Emma Jung and her crippled husband Edmond were present, as well as their oldest grandchild, Clara Klein, who suffered from a rare disease that shut her eyes with swollen lumps. Clara's sister, Alitha, age 15, and her 12-year-old brother Willie born with only six fingers. And too, spinster sisters Selma and Ida Adler, toothless, haggard, and often rumored to be witches but never burned; and Jewish serfs Jacob and Francine Kaufman in their early thirties and childless, rumored for years to be working with other Jews to capture and crucify Christian children, though of course, no one ever caught them in the act. Regardless, like the others, when their flesh met the clear block of yarrow above the flame, they died.

Zolo Bold saw Francine gesturing and talking between tears before her time came. All of the serfs not yet dead ignored her, and then, like those gone before, her naked body spun into the air and slammed violently, face first against the yarrow block that contained the corpse of the Princess von Anhalt. Knocked unconscious by the impact, poor Francine's face and body pressed harder and harder against the clear surface, as if a giant hand crushed her into it. Like others before her, she began to smoke and turn black, and within another moment, to an ashen char that showered as black snow into the fire below.

Zolo watched the horror show, pinned beneath the cold silver beetle. The howls and begging of those awaiting their turn would follow him into manhood, to his very last day, and he fervently hoped Freddie would never know the truth of this dark ceremony in the forest of Anhalt. He must forever block it and never allow her to read his thoughts, never allow her to see the torment and death that restored her to life as the energy of each human soul ripped from its home and flowed into her lifeless body.

Meanwhile, the star-filled yarrow beings danced wildly in their circle, chanting in demonic unison with Temujin Gur, chanting in the Tongue of Ahriman. Each time a serf's body turned to ash, they exclaimed, "*Zhenquron lai om tah!*" and the stars within them illumined to tiny novas, until finally, the last of the serf bodies died and fed the flames with their ash. At this point, the yarrow beings stopped dancing and faced the suspended corpse of the Princess von Anhalt. The stars inside them glowed brighter again, as if all bursting with age at once, and as they did, the floating coffin block glowed. The corpse within shimmered and paled to white, smoothed to a porcelain-like sheen.

Then it was over.

Zolo felt an ease in the weight upon his body. He turned his head to see Freddie's naked body laying atop him, asleep and limp, her dark-haired head on his chest. She looked perfectly formed and healthy, just as he'd seen her upon release from that healing block of ice. In her sleep, she mumbled *Zhenquron lai om tah* to herself, as though dreaming the ceremony of soul stealing.

He rolled his body and rested her on the ground, relieved the terrible ordeal was over, until he saw it: a Gur-like silver beetle, small and sizzling hot upon her lower neck. He gasped and plucked it from her flesh, throwing it into the trees over fifty yards away where it landed with a small flash of soundless light. The beetle thing left a small red scar on her that resembled a yarrow symbol of wavy sticks and dots. It reminded Zolo of Gur's symbols on his red cloak.

Zolo could not deny it. Gur had marked her.

Was this the plan then? Did she die so that Gur could claim a hold on her?

Or was it all just good luck for him?

"KING OF DEMOCRACY!"

Zolo heard the cynical, laughing voice of the Mongolian wizard-god, and glanced up to see him stepping from a line of black trees in the distance, from the place where the beetle had landed with a flash. "Your Czarina whore will live to change history now, after failing so miserably on her own. She is more suited to be my puppet, rather than one for that fool Italian violinist!"

Upon saying that, Gur burst into light with a loud bang and shot to the sky like a streak of meteor returning to Space.

Zolo cursed under his breath and removed his cloak to drape it over Freddie's naked body once more, and gazing up, saw no sign of movement.

They were alone.

Nothing left, only an eternity of cold darkness and starlight.

* Оверман *

FREDDIE SOON FOUND HERSELF IN A WORLD OF WAR TIME, two thousand milliseconds of an hour's struggle to a climax of fury and violence. It took place in a bubble resting upon a chopped and crater-filled oblong of no man's land at least five miles long and fixed between the German and British lines north and south of the Somme. The light in the bubble, dark as the pre-dawn light of France, though illumined by the frozen flashes of shells bursting in the distance and a golden half-moon in the east. The smell was one of blood and wet earth.

Her body had revolted upon arrival, as if spun on a torture wheel. Her feet pushed into the gloppy mud of no man's land, and as her eyes adjusted she noticed the bodies of British soldiers, hundreds of them frozen by death and time, many with surprised eyes wide open and staring at the sky. A few sat upright, due to rigor mortis, their hands extended before them, gripping rifles they no longer held—one of them from a Welsh regiment. He looked like a movie actor, handsome, a cigarette in his mouth. Had he stopped to smoke or been advancing with it dangling from his lips? No matter. As she stared at the corpse, a flash of brilliant light bathed him quite suddenly.

The entire bubble of Zone lit up for miles.

Freddie saw dark and ominous figures hurtling from the source of it, at least six miles away, twenty or more of them flying towards their position, others dropping to the ground and running. They appeared in the distance like black spiders with human legs, and beside them, shimmering points of light like little moons, half a dozen or more, hovering in the air.

"*Dio Soldati,*" Catherine said with a note of fear in her voice.

Gazing up, Freddie saw more lights, star-like and forming in the air, thinning to streaks and opening wide like pockets. Things sprung and flew from those pockets, the likes of which she could never have imagined. Many appeared to be machines, human-like or insect-like, or a thing in-between, and they soared while others dropped to the earth, appendages and weapons clicking out and aiming in preparation for battle.

"Black armor units from Surya," Catherine said calmly. As Freddie would later learn, Surya was a twenty mile long orbital manufacturing and command base for Saravastra's black armor forces ("black" or "magic-black" referring to a vanadium alloy steel coated with a magic shield). Saravastra, in coordination with Mother Yarrows, dispatched black armor units to conflict points via teleportation from Surya. At any one time, over twelve thousand separate black armor weapons of all classes were operational, each one commanded by something called an "artificially intelligent brain" magically joined with the soul of a Warrior Bodhisattva.

"Feel the heat of aria in you now. Prepare for war, princess!" Catherine shouted.

Freddie's breath came heavy and the hearth of her aria smoldered hot, throbbing into her chest and towards her throat with powerful language, and with more feeling of depth than ever. Her pains of transition to the Zone faded and an iron-crushing strength spread to her fingertips. Her senses expanded too, and her mind seemed able to process many more things at once, as well as see possible moves and countermoves while the enemy forces drew near. The sounds of long distance firing and return fire began to fill the air with lightning cracks and cicada-like screeches that hurt her ears, and too, colossal exhalations of heat that flushed her face, and *WHUMP-WHUMP* bellows that felt in her nauseous stomach way too much like heavy British howitzers.

Turning to take the temperature of Catherine's face, she was astonished to see a fantastic figure suddenly appear before her. Her huge black eyes blazed out from a stunningly beautiful Oriental face. She wore a white tunic pinched at the waist and light samurai armor on her upper body and thighs, and she carried a long and gleaming *naginata*, a classic Japanese weapon that appeared like a sword blade fixed to a long wooden shaft. Her long black hair rose up about her head, tendrils of it grasping small metal discs and marble balls which Freddie guessed must be weapons and captured spells. And while she stood there, the light of war boiling hot behind her, Freddie noticed how the echoes of firing stopped and held at one pitch. Lights in the distance no longer flickered. All time moved forward so slowly it created an impression of all things grinding to a halt.

"Sister Itagaki!" Catherine exclaimed with a look of surprise. The two of them hugged for a moment before Itagaki pulled back and said, "I am glad you are here, Czarina. I will be conducting operations unless you say otherwise."

"I do not. You are more experienced at the symphony of battle in the Zone."

"Mandukhai is leading the *Dio Soldati* this time."

"Will you be her death, or shall I?"

"Whoever has the good fortune of ending the monster's existence, I will sing their praises, and if it be me, I will sing of myself," Itagaki said and smiled darkly. She then glanced at Freddie and said to Catherine, "I have never seen you so young, but her eyes have that same fire. Together you will not be defeated. What force can withstand two voices of aria much less one?"

Upon saying that another figure entered their presence, walking up from behind to stand beside Itagaki and glare at Catherine. She was taller than all of them, at least six foot four and with the vague look of a Viking shield maiden: hair long and blonde beneath a shining, nose-guard helmet, sword-steel eyes of merciless stare, but the rest of her was a puzzle to Freddie. Her body fitted with black armor cuirass and greaves writhing with live yarrow symbols, frighteningly reminiscent of Temujin Gur; and her face, tattooed with yarrow sword-symbols that glowed like fierce red scars. Strapped across her back, a black and gold-tasseled scabbard sheathing a great sword, a fully formed yarrow sword, the hilt made of polished gold.

"Aella of The Fianna," Catherine said, returning the glare, "or is it Hervor, ravager of helpless villages? I see you have Tyrfing on your back. How many children and elves has it eaten since last I saw you? But we all know elves do not exist except in poor imaginations."

With irritation in her voice, Itagaki said to both of them, "Save your bitterness and rage for the *Dio Soldati*."

Aella glared at Itagaki, saying nothing, then turned the glare on Freddie, who faced her bravely. She was not afraid of the warrior Wizard Goddess—or so she appeared, definitely more powerful than a spell captain. Aella, to Freddie's surprise though, reached out with one hand to stroke her long dark hair, her eyes never losing their furious steel.

Itagaki shouted at Aella, "Enough! The time lock ends now! *Currículo Tempo!*"

Aella lowered her arm and turned to face the battle, reaching behind her back to draw her sword Tyrfing. Freddie watched as the sword lifted out, turning from the color of yarrow moon-steel to the dark color of blood as it breathed air. Freddie heard it inhaling as it left the scabbard, and once done, it exhaled and Freddie felt the sword breath hot as frigid Artic on her cheeks. It smelled of the Somme battlefield, as if the sword had cleaved the British down and not the German 08 Maxims. The sword spoke to Aella in whispers. Whatever it said caused Aella to turn for a moment and glance at Freddie once more, this time with a puzzled look.

"For Saravastra and Earth!" Itagaki shouted, and upon saying that, she turned and ran towards the oncoming enemy. Other Japanese samurai, both male and female, a hundred or more of them, all powerful spell captains with gleaming *naginata* and magical weapon hair, followed right behind her. They ran to either side of a surprised Freddie. She had no idea they had stood behind her the entire time. They sprang forward at twice the speed of a galloping stallion and leaped, one rank of ten after another thrusting up and rising, each rank forming a flying V formation like brilliant swans soaring at hundreds of miles per hour with a loud war cry of "Banzai!" directed at the oncoming apparition of the *Dio Soldati*. Aella followed, rising above their ranks, her whispering yarrow sword before her.

"*Onna Bugei-sha* they are called," Catherine said with a hint of sadness in her voice. "Many will die today after having lived for centuries. But they can join and combine their powers. That will save some of them."

And as Freddie watched the samurai turning to specks that winked out with a flash, a plague of locusts appeared over two miles away, hundreds of feet high in the golden moon air and roiling towards them like an angry black cloud. "What in Beelzebub's name!" Freddie yelled. She pointed to it and watched Catherine's eyes grew huge and horrified.

"It's ... my God, bodies, the dead bodies of British soldiers, thousands of them."

Upon saying this, Catherine stopped time again with a few Galician words. Once more the war about Freddie stilled to a crawl. Strangely enough though, out the corner of her eye, a few objects seemed to be moving less slowly than before, picking up speed. She did not understand. One of them, a black armor mini-reaper five times the size of the Anhalt World Stormer, actually flew at a walking pace.

"This battle is one of moments within seconds, within moments," Catherine said, her face appearing anxious. As World Makers, we are the fastest. We must unite and take out as many *Dio Soldati* as possible, as quickly as possible, and lock onto the Nicholas Line satellites. But we must move! Aella's sword is possessed by Black Agnes of Scotland, and she will get word to Master Paganini either directly or through the Mother Yarrow grapevine."

"The grapevine?"

"They all talk. They even gossip."

"Why does Aella hate us?"

"She hates me, but you reminded her of a more innocent me. She loves me in the way a man loves, but believes me evil and wants to kill me. She is a hypocrite and I do not have time to talk. We must join the battle and summon The God of The Overman from his Dubai castle."

"But—"

"No time! Feel your aria! *Currículo Tempo!*"

Time resumed. Things not moving began to move. Things moving sped up to a blur. Freddie heard a thunderous rumbling a few hundred yards to her right, as though a new volcano were erupting from French soil. She turned to see an impossibly massive machine rearing up from the earth like a Titan. At full height it stood taller than the Strasbourg Cathedral, over six hundred feet, and the body of it like a black kite the size of at least three hundred English warships. Hundreds of gun turrets of all sizes protruded from the sides, and crescent shaped objects, glistening like white flame, shot forth with a distant *whooooshing* sound from a slit below the crest of the thing and just above the six legs it possessed, three to either side.

It immediately attracted a barrage of fire from the *Dio Soldati* units forming up miles away. Great streaks of energy struck the surface of the black-armor enormity and sizzled as they drilled at its skin. The Titan machine fired back with all its gun turrets at once, the sound and fury raking the air like a roaring cry of hurricane.

"A War Reaper," Catherine said. "Follow me now! Mother Yarrow Maria steers us as one!"

Before Freddie could muster a thought, they both rose into the air and launched forward at hundreds of miles an hour, side by side, not more than a few feet apart and rising high. They imagined the highest limit of their power, streaming out from them, forming a scythe of energy, and they sang their aria deep and strong in the killing wind of their soar:

Tao encher-nos, forte e quente.
Recorrer a fouce
e coller nosos inimigos,
En nome de Ahriman e Saravastraaaa!

(Tao fill us, strong and hot. / Turn to scythe / and reap our foes, / In the name of Ahriman and Saravastra!)

Then the world went insane.

Even what Freddie had seen so far could not have prepared her for this magical death struggle. With the aria spell, she became a scythe of Tao force thick as castle Bärenthoren and over half a mile wide. The scythe, too bright for human eyes, powerful enough to cut the Alps in half or burn Greece to ash, was a hundred times stronger than all the shells fired by the British in six days against the German lines.

Like an army of Anhalt Sun Angels, the two of them hurtled forward, crackling with a billion volts and loud enough to shatter every window in France. Straight and true they flew, towards a flying wedge of the *Dio Soldati.* They cut through waves of British corpses hurtling end over end through the air, their rifles, helmets, bibles, spectacles, pipes, coffee tins, rosary beads, and all manner of other flotsam rolling along with them. The scythes simply turned them to brief sparks, burned out so fast they did not have time to smoke, while behind them, the ranks of the living warriors drew closer.

Multi-armed *Dio Soldati*, twenty feet in height and looking like demonic black knights whose sad-clown faces surprised Freddie, tried to swerve away from the scythe. Many were cut to shreds and disintegrated, fizzling and popping out like damp fireworks. Pieces of others burned or sheared off. Many plummeted in trails of smoke to the earth like fallen angels, sorrowfully screaming on the way down with the voices of both women and men. The moon orbs of the *Dio Soldati*, hovering nearby, each the size of a baby elephant, darted away more quickly from the World Maker scythe, firing a spread of destructive energy lances and bolts as they did so. A few lost their skin to the heat and shriveled with a crunch, though many more were totally consumed as Catherine bobbed the scythe up and down in an effort to do more damage.

Meanwhile, *Dio Soldati* on the flanks volleyed at them with all manner of fire and force. The cries of their spells could be heard, shouted with booming voices above the whine and screech of the killing bolts—but all turned to useless smoke against the scythe of pure Tao. Ten foot long war swords and other magical edge weapons wielded by the six limbs of the *Dio Soldati,* strong enough to cleave tungsten steel or ordinary magic shields like so much macaroni, were swung and hurled at velocities in the supersonic range.

To no avail though. Nothing stopped the princess and Czarina. Nothing could. God Soldiers strong enough to collapse empires in an hour failed to even slow them.

At least five platoons of Master Godfellow's elite perished that day, even more wounded or disabled. Truly one of the worst defeats for his forces—all occupants of the *Dio Soldati* armored suits belonging to the Cadre of The Overman, each one a superhuman man or woman with the power of a Hercules. Though none of his new race possessed magical ability in the way of spell captains, their suits, designed by him for inter-dimensional and interstellar warfare, maximized both sides of the Tao, thus providing a formidable array of magical and non-magical weapons including clusters of war spells and particle-beam disruptors, magical sonics and anti-matter rounds, black-armor plate and force screens, as well as a variety of edge weapons. Against all but the most powerful Wizard Gods and World Makers, they proved invincible, and their sad clown faces were a joke of Godfellow origin.

"Death by clown," he called it. It reminded him of a certain actor who belonged to a traveling troupe in medieval Italy. The man was really a knight in disguise.

All of the *Dio Soldati* divisions believed Master Godfellow to be humorous and of good nature.

They loved him and believed in his vision.

царица

11

Wizard Goddess Rivalry · A New Hole on Mars · The Welsh Corpse

AS EDISON GODFELLOW SIPPED HIS PINOT NOIR AND MUSED on how the poet-singer Leonard Cohen in his old age looked disturbingly like that old buffoon American president from the 1980's, Ronald Reagan, he was joined at his favorite restaurant, *Le Petit Sanglier* in Dubai, by a striking and powerfully built Wizard Goddess—a former Mongolian queen by the name of Mandukhai. She had arrived fresh off a disputed conflict point at the Battle of The Somme. The dining room hostess showed her to his table. He glanced up to see her approach, looking like a cross between a Chinese warlord and a circus acrobat, hung with clinking weapons and smeared with blood—her right eye also missing, and several fingers in the process of growing back.

"Must you wizard goddesses *always* be dripping blood?" he said, smiling and inviting her with a sweep of his hand to sit down.

Never a woman of many words, Mandukhai said dryly:

"No time to bathe, God One."

"One evening, you shall attire yourself in a black sequined gown and we will dance on the patio, beneath the poetry of the Dubai night while listening to Frank Sinatra. *Thus spake Zarathustra.*"

Edison, in joking manner, often made that Zarathustra comment. It came from the writings of the 19th century philosopher Nietzsche. Zarathustra was a prophet who predicted the coming of The Overman. It suited him to imagine himself Zarathustra, wise in the ways of destiny and ushering in a new age for humankind.

Mandukhai sat beside her God One. The golden light of the Himalayan dusk pouring across the dining room of the *Le Petit Sangli-*

er bronzed her skin and made her even more beautiful.

Edison wished her streaks of blood to disappear, and they did so until her skin shone, making her appear like a glowing artifact. He was pleased. He sipped his pinot noir. "Speak to me of the Battle of The Somme," he said. "Who by chance was powerful enough to remove your eye?"

"Itagaki."

"And her fate, pray tell?"

"She was cut in half, but lived."

"And the fate of her *Onna Bugei-sha*."

"Most of them dead. One half of her cried over what remained of their corpses."

"The next time, she too must perish so that the future may live. Thus spake Zarathustra."

Mandukhai's eye bubbled and popped to true form, restoring itself as she spoke further of the conflict. She explained the details of the Nexus Zone battle while her hand of new fingers reached under the table and smoothed up his thigh, and this prompted him to summon the waitress, Angelia Jolie, and order a bottle of 1938 Chardonnay from Burgundy (stolen from a private Napa Valley collection in 1996). While they conversed, Angelina Jolie returned a minute later, glaring like a wild beast at Mandukhai. Edison knew it was Eréndira, once again stupidly attempting to disguise herself and spy on him.

He sighed, and said, "Ahhhhh, such is fate."

But why had he been insane enough to bring them together in the first place? For the trip to Mars, of course. He required two powerful and loyal magical beings to guard his flanks. Also, neither would allow themselves to be bested by the other, so both would give their all in a fight against the common World Maker foe.

Edison knew Eréndira's jealousy could topple whole nations, and between mad bouts of love with her, he tried his best to steer her blistering energy in the right direction. Before she could launch herself at the throat of her rival Mandukhai (who wished to bear him a dozen demi-god children named for Chinese mythic heroes) and thus wreck the entire restaurant and burn the sky island, not to mention overheating his glass of fine pinot, he engaged both of them with these words:

"As the world turns, ladies, the three of us will shortly be on ancient Mars."

"*Mars?* Three?" Mandukhai asked.

"Mars?" Angelina Jolie asked.

Edison pointed at Angelina Jolie and said with good cheer, "No more games. You are unmasked." Upon his last word, she shivered into her true appearance, that of Eréndira Marquez: dark Moorish skin, lustrous black night of hair, big hoops of golden jewelry and a body strong enough to wreck an armada.

The Mongol Queen stood without hesitation to face The Empress of Byzantium. The two of them glared viciously at each other, their breath coming quick, their hands clenching to wicked claws. Neither spoke. The Wizard Goddesses had hated each other with a blood mad fury for centuries and fought several times to a draw. Mandukhai once bit off Eréndira's head and Eréndira once ripped off one of Mandukhai's legs and beat her with it. Another time the two of them battled on the island of Malta in 1685 and wiped out an entire seaside village in the process. Their growls and battle thunder had been heard as far away as Palermo. Human corpses washed up on the Sicilian shore for days.

"Be seated, both of you," Edison commanded.

The two obeyed, despite their tempers.

"Another time, *Mandukhai*," Eréndira said.

"Eat maggots of goat," Mandukhai replied.

In truth though, Edison felt warmly towards both Goddesses. He loved them often, and in the most romantic of places. Once he loved Mandukhai for hours on Titan, on a dark shore of that moon beside a quiet methane lake as the rings of Saturn and the planet's thunder bands rose on the horizon. Another time he loved Eréndira within the bosom of a stellar nursery, in a nebula off the shore of the Milky Way, the two of them several miles tall at the time, though invisible beside the sheer enormity of the birthing suns.

Both of his loves would now help him foil an assassination attempt.

"Who told you of the whore's attempt to slay you?" Eréndira asked.

"Your Lord of Saravastra, the fellow with the violin," Edison said. "Apparently, he falsely believes he will somehow gain by my continued existence."

They all laughed. Edison raised his pinot in a toast.

Business as usual in the war for all time.

Thus spake Zarathustra.

* Оверман *

AS SHE LAY IN THE MUD OF THE SOMME BATTLEFIELD, Catherine looked up to see the half-moon in the eastern sky, at most a few seconds higher than before the *Dio Soldati* assault. She sat up, feeling chilled and soaked by the air and wet earth, and gazed around her. She was alone, somewhere on the eerie moaning field of No Man's Land. And her younger self? Dead before she left Mars—not unlike the hundreds of British corpses now surrounding her. At the moment, the worst thing was the memory of her own resurrection so many years ago in the black forest of Anhalt. It now became clear. She did not witness the deaths of the serf families or the horrible soul ceremony of Temujin Gur, never wished to see it through the eyes of her lover Zolo Bold, just knew at the moment, here on this muddy field, she would not be alive without their sacrifice. A twinge of guilt owned her.

Carrying the guilt is the very least I can do if I am to honor their deaths.

But how was she betrayed on Mars?

Who set in motion the events that led to her death, and those of the serfs? Black Agnes perhaps? Regardless, the battle on Mars to kill Godfellow had been a disaster from the onset. Upon slaying dozens of *Dio Soldati* and crippling dozens more, she and Freddie used their aria to reach through time, via the chrono-defense satellites, and bring Godfellow to the Somme before thrusting him backwards to ancient Mars. She felt and saw herself, above the towers of Dubai, soaring down to a floating sky island and into a small space, the invisible hands of her mind reaching out to grip the World Maker and yank him to where she stood in time-space on French soil as the Nexus Zone battle raged in the background. She recalled a glimpse of Eréndira and Mandukhai. A bit of surprise at their presence, a fleeting moment of panic, then the tug on Godfellow and his arrival like a contained explosion. But she never let go of him, and within a millisecond upon his emergence into that Nexus moment of July in the year 1916, she locked his throat from behind and wrenched up with enough force to rip the Parthenon at Athens from its base. He howled in pain while a flash of brilliant aria, a moment later, transported the three of them to Mars, wrapped in a cocoon of Tao.

Hurtling out of the sky towards the Martian surface like titanic bodies of blinding cosmic force, they hit the planet with enough impact to shudder it from pole to pole and slow its rotation. Earth astronomers would see the crater many millions of years later and name it the Hellas Crater. And the dying glow above that red world, swirling in the towers of hot steam erupting into the atmosphere from a Martian sea vaporized upon impact, they proceeded to skewer Godfellow like a wild game animal. The energy cocoon and the multi-megaton concussion on Mars had not fizzled him down to base atoms, so she and her younger self reacted in tenths of a second by driving power-spiked yarrow swords, seven feet long, into his body. The very force of their impaling thrusts launched them into the Martian air, high above the roaring heat and flames of the impact crater. Her own yarrow sword drove so terrifically into Godfellow's body that it skewered him from tailbone to head, the tip of the blade protruding a full foot from the top of his skull, the blood of his brain bubbling on the steel.

Writhing in a death struggle like mighty gods, their World Maker aria sang and flowed into the blades, and Edison J. B. Godfellow struggled and shrieked in the Martian blue sky like a dying tyrannosaur, enough voltage filling his body to light every city on Earth for a week. Still, death did not come as the huge clouds of boiling steam hid the small sun and giant earthquakes shook the planet below. It seemed Mars itself would die before that jackal Godfellow, for his sheathing of protective spells diverted or negated much of the stupendous aria force brought to bear on him. In consequence, frustration and anxiety began to nip at the Czarina and Princess von Anhalt, and as if his refusal to die wasn't bad enough, the sun itself began to fight on his behalf. It became the enraged and glowing face of Eréndira Marquez, plummeting towards them at a speed of thousands of miles per hour.

Catherine had no time to slow time before impact. Her younger self was struck behind by Eréndira with such force that it drove the two of them down to the Martian surface, though at such a slant that they shot beyond the flaming Hellas Crater.

Now, beneath the quiet moon of the Somme, Catherine remembered the fight, two billion years ago. Her mouth opened to scream as Eréndira's black mandibles snapped deep into her head, the wizard woman's crushing legs locked around her waist while both hands drove growling and thirsty yarrow blades into lungs and heart. Stones on the Martian surface, big as Berlin carriages, smacked her in the face, flying apart to rubble as she and Eréndira dug a small canyon. Then a final pounding boom into a mountain. The Empress of Byzantium, her muscles rippling like a female Samson, wrestled Freddie's body with a death grip. The two of them thrashed over the sand, but no escape. The Princess von Anhalt could not unloosen or shake the snarling Wizard Goddess who had fastened on her like a huge predatory insect, repeatedly screaming "DIE CZARINA WHORE!"

And with mandibles locked, blades driven, muscles heaving with enough exertion to snap a skyscraper, Eréndira broke Freddie's spine.

All went black.

Recalling it now, death had been welcome.

As her younger self died on the Martian surface, her own hands were full with fighting Mandukhai. The Mongol Queen, streaking across the sky like Eréndira, had impacted less than half a second later. The strike and momentum carried them both miles away from the impaled and screaming Godfellow. No time for weapons, they punched and wrestled in mid-air, turning end over end. She hit Mandukhai over a hundred times in three seconds, and the Mongol wizard goddess returned the blows. Beams of steel-melting heat flowed from Mandukhai's eyes to sweep Catherine's body. Catherine spit diamond-corroding acid into Mandukhai's face. One powerful, ring-heavy hand of the Mongol grabbed Catherine by the hair, savagely yanking her head back to break her neck while the other hand dug sharp nails of terrible white voltage into her breasts, and all the while her mouth shouting violent spells with her heavy, man-like voice. One made Catherine's fingers shrivel for a moment while another boiled her eyes. Catherine fired back with words of vicious aria that shivered Mandukhai, and as the combat surged, the two of them grew larger, to groaning, roaring giants a hundred feet tall or more, each attempting to bite and swallow the other. The Czarina's mind was lost to berserker rage, and knowing all the pain and murder the female Mongol stooge of Godfellow had visited upon so many, her desire to slay Mandukhai became psychotic with intensity.

Finally, after nearly a minute of extreme fighting, as the two colossal women clashed like biting hyenas high above a Martian mountain range—the clouds of the Hellas Crater becoming a drifting white plume in the background while massive earthquakes still rocked the planet surface—Catherine recovered enough sense to shout an aria phrase that changed the course of battle.

She imagined it first, and sang, very simply:

Garra os seus ollos, Mandukhai de Mongolia! (Claw out your own eyes, Mandukhai of Mongolia!)

Whereupon, the wizard goddess did just that. Her hands gouged at her own eyes and she shrieked and did not stop shrieking, not even when the face of Edison Godfellow blotted out the entire sky west of their position. An enraged and murderous Czarina glanced up to see the face smile at her, and all went black.

* Оверман *

IN THE DARK SHELL CRATER, THE SMELLS OF BLOOD and mud filled Catherine's nostrils once more. As she considered this, one of the British corpses only a few feet away, suddenly reared upright, rigor mortis having lifted him before her eyes. The helmet fell from the head, and she saw he was a handsome man. He dangled a white cigarette in one hand, his face casual. *Such a strange sight in this twisted field of shocked and dismal corpses.* Though Catherine had witnessed many bizarre things as a World Maker, this particular sight she found eerie and disturbing.

She tried to ignore it and consider how she got there.

Mars was lost. Godfellow lived. But again, how did he know? And now, what difference did it make? The conflict point of battle against the *Dio Soldati* and Mandukhai had been lost also. This must be the case. All about her on the torn French field had returned to that dead quiet night after the July 1 assault. No German forces turned the British right flank. No creeping barrage.

For all my plans and power, what have I produced except for a new hole on Mars?

As she attempted to trace possible lines from Black Agnes to Godfellow, the cigarette held in the death grip of the nearby corpse began to smolder and smoke. It made her take notice. The hand holding it moved. It lifted the cigarette to its lips and inhaled the smoke and blew it out. The corpse said, "Ahhhhhh, such is fate." It then turned its head to stare at her. The handsome face smiled. The body of the corpse relaxed all stiffness. It continued to smoke the cigarette. In a Welsh accent, it said:

"Bloody bad business, this war."

Catherine said nothing, just stared and waited.

"All wars, bloody bad business, eh?" it spoke again, and blew a few smoke rings. "I would rather do without them. My family were sheep farmers, and I hated sheep. That's why I joined the British army. But sheep don't look so bad now, eh?" It chuckled and smoked.

She tried to read the mind of the thing, but she was blocked. No surprise really. She said to it with a flat voice, "Private Zarathustra of Wales, I presume?"

It chuckled again. "So you don't waste time, eh? Alright, fine bird, I am who you believe I am. *Adfyd a ddwg wybodaeth, a gwybodaeth ddoethineb.*"

"Adversity brings knowledge, and knowledge, wisdom. A fine Welsh saying."

"You always impress me, darlin', but you have to learn to properly scheme, eh?"

"Who betrayed me?"

The eyes of it gazed at her body through the cigarette smoke. Catherine noticed for the first time that she was naked and filthy with French mud. *Hard to keep clothes on when gouging out craters and catfighting over Mars.* The eyes fixed on her breasts and moved lower. The Welsh corpse said with a slow and deep voice, "You would be surprised. But you will learn, in time ... it *was all* for the best."

"Stop staring at me, creature."

"You will never win, Czarina."

She rolled her eyes and in that moment, the soldier corpse lunged at her. He threw his body atop hers and pinned her to the ground. The cold mud oozed up to her cheeks. His humorless face of cigarette breath blotted out the moon. She attempted to force him off and her body bucked, but the Welsh corpse could not be shaken. She became afraid. After shelling and death and all manner of supernatural insanity, she now feared a British army corpse intent on rape most of all.

"I want you," it said, "I have wanted you for years, and *that is why* the others hate you because they know my true desire."

"Remove yourself, or I will—"

"Or you will love me, like nobody has loved me, come rain or come Somme."

Catherine bucked again, helpless, and could not feel the aria in her, and she began to panic. How could he diminish her, and so easily? The corpse did not grin or change expression, except in the eyes. The eyes warmed with love, then the corpse buried its face in her neck and bit her.

She screamed.

The other corpses nearby failed to notice.

царица

12

Freddie Loses So Much · Virgin Mary Agony · Necropolis of The Khan

FREDDIE FOUND HERSELF LYING FACE UP ON HER BED in Bärenthoren Castle. All quiet. Before she opened her eyes she recalled the final snap of pain as Eréndira broke her back on Mars. Upon opening her eyes, she glanced down to see Zolo's cloak covering her body, and up to see him sitting on the bed beside her, staring down at her with warm and soulful eyes. He reached out his hand and stroked her cheek. "How do you feel?" he said softly. She replied that she felt a little tired, otherwise fine.

"How did I come here?" she asked.

"I found you outside the walls, laying on the ground, unconscious."

"Just like that?"

"Yes."

"You are a poor liar, Mister Bold."

"I—"

"I see by your face, you are lying or leaving something out, thus creating the effect of a lie."

"I cannot say, I cannot. You must trust me in this."

"How is my father?" Zolo did not answer. Freddie sat up in the bed, her back against the headboard. "I asked you—"

"He is ... no more."

Though she knew it must happen, the shock of it still affected her. She lifted her hands to her face and sobbed. Zolo moved to comfort her and held her shoulders, rubbing his hands up and down her arms. "I am so so sorry," he said. "There was nothing I—"

"He was in your care," she said, her voice muffled by her hands and sobs. "He was in *your care*. I trusted you to watch over him."

"I was unable. It became impossible."

"You are a spellcrafter. You are strong. How could it have been *impossible?*" she said, removing hands from her teary face to stare at him.

"Temujin Gur took me prisoner. It happened during that time."

"How did it happen? Was my monstrous mother involved?"

Zolo told her that upon his return to the castle, he heard talk of Prince Christian's death. Shot by a pistol in the head, in his study last evening. The kitchen staff and butlers say a bitter musketeer killed him over an issue of back pay. The man was crazy. He'd been seen talking to himself and picking fights. Princess Johanna ordered him seized and thrown from the Bärenthoren walls. A funeral forthcoming and Princess Johanna in official mourning, seen by no one but her closest maidservants, and Empress Elizabeth who is comforting her.

"She is probably lying ..." Freddie sobbed a bit more and struggled to regain her wits. "But why did Temujin Gur hold you prisoner? Where did he hold you?"

"In the forest, near where I found your body."

"Why?"

"I do not know. His beetle, his face beetle lay atop me. There was a fire. I heard screams. I could not see ... then he let me go."

"What are you hiding? Do you wish me to *trust you?*"

She could see this question hurt Zolo deeply. His face looked surprised and sorrowful. "Please, princess, you must trust me. I have not betrayed you."

"Fill in the holes in this story and I will trust you."

"Alright then ... You will know sooner or later," he said, staring into her eyes, resigning himself to tell as much truth as he could. "Gur's magic lifted me from the castle and took me deep in the forest last night. He wanted me present when he brought you back to life. He wanted me to tell you what he did, what happened."

"I was dead then? *Really dead?*"

"Yes, you ... your corpse appeared in Bärenthoren Castle first. No one recognized it as you. You looked like a wild animal had ripped off your skin and chewed you in parts."

"I am not surprised, given events," Freddie said, recalling the breaking of her spine.

"He restored you to life with a ceremony that used the living forms of others ... The serfs, the serfs from Baron Eichmann. He killed them, used their souls to resurrect you. I was held down and forced to watch."

"How did they die?"

Zolo hesitated, his face grim. "Do not make me tell you. You know what you need to know."

"Are they all dead then, all of them?"

"Yes, every one, as far as I know."

"I delivered them to a horrible fate," she said, the serfs rising up in her head to plead their lives be restored. "I solve nothing," she said in a low voice, her expression one of sorrow and dejection.

"Temujin Gur chose them. He wanted you to be in pain over it. You *did not* kill them!" Zolo said, reaching out and shaking her slightly by the shoulders. He did not wish her to feel guilt. Pain was unavoidable, but guilt not necessary.

Freddie closed her eyes again. More pain came to her. When would it end? "And what of Babette?" she asked, concerned and looking for some measure of relief.

Zolo's face went quiet and dark. "She ... she—"

"What?"

"She has vanished from the castle. No one knows anything. I have been using Mother Yarrow to search and we cannot find her."

Freddie jumped from the bed, and gripping Zolo by his shirt, yanked him to his feet also. "I will not lose, Babette! I have lost enough! I will NOT LOSE BABETTE!" she shouted furiously at him. "If Mother Yarrow and you cannot locate her, it means she is covered by a spell, and no one here has the power to hide her from a Mother Yarrow but Temujin Gur."

"Yes, I know. I thought that also," Zolo said, trying to stay calm.

"He must be holding her hostage! We must act!"

"I do not know. We—"

Freddie blew up in rage at Zolo's calm and confusion before he could explain himself. She hotly stared at him and yelled, "What do you know about anything? You are a fool! My father's life was in your keeping. You let him die! You were *squashed by a bug* while all of those poor people perished in front of you, and you *could do nothing!* And now Babette has been kidnapped on your watch. Another failure! What good are you? To speak of democracy? What matters that now? For us? ... *For anything?*"

Zolo faced her, stunned to no movement. His face a solid expression of shock, as if he had just witnessed the death of his beloved mother Avizeh.

Freddie let go of his shirt and turned from him, trying to get herself under control so she could think. She said to Zolo without turning around, "You must leave me now, and do not return until I have summoned you. And *do nothing* unless I command it."

Zolo did not reply.

She continued. "Do you understand?"

Zolo ignored her and silently walked to the rear of the bedchamber to access the secret door and escape her madness. She watched him go, her eyes narrowing with anger. "Do you understand?" she called after him. He did not reply, only vanished within the walls of Bärenthoren.

Within less than a minute, Freddie realized the wrong she had committed, and for an instant, even imagined herself a younger version of Princess Johanna. She gasped. Such a thing could not be possible, and yet, the first step towards that condition could not be denied.

Atonement was necessary. But first things first.

* Оверман *

HER ARIA WHISPERED *BABETTE* IN ALL PLACES, from beneath the smallest leaf in Anhalt to mile-deep crevices in Earth, from the shore of Normandy to the peaks of the Alps, but no voice answered back. Using Mother Yarrow to assist in the search, she had flown unseen from the castle upon Zolo's departure. While she searched in a state of desperation, afraid to lose someone she'd dearly loved since a child, she still thought to ask Maria of Pozzuoli about their betrayal to Master Godfellow. She wanted a quick answer, if possible, and she would deal with the details and consequences later.

Maria would only say, *The fault is not mine.*

This response puzzled Freddie, though no time to pursue the matter. She also could not address the guilt now nipping at her mind over yelling so harshly at Zolo. No time for that either.

Damn everything else!

About a half hour later, well beyond the lands of Anhalt, she heard violin music in the air. *Skanda, yes!* It played the dream-creating music, the same tune she'd heard before going to Saravastra for the first time. It emanated from a place deep in the dark forest below her. Without hesitation, she dived straight down for hundreds of feet into the thick branches of the trees and found the music box, the one from her bedside table in Bärenthoren, found it sitting on a thick branch of an old oak above a forest brook. All her hopes for the return of Babette focused on that box, and on what lay beyond in Tibet more than a hundred years in the future.

Master Paganini will know Babette's fate, or he will help me save her. He must!

She reached out to the box as the violin music filled her ears, and as she touched it, her hand also touched a man's face. His skin was a light brown hue in the sunlight, and he smiled at her with a face of soothing warm water. Four golden buttons inscribed with yarrow symbols, the size of small coins, fastened in his flesh: one to either side of his upper cheeks, and two more, one atop the other above his brows. On his head he wore a half moon hat, and on his body, an orange robe. She recognized him as one of Saravastra's spell captains.

The kindly Bodhisattva reached up and placed his hand on Freddie's arm. He pulled her to the ground beside him, as one would a birthday balloon that had floated carelessly to the ceiling. An early morning sun rose in a light blue sky above her. She stood atop a red-tiled patio of some kind, long and wide as the Great Hall, and in the distance, the peaks of the snowy Himalayas. Was she atop a building in Saravastra?

On the surface of this floor, scores of orange-robed Bodhisattva spell captains in their half-moon hats formed a one large yarrow pattern of curls and crescents, sticks and dots, and they all chanted in a low tone, their arms enfolded before them within the broad sleeves of their robes. The sound of a calming Skanda drifted on the wind from the Himalayas—Paganini's 4th Caprice, melancholy in parts, yet hypnotic. Freddie felt at peace as she listened, then an immediate pang of guilt for such thoughts of peace.

How could she allow it? Babette was still missing.

From among the chanting Bodhisattvas stepped Master Paganini. He did not play the violin, yet the music continued, flowing along with the chanting. He wore an orange robe and a half moon hat, just like his spell captains. He did not smile as he approached Freddie, and if she did not know better, she would believe him angry with her. He did not seem a friendly man in the first place, only now, a new edge was visible.

Does it involve the Battle of the Somme? Mars? Master Godfellow?

He beckoned her with his eyes to follow him. They strolled to the east end of the landing, well beyond the big yarrow symbol formed by the spell captains. He stopped and faced her. The sun blazed into her eyes, just above the head of Paganini as if it had arisen from his mind, freshly formed and life-giving, yet ready to burn her to char for her trespasses.

"We have a terrible task ahead of us," he said. His eyes bored into hers so strongly that the sun was forgotten. Perhaps his eyes alone would burn her to char. "We must face the pain of those we love, and rise beyond."

"What do you mean, Master Paganini?" she asked, her voice trembling a bit.

"People we love are in terrible pain. And we must end it."

"Yes, but please tell me. Where is Babette?"

"Once Gur summons us, you will know, and that will be very soon."

"Us? You are coming with me, back to—"

"I am with you, my future Czarina. All of us are with *you now*" he said, lifting an arm and sweeping his hand to indicate the chanting spell captains of Saravastra. "We will be close, with Mother Yarrow Maria as our bridge."

"Then we cannot lose?" She wished to believe that.

"You should know, nothing is certain. The best plans go wrong, even with strong wills and arms behind them. You do *understand that now*, do you not?" he asked, his eyes and voice telling her he knew about the failed plan to kill Master Godfellow.

"Yes," she replied, her eyes falling from his gaze. She suddenly felt ashamed.

"Gur will cross the Nicholas Line. He will use your World Maker aria to hide the two of you from the chrono-defense satellites that Edison and I placed in orbit tens of millions of years ago. He will then resurrect the Lord of The Bow at his necropolis in Mongolia and bond with him."

"Bond with him?"

"Gur intends to place a portion of his soul in the newly resurrected Genghis Khan, so that he may live out the life of an immortal man who will rule the new world with a savagery that will surpass all prior savagery. Nothing could make Gur happier, and once his hero is restored, he will force you to use every drop of your remaining power to destroy our satellites so that no one will ever use them to undo his plan."

"And his plans for me?"

"He will cook you and serve you to the Mongol aristocracy."

"What?" Freddie flared with anger. "I shall eat that monster first! ... But what of Mandukhai?"

"She is loyal. She is in love with him."

"That does not matter now. Send me to Babette. I will kill Gur once—"

"No, you will *not kill Gur*."

Paganini explained the plan. Freddie will do Gur's bidding, help him resurrect the Khan at the Necropolis, but once done, proceed to defy the Mongolian by putting Genghis to death following his resurrection, and of course, whatever else necessary to force retaliation, to stir the Mongol into such a blind rage that he will unleash his full force to annihilate her.

"Gur's temper has always been his fatal flaw, and his hatred for Europeans runs deep. He actually loathes you more than anyone else," Paganini said.

Behind every false smile of Gur, a boiling rage of ancient bitterness, an undying hatred for those he thought harbored a notion they were superior to him, for those he believed to despise or distrust his Mongol ancestry. In his mind too, Freddie symbolized European entitlement and arrogance. Gur will reason, in the flow of mounting anger, that he can deal with the satellites, in one way or another using his own resources, and then he will turn his magic into a lethal and unstoppable blow that will scatter her atoms to the edge of the galaxy. And once he commits to the blow, "We will slow the march of seconds, and march forward with our own power." Saravastra's spell captains and Mother Yarrow Maria, Skanda and the mighty aria of the Princess von Anhalt, will combine their Tao with the colossal force of Gur's rage, and at the moment before strike, Skanda will open a gate to Dubai in 2038 and War Tracker will be incinerated with enough force to burn the moon to vapor.

"War Tracker, yes ... I should have known," Freddie said, dazed by the knowledge of Paganini's plan.

"Yes, War Tracker, my precious World Maker," he said, his face softening to a look that resembled true affection. "The goal has never changed. Only the accursed Gur, working with us, can enable success. He will actually do a good thing, and for the first time in his life."

Freddie paused, and upon considering her overall situation, said to him, "It's odd, Master Paganini, but it seems as though the more World Maker power I acquire, the closer I come to death."

"That is so, and you have already died once. Is that not enough?" he said, his face cooling to stone. "But we will be with you, and Gur will know nothing."

"And Babette?"

"She is alive, but only through the death of Gur will she be safe. As we focus on War Tracker, Gur will be consumed by the fire he helped create. We have much pain ahead of us."

"Much pain, Master Paganini?"

"We will suffer the pain that comes to those we love. All of us here will feel that pain, young woman, through you."

Freddie stared at him. To her, he now appeared as if warming to concern. Was he really though? They both knew nothing was certain. The plan might work, it might not. But if she helped to destroy War Tracker and thereby save her loved ones, she will have accomplished something worthwhile, at long last—or so she wished to believe.

The chanting and violin music brimmed to the front of her consciousness once more. She breathed deeply and walked around Paganini to look down thousands of feet and across to the dreaming cityscape of Saravastra. As before, white gulls of human being, hundreds of them, glided and soared between the soft golden towers, through the sunlit mist and drifting puffs of cloud, and beyond to the snowy mountains. *A godlike city on the verge of eternity.* All was poetry and peace, in a harmony so far beyond the presence of war that she could not believe it possible.

* Оверман *

TEMUJIN GUR GAZED FONDLY UPON THE SCREAMING VIRGIN MARY cocoons rattling in the old torture dungeon deep below Bärenthoren Castle. One screamed with the voice of a man, the other with the voice of a woman. Only minutes before, both occupants had been slammed and nailed inside. In time, Gur knew, their screams would dissolve to whimpers and groans as the iron points piercing their flesh from eyes to ankles drew ounce after ounce of blood, and the relentless, unbearable pain sapped the strength from their naked bodies. Temujin Gur therefore needed to summon the Princess von Anhalt as soon as possible, for he wished her to be a part of the fresh agony. He desired the European bitch to hear the screams, see the quivering Virgin Mary cocoons and the blood running from their toes, and know the people she loved most in the world were dying slowly and painfully while she watched, helpless to prevent it.

A bonus source of pleasure for Gur resulted from the anguish of a Mother Yarrow, her voice calling out to him from across the centuries, begging him to stop. He ignored it, of course, and only smiled to himself. Soon enough, the whole of accursed western civilization would be begging him, The God of The White Mongols—not only for an end to death and pain, but for all manner of things. And they would have to beg, on their bellies, grovel like pitiful snakes. Let one stand and defy him and that one would be tossed into a Virgin Mary. All the bravest and best of white Europe, locked and dying horribly in the Virgin Mary. Tens of thousands of them scattered throughout the countryside from Bavaria to Normandy. Entire forests of Virgin Mary bleeding Europe into the earth.

Yes, yes, the Virgin Mary Forest!

A delightful plan, a dreamy concept. His magic would make them live for many more days. More days of suffering and bleeding, whimpering and screaming. White Mongol poets and bards would record his glory, sing of him to the world. Tapestries would be woven depicting the Virgin Mary Forest and himself as The Lord of The Bow, Genghis Khan, floating above it, frowning down like an angry god. Or he might prefer glorious rays of light beaming from his head, like a wise and benevolent god.

To realize this fondest dream though, he must first summon the Princess von Anhalt.

Gur hated that he must depend on her. *That shriek of a white creature!* He despised the noble feline more than anyone else on the planet. Her defiance and arrogance, her dramatic concern for the wretched serfs, her "born to the royal gold" made him desire her death, and in a most horrible way. Nothing had been more satisfying than the morning he lashed her viciously and bit into her head, whipping her back and forth like a lion with shred of meat. His soothing vision of cooking and eating her with the Mongol aristocracy at once filled him with bliss. What vision could be more satisfying? What revenge more complete? And he would enjoy every savory bite. Her bones would pick his teeth and her skull would weight down papers on his London desk, for he believed some administration of the White Mongol Empire would be necessary— though he detested such matters, being a man of the wild open steppes in his heart.

So it begins!

Temujin Gur allowed the screams of the woman in the Virgin Mary, the nanny of Anhalt, to leak out of the torture dungeon and into the surrounding countryside. Her piteous cries would be heard all the way to the Cathedral of Magdeburg. Gur knew the hated Euro-bitch was nearby, searching, most likely begging help from the accursed Paganini. The sounds of her nanny in deathly pain would bring her flying in soon enough, lure her down to the depths of his personal Hell. Besides, what more fitting place to begin the transformation of the world than among symbols of European savagery and barbarism?

* Оверман *

FREDDIE HEARD THE PITIFUL SHRIEKING OF BABETTE even before she left Saravastra. The sound pierced the ears of her body, sitting in that tree, and it shrilled in her as she turned to say farewell to Master Paganini. He heard it too, through her, and his eyes filled with sympathy. A tear rolled down his face. His words, "much pain ahead" suddenly translated into reality. She let out a gasp and cried out, "Babette, no!" The knowledge that the woman she adored was in such terrible pain drove a cold lance through her. She shook for a moment before she vanished, and Master Paganini would never forget that wide-eyed expression of shock on her young face.

Less than a moment later, Freddie's legs thrust her body up with such violent force that the thick oaken branch, over a century old, snapped and crashed to the ground. Her body sprung from the tops of the forest and into the air, leveling out at two thousand feet and bearing down on Bärenthoren Castle, meteoric as Eréndira plummeting down from the Martian sky.

And while she soared, the anguished screams of Babette filled the world.

Thousands and thousands of birds scattered from the trees and rose to form big black clouds throughout the lands of Anhalt, the birds darting in frantic circles before flying to safety faraway as Saxony. Flocks of grazing sheep and cows for miles around began running and crying as if chased by a pack of wolves. Serfs in the fields froze where they stood, baffled and terrorized, and the residents of castle Bärenthoren behaved in similar fashion. Many knew the screams belonged to Babette, and they crossed themselves and muttered prayers for their own protection, and even the shrewd and murderous Empress Elizabeth, and the tyrant of Anhalt, Princes Johanna, felt the true ice of terror touch their black souls.

Landing in her bedchamber, Freddie followed the screams into the walls. She did not bother to open the secret panel door. She simply smashed through the stone and exploded into the dark hallway that led to the staircase. The entire castle shook with the force of it, and in the distance, the maidservants could be heard screaming. Freddie had caught a fleeting glimpse of Alexander the Great as she sped through the room. She saw his spear and focused on that.

I will be a spear. Yes!

She would pierce the heart of whatever foul thing hurt Babette.

Down the stone staircase she ran, shouting, "Babette! I am coming!" and in moments found herself in the dungeon doorway, smelling the odor of blood and staring at two Virgin Mary cocoons, their metal glimmering in the firelight, trembling with the death-shaking of those imprisoned within.

"God, oh God, ahhhhh ha hahhhh!" Babette screamed like a child on fire, her voice erupting from the Virgin Mary on her right. But who was trapped in the other? And then Freddie knew. She realized the second Virgin Mary victim was Zolo Bold. His agonized and muffled voice shouted to her: *"Go! Do not try to save me!"*

Horror-struck, her eyes wide open and tearing, she could not move or speak. Seconds later, a voice from the dungeon entered her consciousness:

"To witness the anguish of your enemies as they watch their loved ones suffer and die in pain is indeed one of the greatest joys in life."

Temujin Gur! Freddie's eyes followed the source and she saw him standing off to the side. The fires of the dungeon flared at his back, shadows flickering over his smiling Buddha face, his silver face-beetle skittering up and down as if restless. But no time to ponder. The terrible sounds of Babette and Zolo tore at her soul.

"ENOUGH!" she said to Gur, her voice magnified to a wall-quaking volume by her power and fear. "FREE THEM AND I WILL DO YOUR BIDDING!"

"You will do my bidding, whether I free them or no. But I choose not to."

Shaking the walls once again, Freddie shouted her raging frustration at the Mongol wizard in a bellow that sounded like a mad bull elephant crossed with a wounded mother tiger:

"DAMN YOUR BLACK SOUL TO FUCKING HELL!"

"Heart eating hell would suit me better, Princess von Anhalt," Gur said and laughed.

"So shall it be, Mongol goat! I will send you there NOW!"

Overcome by the fury of the moment, and brimming with aria heat, she began to sing, *Morte atopar vostede agora* (Death find you now ...), but suddenly, a thick needle of pain drove deep into the muscle and sinew of her lower neck. Her scream of pain cut off the aria. "What in Hell!" she shouted, gripping at her neck and straining her eyes to see the source of the stabbing pain. Had Gur launched a yarrow dagger into her? "WHAT IS THIS?" she bellowed at him, the wall masonry shaking as dust to the floor.

"You *ungrateful* little Czarina," he said with a quiet voice, and chuckled. "It is a gift from me, a price you pay for having your favorite Mongol goat bring you back from the dead. You do know I saved your life, or has the honorable Senator Zolo failed to inform you?"

Freddie did not answer, only gritted her teeth with the ongoing pain of the dagger-like stab. She cried out again as the pain intensified then lessened, as though Temujin Gur twisted an invisible blade, though only for a few moments.

Gur continued. "Did he also not reveal the deaths of your serf friends? ... No? I burned their souls from them, one at a time, and fed you. They died most horribly so that you could be here."

Before Freddie could respond, Gur winked and her body lurched into the air. She flew forward and spun around, slamming backwards into one of the dungeon torture wheels. Iron clasps snapped hard on her wrists and ankles. She cried out and struggled, but to no avail. Gur's magic sapped her strength, and the wheel began to turn until she was upside down, breathing heavily and beginning to panic. She could hear Zolo struggling in the Virgin Mary, striving to escape to help her, sobbing with his failure, and even through the pain and insanity she felt a razor slice of guilt at the cruelty she'd showed him.

Babette's screams, meanwhile, had died to painful moans and gasps.

Freddie knew the woman she loved was on the verge of death.

"Will you respect my forthcoming request, Princess von Anhalt?" Gur asked.

"Yes, damn you, YES!"

"Good! As follows then. You will accompany me south of the Nicholas Line to a place in Mongolia centuries ago. A minor task really. I simply wish to enact a spell that will change my destiny and free me from this disgusting world of Europe. Will that not be a good thing, Czarina?"

"Yes, yes, *ahhhhh*, blessed God—"

"While I conduct my business, your wondrous aria will confound the damnable sky things belonging to the two wretched Italians. Your Virgin Mary friends here will remain behind to suffer and die unless you complete your task, and if by chance I do not return, ten thousand more of your serf friends on castle estates hereabouts will die from a new black plague. It is all arranged. Also know that your own pain will continue, forever, and your aria will not cure it, for the pain will cancel it with your shrieks."

Over her own breath of panic and the piteous sounds that filled the air, Freddie suddenly heard a whispering voice. It belonged to Master Paganini:

We of Saravastra are here with you. Courage, young woman.

And another voice, that of Maria of Pozzuoli:

I am here also, Princess Friederike!

A small comfort in the midst of a world become a nightmare of suffering death. "Let us get on with it then!" she yelled to Gur as she hung upside down.

"Very well!" he exclaimed, very happy with his success. He spit forth his extra mouths and they fluttered out like fire-yellow butterflies to free Freddie from the wheel. They released the shackles then bit into her arms and turned her upright to face him. She winced at the bites and he licked his lips, tasting her blood with his phantom mouths. "Hmmm, the unique tang of Czarina," he said and laughed again. "If only I could devour you right now!"

She knew what the beast meant, though showed no sign of understanding. She would play along, she must. She watched as Gur lifted his arms and four black yarrow sticks drifted out and up into the air above their heads. Gur muttered a few words in that Chinese-like language, all gravely and alien, and the yarrow sticks spun and began to hum. The tune sounded almost like a slow Caprice by Master Paganini, melancholy yet beautiful. Other sounds too, whispering voices, as if the yarrow sticks spoke to each other.

"Feel your aria! Protect us!" Gur shouted at her, his smiling face replaced by a stern expression. All fun was over. Worlds hung in the balance. "Sing your aria, Czarina! NOW!"

Freddie showed no emotion, just stared at him and felt her brilliant aria once more, this time without punishment, and she sang strong and pure:

> *Nada nos ver,*
> *Nada nos escoitarrrr.*
> *Ningunha máxica saaabe*
> *Vivimos ou respirarrr.*

(Nothing see us, / Nothing hear us. / No magic know / We live or breathe.)

* Оверман*

AS THE TORTURE DUNGEON FADED FROM VIEW, the dying sounds of Zolo and Babette did also. In a few moments, Freddie found herself in pitch blackness, though a floor remained beneath her feet. The air felt cold, much colder than the dungeon in Bärenthoren. A silvery light glowed into being, somewhere high above her. At first, she thought it a moon. Then she noticed, it sprouted legs. Upon closer look, she realized it to be the silver face beetle of Temujin Gur. It filled the air with a moon-silver light and revealed her to be standing in a cavernous room, one at least three times larger than the Great Hall of Bärenthoren Castle.

She glanced around for Gur but he had vanished. To either side of her she saw what appeared to be soldiers on horses. Lines of them facing her, hundreds in rank after rank: Mongol warriors of polished stone wearing moon-gleaming iron helmets with pointed tops, white tufts of horsehair flowing from the peaks, and their bodies fitted with thick, brown-lacquered armor. All carried round wicker shields and gripped tall lances that pointed to the ceiling. Each shadowy face though was different, as if each possessed the soul of a dead warrior, a real man who lived and died in that savage age; and in that eerie light, the hard and violent faces of those long dead Mongols, hundreds of them, all seemed to stare at her.

Would they charge and impale her if she made the wrong move?

Next, she heard a sound, like a small stone striking iron in the distance. She looked across the lines of Mongol cavalry statues, and raising her eyes, saw a figure seated atop what appeared to be a throne. It towered above the statues, set upon a tall marble dais. The figure was sheathed in golden plate armor, head to foot, and rising high in the moon-silvery darkness beyond, a terraced hill, like a black staircase for giants, and on each terrace, the glitter of countless objects.

Then she understood.

The objects were treasures, thousands upon thousands of them made of gold and silver, jewels and rare woods. She peered closer. On an upper terrace, she saw a gleaming, silver tree seven feet high. It grew lion paw roots and sprouted dozens of feather-leaf branches, all of finest silver, balls of golden lemon dangling from its stems. Another treasure was a ship twice as big as the Anhalt World Stormer possessing two masts of solid gold and six sails of thinnest white-gold, its hull of pure ebony inlaid with thousands of rubies. More statues too, of Mongol and Chinese royalty and their court followers, as well as the giant marble heads of conquered kings, mounds of trinkets, coins, bowls, plates, and more.

You stand within the Necropolis of The Khan.

Paganini's voice.

No chance to reply though. Erupting from the air of beetle moon, the words of Temujin Gur echoed down to her and rippled through the Necropolis. "YOU ARE DOING WELL TO HIDE US, OR ELSE WE WOULD SURELY BE DEAD BY NOW."

Freddie said nothing. She seethed inside to make him pay, and the presence of his voice refocused her rage. She felt grateful to possess it. Such rage became a weapon, prepared to ruthlessly strike, and she would prepare her foe for this strike soon enough. She heard Skanda begin to play, deep in her mind, the music muffled as if on the other side of a thick wall, but a rapid and strong Caprice nonetheless.

Paganini said to her:

I will deny him the pain of the yarrow scar. But you must allow the Khan to rise.

Again, Gur spoke, his tone more stern. He wished Freddie to be impressed. "Do you see, sad princess? This man of gold on a golden throne, this man is the Lord of The Bow, Leader of All Beneath The Eternal Blue Sky, GENGHIS KHAN, WORLD SLAYER!"

Freddie replied to Gur by yelling, "He looks more like the ass of a horse smeared with yellow paint!" She knew this comment was bad timing, but her mouth was dumber than her head. The yarrow knife dug in and twisted. "*Ahhhhhh*, damn!" she cried out. Again, another twist, enough to make her sob. Paganini's Skanda grew louder in her mind, more fervent. The pain of the yarrow knife dimmed at once, and she calmed, believing she now heard the distant chanting of those orange-robed Saravastra spell captains.

Or was it the Mongol statue cavalry whispering a war song?

"Careful, you might have to answer to the Khan!" Gur shouted. "NOW BE SILENT!"

She felt a twinge of pain in her neck again, but far less than before. The magic of Paganini had dampened Gur's power. But she must pretend, for Gur's sake. She cried out to prove her pain, and shouted, "I will be silent, Temujin Gur, I swear it!"

"Thank you," Gur said calmly, the voice behind her.

Freddie pivoted in surprise to see him a few feet away, staring and serious as a death toll. "I completed the spell while you stood here like a fool, knowing nothing. I have been gathering souls for a century at least, from European mothers and their children, and I fed them to the Lord of The Bow, like a mother nursing a child."

Freddie glanced up to search for the golden warrior atop the throne, but he had vanished. As she dropped her eyes to refocus on Gur, a figure moved into the light from behind him. Wearing golden armor plate and Mongol warrior helmet, the figure stepped forward to face Freddie. His eyes appeared emerald green in the moon-like light, and the skin of his hands and face, a silvery white. His cheeks were Asian broad, jaw squared and prominent, and his facial expression, cold and savage as a winter of fangs drawing blood. After all, was he not the greatest killer or "World Slayer" the world has ever known? Whatever he was, Freddie remained defiant, returning his cold stare with her own.

The Khan examined her and spoke not a word, his expression unchanged. A second or two later though, it shifted, almost imperceptibly. She detected a growing lust. The thing began to imagine a rape. She knew it! She could see it and she glared at him with a look of pure defiance. The lips of the World Slayer lifted in a slight grin. Her defiance only aroused him further, only caused him to imagine yet more rape.

The Khan is born. You must now begin. Courage, Czarina!

In the World Slayer's face, she laughed, and pointing a finger at him, laughed even louder. Gur yelled, "That is enough, Prussian garbage!" and she felt a slight pinch in her neck. She shouted, "*Owwww ahhhh!*" as though in incredible agony, her face twisting. The lip of Genghis raised in contempt. He growled something at Gur, and to reward his lip and growl, Freddie swung the back of her hand so fast Gur could not react. The force of her blow not only knocked the Khan's helmet off, but spun him around three times and dropped him to the stone floor with a loud clang of armor.

Freddie turned to Gur, smiled wickedly and winked. "There's your golden little prick of a dream!"

The Mongol began with a soundless scream.

Phantom mouths flew with little snaps from his lips, dozens of them, all howling his rage like a chorus of hysterical demons, while Fracas Machines small as hornets, poked their big-eye heads from pockets suddenly opening on Gur's face. They unsheathed themselves, sprouted legs and leapt into the air, angrily speeding towards Freddie with a shrill screech as Gur shouted, "GOD WHORE OF EUROPE, NOW YOU—"

He never finished that sentence.

A loud, flesh-cracking slap knocked him backwards for several feet—her strength and speed many times more than when last they clashed. His furious face bugs and howling lips zipped at her from all sides, stinging and biting and stabbing. She imagined them flaming cinders, and with warm aria, sang *Servos de Gur, queimar en cinzaaasss!* (Servants of Gur, burn to ash!). The swarming little pests flashed and fell to the floor, writhing in flame.

This pause to burn lips and bugs, however, allowed Gur to react.

As the little Fracas things fizzled, Temujin Gur's mouth opened to ten times its normal size. It gaped to a hellish black hole and exploded with a sonic howl of rage, loud as the English shellfire at the Somme. The howl boomed so loud it battered her insides and head as if she were being struck by a dozen iron maces at once, and if not for her strength, this howl of Gur would have pulped her to a boneless fish. She groaned and stumbled backwards as he poured it on her, wave after wave, the volume curling metal and bursting the hundreds of stone Mongol warriors to dust.

Then at last, the blast of loathing subsided.

Freddie thought she heard the sounds of things collapsing, broken treasures echoing in the dark, and unable to stand on her feet a moment longer, she slumped to her knees. Her head was down, her body throbbing into one giant bruise. She glanced up just in time to see Temujin Gur towering over her, tall as three men, his head of black hornet-skin glistening in the beetle moonlight and looking like a cross between a praying mantis and a birthing lycanthrope. Before she could gather her senses, his snout snapped down, biting deep. Dagger-long teeth pierced her body from face to groin, the mouth grinding in an attempt to chew and swallow.

Freddie's legs kicked and she screamed in fury within his black mouth, her mind struggling for aria. She yanked one of his teeth out with a loud pop and drove it deep into his fleshy black tongue. A dark ichor gushed from the wound, soaking her and reeking of foul sewer. In retaliation, he boomed forth with a dragon roar of iron-melting flame that singed her flesh and crumbled her clothes to dust, the black stains of tongue burning off to steam. Following that, he jerked his head and released her with a force that hurled her body through the air to smash into the Khan's throne dais. She impacted with such velocity that she cracked the ton-heavy marble. Days earlier, the Princess von Anhalt would have been seriously hurt or crippled, only now, it did not even slow her.

Her body smoking and bruised, Freddie stood to face the oncoming monstrosity of Temujin Gur, or what was once Temujin Gur.

She dodged and leapt aside as the thing lunged and snapped at her with newly grown fangs, she imagined the golden treasure of Genghis Khan filling its mouth, ramming down its throat, and her aria sang, *O tesouro de ouro de Khan,cubrir esa boca!* (Golden treasure of the Khan, fill that mouth!), whereupon hundreds of pounds of gold coins, plates, goblets, statues, and all else shot at the speed of sound from all over the Necropolis and straight into that thunder-roaring maw. The sheer force behind the mass of plummeting metal knocked the Gur thing backwards and down to the floor on its back. Hands of black talon desperately dug at the golden horde stuffing its snout, and it tore out chunks as fast as possible, legs kicking as it did so—giving it the overall appearance of a child having a tantrum.

While it choked and growled and struggled, she taunted it. "I will never be killed by a weak Mongol dog like you!" The Gur thing squirmed and squealed with even more anger as it clawed wildly at the golden mass boring down its throat like a driven spike. "And your precious monster, Genghis Khan, will PERISH BY MY HAND NOW!"

Freddie flew to where The Lord of The Bow slowly stood to his feet. She snatched him up and whipped him around to face her, hoisting his body high as she had Baron Eichmann. She wanted to stare into his emerald eyes before she killed him, boring in her own hatred, for she knew Gur's soul resided in this Khan creature, and too, she knew him as the greatest murderer of all time. Meanwhile, behind the World Slayer, she heard the golden horde vomiting free of Gur's maw, finally dislodged by his powerful magic. And as she turned, a dozen black yarrow sticks launched from his dog-bug head and arced down to the floor, expanding into human-like shapes upon contact.

The dancing banquet demons!

No time to waste. Three feet of yarrow sword formed in Freddie's hand, and to her surprise it whispered, *Drive me deep*. In a tenth of a second, she drove it up beneath the Khan's ribcage and into his spine until it jutted from his back for a full two feet. The body of the Lord of The Bow jerked a few times and his mouth gurgled out, "*Fuck you, whore,*" and he tried to spit in her face, but died with a final spasm, blood coursing from his mouth; and with Gur and his raging imps only a half moment from contact, Freddie did the unexpected. Like a shell from a British siege howitzer, she flew straight into the oncoming Gur with the Khan's impaled corpse held before her. Her blood-splattered yarrow sword pierced Gur in the chest, and her impact, strong as a herd of charging bull elephants compressed into one solid strike, drove him backwards across the room, the Lord of The Bow pinned to his body like a macabre brooch.

Freddie somersaulted away and rose up to watch Gur shriek like a terrified child and clutch frantically at the corpse of his future. His talons grasped and pulled at the sword with the Khan's body attached, howling horribly as he did so while the swarming yarrow demons shot bolts of black flame at Freddie's back—the same fire that had burned her unconscious as she lay impaled on the spear of Alexander. The bolts sounded like brief and loud rushes of wind as they spat through the air. She cried out in genuine pain, unable to avoid a few licks of the black fire.

The demon things sprung at her next, their insides radiant with churning red orbs and hundreds of tiny stars. Saravastra knows what those red things were! Distant suns about to burst? But no time to ponder. With an aria of *Tempo ser lenta* (Time be slow) she dodged their leaps and ducked the bolts of black flame. They moved in slow motion now, and for the first time, she looked deep and saw that the stars were actually the tiny glowing faces of women, men and children of varying races: African, Asian, European, Indian, and others she did not recognize. All the faces evidenced a terrible agony. Each black demon then was a star cluster of souls in pain, chained by Gur's magic to servitude and torment.

What kind of Hell must that be?

Freddie realized the time had come to force Gur's hand for the final blow at Dubai, and to end his miserable existence forever. She rose higher into the air and twisted around to face him, her fists clenched, her hair wild and churning about her face. She imagined her aria of Tao creating a protective bubble of hot magical force, and she sang loud and strong enough to overwhelm the slow-motion noise of a blustering Gur: *Unha burbulla quente de Tao, protexer o meu corpo.* (A bubble of hot Tao, protect my body.) And she added, *E serve-me ben!* (And serve me well!).

She watched Gur's form suddenly collapse to his usual appearance. Even with time slowed, the transformation back to the smiling Buddha face appeared rapid and bizarre. Once done, he also rose into the air, though more slowly, and his yarrow demons turned as one to face her. Gur had not yet realized how slow he moved in comparison, and she would take full advantage. Freddie projected her heat at him, just a moment's flash, hot enough to ignite a tree and enrage him even more. He growled and clenched his teeth as the burst of heat washed over him. She returned her time to normal with the words: *Tempo ser natural!* And shouted at him from across the cavernous Necropolis: "I will kill you, goat fucker, before you can even touch me! Do you hear? I will free your imprisoned souls and forever end your plans to restore your child eating rapist god! Such a sad plan, and from SUCH A STUPID FOOL!"

"AND I WILL BURN YOU TO SMOKE AND BREATHE YOUR SOUL INTO MY BLOOD!" he shouted back, his eyes delirious with insane anger even though his face still smiled in a parody of itself—a sight the Czarina of years to come would never forget, and one nobody could believe unless they actually saw it.

"Not even all your power can harm me, goat man! I DEFY YOU! Use it to burn me and see how foolish and weak you are!"

She shouted that and heard Paganini's voice, the Saravastra chanting of the spell captains louder than ever, and the violin music of Skanda rising to crescendo with a haunting and violent Caprice.

We are ready, Czarina. The moment is now.

Mother Yarrow Maria: *Strike true, warrior daughter!*

Paganini again: *Once he attacks, slow your time, get behind him and unleash your aria as you did against the Dio Soldati at the Somme. We will take care of the rest.*

"For Earth and Saravastra!" she shouted as she faced Gur.

Temujin Gur's yarrow demons thinned to sticks and snapped back to circle their master. As they did so, the sticks let loose a chorus of misery, as if the thousands of imprisoned souls cried out at once for mercy. Oblivious, Gur raised his arms and barked his Tongue of Ahriman, and it sounded to Freddie like:

"ZHENG YAO GUR, ANNO LAI, CATARCLUC, CAHHHH!"

A bubble of red-glowing force enveloped him, and the yarrow sticks as well, reminding Freddie of the red suns in the black demon bodies. The glowing sun-force brightened until the entire treasure collection in the ruined and smoking Necropolis blazed with a fierce red light and began to melt and drip like so much golden blood running from a hot wound. Gur continued to cast spell, though his voice was muffled by the sound of the superheated air beginning to crackle.

Freddie's bubble protected her, matching Gur's heat, forcing him to increase his own to ever more murderous and destructive levels. She caught a glimpse of the golden corpse of Genghis Khan, now like a little lump of butter dissolving in a hot skillet, and as it did, the very stone walls of the Necropolis began to smoke and run like thin lava to the floor, mixing with the melting treasure until, moments later, Freddie hovered above a lake of molten mass, the air thick with swirling and poisonous vapors. Over it all, she shouted, loud enough for Gur to hear through the unfolding chaos:

"I AM STILL ALIVE, GOAT FUCKER, AND I WILL BITE YOUR HEAD OFF ONCE YOU ARE DONE PLAYING!"

Freddie sensed Temujin Gur ready to explode, in every sense of the word. All her instinct and senses said NOW! *Tempo ser lennntaaa!* (Time be slow!) She darted up and behind the bubble of Gur's magic, now wide as a house and throbbing with giant tongues of flame, as if Gur had siphoned the sun itself. Lowering her body behind him, she witnessed the ultimate eruption of his raging hate: an enormous, sun-like flare birthing quickly despite the slow of time. She knew it capable of blowing out the side of the mountain and incinerating the Earth all the way to Peking.

But that would never happen.

Skanda and the yarrow-chanting Bodhisattvas reached full crescendo with enough power to crumble the Andes mountain range while Mother Yarrow Maria on her own exerted enough magical strength to sink the island of Crete. And Freddie unleashed her full aria Tao, sufficient to vaporize the Arctic Circle with enough left over to reroute the Nile.

As a result, Peking was saved.

* Оверман *

EDISON DANCED WITH MANDUKHAI BENEATH THE DUBAI MOON to the tune of "You Make Me Feel So Young" by Frank Sinatra. He loved that old Sinatra, as much as he loved Leonard Cohen's dark songs with words like, *"I've seen the future brother, and it's murder."*

Mandukhai looked stunningly beautiful, dressed in a black sequin evening dress which fell only to her upper thighs, low cut neckline, and transparent black chiffon sleeves. The two of them danced slowly, cheek to cheek, on a Mediterranean blue-tile patio atop *Le Petit Sanglier*, surrounded by Babylon torches big as giraffes, and in the distance, the grand sky towers of Dubai twinkled with thousands of lights, lines of aero cars flying silently between them and filled with the Overmen—his Sorcery Star pilots, *Dio Soldati*, empire administrators, Dyson Sphere engineers, and so forth. All part of his master plan. Any humans remaining alive would do whatever menial tasks made sense while clever, personable robots like Angelia Jolie took care of all else. The concept of it made him feel so at ease, and happy as a true World Maker should be.

Mandukhai stared into his eyes with her own loving eyes full of war and massacre and hot sex on Titan while Sinatra sang, *"You and I are just like a couple of tots, running across a meadow ..."* as he smiled at her with teeth brilliant as a sunlit glacier. She smiled back and leaned closer to gently bite his ear. Later, he knew the sex would be free fall. Float down, back up, and do it again as the wind rushed in their faces. She bit his ear, the feel of it tickling his toes, and the Dubai night turned to day, and even brighter, as if a nuclear warhead had detonated in the sky above the city. He heard a distant, echoing boom, and felt a flash of heat on his skin, hot enough to singe the delicate ends of Mandukhai's hair and make his pinot noir undrinkable.

Next, a roaring crack in the distance, getting louder and drawn out, as if an impossibly large thing prepared to topple. He sighed, a bit peeved for being interrupted, and said to an alarmed Mandukhai, "Oh, what now?"

He released her, turned and walked to the far end of the patio to gaze over the city. He saw one of the Dubai towers to his right, faraway and well over two miles high. Severed in the middle, the upper portion fell towards the earth.

A broken colossus, the fall slow and unreal.

Edison scanned to his left and saw his own tower, the top of it gone, at least thirty floors vanished. The crown of the structure was blackened and in flames. He strained his acute vision, strong enough to see the beak of a small sparrow twenty miles away, and noted War Tracker gone.

A chill claimed his body.

For the first time in centuries, Edison Godfellow felt a surge of fear.

I am afraid. I do not believe it, and yet, it is so.

Upon completion of that thought, all about him faded.

Even Mandukhai.

His dream towers of Dubai evaporated, and the sky islands, aero cars, the grand palaces on the sea like luminous crustaceans, all gone. He floated in dark space, in the cold night air above a different Dubai far below him, one much smaller, depressed and dim with not even one building above ten stories. The past had changed his future to this future, and one in which oil and military money obviously mattered far less. Without War Tracker to act and dispatch the medicine of force to heal the wounds in time, a crucial conflict point had obviously turned to the benefit of Paganini and those moon-hatted imbeciles of the Pan-Buddhist Democratic

Union. Though which one? Dozens of conflict points could be going on at any one time, from assassinations to battles to kidnappings.

Perhaps that cursed Battle of The Somme again?

But how had Paganini been able to muster enough focused force? It seemed impossible, since the energy necessary to pierce the screens that protected War Tracker would have required at least 200 megatons per square centimeter. Edison knew the Czarina, or two Czarinas must be involved, along with Paganini and his blathering moon-hatters, a few Mother Yarrows perhaps, and God knows who or what else!

Regardless, the memory of history on this Earth was no more. Fortunately, his own memories remained whole, since he kept himself above and beyond the fickleness of time. What did Kipling say in the poem "If"? *If you can breathe not a word about your loss, but begin again with worn out tools?* Something like that? He wasn't too old to learn from mistakes ... or might he be mistaken?

A man has got to know his limitations.

Man or no, a lack of memory at the moment would be a good thing.

царица

13

World Stormer Prediction - Peter the Great - A New World, For Now

BABETTE WOULD NEVER REMEMBER THAT HORRIBLE TORTURE in the Virgin Mary. Upon Gur's death and the destruction of War Tracker, Freddie returned to the torture dungeon only a moment after she had joined Gur in the Necropolis of The Khan. She freed Babette and Zolo, and healed them, erasing all memory from Babette and causing her to sleep once more. Zolo though, wished to keep his memory, and she agreed to his wishes, hugging him for minutes on end and asking his forgiveness.

"Let us make love to celebrate a blackness gone from this Earth," and she kissed him long and deep, and he returned her love in a magnificent way until, by whispers of magic, they found themselves lying in wild grasses atop a foothill of the Alps, gazing over the Mediterranean under a full moon night. The town of Menton, France in the distance, torch lit and serene.

Both Mother Yarrows, Margaret and Maria, closed their eyes to it, not wishing to gaze upon the lovemaking. Allowing privacy when necessary was a core principle the Mother Yarrows lived by, and one dictated by Saravastra, though a few broke the rules at times and closely watched intimate encounters. Many Mother Yarrows lived lonely lives in their time, and the lives they mentored and cared for in the future meant everything to them. A few felt a right to experience even sexual love as intimately as possible.

A small reward of sorts, or so they believed.

Before the night on the Alpine foothill came to an end, Freddie said to Zolo, "Your sense of rightness and compassion are greater than mine, as is your sense of loyalty and destiny. Though I lost my temper with you over the death of my father, and the serfs, I know those terrible events had to take place. And I know you suffered through them, and later, because of them, suffering too because I could not realize the truth and unfairly blamed you ... There has been *too much* on your shoulders, Mr. Bold. Please forgive me for being such a terrible selfish bitch."

"I understand," Zolo said, "And I would have felt the same as you."

"You are the strongest man I know, and in every way that truly matters. I love you, Zolo Bold," she said as the lights of Menton winked out and stars whispered from eons away and the townsfolk dreamed their dreams of seas and meadows.

* Оверман *

THE FOLLOWING MORNING, FREDDIE TOOK BABETTE for a stroll outside the castle—the day fresh, and the rolling hills and fields of Anhalt still foggy in the warming sunlight. Freddie held her arm and listened to her nanny's chatter. She still had not spoken to Babette since Gur knocked her down with spell and branded her with yarrow symbols.

"I heard you, darling, in your room. It sounded like you were being attacked!" said Babette.

"I was, and you were brave to try and rescue me."

"I would give my life for you, *lapooshka*," Babette said, small tears in her eyes. "Was it that horrible Mongol wizard of the Empress?"

"Yes, but we have nothing to worry about now. He has gone."

"Forever, I hope. He turned the whole castle into one never ending nightmare. Bleeding walls and phantoms and floating corpses and God knows!"

"Be calm, my darling."

"I will, I will ... It was just so terrible. And now Empress Elizabeth has her servants out on the walls banging pots and calling his name. They say she is hysterical."

"What? That's *ridiculous*," Freddie said and laughed softly.

"But I do miss your father, *lapooshka*. He was a good man, and always kind to me, a good word to everyone. Fair to the servants. I cannot believe that maniac shot him for a pay grievance. Your father *never* would have cheated anyone."

Freddie held back a sob. She did not wish to upset Babette. "I know. I loved my father, and I have yet to grieve for him the way I should, but I know my mother—"

Babette interrupted with a raised arm and a pointing finger. "Look!"

Freddie followed the path of her finger to see a number of men outside the castle walls with big hammers. They began to swing the hammers at a pile of metal and shiny glass in a big pile along the wall. The sound of their hammer strikes sounded like *ponk, punk, pank*—little nips of sound coming over the field to where they stood.

What was it?

The Anhalt World Stormer!

Freddie could see what they worked to demolish. "Wait here, my darling!" she said to Babette, and she ran at a normal speed across the field towards the scene. In a minute, she stood before them, anger in her eyes. The men, Bärenthoren servants, various butler assistants and "scrubber boys," looked up at her and stopped swinging the hammers. They appeared dazed by her stare, confused, even anxious. Freddie knew their predicament—stuck between Princess Johanna's wrath and her own. She felt sorry for them, and her temper quieted.

"I suppose my mother gave orders this be destroyed?" she said to them.

"Yes, princess," a man said. The voice came from her right side. She turned her head to see the depressed and thin face of Benjamin Barth, the servant who had asked for her help to thwart Baron Eichmann. It seemed like centuries ago, yet the sight of him struck her dumb. The realization of his grief, and the reminder of those many deaths to restore her to life, cast a darkness over her thoughts.

What can I possibly say?

All of them stared at her.

They must be wondering if I am going insane.

"Benjamin ... I ... Come here for a moment, I wish to speak," and she turned to the others and said, "Please be still."

Benjamin, walking like a zombie, joined her and she led him by the arm out of earshot of the others. "Benjamin, *please please* forgive me. I have been ... gone, and my life in danger. I heard ..." She found it hard to say. He just stared at her with a look of shock on his face. "I heard something about the serfs of Eichmann vanishing, or ...?"

"No one knows," he said with a flat voice. "I think they are dead. I wish I were dead also, but I do not have the courage."

"Your sister, Daniela—"

"She was not one of them. Baron Eichmann kept her for himself. For his passions."

"What? His *passions?*"

"She is his slave."

"My God, Benjamin, I did not know," she said, growing enraged by the news. It seemed, even on this beautiful morning, rest would not be forthcoming. So be it. She reached up to hold his face with her hands, and said to him, "By tonight, dear Benjamin, she will be free of Eichman and he will be gone from this Earth, as well as his wretched wife, and they never will hurt anyone else. Danilea will return and live with you here. You have my word. You will see her tonight, *I swear it.*"

Benjamin Barth fell forward into her arms and sobbed and sobbed.

Upon holding him for a time and rubbing his head, she asked one of the servants to escort him to his room, whereupon she ordered the rest to leave the World Stormer and attempt to demolish it no longer. In response, one of them nervously said to her, "But princess, your mother will—" Freddie cut him off and said, "Do not fear. I will settle her soon enough."

The servants walked slowly back into the castle, all of them looking depressed. Freddie decided she would later use aria to re-store the Anhalt World Stormer and place it all shining and new in the Bärenthoren Great Hall where her mother could not miss it. Freddie would tell her, "I saw Temujin Gur make it appear, then he laughed and vanished!" And just when Princess Johanna was ready to explode, the World Stormer would raise its machine barrels and fire a few rounds in her direction, thus causing her to run scream-ing in terror from the hall.

Freddie found it odd, especially after all she'd been through, that the idea of provoking her mother still found great appeal. She gazed down at the broken tubes, the electric spats and barrels and cylinders, the twisted and pounded black chassis of the World Stormer. Her father's most wondrous invention—a bit of matter that was part of a whole beyond the power of any god or God; and just like the castle Bärenthoren, like the living woods and grasses beyond, like the water in the ground and in the sky: all born of stars. The wandering between one time of Earth and another made her look inside herself for a universal constant, and in the madness of swirling Time, she found it in the simple thought of the night sky, in that timeless void of all creation.

She knew that one day she would stand in this same place, per-haps a million years from now, and nothing would be left of An-halt, or the castle. Even the dust of it would have long since been blown by winds to other lands, of no more consequence than the echo of a voice dying in the mountains. But the stars would still be unchanged, the eternal need for creation still there, twinkling down forever.

* Оверман *

A MAN WHO LOOKED LIKE A DUCK WITH A DROOPING BEAK faced Freddie in the main castle doorway off the courtyard as she escorted Babette back into the castle. Though she could hardly call him a man. More of a boy. His face very pale and slack, long soft nose, small dark eyes—an ugly face with a look of stupidity about it. He wore a purple velvet waistcoat, a white shirt beneath, and a big gold chain hung about his neck. He carried a riding crop in one hand, and his breath reeked of alcohol. He stared at Freddie's clothing with his drink-glazed eyes, saw her white riding pants and high leather boots, and his face sneered. Apparently, women dressed in such a fashion greatly offended him. He next turned his gaze to Babette and sneered again. Apparently, the sight of a servant offended him also.

He raised his riding crop to rest in his other hand, and said to Freddie with a voice that sounded like a Russian woman with nasal blockage, "What means these pants of yours? Are you a servant here, or an elected king of peasants?"

"I am who I am, sir, and my pants are not *your concern*," she answered in a forceful way in an attempt to put the little ass in his place. Freddie was determined to get around him without haste and escort Babette to her bedchamber. Whoever he was, he must be the son of a Russian nobles, though she'd never seen him before. The droopy duck face lifted his riding crop and smacked it into the palm of his hand, staring at Freddie with theatrical anger. She laughed to herself, but watched him with a cold face.

Does this ass pickle desire to strike me?

"What are you about with that crop, sir?" Freddie asked.

"I have been lashing my hounds!" he exclaimed, his stinking alcohol breath punishing her while his eyes brightened with the announcement, as if the memory of lashing hounds excited him. "I court marshaled one and hung another from the walls for disobedience."

"Why would anyone favor the harming of animals?" she asked him, her tone a mixture of disgust and curiosity. She noticed the head of a toy soldier sticking out of his waistcoat pocket. *Is the ass pickle playing with toy soldiers also?*

The pickle answered with an air of contempt, "I take no special pains to beat dogs any more than serfs, *miss peasant queen* ... All must be disciplined."

"And with help from that soldier in your pocket? Do you *fancy* yourself a general?"

"I like toy soldiers," he said indignantly. He then removed the soldier from the pocket and lifted it up to Freddie's face. A Prussian dragoon in white coat and tri-cornered black hat. The soldier pointed a musket at Freddie's nose. The duck-faced pickle shook the soldier back and forth and said, "Pow! Death to peasants! Pow!"

Freddie glanced at Babette who returned the look, both of them having the same thought at once:

Is this little ass pickle insane?

Tired of his smelly breath and childish stupidity, Freddie pushed her way past the boorish ass pickle as he continued to point the dragoon at her and say, "Pow!" and walked with Babette up the grand wooden staircase to her room. Like in old days, Babette would later come to Freddie's bedchamber with a mug of warm milk and a bedtime story. So simple yet so relaxing, and right now, she desired that over any grand city floating on the edge of forever.

Other servants passed them on the staircase or in the hall, and whether maids or butlers, they greeted Freddie respectfully, as usual, but stared at Babette as though seeing a circus freak. This behavior alarmed and irritated Freddie. As she would later learn, the servants recalled Babette's voice crying out in terrible pain, a voice so loud that it rattled the castle and boomed over the Anhalt fields. Rumors said Babette had been engaged in an act of extremely painful love making with Temujin Gur, the Mongol wizard of Empress Elizabeth, thus her many cries and moans. A rumor begun by Princess Johanna's maidservants transformed Babette to a horse, since everyone knew Mongols preferred to mate with horses. Regardless, everyone agreed that Temujin Gur, upon having his way with the screaming Babette slut, ascended from the castle in a state of disgust. Babette, however, remained behind, implanted with his demon seed—perhaps even carrying a human horse monstrosity in her womb.

Those were the rumors, and Freddie vowed to put an end to them.

How easily these people substitute harmful rumor for any show of sympathy or support, and without the slightest attempt to learn the truth.

The foul talk not only wounded Babette deeply, it also tainted the air of the castle and interrupted the healing peace Freddie sought. And too, for the first time, it created a bias in her against the castle servants.

The Princess von Anhalt could not deny it.

Is there even one among them with sense or heart?

* Оверман *

DECIDING TO NOT KILL A CHILD, EVEN IF THAT CHILD was Adolph Hitler, Saravastra's war strategy office, working with Paganini, dispatched the Czarina Catherine to prevent Hitler's father Alois, in 1876, from officially changing his surname from Schicklgruber to Hitler. Too many battles had been fought in the Nexus Zone over the body of the child Adolph, and an Extinction Event threatened. Saravastra believed it would be similar to the devastating one that erupted over Hitler's failure to enter art school (the "Mein Kampf Point"), an Event that resulted in much loss of heroic life and black armor hardware. With a simple bit of aria then, one of the greatest mass murderers of history was castrated of his genocidal dreams even before he was born.

Heil Schicklgruber?

Dubai and Master Godfellow had failed to account for such a simple occurrence, and therefore placed no prior spell to defeat it; and the plan, subtle and brilliant in its conception, succeeded, for as all Saravastra knew, Dubai ceased to exist the moment the name change did not occur. Master Godfellow's dream world of the Overman literally evaporated beneath his feet. The Bodhisattvas of Saravastra, given to stoicism and chants, broke forth in joyous yells that echoed throughout the towers of their fabled cloud city. Paganini himself laughed heartily, and in his office overlooking the Himalayas, as the white birds of human soared in the distance, he and Catherine toasted the new future with a glass of Italian red wine.

"To Herr Schicklgruber!" she said, raising her glass.

Paganini smiled and relaxed in his straight wood chair. Catherine had never seen him so comfortable upon such an uncomfortable chair. He was like a new man. She continued, "It's hard to believe, Niccolo. I wish I could have seen the look on that bastard's face when Dubai winked out."

Paganini nodded and related to her, between bouts of chuckling to himself, that Adolph Schicklgruber's early attempts at politics failed miserably. His opponents nicknamed him "Adolph Pökel-ficker" (pickle fornicator).

Catherine laughed so suddenly that a mouthful of wine sprayed out of her mouth and into the air.

"And that sealed his fate!" Paganini said, and summed up for her the time-ripple effects of the name change. The act of Pentagon, the American drone fleet, did not evolve in the 21st century to dominate and enslave Earth with Master Godfellow's help because the evil bitterness of one sick man a century and a half before never claimed a foothold in Europe. Countless millions of lives were saved, the Holocaust prevented, and World War II avoided. And with War Tracker now out of the picture, response would be very slow. "Edison will need time to regroup and pick up the pieces," Paganini said. "He will retire, most likely, to his City of Traps."

Catherine had heard of the place. The City of Traps—Godfellow's land of his own creation—before Dubai, beyond Dubai. A thing of rumor and myth somewhere between a medieval courtyard in Barcelona and the methane lakes of Titan: a hellish paradise without sunlight and wide as Crete, long as the French coastline from Nice to Cannes. No one truly understood the why or how of it, or even precisely where it could be found, just that it existed.

"Saravastra's War Strategy Office will now conduct other actions," Paganini said, "and at a dozen or more points, keeping the pressure up." Even the Somme would be fought again, now that they knew the German counteroffensive worked—the WSO strategy being to strike often and interweave events in such a manner as to keep the enemy off balance, thus assuring the kind of peaceful future Godfellow hated most. And as a precaution, an *observador paciente* kept watch over Hitler's father Alois, to make certain he did never changed his mind about changing his last name—such a precaution necessary, for sooner or later, Master Godfellow or his forces would realize the source of the new time stream.

Catherine's good humor began to fade at the thought of it.

When will the madness stop? Of course they will come, because their leader is still alive.

Despite the great victory that stalled Godfellow's plans, she might have killed the supreme bastard on Mars if not for a betrayal. His death simply made more sense, as she and Mother Yarrow Maria believed. But their entire venture was a miserable and embarrassing failure. All she could show for it was a new hole on Mars and the memory of an attempted rape in the mud of the Somme. What did the sex maniac Godfellow say after he leapt upon her? *"I've seen the nations rise and fall, I've heard their stories, heard them all, but love's the only engine of survival."* And following her crushing blow to his groin with her knee only seconds later—a blow which broke the spine of the corpse and jammed its tip up and through the dead Welsh brain—she pushed him away; and as she lay there, cold and filthy, the fallen corpse only ten feet distant rolled onto its side facing her, lit another cigarette, and said with a passionate voice:

"I love you more than anyone, Czarina."

Her aria magically eased her mind out of the trauma of being raped by a World War I corpse, and she decided upon doing so that she needed a vacation. Due to her new hatred of cigarettes, still tasted on her lips, she fantasized ending the tobacco industry in early America before it could take root and poison millions, but she knew Saravastra would not sanction such a thing—too many variables to consider.

* Оверман *

FOLLOWING HER TOASTS WITH PAGANINI, ALL OF SARAVASTRA celebrated in a grand hall known as The Hall of Patience, located within the Mother Tower, one of the city's tallest structures. Every spell captain and ally of the Pan-Buddhist Democratic Union (PBDU), human and inhuman, attended the new utopia party. Magogs, looking like giant horned devils, brought their growling children. Wizard Gods arrived in uniquely artistic and powerful forms, several blooming out to as many as seven bodies that walked, floated, and danced. Bodhisattvas landed in their black-armor war machines, the metal of them scarred and smoking as the white wisps of their souls rose from these machines to join their bodies awaiting them in lotus position atop a stage. Warriors from other eras strolled the hall, drinking whiskey and ale, or a concoction of black fumes reportedly "made in Hell." Leaders of the PBDU formed a line of hundreds of supporters chanting and carrying on high their yellow and black PBDU flags—their symbol being a Buddha seated in lotus atop an eagle. And over it all, Paganini's violin played delightful and uplifting music.

All were happy, all shouting or laughing.

A victory speech by Paganini was rumored to soon take place.

Catherine stood atop a jade balcony in the Mother Tower, looking down on it all, and a gloom descended upon her. The Saravastra celebration seemed premature, even foolish, and false in a sense. Why? Because *Godfellow was still alive*. The night threatened to rise once more. But did the realization of such reality make her a negative person? A pessimist? The death and destruction of the 20th century threatened to reassert itself. The truth of this fact could not be avoided. Who would be celebrating then? None but the hyena Godfellow and his drunken Overmen, and on a Dubai Sky Isle while Sinatra played in the background.

Such thoughts canceled her festive mood. She felt disgusted and had no wish to join the celebratory party at Saravastra, so upon the edge of a mighty cliff on the Big Sur coastline in California, during a Pacific sunset in 1579, she sat, watching the *Golden Hinde*. The ship of Sir Francis Drake sailed not more than a mile offshore. She marveled at the beauty and simplicity of the craft. It looked to her like a small wooden flowerbox sprouting huge white blooms: a ship of two large masts with two broad sails each, a smaller lateen mast on the stern, and another on the bow. All sails full, all snapping in the Pacific wind, pink-hued in the sunset.

Might this be the real utopia?

As she watched and breathed deeply the clean, pure air of California, a man strolled up and sat down behind her. She did not turn to see his face. She already knew his identity. He too watched the *Golden Hinde* for a few moments and said to her:

"Why did you keep secret your plan to kill Edison Godfellow?"

The man was Niccolo Paganini. His voice was quiet, certainly no longer happy.

Catherine answered him, her voice emotionless. "Because you would have said no to the plan. But bold results call for bold action."

"True, though it was not his time. We at Saravastra know that."

"So all of you prefer the continued insanity of time war?"

"Czarina, I prefer a future of peace."

"Then why not let loathsome scum die, Niccolo? Why?"

"There are reasons ... We cannot tell you. You must believe me, it is vital that he lives to fulfill a destiny. The entire future of this planet depends on it."

Catherine paused to control her temper, and said to Paganini with irritation in her voice, "Perhaps, Niccolo, this is all really about *you finally besting* Godfellow, and he being around to see it. If he's dead, thumping your chest over his body is far less satisfying."

"You know that is absurd," Paganini said with a touch of hurt.

"Then why? Why keep him alive to plan more war and domination?"

"Must I repeat myself?" he asked, his voice emotionless once more.

"Who betrayed us then? Black Agnes?"

"Black Agnes talked to several Mother Yarrows about seeing your younger self at the Somme. I was informed and personally heard the thoughts of Maria of Pozzuoli. She cannot hide them from me. She tried."

"So ... you told Godfellow of our plan?"

"Yes."

A long pause as the *Golden Hind* sailed further south and the sun dipped below the western horizon. "You betrayed me, Niccolo. You allowed me to die, and those serfs sacrificed to bring me back to life, and I feel like hurting you," she said with a cold voice.

"You betrayed our cause, Catherine," he replied in a matter-of-fact tone. "The last World Maker of aria died because she acted foolishly."

"Because you gave her up to Godfellow to be murdered?" she asked, turning around to face Paganini in the gathering darkness.

"No. She was unaware of his many protections, and she was overconfident."

"But now I am supposed to *trust you*?"

"Always trust we believe in a cause, and will do right by that cause. And so you know, Dubai is no more and Edison is without War Tracker. A new time stream is in place, which you made happen. Do you fully comprehend the magnitude of our victory?"

"So War Tracker is forever gone from our lives."

"No ... We have it captive, on Surya."

"*What?*"

"The force we brought to bear only pushed War Tracker beyond Earth's gravity and injured it. We now hold it prisoner."

"Then you can use it—"

"No. Without Edison it lies and squalls like a child. It will take him years to create another one."

"I see, well, I have no choice but to be your good little soldier, Niccolo."

"You make your own choices, Czarina."

* Оверман *

Saravastra Sept 4, 1898.

Niccolo and I argued last evening while I attempted to relax at Big Sur and watch the Golden Hind sailing south. I love Mother Yarrow Maria, and her presence is a reassuring one, though she can keep no secrets because Niccolo will not have it. I reminded him that I died after confronting Godfellow, and in effect, he had been the one who condemned me to that fate. My youthful and naive self was killed by Eréndira, sent by Godfellow, and all because of Niccolo. She and I might still have failed to kill the pompous God One on Mars, but at least those monsters Eréndira and Mandukhai would not have been present. And as I consider it further, 'God One' is an appropriate term for the likes of him, for like an Old Testament Jehovah he brings wrath and manipulates whole nations, laying waste without conscience. Most strange though, this time travel business, especially when one considers the way in which the altered past can suddenly inflict guilt and other terrible memories never before possessed.

I know that as Czarina I will raise a feudal Russia from the muck of ages, and do many good things to alleviate the people's suffering. This future I see for myself, but at what cost? Who can possibly understand what I must endure? I read about myself in books, in libraries and other places in future years, though only my memoirs hint at the true insanity of life with Peter. Though I find it still unbelievable, I am now one of the four most powerful beings on this planet and yet I must endure an infantile hell created by a moronic fool. Only my escapes in time at the request of Saravastra and Niccolo provide any relief, and the adventures I experience, however fruitless or meaningful, are well received by me. Anything is good substitute, even Virgin Mary torture when compared to the maddening presence of "the whelp" as so many call him.

I will say, being raped by a dead soldier at the Somme is not a thing I would wish to replace the painful presence of Peter, though such a comparison illustrates my point; and Niccolo will not allow me to use my yarrow magic or aria to change Peter in any way. I often believe Niccolo wishes me to suffer, that the suffering of life with Peter makes it all the more easier for the Lord of Saravastra to chart my courses since I always welcome his tasks, and no more so than recently. Why? Because the whelp has become even more intolerable than usual. He works at training his hounds, or so he calls it, lashing the poor animals with his whip, yelling at them and chasing them through the castle in Moscow. Those of the dogs that tire and attempt to run away or lie down are relentlessly beaten, and the poor things howl so loudly! Once, as I listened to one of the doomed animals whining and crying, I opened the door to his room and pleaded for the poor beast, but that only caused Peter to rain blows with renewed vigor. Unable to view the cruel sight, I moved to my bedchamber in tears. I cannot tolerate the sight of animals in needless pain. Peter later witnessed my sadness, and this only made him threaten to injure the hounds even more.

No room can be found in his whelp soul for pity. If possible, I would have sung aria and turned him into a hound and beat him myself, however, I do not think this would have taught the sadistic creature a lesson. Only his end will put him out of the world's misery. It sounds cruel perhaps, though I must say I welcome the opportunity to engineer his final minutes on Earth. History records that I will do so, and all of Russia will support me. I can only look forward to such a day and it cannot arrive soon enough.

Speaking of endings, my conflict with Niccolo has caused me to dwell once more on the vision of my end at the hands of Fracas Machines in the Himalayas. For the first time, I feel more strongly than ever in the possibility of this event coming true. For years I believed it more of a hoax on the part of Temujin Gur, and Niccolo has sworn this circumstance, but now I am more inclined to believe Niccolo would actually have me killed, or at least, allow me to die if he believed such a thing necessary.

Do World Makers really die though? Niccolo and Godfellow, and others, have been alive since the Bronze Age, and yet, I know my Asian predecessor was turned to salt and digestion at the hands of the Dio Soldati. So many things I do not fully comprehend. I do not even know why or how I became a World Maker. I still do not understand Ahriman, or the real substance of his being. At times I consider him a dark illusion created by Godfellow and Niccolo to frighten me. I doubt this is the case though. He is our source, our father in a manner of speaking, as Niccolo says, but what does that really mean? Am I not born of my mother and father, or was I placed in a demon womb by Ahriman, or born of an unholy union of a thing inhuman with a human? I cannot say. I do not doubt my wicked mother would consent to uniting with a demon if the prize were sufficient, and often, I believe she was truly sired by one. Whatever the real truth, I desire to know the nature of Ahriman. He is evil, most certainly, far more evil than Godfellow. My senses alert me to this, and Mother Yarrow Maria knows it also, and Niccolo avoids me when I seek more information about him.

I might aria this Ahriman into a reality I can witness, though I fear such a thing, deep and colder than I fear the potential of my last day. The fear is like an instinct I cannot avoid or deny, and perhaps Ahriman himself placed it within me as a clever mechanism to prevent my searching, thus enabling his mystery to continue without respite.

One day, the truth must come out. Perhaps, on that day of knowing Ahriman, I will be powerless and driven to leap from the cliff by Niccolo's mechanical pets, or perhaps I will know nothing at all, and be driven to my death regardless. Or perhaps, such a thing will not happen. Regardless, I fervently wish to know, one way or another.

* Оверман *

BARON EICHMANN AWOKE AT 3 AM TO THE SUN RISING EARLY. He got out of bed, his wife grumbling in the background, and in a blinking daze stumbled towards the window of his tower bedroom. He pulled the curtains and a spear of sunlight blinded him. He cursed and held his hand before his eyes. Next, he heard a distant singing, a woman's voice, brilliant and pure, echoing over the fields. The words he could not understand. They sounded rather like Latin, and it reminded him of an opera, though he didn't know which one.

As his wife became angrier, he saw the sun itself, only not the one he expected. It appeared to be floating above the earth, not more than half a mile from his castle, and it moved slowly, from north to south. And he felt it ... *Heat!* The window before him grew hotter and he backed away. He heard faint screams from somewhere outside and the roof of the castle stables, far down and to his left, suddenly erupted in flame. The woman's singing voice entered his bedchamber like a fall of smashing plates and the window exploded. The spear of sunlight charred him in less than a moment. He fell to the floor as a blazing ball of flesh, and his wife, the infamous Baroness, allowed only half a scream before she too burned and blackened.

For miles around, the peasants thereabouts were stirred from their beds of straw by the light and distant explosions as heat detonated ammunition stores. They stepped outside to see Baron Eichmann's castle in the distance, going up in flames, and an odd little sun looking like a big bright star from their vantage point, moving in a circle about the castle. And it would be said among them for the rest of their days that they witnessed the Anhalt Sun Angel, returned once more to avenge the poor and downtrodden. Even God's mercy has limits, and the Sun Angel was the instrument of God. None could deny it. They fell to their knees and gave thanks to Heaven and many wept like children to see such Old Testament justice. A few even said they would hang Father Brum, the parish priest, if he did not bless the holy event.

Unknown to them, the Anhalt Sun Angel had considered the fate of the Baron and his evil wife for at least an hour before acting. She contemplated turning them both into serfs without fingers, or perhaps grass snakes with memories of humanity, but in the end, she felt the Anhalt Sun Angel would send a clear message to the other tyrants.

The Angel's aria had carried her swift as thought to Eichmann's castle where she found Benjamin's sister tied to her bed with a rope, and terribly bruised about the arms and face. The Angel healed her with aria and made her sleep as she flew her to safety at Bärenthoren Castle. She asked Babette to watch after her, then returned and freed the remaining servants under the thumb of Eichmann, removing them quietly from the grounds as they slept. Once finished, she rose like early dawn just west of the Baron.

Satisfied with the knowledge that he would never again harm anyone else, she lingered among the moonlit clouds, soared in the night air to cleanse herself, finally approaching Bärenthoren Castle with the eyes and height of a hawk. To her surprise, she saw more fires far below her, this time atop the walls and towers of Bärenthoren, and at four A.M. in the morning. She could not figure it at first.

Was the castle burning?

No. The flames came from torches, lots of them.

Drawing closer, she saw that men held the torches, scores of them, and women too—the castle servants, guards, and even Russian noblemen who had joined the train of Empress Elizabeth in her pilgrimage to Bärenthoren. A tiny figure moved among them, gesturing frantically, hopping and darting. She focused more closely and saw it was Empress Elizabeth in a hoop skirt and tilted wig, a big brass monocle dangling awkwardly from her face by a leather strap. She appeared to be conducting a symphony as she moved among the figures, encouraging and directing them, and as the Anhalt Sun Angel dropped lower to the walls, she heard the voices of this symphony. All of the figures holding torches chanted, "*Mirzaaa Gur, Mirzaaa Gur*" without pause.

Landing unseen among them, she observed Empress Elizabeth who appeared to be disheveled and exhausted by an attack of panic. Obviously, her panic meant she feared for her future without Temujin Gur. Too bad! The Empress leaned back against a stone wall that faced the parapets, breathing heavily. Her maidservants hovered around her, nervous and unsure as pilot fish afraid of their mother shark. A wrong word or move on their part might condemn them to beatings, or worse. As Freddie watched from only a few feet away, the Empress lifted one shaking hand and held the huge brass monocle tight to her right eye, and said in a heavy whisper, *"God One, please answer me. Temujin Gur has disappeared ... God One, do you hear me?"*

No answer.

The Empress, looking desperate and angry, sharply waved her maidservants away. They scattered like nervous pigeons. She then turned her mouth close to the stone wall and as the voices endlessly chanted in the background, she spoke again in a heavy whisper, *"Why do you forsake me, God One? ... What can I do to please you? ... I beg you, answer me. Temujin Gur is gone."*

The invisible Sun Angel laughed to herself. The Empress would be waiting a long time for Temujin Gur, not realizing of course that his atoms floated somewhere on the winds of Time between the 13th century and the demise of Dubai.

She turned to glance around the castle walls. In the near distance, she saw her mother, Princess Johanna, standing beside a Prussian noblewoman, a frequent companion by the name of Countess Rothschild. The two of them kept perfectly still in a dark corner, away from the general circus. Both stared at the figure of a young nobleman cavorting about without a torch, high stepping and flinging his arms in the air as if drunk, shrieking for Temujin Gur with voice of a strangled cat. The figure belonged to that of the incredibly stupid and annoying ass pickle she'd met after walking with Babette. *Who is he? What is he?* She imagined turning him upside down in mid-air and jerking him like a saltshaker. Her attention returned to her mother.

She watched her mother's lips move.

Princess Johanna's eyes never strayed from the crazed ass pickle as she remarked to the countess beside her, "There dances *my door* to the royal Russian court."

The Countess Rothschild grinned, glanced sideways and said, "Please do not forget your friends when you arrive. Will you actually be able to live with your daughter as Czarina?"

"No longer than fate demands, dear countess," she replied with a slithering voice. "No longer than fate demands."

* Оверман *

THE DAWN SUN ROSE TO FACE EMPRESS ELIZABETH as she brought an end to the chanting torch vigil on the battlements of Bärenthoren Castle. She angrily dismissed everyone and commanded them with a hoarse voice to speak of the event to no one, at the risk of their lives. All about her nodded and croaked their responses with dry voices, especially since most of them were parched with thirst, except for the Empress who drank goblets of sparkling sweet water brought to her by royal maidservants throughout the ordeal.

Princess Johanna retired at last to her gold-spackled bedchamber and was changed into nightwear by her own maidservants. She dismissed them as usual with insults and face slaps, and once in bed, breathed a deep sigh. She closed her eyes and felt herself drifting down, deeper and deeper. Soon enough, the sea wavered above her, dark and swimming with horrid dark shapes and snake-like things. Was she dreaming already? How could she breathe? She struggled to open her eyes, to come out of the dream, but she could not.

The dark closed in around her and she felt a terrible pain in her head.

She shot through the water backwards, her body flapping as a powerful force tugged at her, and she awakened to the ceiling of the castle hallway moving before her eyes, the pain still in her head. She suddenly realized, she was being savagely yanked down the hall by her hair!

She squirmed and fought to no avail, yelled at her invisible tormentor to stop. Who could it be? Who would dare? Her body continued to be dragged and the pain so intense she began to weep.

Despite all that, she could not guess the fate that awaited her.

* Оверман *

ZOLD BOLD COULD NOT HELP BUT RECALL THE PAIN of the Virgin Mary, those hundred bloody nails piercing his dreams, even as he reclined upon his couch in the cloud-encircled Mother Tower deep in Saravastra. Such pain recalled by the body, yet in such a place of tranquility. It would remain in him, permanent nails piercing his flesh, and he wanted it that way. But why? Why the wish to lock that pain in his blood and mind?

Am I punishing myself for betrayals? Failures? For weakness?

He wasn't certain of the answer, though he welcomed the distractions of war and love to ease the memory. Most of all, he welcomed the thought of coupling with the Princess von Anhalt off the shore of the Mediterranean night. *Her naked form, as it had been during the twilight of the ice pillar, yielding to my touch, and her breasts, her hair, God of All Things ...* What offspring they might create if given the time? He wished her to bear his child, a son perhaps, or a celestial daughter who would tame worlds and force goodness on evil nations the way the Anhalt Sun Angel forced justice on Prussia.

If he died then, as Temujin Gur had said, his daughter or son would survive him, perhaps even fight for liberty in the Americas and beyond, perhaps even avenge him. Master Paganini said he would not die, that he only appeared to die in order to trick Gur. Perhaps that was so, though he could not trust Paganini any longer—not because he believed him evil or selfish, but because he knew the Lord of Saravastra would say or do anything to support his cause. After all, had he not demanded Zolo act the same?

A rumbling noise distracted Zolo. It reminded him of the celebratory party he was supposed to attend, the one being thrown by Master Paganini and the PBDU now that the 20th century had been saved from a devastating world war; and all manner of beings, both magical and non-magical, arrived in droves to represent the living Tao and speak of utopia.

He heard the rumbling again.

It sounded like words he could not understand—perhaps an alien magic language—and he stood to his feet. The sound emanated from above, like thunder. He stared out his window, and in the titanic blue sky above the red-tile roofs of Saravastra's mighty towers, he saw bright stars, wafer-like airships, and gauzy, air-filled bodies drifting and falling towards the city.

Were they from worlds beyond his knowing? Did the new utopia really matter to extraterrestrial beings of magical Tao? Or non-magical for that matter?

There was so much about the Tao, and the universe itself, that Zolo found incomprehensible, so much that made him feel like a motherless child again staring at a magic city floating in the clouds. He watched in a daze as the slowly falling objects whispered to one another, as if sharing news or sorrows, and he truly understood nothing of their language, though for an inexplicable reason he felt a sudden sense of urgency. His hand began to tremble. He heard the words of thunder again and all about him grew dark, even the sky outside.

Then it was over. Something enormous had eclipsed the sun for a few moments.

But what?

All quiet in the Mother Tower though.

The alien creatures of Tao continued to drift down from the black heavens.

Had they seen the thing? Were they talking about it?

As if in a daze, Zolo found himself walking through the Mother Tower, a bustling place of living energy overly crowded with bodies and noises and aromas in a way he'd never known. As he went, he heard low-toned conversations among a few passersby that contained phrases like "that sudden darkness" and "those thunder words" and too, a name that chilled him, "Ahriman."

So was that mysterious god of gods the cause of the eclipse?

No answer possible, though perhaps Zolo would know the truth soon enough.

Moments later, he arrived at the "Hall of Patience" whose cloudy ceiling rose higher than five Saravastra towers stacked one atop the other, the Hall itself ten-times-ten as wide and deep as the Great Hall at Bärenthoren. He strolled onto a broad balcony carved of purest smoky jade and gazed down on the colorful throng roiling and rippling like a great storm band on Jupiter. No Ahriman to be seen. However, he did see bright yellow PBDU flags being carried on high by Saravastra spell captains, all to celebrate the arrival of utopia, and Magogs too, towering above all others like goliath-sized trolls sprouting wicked scarlet horns. Zolo had never befriended one of them and he'd even heard tales of them devouring humans and lesser creatures, but Master Paganini used them effectively in combat operations against Master Godfellow's forces. They grew like mussels in cluster beds on a Martian-like desert world many light years away, and their hides were practically impenetrable, their individual strength like a team of giants. Swirling among them were many hundreds of spell captains, Wizard Gods, and Bodhisattvas in their robes and half-moon hats, as well as other warriors of all kinds and species clanking about in amplified black-armor, and filtering through and above it all, Paganini's *La Campanella*, violin music that sounded to everyone like peace and victory.

Zolo tried to absorb it all, to realize a sense of relief or accomplishment in the presence of such joy and victory, but the question of possible doom still nagged at him.

How can I be more selfish? And yet, I must know.

As he turned his head, his eyes caught sight of a woman he recognized, standing upon an adjacent balcony, also gazing down at the celebration. His mind stuttered and stopped at the sight of her as though he'd seen the moon itself plummeting to earth. She seemed sad, possibly a bit angry, yet still regal, powerful and stunning in appearance as befits the most powerful World Maker on the planet: Catherine II of Russia. He'd been in her presence once before, also at a distance, and Master Paganini strictly forbid him from speaking to her or communicating with her in any way. "She belongs to a time and place that must never influence Zolo Bold," he said. Still, he could not help but fixate on her.

Princess Friederike my love, it is you.

And did not Freddie herself speak with Catherine? Did they not all work together to struggle against the machinations of Master Godfellow and his cohorts? Of course, they did. So why should it be such a terrible thing if he spoke with Catherine, just to learn the truth of his own fate? And she wasn't far away. A simple leap from his balcony to hers would cover the space.

She might refuse to speak with me, but still …

Before he could consider it further, a voice within interrupted him, the voice of Margaret of Anjou:

YOU CANNOT CONFRONT CATHERINE OF THE RUSSIAS.

Why not?

HAVE YOU NOT BEEN TOLD BY MASTER PAGANINI THAT YOU ARE FORBIDDEN?

I have a right to know my own fate, Mother Margaret.

EVEN I DO NOT KNOW MY OWN FATE, ZOLO BOLD.

Have you been told by the world's darkest wizard that you will die by his hand?

I HAVE MUCH TO LOSE IF YOU COMMIT SUCH AN ACT, AND THOUGH I LOVE YOU, I CANNOT ALLOW IT. AND THERE IS NO NEED, FOR THE ANSWER COMES YOUR WAY.

It comes my way?

FORGIVE ME, ZOLO. I DO THIS ONLY FOR YOU, AND I WILL DO MY BEST TO HIDE THIS MOMENT FROM THOSE WHO MIGHT IN-TERFERE.

Zolo felt a hand on his shoulder. He turned to see a man a bit taller than himself, a man who looked as if he'd wandered the wastes of Earth and fought demons every step of the way, a man with a black gaze like the walking dead, though with enough melancholy in the eyes to attest to the real blood still warm in his body. His face, grimy and unshaven with a few weeks of beard; his hair dark, poking out from beneath a dirty red bandana, disheveled and crusted with sand. He wore a long-sleeved white silk shirt, filthy and tucked sloppily into a wide leather belt which upheld a pair of classic black Persian salvar, or long pants. On his feet he wore the remains of Roman-like leather sandals laced above his ankle.

Zolo observed the man closely, up and down, and it took him nearly ten seconds to realize the identity of this stranger. He swallowed hard and gasped as the two of them connected, eye to eye. The man's face produced a weak grin, though the rest of his body remained motionless ... But wait. Could it be the truth, or a convenient illusion placed before him for the purpose of distracting him from Catherine?

NO ZOLO, HE IS THE MAN YOU WILL BECOME.

The man spoke next. "I hear Mother Yarrow's words," he said. "I hear her voice now for the first time in many months. She tells me this weed of apparition placed before me, is me ... the boy I once was."

"I ... I am Zolo Bold," Zolo said. He reached out to touch the man before him, to make certain he was not an illusion. The man winced ever so slightly, as if his entire body were in pain, and Zolo said, "Mother Yarrow brought you here to—"

"I know why I am here," the man said, his face grim as Siberian twilight.

"Then—"

"You will live beyond the age of 46."

"Temujin Gur said—"

"Gur is not the final judge of our fate, but he may arise once again. I cannot say."

"He is dead. Master Paganini and the Princess von Anhalt killed him."

The man sighed and grinned weakly again, then he said, "The blackest of wizards live in Time's hollows and crevices. He is alive somewhere. A version of him could be here, even now, disguised as one of the revelers. You can never be sure ... and you are *never* completely safe. I know. He almost killed me."

Is all this true, Mother Yarrow?

She did not answer. Zolo blinked. The man was gone. Only a few grains of sand remained behind on the floor where he'd stood.

Zolo glanced over at the balcony nearby. Catherine was gone too.

Mother Yarrow?

Still, she did not answer.

THE END

---

www.ingramcontent.com/pod-product-compliance
Lightning Source LLC
Chambersburg PA
CBHW021956170626
46808CB00001B/172